SUSAN JOHNSON

The only author to ever receive an unprecedented
''Six Stars'' from *Affaire de Coeur*

''She writes an extremely gripping story . . . with her
knowledge of the period and her exquisite sensual scenes,
she is an exceptional writer!''

—*Affaire de Coeur*

''Her romances have strong, intelligent heroines, hard,
iron-willed men, plenty of sexual tension and sensuality
and lots of accurate history. Anyone who can put all that
in a book is one of the best!''

—*Romantic Times*

SWEET LOVE, SURVIVE

''Magnificent . . . rich . . . dazzling . . . a sensual, loving
story.''   —*Affaire de Coeur*

''Fascinating . . . The author's style is a pleasure to read
and the love scenes many and lusty!''

—*Los Angeles Herald Examiner*

BLAZE

''Appealing, sensitive and sensual . . . Ms. Johnson is one
of the most eloquent and erotic writers I've read. Her
research is thorough, pertinent, and intertwined with an
exquisite love story.''   —*Affaire de Coeur*

Winner of the *Affaire de Coeur* Golden Certificate
''for the quality, excellence of writing, entertainment and
enjoyment it gave the readers . . .''

Berkley books by Susan Johnson

BLAZE
SILVER FLAME

SILVER

FLAME

SUSAN JOHNSON

BERKLEY BOOKS, NEW YORK

SILVER FLAME

A Berkley Book/published by arrangement with
the author

PRINTING HISTORY
Berkley edition/March 1988

ISBN: 0-425-10689-6

A BERKLEY BOOK® TM 757,375
Berkley Books are published by The Berkley Publishing Group,
200 Madison Avenue, New York, NY 10016.
The name ''BERKLEY'' and the ''B'' logo
are trademarks belonging to Berkley Publishing Corporation.

PRINTED IN THE UNITED STATES OF AMERICA

10 9 8 7 6 5 4 3 2 1

One

———————————————◆—————————————————

Helena, Montana
January 1889

VALERIE STEWART SAW him first when he walked into the music room, and her eyes opened appreciably in surprise.

Trey Braddock-Black at an afternoon piano recital.

It had to be unprecedented.

Her small start of surprise set up a flurried chain reaction of swiveling heads, and Erik Satie, Emma Peabody's newest discovery from Paris, momentarily lost his audience's attention.

Montana's most eligible bachelor stood near the door with one shoulder resting against the pale gray wall, his arms crossed negligently across his chest, and smiled a slow upcurving of acknowledgment. He was familiar with being conspicuous—whether for his scandalous reputation, his handsome half-breed looks, or his family's considerable wealth, Trey Braddock-Black was habitually scrutinized.

He dipped his head in a small measured nod to the room at large, his long black hair sweeping forward briefly with the movement. Reminded of their manners, everyone quickly looked back to the bearded young man with the pince-nez, playing his newest composition on Emma Peabody's grand piano. And for the next twenty minutes Emma's guests studiously avoided overt glances at Hazard Black's disreputable son while busy minds silently contemplated which female had lured Trey to this afternoon recital. There was no question in anyone's judgment that his unusual appearance was prompted by a woman.

Emma's music room was large, its dove-white walls detailed in gilded molding, the parquet floor of a plume and fret motif laid by Italian workmen who had recently refurbished the Tsar's palace at Tsarskoye Selo. Elegant banquettes covered in delicious yellow cabbage-rose silk print were informally arranged as in a drawing room with pretty, painted caned chairs from Venice scattered between the banquettes and small tables punctuating the whole so no guest need reach far for a glass of champagne or a sweet.

Among the heterogeneous guests, numerous fashionable young ladies, beautifully dressed by their mothers with their daddy's money, languorously disposed on the yellow silk banquettes, their long, full skirts draping in colorful folds, their bonnets frilled and beribboned, appeared like so many colorful blossoms. With the melodious purity of Satie's music swelling and flowing through the luxurious room, assessing glances strayed past the politicians, businessmen, and bankers; glossed over the matrons and dowagers; and dwelt occasionally with studied scrutiny on one or the other of the pretty young ladies. Who had he come to see?

The pretty young ladies were in universal accord—their covert glances were on the tall, dark man leaning against Emma's wall.

So when Satie finished, when the polite clapping subsided, surreptitious reconnaissance watched and waited to see the woman.

It was a moment only before Valerie Stewart, elegant in burgundy velvet and a stylish bonnet of silk azaleas, rose and walked over to Trey.

A concerted consensus pronounced a silent *Ahh* while the young ladies democratically reflected, *Damn*.

Valerie stood very close like she always did, he thought, so one was aware of her fine breasts.

"Good afternoon, darling, you look"—Valerie paused suggestively while her kohled eyes traveled leisurely up Trey's tall, muscular form arrayed in Saville Row's finest tailoring—"well." Her sentence ended in a lush, purring resonance.

He wanted to say, "You can't eat me alive right here in Emma's music room, Valerie, dear," but it would have been presumptuous and ill-mannered, so he smiled politely and said instead, "Thank you, and you're beautiful as usual, Valerie." Her dark hair and pale skin was enhanced by the rich burgundy. "Did you like Erik's compositions?"

Waving her kid-gloved hand dismissively, she made a small moue. "They all sound the same, don't you think?" Valerie's appreciation of the arts was confined to being seen at the right receptions and recitals and understanding the finer points of jewelry appraisal.

Trey's pale eyes widened momentarily in a swift reflex action at her crass simplicity, or more aptly, he decided an instant later, her crass discourtesy. "No, darling," he murmured, his deep voice tinged with a cultivated insouciance, "they all sound remarkably different."

Looking up at him from under her heavy lashes, her face delicately tipped so her best side showed to advantage, she turned the conversation to her favorite topic—herself. "Have you missed me?" It was a flirtatious, coy phrase, breathed in a husky, intimate tone.

"Of course." The required responses came effortlessly. Pushing away from the wall, he glanced over the silk azaleas on her bonnet to the group surrounding Satie at the piano.

"When can I see you again, darling?" Her voice was honeyed, and she moved a step closer so her scent filled his nostrils.

"Later," Trey said evasively. He was here to see his friend, not flirt, and taking a half step, he began to move around her.

Lifting her closed fan fractionally, Valerie blocked his movement. "When later?" she inquired with a pretty pout.

"Valerie, dear," Trey said with a quick grin, touching her arms lightly, "you pout beautifully, but I came to Emma's today to see Erik. Come with me," he invited with a well-bred courtesy, "and talk to him."

"He's only a second pianist at a Paris club," she replied disdainfully, her values based on money, position, and dress, "and odd and disheveled . . . and bohemian. Why would I want to talk to him?"

"He's also an imaginative composer," Trey said quietly, annoyed at her bourgeois attitude. "Now, if you'll excuse me . . ." and he moved her gently out of his way.

Trey had met Erik Satie at the Chat Noir in Paris the previous year, and when he'd gone up to compliment the

pianist on his virtuosity, they'd discovered much in common.
Born within months of each other, both were enamored of the
piano, detested Wagner, adored Chopin, and resisted the
conservatory method of training. Largely self-taught as a
pianist, Trey was instinctively attracted to the eccentric young
composer who dressed à la bohème, affecting flowing tie,
velvet coat, and soft felt hat. Whenever Trey was in Paris,
they made the rounds of the clubs and salons, and then in the
wee hours, in Trey's lodgings over Pernod and brandy, they
practiced Satie's newest works. Largely through Trey's enthu-
siastic insistence, Satie had been introduced to Emma Peabody, the arbiter of avant-garde music in Helena.

A tall, ramrod-straight, gray-haired dowager, Emma spoke
in blunt, brusque phrases, but she knew music, and she'd
been a friend to Trey since his childhood. "Got out of her
clutches, I see," she said gruffly as he came up to greet her.
"You were late."

"Which do I answer first?" Trey said with a boyish grin.

"Neither," she replied curtly. "Can't tolerate Valerie.
Detest lateness. Hate excuses worse. And don't try to bam-
boozle me with that charming smile . . . I'm too old. Save it
for flirts like Miss Stewart over there. He's good," she
abruptly declared with a nod of her chignoned head, as if she
were buying Satie at auction. "Damn good."

"I *told* you." Emma had been reluctant at first when Trey
had suggested Satie for her annual recital, feeling he was too
outré, and his soft reproof was amused.

"What do you know, you young pup?" she harrumphed.
"You're still wet behind the ears."

"Know enough not to like Wagner," he replied genially.

"Smart boy. Damn sauerkraut mock heroics. Ruined music
for a decade." Emma's face always colored up when Wagner
was discussed, and Trey soothingly distracted her.

"Unlike Erik's work. I thought the *Gymnopédies* was particularly fresh."

Emma's color subsided; Wagner's deficiencies were discarded in favor of Satie's splendid talent. . . . "His work is
hauntingly simple," she agreed, "and bold too," she added
with a brisk nod. "And then his passages of medieval disso-
nance appear, and it seems as though one's transported to
another time. How does he do it?"

"Pernod," Trey said, his smile roguish, "for starters."

"Wicked boy." And she clipped him a stinging thwack on

his arm with her ivory fan. "You're going to have to mend your disreputable ways someday." But there was a smile behind her brusque words, and her snapping brown eyes were filled with affection.

"Just so long as 'someday' remains in the vague future," Trey replied teasingly. "Come now, I want to give Erik my compliments, and you can tell him he's worth another five thousand to you because of the *Gymnopédies*."

Placing his hand lightly under her elbow, he began guiding her around the clusters of music lovers scattered throughout the high-ceilinged music room.

"I'm already paying him more than Liapounoff," Emma protested as they skirted the governor and his wife with a smile and a nod.

"There," Trey murmured, lifting a glass of champagne from a passing tray and handing it to her, "my point, exactly. He's better than Liapounoff."

"If you think he's worth so much, you pay him." And she drained her champagne in a single swallow, her style of drinking much like her speech syntax—unceremonious and direct.

Trey politely relieved her of her empty glass, set it in a potted palm they passed, and, turning back to her, said, "He won't take money from me. Besides, Emma, my sweet," he said with a lazy drawl, "you can't take it with you."

Stopping abruptly, she turned to him and, looking up into his finely modeled face framed by long, sleek hair the color of midnight, inquired tartly in that flinty, businesslike tone that had made the bank she owned first in the territory. "What are you going to do for me if I sink another five thousand into your friend?"

He replied in quiet, measured tones that wouldn't carry. "I'll come to one of your dinners and entertain that grand-niece of yours you're always pushing at me." And when he broke into a smile and winked, a déjà vu image of his father twenty-some years ago flashed into her mind: every woman had wanted him—like this boy.

"Poor thing thinks she's in love with you," she said with candor and one arched brow of appraisal. "I'll give you *all* my money if you marry her. Going to give it to her, anyway," she added frankly.

"Lord, Emma," Trey replied, looking shocked not by

Emma's bluntness but at the thought of marriage, "do I look like I'm up for auction? I've more money than I need."

"But you haven't got a wife," she amiably pointed out.

"And I don't *want* one!" His voice had risen enough to draw attention to them, and casting his heavy brows up in exasperation, he carefully lowered his voice and murmured, "Come *on*, Emma, don't make it so tough. Just give Erik the extra five grand, and I promise on my father's coup stick to be so nice to your grandniece, she'll smile for a week."

"Conceited rascal, you're too handsome—like your father. I knew him before he met your mother, you know, when every female in Virginia City had decided they'd liberalize their attitudes and invite an Indian to dinner."

"It's not the looks, Emma. Women just want what they can't have. They see it as a challenge," he demurred, genuinely unpretentious for a man who had every reason to be vain.

"Someday you'll find someone you'll want to marry." Emma believed in having the final word.

"In the meantime . . . we're talking five thousand dollars." The last thing in the world Trey Braddock-Black cared to talk about was his marriage; that subject was on his list of priorities immediately after a month's stay in Antarctica.

"Dinner at my house . . . tomorrow night."

He grinned and put out his hand. "You have," he said very softly, "yourself a deal."

"I'm going to see him later," Valerie was archly saying to Cyrilla Shoreham over a silver tea-service set on a small chinoiserie table between their chairs, "if you must know."

"I *don't* believe you."

You snide little bitch, Valerie thought, just because he's never looked your way. "Would you like to tag along? I could hide you in the closet," she answered in blasé affectation.

"Are you going to *Trey's*?" Cyrilla asked, wide-eyed and fascinated.

"He invited me over." Valerie adjusted the lace at her cuff and reached for her teacup. "We're very dear friends," she murmured, showing her fine white teeth briefly. "I thought you knew. In fact"—she waited theatrically for a moment—"I think he's going to propose to me soon."

"No!" Cyrilla's gasp was so strident, several heads turned in curiosity. "I don't believe you!" And this time her doubt wasn't spiteful envy but thunderstruck astonishment.

Valerie shrugged a delicate, ladylike lift of her shoulder. "You should," she replied complacently. "He's quite fond of me."

The object of her conversation found himself disconcerted an hour later when he and Erik walked into his town apartment to find Valerie waiting.

"How did you get in?" Trey asked in a quiet voice, making a mental note to have a word with the manager.

"Harris let me in." Valerie's smile was gracious, her pose collected, as if she lounged every day on Trey's bargello banquette. The problem was, of course, on many occasions last fall she had lounged, usually nude, on that exact banquette.

But Trey hadn't seen her for some time; he never saw women for any length of time, allaying the universal female tendency toward possessiveness. "Erik, allow me to introduce Valerie Stewart," he said smoothly, his expression bland, the small irritation of having his privacy invaded invisible. "Valerie, Erik Satie."

Nodding slightly to Satie's bow, Valerie smiled up at Trey. "Will you be long?" Her inquiry was rude and pointed.

And for an awkward moment Trey debated being rude in turn.

"If you had other plans . . ." Erik began, looking uncomfortable and more rumpled than usual in one of the twelve gray corduroy suits he favored.

"No," Trey quickly responded. "Sit down, Erik." He gestured toward the liquor cabinet. "The Pernod's over there." Then, turning back to Valerie, Trey offered his hand. "Could I speak with you privately?"

Their discussion in the foyer was brief.

"Erik's only here for two days," he said.

"But you said you'd see me later," she replied.

"I'm sorry if you misunderstood," he said. "We're going to practice one of Erik's new compositions."

"*When* will I see you?"

He didn't feel she would respond well to never. "How about a little bibelot from Westcott Jewelers as a token rain check?"

Her eyes lit up, and his smile was one of relief. He despised scenes.

He brushed her cheek with his fingers, his mind already back on musical scores. "Run down there now and pick out whatever you like. I'll call them and tell Westcott you're coming in."

Reaching up on tiptoe, she kissed him. "You're a darling," she cooed happily.

"Thank you," he said.

Three days later, after having seen Erik off, Trey and his two cousins were comfortably disposed in the parlor of Lily's sporting house, contemplating between drinks and idle conversation the gathering dark clouds visible through Lily's swagged and fringed bow windows.

"There's a storm coming in over the mountains with that shift in wind. The cattle were turned around already this morning on our way into town. Finish that drink and then let's head out."

"Let's stay the night instead," Trey replied mildly, pouring himself another drink. "No reason to go back home tonight."

His cousins, Blue and Fox, exchanged dark, silent glances of futility and understanding. They both knew why Trey was in no rush to return home. His parents' party that night included Arabella McGinnis, another woman who without subtlety regarded their cousin as her prospective bridegroom. After having to deal with a persistent Valerie and then Emma's grandniece, Trey wasn't in the mood for cloying women. That was one of the reasons they were at Lily's.

"You don't really want to dance attendance on sweet young misses tonight at Mama's dinner, now do you?" Trey asked. "An honest answer; no duty replies."

And at Trey's wicked grin they both broke into smiles. It wasn't fair, putting Lily's up against dinner companions who blushed coyly at every bland comment and giggled when they weren't blushing. "You make the excuses tomorrow, then," Blue said.

"No problem. Mama knows how insufferable Arabella can be, and if father and Ross McGinnis weren't business associates"—he shrugged negligently—"hell, I wouldn't have to put up with Arabella's simpering pursuit."

"I thought you liked luscious blondes."

"I do, but I like a touch of brains too."

"Since when?" the two other men drawled in unison.

Trey's dark brows rose slightly. He knew his reputation, and they were right. He liked women—for offering life's greatest pleasure. It wasn't their minds he was primarily interested in. "Point taken," he said. "Now could we change the subject?"

"Rumor has it Arabella's been sleeping with Judge Renquist."

Trey smiled. Him too? He knew for a fact that she had enough voluptuous blonde energy to entertain an army. Just as well. Maybe she'd be deflected from her matrimonial plans. He was running out of polite excuses. "It's Tuesday, and there's a damn blizzard brewing outside," Trey said, intent on discarding the topic of Arabella. "Why are we knee-deep in rich old men?"

"They're selling two Chinese girls tonight, I hear,"[1] Blue said.

"*That's* why Lily's is so full, even in this hellish weather," Trey replied, his pale eyes scanning the room.

"Have you ever seen a sale?"

"No. Have you?"

"No."

"Are you going to bid, Trey, honey?" the curvaceous brunette snuggled against him murmured playfully.

"Lord, no," he said, lifted the last of his liquor to his mouth, and drained the heavy cut-glass tumbler.

"I didn't *think* you liked yellow flesh," the dark-eyed woman breathed in a throaty voice.

He laughed and glanced down at the woman held familiarly in the curve of his arm, amusement spilling out of his luminous eyes. Setting his empty glass aside, he signaled for another bottle, then said with a half smile, "You're talking to the wrong person about skin color, Flo, darling."

Trey Braddock-Black was proud of his Absarokee lineage. And to those who looked with contempt at skin a shade different, he took special pleasure in reminding them who he was. "Hazard Black's son," he'd say. "We used to own Montana." And damn near still did, some pettishly thought. The original gold from his father's first mine; the newer copper reserves, enough for twenty lifetimes; his mother's wealth; Hazard Black's power; the private Absarokee army at his back that Trey called "family"—all contributed a certain arrogance to the young man, who, back from four years of school out East, seemed intent on playing now, as hard as he worked the small empire that would someday be his.

Trey and his two companions had been drinking in Helena's finest brothel since they'd stamped in, cold and snowy, across Lily's imported pink mille-fleur carpet early that afternoon. "Need a brandy to warm my blood, Lily, darling," Trey had exclaimed, pulling off his heavy buffalo coat. "Not fit for man or beast out there today." His two friends had discarded their fur-lined coats as he spoke to the well-preserved blond proprietress of the plush sporting house, but they kept their guns holstered low on their hips, and their eyes held a curious alertness.

A fine brandy, French and dear, was promptly produced, and the three men were on their second bottle now. The gray, chill afternoon turned early into a winter twilight, and by the time dusk had settled, each of the men had one of Lily's pretty girls beside him. The parlor had filled as evening approached, and light piano music mingled unobtrusively with the low murmur of conversation, expensive cigar smoke, and the scent of high-priced cologne. Lily's establishment was the type that catered to rich men's pursuit of pleasure. It was cozy, costly, and handsomely decorated with authentic rococo furniture and large urns of hothouse roses . . . not as refined as Madame Pompadour's Petit Trianon, perhaps, but a very close approximation for the windswept prairies of Montana.

With a freshly refilled glass, Trey looked comfortable in the scented, gilded room, sprawled dark and powerfully lithe on an embroidered settee like any spoiled prince of the realm. Although a half breed, he was endowed with all the magnificent classic beauty of his father's Absarokee forebears: a straight finely proportioned nose; bone structure so splendid any sculptor would weep with envy; heavy, dark brows that slashed above deep-set, restless eyes remarkable for their silver luminosity; and his tall, broad-shouldered frame for which the Absarokee were justly famous, revealed beneath its elegant sprawl, an unmistakable impression of raw strength.

Conventional society was graced occasionally by this handsome scion of fortune—too handsome for his own good, many said—and young misses had seen him as an enviable prize since he'd entered adolescence. But Trey conducted himself a shade too recklessly, in too many bedrooms, to please wary deb fathers, although he tantalized their daughters with a careless, indiscreet charm that left them all breathlessly eager. Not withstanding his wildness, deb mothers considered him eminently suitable. Millionaires were popular son-in-laws.

He preferred Lily's quiet parlor, though, to dalliances with willing society misses; he enjoyed her unaffected, open friendship, and occasionally he took up with one of Lily's young ladies. With his dark good looks, audacious charm, and exceptional skill and endurance in bed, he was universally adored at the Petit Trianon of the prairies.

"Dammit, Lily!" a well-tailored older man, one of the new cattle barons, said, remonstrating his hostess in a slurred bellow. "You said seven o'clock for the sale. Damned if it ain't half past already."

"Relax, Jess," Lily replied calmly, the glow of the painted lamp globes producing a shimmering sparkle in each tiny facet of her diamond ear drops. She smoothed a hand across the trim waist of her Worth gown and added, "Chu's a little late, is all . . . He'll show up. Besides, Jess, sweet, this is only a service I offer, to satisfy my clients. I've no personal stake in it, or control over his timetable."

The sale of Chinese girls was more common in China Alley than at Lily's, where it was rare and only presented when customer requests became insistent. In China Alley the phenomenon was prevalent, supported by several thousand years of tradition that not only approved but also endorsed, the expediency of disposing profitably of unwanted daughters.[2]

Trey had heard of the sales before but never had seen one. Immune to the motive inspiring acquisition of another human being, he'd by choice never attended an auction.

Tonight, by chance, he'd see his first.

Two

TEN MINUTES LATER the paneled double doors opened, and Trey, with no more than simple interest, turned his head to survey two young Oriental women entering the warm, perfumed room. They were small, fragile, dressed in bright quilted silk jackets and black silk trousers. Their eyes were demurely downcast, servitude as inbred as ancestor worship.

The bidding was immediate, rapid, and spirited.

Trey's stomach tightened momentarily, even though his pleasant alcoholic haze mitigated the sharper edges of reality. He shrugged then, to brush away the brief unease, telling himself that life at Jess Alveen's palatial ranch or Stuart Langly's mansion on the hill might be an improvement over a China Alley existence.

But when it was over and the actual exchange of currency was taking place, he suddenly lifted Flo from his lap and, rising from the damask settee, softly said, "Be back in a minute." Skirting the table behind them with a short nod of greeting to the two men his father's age seated there, he walked into the adjoining dining room.

When Trey rose to leave, both his companions followed him with their gaze. But seeing him stop before the broad bay windows, they quickly perused the empty dining room with

sharp-eyed glances and, assured of his safety, turned back to
their lady friends. The men with Trey were bodyguards in
addition to being relatives and friends. Hazard Black had his
share of enemies, and his son had inherited them. There were
a score or more of influential men who resented Hazard's
power and influence in his corner of Montana, and most of
those wouldn't be adverse to Trey's demise. If it was properly
accomplished, of course, with no witnesses. So Trey often
rode out with bodyguards. A nuisance, he complained. Practicality, his father responded. A necessity, his mother insisted,
her own memory long, and four small graves in the family
cemetery mute testimony to her insistence. Trey was her only
child to outlive childhood, and she protected him as only a
mother can her last surviving child.

Standing before the large beveled-glass window, Trey
watched the heavy snowflakes fall from the dark sky and
heard with vague displeasure Chu and Alveen and Langly
conclude their business transactions. When it was over, he
felt himself breathe more naturally again, and shaking his
head slightly to clear away the brandy, he turned from the
blustery landscape outside to return to the parlor.

He heard her voice before he saw her.

She spoke in short, swift phrases with a slight accent. And
it wasn't Chinese.

"I want it understood. Only three weeks are for sale. An
indenture, so to speak, for three weeks. No more."

Trey was in the archway dividing the two rooms when she
finished speaking, and he saw her cast a direct, unflinching
glance around the crowded room. Their eyes met for a brief
moment, but her heavily lashed gaze was sweeping the room
and didn't linger.

She was as slender as a willow, dressed unwomanly in
worsted trousers, worn boots, and a faded flannel shirt.
Her heavy hair was wild like a tawny, turbulent waterfall, and
her eyes, in the brief time they'd held his glance, were as
green as springtime. Her skin was golden, not pale; she'd
been outside under the sun, and it suited her proud, straight-
backed stance and splendid, fine-boned face.

But she looked very young with her long, tumbled hair,
and if it had been tied back with a pink silk ribbon instead of
half falling over her forehead, she would have passed for

fourteen. A very luscious fourteen despite the camouflage of rough men's clothing.

"Is it understood?" she added, lifting her chin a fraction, an indomitable, small fury in the midst of heated, scented wealth.

Trey could almost see the flare of excitement ripple across the room at her words. She didn't realize the three weeks she insisted on made it much easier for anyone to bid for her. A white woman had never been auctioned before. It would have been unethical even in this frontier society where *ethical* was loosely interpreted as personal expediency. But to set up a sweet, pretty young thing in a discreetly selected hotel for three weeks—hell, that would soothe anyone's transient fit of conscience.

His cousin, Blue, came up to Trey as he stood in the doorway. "What do you think of that?" His straight, fine chin lifted an inch in her direction.

"*Ítsikyà·te batsá·tsk*," Trey replied quietly, "Very nice," his pale, light eyes intent on the small woman.

"Unheard of, apparently."

"But damned profitable, I expect," Trey said, his gaze taking in the covetous expression on every male face in the room.

She was desperate, and that's why she was standing here in this gilded brothel, the cynosure of men's eyes, her heart beating like a drum. The food had lasted six months after her parents died, but it was almost gone, and she had to provide for her young brothers and sisters. Three days ago she'd left them with enough food to last a month and promised she'd be back then with supplies and money. The oldest and their provider, she'd come to terms with the circumstances and had come to Helena to sell the only thing of value left—herself.

So here she stood, hoping she'd make enough money to feed her brothers and sisters until the summer crops were in. That was seven long months away. Her fingers curled into fists to still the desperate fear. Please, God, let them want me. . . .

Jess Alveen, evidently in an amorous mood that night, began the bidding with five thousand dollars—twice what he'd just paid for the Oriental woman.

The young tawny-haired girl's eyes widened momentarily as she stood center stage, but the surprise was so quickly shuttered, Trey wondered a second later if he'd imagined it.

The offers went up in increments of a thousand until only Jess Alveen and Jake Poltrain were left bidding, and then, finally, only Jake Poltrain. A hush had settled on the room when Jess dropped out, an uneasy, restless silence, for everyone had heard of Jake's unsavory excesses with women. Rumor had it that alcohol and bouts with opium had unmanned him, and cruelty was his transient cure.

Chu's keen eyes surveyed the room. "Twenty-five thousand once, gentlemen." His glance swept the crowd inquiringly. "Twice." He had already formed the word *sold* with his lips and Jake Poltrain had taken one step forward when Trey pushed away from the doorjamb dividing the parlor from the dining room and said, "Fifty thousand."

The shocked gasp that exploded in the small room was a reflexive combination of relief and thunderstruck awe. All eyes swiveled in fascination toward Hazard Black's audacious son. Trey had a reputation for extravagance, but this far exceeded any of his previous prodigality.

Standing at ease from the sheen of his hair to the toes of his exquisite boots, he stood calmly waiting. And all the men who had known him since childhood recognized the familiar composure. And the pleasant half smile. And the arrogance.

"I have a fifty-thousand-dollar bid," Chu said, allowing his avarice to show in the faintest of smiles on his normally inscrutable face. "Would you care to remain in the bidding, Mr. Poltrain?" he politely asked.

Jake Poltrain's face turned a livid magenta, and if corrosive looks were lethal, Trey would have been measured for a pine box. The heavyset man directed a look of pure hatred at Hazard Black's only child. It was a naked loathing, furiously nurtured by several unprosperous disputes over grazing rights on Indian land. He had never won against Hazard.

For a moment the silence was thick with challenge.

Poltrain was keeping the fury under control only with great effort, the tension evident in the grim slash of his mouth and the flare of his nostrils. But he had no intention of taking on Hazard's son, who, he very well understood, could outbid a banker. There'd be another time for his revenge and he'd choose it. Jake's bull-like shoulders lifted in a shrug, and expelling the held air in his lungs, he breathed a malevolent, brusque, "No."

"Very well," Chu continued, as if he auctioned off fifty-thousand-dollar women every day of his iniquitous life. "The girl is yours, Mr. Braddock-Black, for fifty thousand dollars."

The disquietude was instantly dissipated now that Jake Poltrain had been blocked. No one would have cared to see the young girl fall into his hands for even three weeks, but twenty-five thousand dollars was a lot of money, and no one had felt Christian charity demanded that much of a sacrifice. For Hazard Black's young cub, though, even fifty thousand wouldn't cause any hardship. His mother alone had brought twenty-two million dollars into her marriage, and those were 1865 dollars, which were worth considerably more than the current federal notes after two national financial panics in six years. And his father's gold mines and the copper and the cattle and the high-priced horses they bred. Hell, his father's business agent wouldn't bat an eyelash when he audited the check.

Then all thoughts turned to the pleasant diversions Trey's fifty-thousand-dollar pretty would confer for such a benevolent sum. Damn if they all couldn't think of a thing or two *they'd* like for fifty thousand dollars, was the universal masculine reflection, and several ribaldly vocalized their sentiments.

"Looks like you're going to be busy, Trey, in the next three weeks," Judge Renquist declared jocularly.

"If you need any help, let me know," another older wag asserted.

"Remember to sleep once in a while, son; otherwise, you'll never last out the time," a third voice suggested wolfishly.

"She looks a mite scrawny."

"Looks like an angel, more like," Jess Alveen emphatically stated, and most in the room unanimously, if silently, agreed.

Trey had bid against Jake Poltrain intuitively, with no overt intention of making the tawny-haired girl his mistress. It had been an impulsive act of charity or courtesy, perhaps; or retaliation against an old enemy. But as he stood there watching her and listening to the men's graphic comments, the image of the slender girl began to entice him. Her tumbled hair was silky and long, halfway down her back . . . long enough, he thought with a warm surge of pleasure, to cover her breasts. Would she be experienced, he wondered, or more aptly, how experienced? he mused with kindling anticipation. Anyone selling themselves at Lily's was, by definition, "experienced." Trey saw her small hands clench again at a particularly vivid suggestion and decided that unlike the Oriental women, perhaps self-deprecating humility wasn't in her nature. Abruptly he broke into the bawdy repartee, his rich voice putting an end to the lively discussion. "Thank you, gentlemen," he smilingly acknowledged, "but I think I'll manage without your assistance." And then his gaze traveled over the heads of Lily's guests and met stormy green eyes. "Maybe . . ." he added very softly, under his breath, but his light, silvery eyes were full of amusement. With a record of unremitting success in the boudoir, Trey Braddock-Black never seriously doubted his ability to charm women. Even women dressed like men.

Chu had taken the girl with the honey hair by the shoulder and was pushing her ahead of him in Trey's direction. As they approached, Chu said, "Should we go into the dining room to settle?"

"Fine," Trey replied, and, glancing quickly at Blue, smiled a swift, boyish smile prompted by his besting of Poltrain, his brandy-induced cheer, and the prospect, suddenly fascinating, of seeing the unusual young woman at close range. Very close range, the brandy-heated blood coursing through his veins suggested.

After they were seated at one of the small tables, Chu spoke first. "This isn't one of my customary sales. The woman asked me to serve as her agent. My percentage is twenty-five percent. The rest of the money is hers."

Trey called for pen and ink, and Empress watched him write the bank draft for Chu. It was her first opportunity to see Trey Braddock-Black in person. He was far too handsome, was her first assessment. Staggeringly beautiful when so near, with glinting silvery eyes that seemed to have a life of their own, restless and alive, like windows into a secret paradise. His long woman's lashes swept up for a moment when he asked Chu a short question, and he caught her staring at him. He smiled, and the uncommon warmth was a tangible thing.

Not only too handsome but too charming. The world had been kind to him, she thought, hastily dropping her gaze. He was very much at ease—familiar, no doubt—with women staring at his good looks. She should have smiled back at him, she realized an instant later, but tonight was too intensely emotional for her polite reflexes to be operating properly. Tonight was her Armageddon of sorts. An ending. And a beginning . . . a future for her family.

When her gaze dropped precipitously before that devastating smile, she found herself looking at the fine wool of his shirt. It was a delicate merino in a soft wine tone. She had had a dress in that fabric once, long ago in France. It seemed like another world away . . . her life before Grandmère had died, before the duel, before the hard times had begun. She shook away the melancholy with an effort, reminding herself that only the future mattered. Only the next three weeks were a priority now, and the extravagant sum of money she'd be bringing home.

Chu was politely bowing and taking his leave, Empress noted, and she squared her small shoulders.

The woman had been silent during the transaction, assessing him with those enormous green eyes. Trey wondered briefly what calculations were clicking away behind those intense, vigorous eyes. Turning back from bidding Chu goodbye, his question was answered, for she said bluntly, "I want my share in gold."

It stopped him for a blank moment. Too much brandy for too many hours, plus the sudden demand on a snowy evening long after the banks had closed, took a second to register. His mind raced over the feasible options, and none produced $37,500 in gold at this hour of the night. "Listen, darling . . ." he began, giving her his full attention for the first time since they'd walked into the dining room.

"I'm not your darling." Her voice was softly defensive, her lush green eyes provocatively assertive.

Trey's dark brows shot up, his eyes widened with interest, and another non-plussed moment passed in which Trey restrained himself from remarking that for fifty thousand dollars she was anything he cared to call her. "Forgive me," he said instead, smiling faintly at her brash courage and small set chin. "Do you have a name, then?" he said on the mildest note of inquiry, his pale glance sliding down her throat to the tantalizing juncture where worn flannel met her sun-kissed flesh.

"Of course," she declared in the same quietly commanding tone.

He waited expectantly, his gaze roving slowly upward again until his insouciant eyes met her slightly forbidding

ones. It didn't appear as though the lady would be lukewarm
to bed. More like making love to a very small wildcat, he
casually concluded. And his desire stirred at the prospect. All
of the women in his vast and varied past had been obligingly
willing. And while making love was a pleasure whatever the
circumstances, his interest was piqued by this very expensive
and feisty little chit, independent and self-assured enough to
offer herself for sale without any feminine trappings of silk or
satin, ribbons or bows.

As the silence lengthened between them, with the man who
was rich enough to pay a fortune for three weeks of her time
calmly gazing at her, she reluctantly said, "Empress Jordan."

The little beauty was full of surprises. She said the name as
though she inherently deserved the title, and a kingdom to go
with it. A Gallic kingdom from the sound of the softly
pronounced name. His luminous, tolerant glance surveyed
her. "Well, Empress," Trey said quietly, "the banks are
closed now and Lily doesn't keep that amount of gold on
hand, but if you'll take my bank draft now, we'll go across
the street in the morning and have Ferguson count out the
gold for you. Will that do?" He leaned back in his chair,
looked at her with interest, and added in a needless aside,
"I'm good for it. Rest easy."

Even living back in the mountains with her family in a
secluded valley, Empress had heard of the Braddock-Blacks.
Who in Montana hadn't? She reflected for a moment, torn
between urgent necessity and blind instinct. Exhaling quietly,
she said, "Very well. I'll accept the bank draft until tomorrow morning."

"Thank you, darling," Trey replied ironically, "for your
exquisite faith. . . ."

And this time she didn't correct him.

"So . . . here you are . . ." he said very slowly a moment
later, handing her the check. His deep voice was rich with
suggestion, but for a moment after his fingers released the
check, he did nothing more, as if in deep contemplation.
Then his hand, callused across the top of the palm like a
working cowboy's, dropped back on the table, and his dark
brows rose slightly. "Should we?" He gracefully gestured
toward the hallway leading upstairs.

He saw her swallow once before she replied in a curiously

unsure voice, ''Yes . . . all right.'' And she hurriedly stuffed the check into her shirt pocket.

Trey rose and, walking around the narrow table, pulled her chair back as she stood. Looking down at her from what appeared to be an enormous height to Empress's suddenly frightened mind, he offered her his arm. Shaking her head, she looked away. Tactfully he suggested, ''Perhaps you'd like to go on ahead. It's the second door on the right at the top of the stairs. I'll send a maid up with bathwater for you.''

''Bathwater?'' Empress queried in a tiny voice. She could feel the strength of his presence, the concealed energy lightly controlled, even though he hadn't touched her.

''And a robe,'' he added. ''I'm not partial to your range clothes.''

Empress drew herself stiffly erect for a moment to offer a sharp retort to the slur on her attire but immediately thought better of it. After all, he was paying her $37,500 in gold tomorrow morning, and visions of how that fortune would aid her family stifled the words in her throat. Her blood was as blue as his, bluer if quarterings mattered, which they didn't, out here on the rough frontier where survival depended on gold—on her—at the moment. Not on any aristocratic background, however fine its pedigree. ''Will you be long?'' she asked to cover the flurry of her insecurities and trepidation.

''No,'' he said, his tone low and heated. ''I won't keep you waiting.''

Striding back into the parlor, Trey conferred briefly with Lily, who immediately sent a maid scurrying off. Then he pleasantly accepted the good-natured masculine teasing directed at him. Ignored the black hatred of Jake Poltrain's drunken gaze, and drank another half bottle with his cousins before he excused himself and ascended the stairs.

Three

───────────────────·■■■··■■■·──────────────────

HE KNOCKED ONCE before he opened the door and walked in
with a loose-limbed grace that accented paradoxically both his
leanness and his power.

Empress was stepping out of the tub into a large towel held
by the maid. Lambent firelight gilded her slender form and
glistened sleekly down the silky length of her hair. Trey's
breath caught in his throat. Her slim, full-breasted body was
framed by the large white towel all lush, opulent curves and
satiny flesh, like a golden Venus. An experienced man, he
considered himself beyond surprise apropos of beautiful nude
women, but even he was struck by the perfection that had
been hidden under the plain, mannish garb.

With a nod of his head he dismissed the maid, his eyes
never leaving the arresting beauty of the young, naked woman
before him, bewitched by the powerful sense of innocence
she evoked. Perhaps it was the setting. One didn't expect
such delicate purity in a brothel. Or maybe it was the white
lilac fragrance wafting toward him from her damp hair and
skin. The scent was springlike on this stormy winter night,
unblemished, like the woman who reminded him too vividly,
even in his pleasantly brandy-warmed state, of a young child.
Suddenly he wasn't sure why she struck his sensibilities so,

for her body was very unchildlike. It was, in fact, very rich and womanly, like one of Lily's extravagant twenty-course dinners that provoked every bodily sense with tantalizing guile. It was her eyes, he finally decided—they were frightened and much too large with apprehension. So he said without thinking, "Don't be frightened. I don't have Jake Poltrain's tastes."

His cryptic words were anything but soothing, he realized immediately, for her hands trembled slightly at her sides. But her chin came up like it had downstairs, and he recognized the same intrepid mettle. As if some small, inner voice indomitably resisted the fear. "I won't hurt you," he said very softly. "You're perfectly safe."

Whatever inner anxiety had prompted the fright was apparently resolved, for she replied calmly while she reached for a towel hung near the fire, "Safe, I suppose, only if liberally interpreted, Mr. Braddock-Black. But warm and clean, certainly." And tossing the towel over her head, she bent over and began rubbing her hair dry.

Crossing the distance separating them in three swift strides, Trey pulled the towel away, tossed it aside, and said in a level voice, graphic with self-control, "I *won't* hurt you, I mean it."

Straightening, she stood before him, unabashed in her nudity, and raising her emerald eyes the required height to meet his so far above, she said with Byzantine inflection, "What *will* you do with me, Mr. Braddock-Black?"

"Trey," he ordered, unconscious of his lightly commanding tone.

"What *will* you do with me, Trey?" she repeated, correcting herself as ordered. But there was more than a hint of impudence in her tone and in her tilted mouth and arched brow.

Responding to the impudence with some of his own, he replied with a small smile, "Whatever you prefer, Empress, darling." He towered over her, clothed and booted, as dark as Lucifer, and she was intensely aware of his power and size, as if his presence seemed to invade her. "You set the pace, sweetheart," he said encouragingly, reaching out to slide the pad of one finger slowly across her shoulder. "But take your time," he went on, recognizing his own excitement, running his warm palm up her neck and cupping the back of her head lightly. Trey's voice had dropped half an octave. "We've

three weeks. . . ." And for the first time in his life he looked
forward to three undiluted weeks of one woman's company.
It was like scenting one's mate, primordial and reflexive, and
while his intellect ignored the peremptory, inexplicable compulsion, his body and blood and dragooned sensory receptors
willingly complied to the urgency.

Bending his head low, his lips touched hers lightly, brushing twice across them like silken warmth before he gently slid
over her mouth with his tongue and sent a shocking trail of
fire curling deep down inside her.

She drew back in an unconscious response, but he'd felt
the heated flame, too, and from the startled look in his eyes
she knew the spark had touched them both. Trey's breathing
quickened, his hand tightened abruptly on the back of her
head, pulling her closer with insistence, with authority, while
his other hand slid down her back until it rested warmly at the
base of her spine. And when his mouth covered hers a second
time, intense suddenly, more demanding, she could feel him
rising hard against her. She may have been an innocent in the
ways of a man and a woman, but Empress knew how animals
mated in nature, and for the first time she sensed a soft
warmth stirring within herself.

It was at once strange and blissful, and for a brief detached
moment she felt very grown, as if a riddle of the universe
were suddenly revealed. One doesn't have to love a man to
feel the fire, she thought. It was at odds with all her mother
had told her. Inexplicably she experienced an overwhelming
sense of discovery, as if she alone knew a fundamental
principle of humanity. But then her transient musing was
abruptly arrested, for under the light pressure of Trey's lips
she found hers opening, and the velvety, heated caress of
Trey's tongue slowly entered her mouth, exploring languidly,
licking her sweetness, and the heady, brandy taste of him was
like a fresh treasure to be savored. She tentatively responded
like a lambkin to new, unsteady legs, and when her tongue
brushed his and did her own unhurried tasting, she heard him
groan low in his throat. Swaying gently against her, his hard
length pressed more adamantly into her yielding softness. Fire
raced downward to a tingling place deep inside her as Trey's
strong, insistent arousal throbbed against the soft curve of her
stomach. He held her captive with his large hand low on
her back as they kissed, and she felt a leaping flame speed
along untried nerve endings, creating delicious new sensa-

tions. Her nipples peaked hard, and there was strange pleasure in the feel of his soft wool shirt; a melting warmth seeped through her senses, and she swayed closer into the strong male body, as if she knew instinctively that he would rarefy the enchantment. A moment later, as her mouth opened pliantly beneath his, her hands came up of their own accord and, rich with promise, rested lightly on his shoulders.

Her artless naïveté was setting his blood dangerously afire. He gave her high marks for subtlety. First the tentative withdrawal, and now the ingenuous response, was more erotic than any flagrant vice of the most skilled lover. And yet it surely must be some kind of drama, effective like the scene downstairs, where she withheld more than she offered in the concealing men's clothes and made every man in the room want to undress her.

Whether artifice, pretext, sham, or entreating supplication, the soft, imploring body melting into his, the small appealing hands warm on his shoulders, made delay suddenly inconvenient. "I think, sweet Empress," he said, his breath warm on her mouth, "*next* time you can set the pace. . . ."

Bending quickly, he lifted her into his arms and carried her to the bed. Laying her down on the rose velvet coverlet, he stood briefly and looked at her. Wanton as a Circe nymph, she looked back at him, her glance direct into his heated gaze, and she saw the smoldering, iridescent desire in his eyes. She was golden pearl juxtaposed to blush velvet, and when she slowly lifted her arms to him, he, no longer in control of himself, not detached or casual or playful as he usually was making love, took a deep breath, swiftly moved the half step to the bed, and lowered his body over hers, reaching for the buttons on his trousers with trembling fingers. His boots crushed the fine velvet but he didn't notice; she whimpered slightly when his heavy gold belt buckle pressed into her silken skin, but he kissed her in apology, intent on burying himself in the devastating Miss Jordan's lushly carnal body. The last trouser button slid out, and his maleness sprang free. His wool-clad legs pushed her pale thighs apart, and all he could think of was the feel of her closing around him. He surged forward, and she cried out softly. Maddened with desire, he thrust forward again. This time he *heard* her cry. "Oh, Christ," he breathed, urgent need suffocating in his lungs, "you can't be a virgin." He never bothered with virgins. It had been years since he'd slept with one. Lord, he was hard.

"It doesn't matter," she replied quickly, tense beneath him.

"It doesn't matter," he repeated softly, blood drumming in his temples and in his fingertips and in the soles of his feet inside the custom-made boots, and most of all in his rigid erection, insistent like a battering ram a hair's breadth from where he wanted to be so badly, he could taste the blood in his mouth. It doesn't matter, his conscience repeated. She said it doesn't matter, so it doesn't matter, and he drove in again.

Her muffled cry exploded across his lips as his mouth lowered to kiss her.

"Oh, hell." He exhaled deeply, drawing back, and, poised on his elbows, looked down at her uncertainly, his long dark hair framing his face like black silk.

"I won't cry out again," she whispered, her voice more certain than the poignant depths of her shadowy eyes. "Please . . . I must have the money."

It was all too odd and too sudden and too out of character for him. Damn . . . plundering a virgin, making her cry in fear and pain. *Steady, you'll live if you don't have her,* he told himself, but quivering need played devil's advocate to that platitude. She was urging him on. His body was even more fiercely demanding he take her. "Hell and damnation," he muttered disgruntedly. The problem was terrible, demanding immediate answers, and he wasn't thinking too clearly, only feeling a delirious excitement quite detached from moral judgment. And adamant. "Bloody hell," he breathed, and in that moment, rational thought gained a fingertip control on the ragged edges of his lust. "Keep the money. I don't want to—" He said it quickly, before he'd change his mind, then paused and smiled. "Obviously that's not entirely true, but I don't ruin virgins," he said levelly.

Empress had not survived the death of her parents and the months following, struggling to stay alive in the wilderness, without discovering in herself immense strength. She summoned it now, shakily but determinedly. "It's not a moral dilemma. It's a business matter and my responsibility. I insist."

He laughed, his smile close and deliciously warm. "Here I'm refusing a woman insisting I take her virginity. I must be crazy."

"The world's crazy sometimes, I think," she replied softly, aware of the complex reasons prompting her conduct.

"Tonight, at least," he murmured, "it's more off track than usual." But even for a wild young man notorious as a womanizer, the offered innocence was too strangely bizarre. And maybe too businesslike for a man who found pleasure and delight in the act. It was not flattering to be a surrogate for a business matter. "Look," he said with an obvious effort, "thanks but no thanks. I'm not interested. But keep the money. I admire your courage." And rolling off her, he lay on his back and shouted, "*Flo!*"

"No!" Empress cried, and was on top of him before he drew his next breath, terrified he'd change his mind about the money, terrified he'd change his mind in the morning when his head was clear and he woke up in Flo's arms. Fifty thousand dollars was a huge sum of money to give away on a whim, or to lose to some misplaced moral scruple. She must convince him to stay with her, then at least she could earn the money. Or at least try.

Lying like silken enchantment on his lean, muscled body, she covered his face with kisses. Breathless, rushing kisses, a young girl's simple closemouthed kisses. Then, in a flush of boldness, driven by necessity, a tentative dancing lick of her small tongue slid down his straight nose, to his waiting mouth. When her tongue lightly caressed the arched curve of his upper lip, his hands came up and closed on her naked shoulders, and he drew the teasing tip into his mouth. He sucked on it gently, slowly, as if he envisioned a lifetime without interruptions, until the small, sun-kissed shoulders beneath his hands trembled in tiny quivers.

Strange, fluttering wing beats sped through her heating blood, and a curious languor caused Empress to twine her arms around Trey's strong neck. But her heart was beating hard like the Indian drums whose sound carried far up to their hidden valley in summer, for fear outweighed languor still. He mustn't go to Flo. Slipping her fingers through the black luster of his long hair, ruffled in loose waves on his neck, she brushed her mouth along his cheek. "Please," she whispered near his ear, visions of her hope to save her family dashed by his reluctance, "stay with me." It was a simple plea, simply put. It was perhaps her last chance. Her lips traced the perfect curve of his ears, and his hands tightened their grip in response. "Say it's all right. Say I can stay. . . ." She was murmuring rapidly in a flurry of words.

How should he answer the half-shy, quicksilver words? Why was she insisting? Why did the flattery of a woman wanting him matter?

Then she shifted a little so her leg slid between his, a sensual, instinctive movement, and the smooth velvet of his masculinity rose against her thigh. It was warm, it was hot, and like a child might explore a new sensation, she moved her leg lazily up its length.

Trey's mouth went dry, and he couldn't convince himself that refusal was important any longer. He groaned, thinking, there are some things in life without answers. His hand was trembling when he drew her mouth back to his.

A moment later, when Flo knocked and called out his name, Empress shouted, "Go away!" And when Flo repeated his name, Trey's voice carried clearly through the closed door. "I'll be down later."

He was rigid but tense and undecided, and Empress counted on the little she knew about masculine desire to accomplish what her logical explanation hadn't. Being French, she was well aware that *amour* could be heated and fraught with urgent emotion, but she was unsure exactly about the degree of urgency relative to desire.

But she knew what had happened moments before when she'd tasted his mouth and recalled how he'd responded to her yielding softness, so she practiced her limited expertise with a determined persistence. She must be sure she had the money. And if it would assure her family their future, her virginity was paltry stuff in the bargain.

"Now let's begin again," she whispered.

"Let's not," he said, groaning.

"Tell me if I'm doing things wrong."

"Empress, darling," he murmured on an indrawn breath of monumental restraint as her bottom moved gently beneath his hands, "you're doing everything exactly right."

"You have to teach me."

God in heaven! Carefully Trey said, "I shouldn't."

"Better you," she said very softly, "than Jake Pol—"

"—train," he finished with a sigh. "You're serious, then."

She nodded, and tumbles of sun-streaked hair slid delicately across his chest. His hands glided up the warm satin of her back, and Jake Poltrain's name helped make the decision.

"You can stop me anytime. Up to a point," he said. He didn't know how much she knew about men.

"I don't want you to stop." Invitation, lush and sweetly scented.

He took a deep breath. "In that case, kitten, I'd better get undressed. The teaching," he murmured, "will require a little time."

"Let me do it." She smiled at him, gratefulness in her eyes.

His dark brows lifted inquiringly. Had he misunderstood something?

"Undress you," she replied to his searching glance.

He hesitated for a moment, uncertain whether the experience appealed to him. After all, she was a rank tyro, and it could prove awkward.

"I won't hurt you," she promised impudently, a mischievous grin on her face.

He threw back his head and laughed. "Oh, hell," he said a moment later, his smile still wide, "everything else is going to be new tonight . . . why not."

But she wasn't awkward, and she wasn't timid, and from the first moment her hands touched his belt buckle, he felt a pleasure stronger than he'd ever experienced. He lifted a little to help her pull the belt free and then waited, a curious anticipation tantalizing his nerves. Why did her touch leave him tautly expectant . . . tense with wanting her? Was it the novelty of her virginity? Was he aroused because of a strange, sweet innocence that had never interested him before?

She reached for the top button of his shirt, and slowly undid it. The buttons were bone, pale, finely polished, an animal of some kind carved in their centers. The design was exquisitely intricate, hours of work lavished on each individual button. Empress gently ran her fingertip over the couchant animal. A mountain lion? A puma? It was too dark, though, she reflected idly. "A black cougar."

She hadn't realized she'd said it aloud until Trey softly replied, "My good-luck charm."

Her eyes lifted to meet his. "They're beautiful," she said, and her mind diffidently included the warm, silvery eyes staring into hers.

"But outclassed tonight, darling," Trey murmured, his attention on her exquisite face.

Empress blushed at the low, heated compliment, at the

desire flaring like fire in his gaze, and in a small nervous flurry she unbuttoned the last button on his shirt. Taking a calming breath, she reminded herself why she was there, the sacrifice to expediency and what was at stake, then forced her girlish tremors aside. The transient flutters displaced, she slid his wool shirt down and, brushing her palms over his powerful shoulders, said, "You're very strong."

"And you're very . . ." He wanted to say *desirable,* so damned lush and desirable that he wanted to push her down on the bed and take her that instant without preliminaries. ". . . good at undressing me," he murmured instead, smiling a lazy seductive smile that lit his pale eyes with flashes of gold.

"I've a baby brother to practice on," she replied frankly, with her own faint smile and a teasing lift of her ragged, dark brows.

The prosaic frankness astonished him for a moment.

It should have curtailed the sensuality she provoked in him—the mention of home and family and baby brothers— but strangely it added erotic mystery to the fragile beauty who knelt naked beside him, undressing him with a languor that he couldn't decide was deliberate or artless. She was curiously unabashed, and that tinged the whole bizarre circumstance with a rich opulence. As if a precocious nymph had appeared in disguise on a snow-swept winter night in Montana to please him and pleasure him and teach him a new meaning of sensation.

"Do you have brothers?" she quietly asked, tugging his shirttails out of his trousers.

"No."

"Sisters?"

"No."

"I've both," she said.

He was about to answer politely, or at least make the attempt with the focus of his mind absorbed so raptly in the pleasure coursing through his body, but her small hand slid down his bare stomach and brushed lightly over his pulsing erection, and he forgot what she'd said.

"You like that, don't you?" Empress whispered, watching Trey arch his back slightly in reaction, hearing his low groan of pleasure.

He couldn't tell when he opened his eyes whether she was teasing or candid, but he knew if he wasn't going to hurt her in this denouement she called a business matter, and which he, in the small pockets of logic remaining in his brain, saw as madness, she was going to have to be readied, and very soon.

"I like it," he agreed in a husky voice, a smile spreading across his face. "Now come here, Empress, and tell me what *you* like." Reaching out, his palm drifted over the soft curve of her breast, slid upward, and, grasping her lightly behind her neck, he pulled her head down to his and kissed her . . . a deep, intrusive, heated kiss that ate at her mouth and lips and caused, he noted with satisfaction, her breathing to change.

"Is it always so nice?" she whispered when his mouth lifted from hers, blissful well-being inundating her mind.

"It gets better"—he smiled a little—"guaranteed."

She looked down at him lying in casual disarray beside her, half dressed. "Could I have that in writing?" A touch of impishness sparkled in the sugary depths of her eyes.

"Of course," he murmured, laughingly self-confident. "Along with a few other things . . . ." He was accustomed to giving women pleasure. He knew exactly what to do.

"Are you always so confident, Mr. Braddock-Black?"

"Trey," he whispered. "And . . . yes." His hand was fitting itself comfortably over the curve of her hip. He'd have to remember to go slowly so she would remember the pleasure of the first time and not the pain.

"So modest." Her grin was light and teasing.

"Yes," he said again with his own disarming smile. "I think we make a perfect pair. *Your* modesty is the same, right?" Being nude caused her no embarrassment, but after all, selling yourself before a jaded group of wealthy men was the antithesis of modesty or, in any event, thought-provokingly unique.

"Would you like me to be modest?" Empress asked, entirely natural and willing to please. "I'm not sure how to act. I could put that robe on and turn out the light."

Trey laughed again, amused at the notion that he might prefer his sex in the dark. "Lesson one, pet," he said pleasantly. "Modesty is misplaced in the bedroom."

"Oh, good. Then may I kiss you again?"

How young she looked when she said that. His gaze dwelling lazily on her held a disarmingly friendly appeal. "Let me get these boots and trousers off, and you can do whatever you like."

"I don't know how to do anything else."

Sitting up and swinging his long legs over the side of the bed, Trey bent to pull his boots off. He half turned his head back and smiled at her. "By morning," he said very softly, "you will."

He began by kissing her, his warm mouth like heaven, she thought, as it caressed the curve of her shoulder, the corner of her mouth, her eyes and lashes and tender earlobes. He kissed her where the swell of her breast met the trim neatness of her ribs, and where the full softness flowed into the small hollow under her arm. He kissed her fingertips and the smooth soles of her feet, and when he moved upward slowly, easing his long body over her slender form, she felt as though she were floating on a pink-tipped cloud, and the heat coiling deep inside her was enough to illuminate the universe.

Trey kissed her on her mouth then, lying gently on top of her, feeling cool on her heated skin. "I'm warm," Empress whispered.

He looked down at her, at the rosy glow on her cheeks and the blush sliding down her throat, and said, "That's nice." He was moving by inches and degrees, conscious in an odd way that he was responsible for more than just her pleasure tonight, touched somehow by her innocent giving of herself. He'd always played at love, lushly and expertly but lightly, his mind and emotions uninvolved. It was a game where skill, opulence, sensation, all contrived to enhance the most exquisite sport of all—*amour*. A new element overshadowed his familiar responses tonight. Caring, perhaps . . . more: a feeling for her courage and open giving. Somehow it changed the game.

"You're very . . . large," she breathed, tracing her fingers down his chest and flat stomach, stopping just short of the elusive object of her sentence. "Will it hurt?"

Her eyes lifted, and he found himself momentarily at a loss for words. "No," he finally said, wondering if she'd hate him later for the lie, "it won't hurt."

"I'm glad it was you there in the parlor," she whispered, her gaze softly heated and direct. "I'm really glad." And she lifted her mouth to kiss him, wanting to stay on her pink-tipped cloud.

"I wanted you more than anyone else," Trey murmured, and he realized suddenly that it was true. It wouldn't have had to be Jake Poltrain wanting her. Any one of them down there would have elicited the same response. As an Absarokee, he was attuned to his feelings and personal vision and earthly energy, and he knew. She was written on his fate—delicate, strangely asexual, yet erotically provocative in her man's garb—and he had had to have her.

"I want you. Am I saying it right?" she inquired in a lushly throaty tone. "I'm floating on a soft, heated cloud right now. You're very good," she murmured, tightening her arms around him.

"Move over, Empress, darling," Trey whispered, brushing his mouth across her half-parted lips. "I'm climbing on your cloud."

She was *his* cloud lying beneath him, perfumed with lilac, warm as sensuous longing, arching her back slightly to feel the solid strength of him poised lightly above her, his elbows politely taking the majority of his weight. Her erect nipples teased the hard muscles of his chest, and her full breasts moved silkily against him as her hands gently stroked his back. It was as if she'd set a brush pile ablaze inside his body, and the flame spread so swiftly with each new kiss and gentle movement, it outstripped the wind.

It had been too long since he'd first walked in to see her rising from her bath, too long for his arousal despite the halts and delays, too long to play with teasing kisses. He was past waiting suddenly, past politeness and better intentions. She would have to take him now.

His mouth came down on hers, out of control, barbaric in its plundering invasion, and she yielded to his onslaught, at first with a sighing welcome, as if she'd waited for him all her life. But moments later her hands clung to his shoulders with a madness of their own, and she lifted her hips tentatively against his maleness, enticing him to enter her, reaching for surcease to the trembling desire flooding through her to the tips of her quivering toes. She ached for him, yearned for him, heated, damp, and swollen, was ready for him.

Nothing mattered to either of them now but putting out the fire. All the alien, labyrinthine reasons for being in each other's arms disappeared abruptly, burned away by an astonishing sense of joy and wanting so relentless and powerful, there was no turning back. Stroking the softness of Empress's inner thighs, Trey gently pushed them apart, settling his lean hips between her legs. Then his fingers touched the moist, heated entrance to his paradise and slid lushly over her wetness.

Empress gasped, holding her breath while the exquisite

sensations spread like sweet wine through her senses. "Do that again," she breathed shakily when reality at last returned minimally at the edges of her mind.

He did, and she thought she would die.

"Can you die of pleasure?" she whispered with a sigh into the curve of his shoulder. "*How* do you know—" But Trey's expert fingers slid in farther, curtailing the question, for Empress was suddenly lost to everything but the hurtling ecstasy.

"You're beautiful," Trey said softly, stroking gently, so the world spun away for Empress into a golden rapture of feeling. "Wet and hot and beautiful," he added in a husky rasp. "I can't wait. Hold me now, darling." Fitting himself where his fingers had tantalized, he drove into her tight, velvety sweetness. He felt her go rigid beneath him, but it was over and he lay quiet inside her then until she relaxed, the quick, thrusting pain dissipated. His hand closed on her hips, as if he could brush away the hurt with the drifting warmth of his fingers, and a moment later he began moving inside her, delicately testing the limits of her pleasure or pain. He took his time, his frenzy gone now that he was where he most wanted to be, carefully slid upward only to withdraw as carefully, murmured love words, stroked and fondled until he felt her glide lusciously around him and heard her whisper in a quiet entreating voice, "More . . ."

He obliged, gallant and sure, in a deepening rhythm she met with arched hips and strong arms pulling him close. Her breathing was ragged with passion, his own unquiet as they touched each other in an uncontrolled penetration and greedy taking until she was feverish beneath him and around him, frantically shuddering so near the brink, he knew it was only seconds more. His hands slid down her slender hips and under her silky bottom, and he pulled her meltingly into his next, slow deliberate downthrust. Feeling her first tiny convulsion begin when he was buried deep inside her, he let himself at last fill her with the hot desire she'd roused in him from his first glimpse of her in Lily's parlor. And she clung to him while the tidal wave of enchantment swept over her. And softly cried out his name. And left bloody half-moons from her nails on his shoulders.

Moments later, orgasmic but not sated, Trey lay inside her, intoxicated by a curiously restless passion, desperately wanting more of her. Two weeks, six days, twenty-three hours, he thought, and bending his head to kiss her soft warm mouth, he knew he was going to wear himself out and wear her out and feel every acute, sensitive, earnest, sharp, shimmering flavor of love in the next three weeks.

He didn't question the fact that this sensation was staggeringly unique in his experience; he only looked forward profoundly to the ensuing delight. He had found his mate—at least his mate for a transient number of weeks—and with primordial instinct, by taste, feel, touch, he wished to make her his . . . again.

Empress said, "Stop," breathless and panting after the third time, and startled, shaking his damp black hair out of his eyes, Trey stopped and looked at her as if she were from another planet. He saw her then with different eyes; she refocused, beautiful, rosy, half smiling at him. "You don't have to work off the entire fifty thousand tonight," she said, her glance warm and friendly.

"You're different," he replied, not answering her statement, explaining instead, however vaguely, a measure of her allure. He could feel the air on his skin. His nerves, in an unaccustomed fashion, were oversensitized, exposed.

She didn't tell him she *felt* different, because her feelings were too chrysalis and undefined. But she felt as though something of immense importance had happened to her, and it wasn't the denouement. She couldn't say exactly what it was, but she knew this night would forever divide her life into before and after. It was very strange—as if she'd come alive tonight, as if she had immense new powers, a new secret nature that flowed beyond the confines of what had been until now a sheltered young girl's life. "I'll be here tomorrow," she said, pleased with the sudden discovery of her new inherent powers, and reached up to brush a sleek wave of black hair from Trey's forehead.

He smiled. "I'm sorry. You're right. Damned selfish of me." And with a brushing kiss across the tip of her straight nose, he rolled away and sprawled on his back.

"You needn't be sorry," Empress replied, half turning on her side and supporting herself on her elbow. He was quite beautiful, she decided, looking down at him lying selflessly natural, her glance examining him from his handsome face down over his heavily developed shoulders, across his torso covered sparely with taut sinew, to his trim hips and long, muscled legs.

"I'm not really," he answered with a quick grin, his eyes wide and calm and smiling. And lacing his hands under his head, he added, "I'm not sorry at all. You're unbelievable, you know."

"Thank you. I didn't know, of course . . . had no way of knowing . . . although, Mr.—"

"Trey."

"Trey, you're probably the one to thank. I expect women like you. . . ." She was intelligent enough to realize that all men weren't as skilled and tender, or so gentle. Even as inexperienced as she was, she knew she had by a small miracle fallen into the hands of a man who oddly blended power and sensitivity.

"I suppose some do," the man who had a reputation for extraordinary charm with women, in and out of bed, modestly replied.

"Do you do this often?" It was asked out of curiosity and naïveté.

He paused. What do you say to a newly ravished virgin—or anyone, for that matter—asking such a pointed question? How do you politely say, "I don't know what you mean by 'often.' Is your often the same as my often?" *I think this is one of those questions a gentleman is never supposed to answer,* he decided, remembering some advice on modesty and courtesy given him long ago by his father. He smiled. "I'd be happy to do it as often as you like. We'll send down for food if I start tiring."

"You enjoy me," she said with a small pleased smile.

Unclasping his hands, he reached for one of hers and said, "Clever of you to notice."

The look she gave him was new, part coquette, and delightful.

He squeezed her hand gently in unspoken intimacy, as if they were old friends. "Are you tired?" he asked out of solicitude but also out of an interest in changing the subject from his amorous activities.

"No, not really. Could we rest for a while, though?" she asked matter-of-factly, as if she were only requesting a short break from her job duties.

Trey settled back against the pillows, her hand still in his. "Tell me about yourself."

"You tell me about yourself first," Empress answered

softly. She preferred anonymity, for once she left in three weeks, she intended to obliterate this interval.

Understanding her reluctance to divulge the details of her life, he politely acceded to her request, although her faint French accent was intriguing. They lay in bed side by side, her hand curled comfortably in his, and Trey was telling her about the Absarokee and his father's clan when there was a knock at the door. Not diffident but curtly hard. And a deep masculine voice asked, "Are you decent?"

Trey's voice, a shade deeper and laced with amusement, answered, "No, but come in."

Empress slid under the covers when Blue walked in.

"She's shy," Trey said smilingly.

"Really," Blue replied in a mockingly ironic tone, thinking she wasn't too terribly shy, since she was obviously naked under the blankets. Leaning one shoulder against the door, he said, "Poltrain's talking big downstairs. Thought I'd let you know," he explained. "It's the liquor, too, of course, but you know how he feels about us and your family. Maybe Fox and I should guard your door tonight. He's madder than hell about you outbidding him and is talking about settling the score with you. This one and all others too."

"Don't worry," Trey responded calmly. "He won't try anything at Lily's. It's just whiskey talk. And I know how you've been looking forward to seeing Kate. So don't let Jake spoil your night. I'll see you in the morning."

"Sure, now?"

"Positive. Hell, I'm as safe here as I am at home."

Blue's glance surveyed the curved body under the covers. "How's everything?" he asked cryptically.

"Fine. Just fine." Trey's mouth curved into a smile. "Really *really* fine," he added softly.

Blue pushed away from the door. "See you in the morning, then."

"Not too early." Trey nodded in Empress's direction.

"Would afternoon be better?" Blue asked with a grin.

"Afternoon," Trey gently agreed, "would be much better."

"*Ìandirúxua, tsitsétse,*" Blue said with a teasing smile. ("Remember to get a little rest.")

"*Ahú•cĭ•a biháwim co•bi•céky,*" Trey replied cheerfully. ("Plenty of time to sleep when I'm dead.")

Trey flipped the covers back after Blue quietly shut the door and pulled Empress into his arms. "Blue's like a brother to me. Meet him next time. You'll like him."

Twisting her head to look up at him, Empress said, "It's embarrassing."

"No one cares about 'embarrassing' here. And Blue and Fox are almost always with me, so . . ."

"I might as well meet them."

"Might as well," he agreed.

"Why are they always with you?" She'd heard the rumors about the Indian troubles with Hazard and the big cattle interests, but only barely. Too isolated up in the mountains and too immersed in her own struggle for survival, Empress hadn't the time or energy to be concerned with wealthy men's problems.

"Bodyguards."

She looked at him with a tilt of her brows. So it was true. "Who wants to kill you?"

"It's nothing personal," he replied with a smile. "It's just that I represent my father's interests, and a lot of people don't like Indians like my father who haven't been robbed of their land"—his smiled widened—"and think they're as good as a white man. We're supposed to be content to stay on the reservation and live on the government's dole. That's provided any of it gets through the gauntlet of thieves operating the Indian Affairs Department. My father chose not to. He also controls a large tract of land many people would like to get their hands on." He shrugged. "So I have bodyguards when some of the threats become overt. It's a nuisance sometimes, but—"

"Have you ever really needed them except as a deterrent?" The notion somehow seemed out of place in the wilds, or here in this gilded brothel, and for a moment her eyes were wide with inquiry.

Gazing at her, Trey wondered if she'd only come to Montana recently and didn't understand all the convoluted political intrigue or the style of justice prevalent on the frontier. "Occasionally," he said mildly, but his eyes for a brief second lost their charming warmth, and precise memory recalled too many lessons learned concerning human treachery and greed. It was a conversation he didn't care to continue. "By the way," he said abruptly, circumventing details about the people after his half-breed blood, "we'll move to my apartment tomorrow. It's less public. And you'll need clothes."

"I have clothes."

"We'll have them burned," he said pleasantly.

However pleasant his tone, it was a brutal reminder of her position. "You're the master, I suppose," she replied, ruffled and touchy. "At least for the next three weeks." And rolling away, she sat up and glared at him.

He smiled lazily, finding her as beautiful out of temper as in, and, idly reflecting on the perfect curve of her narrow waist, declared, "In that case, I'll have to take advantage of my authority. I can't recall ever being a master before. Will I need my quirt?"

"I *wouldn't* recommend it," Empress replied in a softly honeyed tone, her eyes basilisk green.

"Good, I can have my way without it. Thank you, darling, for being so understanding," Trey teased lightly, sliding down a fraction on the pillows piled behind his head. Stretching, he arched his back, then settled back into the down mattress. "Some velvet gowns and a cashmere wrap, I think," he began, ticking off the items on his bronzed, lean fingers. "It's so cold this time of year," he added with an indulgent smile. "A few silk nighties . . . Is silk all right, or would you prefer flannel?" he asked the woman who continued to look black daggers at him. "And a fur cape for driving. Do you like sleigh rides?" Silver eyes traveled slowly downward, taking in the full richness of Empress's opulent form, then unhurriedly returned to hold her glance with his. His thoughts were suddenly absorbed by an erotic image of Empress lying on furs in his red-lacquer sleigh.

"You needn't spend any more money on me," Empress retorted heatedly, the litany of elegant clothes sounding in her ears like chaffing charity.

"I'd like to see you dressed like a woman. Humor me, sweet."

She didn't answer for a long moment, feminine vanity warring with a powerful self-determination. Practicality interceded at the last: She was in no position to fight Trey Braddock-Black. "It's your money," she replied curtly.

"True," he said, entertained. "Do you have a preference in furs? Something dark, perhaps, with your coloring. You'd look luscious spread out on dark sable or black mink. . . ."

"I thought the fur was for sleigh rides," she reminded him pointedly.

"We'll get one for *after* sleigh rides too," he said with a very private kind of smile. "Tell me your favorite foods," he went on casually. "I'll have the apartment stocked. You needn't be this thin."

She stared at him for a moment, her gaze clear, unplacid green. His own, instantly accommodating, shone a twinkling silver. "I adore slender women," he said. "Now flowers," he continued deftly. "What kind of flowers do you like?"

"*Flowers*?" Empress exclaimed in shocked surprise, the sound of the blizzard howling outside making talk of flowers outrageous. "You can't mean it."

Trey had learned long ago there was very little that couldn't be bought if you put your mind to it. "Depends what you like. What do you like?" His tone was calm.

"You could never get them now," she blurted out. As if one could get forsythia in the middle of winter in Montana!

But when, at his insistence, she'd told him, he said he'd try.

It wasn't supposed to be like this, she thought, bewildered. She'd seen her indenture as a sacrifice to be endured, clench-teethed and detached, a compliance without enthusiasm. It wasn't supposed to be lingering warmth from this man's touch, and comfort like she hadn't considered for five long years. It was supposed to be conflict in her heart and mind and soul. Instead, it was enchantment luring her into silvery eyes and the knowledge that blissful pleasure was only an arm's length away and waiting for her. "Come here," he said, his voice low, as gentle as flute music in the twilight. He held out his hand. And she went to him because she couldn't help herself.

A moment later, lying within the circle of his arms, she tipped her chin upward on his chest and quietly breathed, "Such extravagance seems . . . somehow sinful." She didn't mean it in a moralistic way but only in relation to the dire poverty of her existence the last few years.

"Speaking of sin," Trey murmured, sliding his hands down the curve of her spine, "you're tempting as sin yourself, lying here all indolent and warm and new. Would you mind . . ." He smiled faintly into her upturned eyes. "I mean, if you've rested enough . . . I have this unaccountable urge—" Stopping, he raised one dark brow, his pale eyes assessing. "Well, not precisely unaccountable. You're delicious . . . and I'm mad for you." He couldn't explain that "unaccountable" was only in terms of all his previous urges

and temptations apropos women and love. Love for him
had always been sportive and sumptuous but never, *never*
urgent. That was why this current wanting struck him as
unaccountable. He wanted her beyond the usual playfulness
or dalliance or casual taking. He wanted her without discretion, like a young boy wants his first taste of love, or like an
insistent child wants to touch a rainbow's tail. He wanted her
beyond reason and logic. He wanted her . . . now.

She meant to say no at least the first time, to show that he
couldn't so easily have his way with everything in the world,
that he couldn't be a spoiled child of fortune *always,* that she
had some control in this bizarre relationship which he saw as
an enchanting whim.

But he whispered heated love words that started the fires
kindling in her. Told her in intoxicating detail what he was
going to do to her and how she'd feel and where she should
look if she wanted to see how much he wanted her. And
when she looked, he told her how long he was going to make
love to her. He caressed, stroked, fondled, petted, and made
her forget for a transient time that the real world wasn't all
silken touches, luxury, and ease.

Or was it? she wondered dazedly short moments later,
charmed and inveigled past sense or reason.

He teased her, calling her *"baš icbí•wicgye ditsirá•tsi,"*
which he'd translated as "my fierce kitten," when she'd
cried for him frantically. He whispered he'd take care of her
. . . and all her needs. "Stay with me," he murmured heatedly, and he'd not meant the three weeks. But he wasn't
completely sober, she knew, because the taste of brandy was
heady when he kissed her. He may be different in the morning. But right now, with his mouth trailing down her throat,
she didn't want to think about morning or any of the hundreds
of problems in her life. She didn't want to think at all.

Trey's mouth slid down her smooth stomach and slowly
drifted between her legs. Resting his cheek against her warm
thigh, he looked up at her. *"Baš icbí•wicgye ditsirá•tsi,"* he
whispered. "Show me where you want me to touch you."
And taking her hand, he languidly kissed each fingertip while
the weight of his head pressed against her thigh. Then sucking gently on her last finger, he released her hand from his
mouth and guided it the few inches toward the heat pulsing
between her legs. "Here, fierce kitten?" he asked softly,
sliding her small hand across her rosy, distended flesh, swollen

and throbbing from his use of her and her need for him. "Tell me . . ."

"Oh, God . . ." she breathed as stabbing pleasure flooded her mind. There was no escape from the sensation. No comparison in all the former days of her life; no answer to the blind yearning, no argument, no excuse. "Please, Trey, I need you," Empress cried softly.

And together they explored the delirious limits of passion.

Hours later, despite Trey's glib words to Blue, he drowsily held Empress in the circle of his arms. She had sleepily said, "Thank you," to him, a compounded gratitude: for the money; for the future her family now had; and strangely, where she should feel remorse—a muffled thank-you murmured into Trey's warm chest . . . for the way she felt—wonderfully safe. And only in that instant did she realize how dreadfully frightened she'd been standing in Lily's parlor. But no more. Breathing trustfully in Trey's embrace, she slept.

He'd watched her then, lightly stroking the soft, sun-streaked curls coiled over his body, gazing at her lacy lashes, shades darker than her hair, lying like silk on her cheeks, deciding with a casual certainty as his glance traced the fine delicacy of her features that she was more beautiful than any woman he'd ever seen. It was an objective assessment made by a man who'd seen a great many beauties of the world—at close range. And for a virgin—he smiled faintly and tucked an errant tendril behind her ear—well, she'd disproved all the stories about green virgins. "Good night, fierce kitten," he whispered. His voice was tender, for the words meant much more.

My Lord, he was tired, a sweet, ringing weariness of contentment, and very soon exhaustion overtook him, too, and he fell asleep peacefully.

Four

IT SEEMED ONLY seconds later, although some time had passed, when Trey felt someone shaking him awake. His fatigued, vaguely inebriated brain took a hazy moment to recall exactly where he was. Then his eyes snapped open and he groaned silently.

Flo was standing over him, vivid in crimson silk, holding a half-empty champagne bottle, whispering in a voice that would carry a mile in the storm blowing outside, "Move over, Trey, honey, I brought champagne."

He looked quickly to see that Empress still slept, relaxed fractionally when he saw she did, then whispered back, "It's late, sweetheart, and I'm tired. How about some other time?"

"Nope," Flo replied with a wobbly, back-and-forth motion of her head. "Don't want to wait. Want to have a teeny, tiny drink with you," and so saying, she tipped the bottle up and swallowed a large gulp. "Here, your turn," she offered cordially with a tipsy smile.

"No thanks," Trey politely refused, warily watching her sway beside him. "My head's slightly sore from the brandy."

"Champagne's better for hangovers," she observed with a studied wink. "Same as two women are better than one. And if you're not going to move over, I'll have to sit on her."

Trey rolled a swift half turn away, protecting Empress in his arms, and just narrowly averted being fallen on.

"Hi there," Flo said cheerfully, dropping abruptly beside him in a flow of red silk and lace. "You look awake now. Wake up the little lady and let's all have a drink of bubbly."

Sighing, Trey took the bottle held out to him and drank.

"Give her some too," Flo insisted, her voice gently slurred, and generously waved her arm toward Empress.

"Let her sleep."

"Hell, no. Let's see what fifty thousand buys. I've never seen a high-priced whore like that, Trey, honey. I want to see."

"You're drunk, Flo."

"Well, so are you."

He probably was, but not as drunk as she. He had sense enough not to argue. "Good champagne," he said instead, and handed the bottle back to her.

"You gonna wake her?"

He shook his head and smiled.

"Since when don't you like a menage à trois, Trey, lovey?"

"Christ, Flo!" he exclaimed softly, at loss for an explanation to her frank declaration.

"She somethin' special?" Flo asked, mildly pugnacious.

"No," Trey replied, thinking better of it. "Maybe," he relented. Then, exasperated, he exclaimed, "Lord, Flo, I don't know!"

"Don't *know*, don't *want* to, everything's 'don't' with you tonight. Don't 'don't' me anymore, sweetie pie. If you won't wake her, I will!"

But he was out of bed with Empress in his arms before Flo could maneuver upright with her voluminous skirts, her tight corset, and the bottle she still held. Knowing what she wanted to hear, he said, "Stay there, Flo. I'll be right back." Lean, lithe, and naked, he carried Empress into the small adjoining dressing room. Disturbing her as little as possible, he put her to bed on the pastel brocade chaise. Satisfied she was tucked in and warm, he carefully shut the door between the two rooms and reached for his trousers from the floor where he'd dropped them. It wasn't until he was buttoning the last button at his waist that he glanced back at Flo. "Damn," he mut-

tered under his breath. She wasn't going to be easy to handle—
she never was, after drinking champagne, he recalled resignedly.
This was going to require a certain degree of diplomacy, for
Flo had taken the opportunity to undress while he put Empress to bed. She was drowsily lounging against the lace-
trimmed pillows like a graceful houri.

Her lashes lifted, and her gaze slowly focused on him.
"Come kiss me, Trey, honey. I missed you tonight." The
bottle was gone, her voice was inviting, and she smiled like
she had so many times before.

"Flo, sweet darling . . ." he began placatingly, keeping his distance. "It's . . . I'm . . . Blue's likely . . .
Blue's waking me early in the morning, love," he decided
sounded best. "And I'm damn tired. Be a dear now and put
on your dress. I wouldn't be much good to you, anyway. I'm
beat."

"She must be a hot piece." Her throaty contralto was
sweetly acid.

"I didn't mean that," he explained hastily. "It's just late."
Picking up Flo's rumpled dress, he walked over to the bed,
kneeled on the blush velvet, and held it out to her. "We've
been friends for a long time, honey. Get dressed now and
we'll talk in the morning. How's that?"

"Don't like it," she said, pouting, tossing her dark hair
over her shoulder with a flick of her braceleted wrist.

"Let me dress you," Trey murmured, moving nearer.

"That sounds better," she purred.

He'd put her dress on, carry her back downstairs, and Lily
could have Flo put to bed. He didn't want to argue with her
here. She was champagne-drunk and erratic. And oddly,
with feelings he didn't analyze, he didn't care to have Empress Jordan find him arguing with a nude, inebriated woman,
after he'd just—oh, hell, he didn't know exactly why. He
simply wanted Flo out.

He was facing Flo, so he didn't see the door she had left
ajar ease open, allowing three inches of gun barrel to protrude
into the room. He was reaching toward Flo with the dress
skirt spread out in a red silk fan, to slide over her head, when
he saw her eyes widen in terror.

He was about to calm her, tell her he'd never frighten her,
when a faint warning vibration tightened his stomach. A
second too late. Before the unconscious alarm had traveled

halfway to his brain, something slammed into his back like hot, corrosive acid, and exploding pain shrieked through his senses, at the same time the sound of the blast struck his ears. He saw and heard and felt the excruciating nightmare of hell vividly in the first person and dimly heard the unearthly screams. Flo's, he recognized. And a second later his failing brain suggested that the low, deep animal cry was his. Just before the corridor he was racing down to escape the suffocating agony closed into black darkness, one nerve receptor, still operating under the smothering torment, sent the message through. *A shotgun blast. He and Flo were shot.* He forced his eyes to move, but the effort was like moving a mountain by hand. *My God. Flo's dead.*

Was he dying too? Don't tell Mother, he thought. Then a crushing darkness buried him.

Empress was the first one to see them.

The roar of the gunshot and the tortured screams were bringing everyone in the house to the room, but Empress tore open the dressing-room door and saw them first.

Her skin chilled to gooseflesh as she looked in on the bloody scene. In the dim glow of lamplight the room was utterly silent, the horror of shrieks piling into a crescendo of anguish, only wispy echoes in her mind. The bed and wrecked bedclothes were splashed, splattered, splotched, and puddled with blood.

There was no question, she thought, her eyes wide with horror. The woman was dead. The pattern of shot catching Trey in the back had exploded in her face, and from that distance the cluster was tight. Empress shut her eyes and took a deep, steadying breath before she dared look at Trey. Dear God, she silently prayed, not all that generous warmth and beauty and teasing laughter dead. Let him still be breathing. Please, God!

Opening her eyes, she clutched the blanket from the chaise more securely around her and, trailing white wool across the blood-drenched carpet, ran toward the bed.

He was ripped apart, ravaged by the exploding pellets, lying facedown on the silk sheets in a widening field of blood. His long black hair half covered his face, scarlet rivulets tracing vivid rivers down its satiny length, spreading fingers of liquid death, red and black and spidery across his fine features.

Reaching for his wrist, trailing over the side of the bed, she frantically searched for a pulse. Her fingers explored his strong, muscled forearm slowly, carefully. Nothing. Her heart was thudding in her chest. Don't panic. Try again, she told herself. And she prayed. This time, after what seemed endless breath-held moments, a faint pulse beat—only once. Had she imagined it? Had she wanted him alive so badly that she'd willed the feeble beat? She waited, her eyes transfixed on the small spot of dark skin beneath her fingertips. At last—a second weak flicker of life. Tears came to her eyes, and she said very softly, "Thank you."

Two minutes later the room was filled with people, noise, and confusion, and three minutes later Blue and Fox had cleared it.

"We have to get him out of here," Blue said, his dark glance scanning the two windows facing the street. "There's too many people and only two of us," he added, motioning Fox to hand him a blanket from the far side of the bed. Then he gave a curt order for Fox to get their buffalo coats and began wrapping Trey in the blanket.

Empress had been unceremoniously brushed aside when Blue ran into the room, and she now stood at the foot of the bed watching his capable hands gently cover Trey's torn body. "Where are you taking him?"

He looked at her, a brief cursory glance. "Home."

"You can't," she exclaimed softly. "Those wounds! He'll bleed to death if you—"

"Not in this cold he won't."

"I'll go with you. I can help."

"No," he said. He didn't ask why she hadn't been in bed with Trey. Why Flo had been instead. He only worked feverishly to swathe Trey completely, oblivious to the dead woman sprawled across the bed. He didn't care what had happened in this room with the women. He only knew Trey was in peril here and had to be taken out. "We're going home." Blue said it very low in Absarokee, his mouth near Trey's ear. The whole side of Trey's face was smeared with blood. To anyone else no visible response would have been apparent, but Blue was watching closely and saw the trace of movement under Trey's closed eyelids. "Home," he repeated in his native tongue, and picked Trey up in his arms like a child, calling on all his adrenaline-flushed strength to lift the man as large as he.

Trey was covered in buffalo robes downstairs, and against Lily's frantic, impassioned pleas, they left with him. "Call the train," she'd argued, but they both knew the Arrow Pass drifted first in a storm, and the train wouldn't get through until the tracks were shoveled clear. "I'll get Doc McFadden," she'd insisted, but neither of them trusted white men much.

Mounted on their strong ponies, they rode north, Blue holding Trey, and Fox breaking trail through the heavily drifted snow. It was a superhuman effort by both men and beasts, forcing their way through blizzard winds, subzero cold, and mounting snow. They stayed on the high ground although the wind was fierce, cautious to avoid the dangerous, hidden ravines and coulees where loosely piled snow could bury a horse and man.

They ignored the strange girl from Lily's, dressed in her range clothes again, struggling behind them on her cow pony, too intent on their own urgent passage through the angry, swirling storm.

But at the ranch house it was she—small, snow-covered, blue with cold—who gave orders how to carry Trey upstairs. They left dark, melting puddles of snow up the Turkish-carpeted stairs and down the long corridor to Trey's bedroom.

Her name was Empress Jordan, she announced softly to the horror-stricken inhabitants of the house, although no one asked, with Trey's white face and bloody, ravaged body near death. The last name, Jordan, she pronounced with a French inflection. Trey had bought her that night, in Helena, she shocked them by saying, the faint trace of Gallic accent lending even more incredulity to her calm statement.

They didn't have time to heed her—Trey's lifeblood was draining away. But hours later, when the ranch doctor gave up, the delicate girl with tawny, tumbled hair and worn clothes moved out from the shadows of the upstairs hallway and said into the hushed mourning sadness, as palpable as orchestral dirges, "I know folk medicine from my mother and might be able to save him."

All eyes riveted on the fey young girl; shock, disbelief, and chrysalislike traces of hope illuminated in varying degrees on the faces assembled before her. She saw the heartbreaking look of yearning pass between mother and father and saw Hazard's brief nod.

Blaze spoke first, "He's our only child. If you can do anything—" Her voice broke, and fresh tears spilled over. Beseechingly she looked at Hazard, who folded her in his arms. Then his eyes came up and held Empress's in a dark, direct gaze.

"Whatever I have," he said quietly, "is yours, if you save him."

She was in there now, desperately working over Trey.

The doctor didn't expect him to live through the night.

Five

―――――――――――――――

"I NEED MY saddlebags," Empress had said quietly in response to Hazard, and a servant had taken off at a run down the hall.

All the rest she required—the boiling water; clean bandages; crockery to mix her medicines and poultices; the bizarre request for a dozen eggs beaten into a froth with cream and vanilla—had appeared in Trey's room within minutes. Stripping off her damp jacket and pulling off her wet boots, she'd said as politely as possible to the crowd of family, friends, and servants assembled in the room, "I prefer working alone."

All the faces registered differing combinations of shock and wariness, but Hazard and Blaze, standing at their dying son's bedside, never questioned her motives. Trey's breathing was no longer apparent. Only by carefully watching his chest could the faintest motion be detected. And at terrifyingly long intervals. As if his brain, still marginally functional, would occasionally remind the lungs that they needed air. And when the message slowly arrived through shattered and damaged routes, the lacerated remains of Trey's body would attempt to follow the instructions.

Hazard squeezed Blaze's hand.

She looked up at him, her face wet with tears, and it took

every ounce of strength he possessed to keep his voice steady. He had always been her rock; he couldn't let her down now, although his heart was breaking. "She's going to take care of Trey now," he said, and tugged gently on her hand.

"He can't die, Jon. Tell me he won't die." Her plea was a desperate cry for assurance.

Hazard looked at their last surviving child. Their firstborn, who represented so many memories of their love—the baby who could have been killed by the Lakota but wasn't; the strong, plucky child who had survived all the feared childhood diseases that had taken their other four children. Their only child they hadn't had to wrap in white velvet and lay in a small coffin with their favorite dolls or toys or warm, soft blanket.

Hazard's eyes turned back to Blaze, and he answered in the only way that wouldn't break her spirit. "He won't die," he said, thinking that if Trey did, he'd feel like dying himself. He wondered if it was a penance for having too much—the deaths of all their young children. An austerity bred in him by his Absarokee upbringing at times questioned the necessity for all this material wealth.

They had had too much, he sometimes thought. Life was too rich. Their love too grand. Five beautiful children, and power and land and wealth. Then, one by one, the children had been taken from them. One son dead of diphtheria. Another two years later with the same strangling illness, although they'd fought it with every remedy, every prayer, doctors brought in from Chicago. Then, five years later, when Chloe and Eva had died within hours of each other, after they had survived the pneumonia and were seemingly on the mend, he'd feared for Blaze's sanity. He'd held her for two days, afraid he'd lost her, too, terrified at the blankness in her eyes. He'd talked and soothed and cajoled, promising the world to her, not letting her know their two daughters had been buried, desperate with his own fear.

It was Trey who'd finally broken through the barriers. He'd been away at school and had been sent for when Chloe and Eva became ill. When he'd come into the room, Blaze looked up, and tears ran down her cheeks. They'd been the first sign of emotion Hazard had seen in two days.

"I'm home, Mama," Trey had said, and held out his arms.

So, if there was a balance in the natural order of things, if gains required loss, he and Blaze had paid dearly for their wealth. And if Trey died this stark winter night because of the enemies out for his blood, he felt a terrible gut-wrenching need for vengeance. Jake Poltrain wouldn't live out the day.

The anger mitigated the vast, empty helplessness. He'd known when the doctor took too long to answer his questions. Hazard had seen enough men die in his life to recognize the color of death. He'd known then how slim the chances were. How infinitesimal the hope for their son.

He led Blaze to the door, willing to do whatever was required to save his only child. "We'll be right outside if you need anything," he said.

"I don't want to leave," Blaze exclaimed abruptly, rebelling against stoic acceptance. Turning, her glance briefly touched on Empress and then went to Trey's still form. "I can help." Her voice was suddenly firm, her eyes shiny with tears but determined. "You can't do it all alone."

Empress debated momentarily. The beautiful flame-haired woman, dressed in the height of fashion, looked at first sight as frivolous as a butterfly. Large sapphires sparkled at her throat and ears. Her cut velvet dress was recognizably a Worth, blue as a summer sky, sumptuous as a queen's ransom. Had they been entertaining, or did she dress so for dinner every night out here on the frontier? It seemed another age ago when her own mother had a wardrobe from Paris's best couturier. But she knew her mother had possessed a strong spirit beneath the genteel facade, and perhaps this woman did too. "It may be fearsome to watch," she warned cautiously.

"I've watched four of my children die," Blaze said quietly. "Nothing is more fearful than that. Tell me what I can do to help," she said, finishing with a resolute lift of her chin. "What we can do," she amended, looking up at Hazard.

Hazard's fingers tightened on his wife's small hand, and with an apologetic smile at Empress, he said, very softly, "He's all we have."

"If I'm doing something for Trey," Blaze explained, "it's like . . . somehow—" Her eyes filled with tears, and she finished in a trembling whisper, "He'll know we're here, and he won't die."

Empress understood. Medicine could cure on its own merit, but everything she'd learned from her mother and grandmother, who knew the old herbals by heart, verified that people lived who hadn't the barest hope of survival, and others died who shouldn't have. And the difference was their will to live, or caring human contact, or whatever one wished to call that small spark of inextinguishable energy that passed between human spirits.

"Then first," Empress said, "we have to make him comfortable, take away the pain so his body can begin to heal. You can help. Have some ice brought up to keep the eggnog cold. We'll feed that to him all night."

Empress dissolved the sleeproot and pipsissewa powders in a small portion of the eggnog mixture. And then they took turns in the laborious process of dripping it into a small funnel attached to a hollow reed, placed far back in Trey's mouth. His swallowing reflex took care of the rest.

An hour later, one cup of the eggnog had been administered.

"We have to get a poultice on the wounds," Empress explained, "now that he's sedated." The doctor had extracted the shotgun pellets—at least as many as he could find—and although therapeutic, it was weakening to the patient. Trey had lost considerably more blood.

Empress took dried yarrow from her saddlebags and added enough boiled water to make a thick paste. Hazard helped turn Trey so the wounds on his back could be treated. It was a gruesome mass of bloodied flesh, which Empress gently dressed with the poultice, then wrapped with bandages.

"Now some yarrow tea for him," she said, and Blaze helped brew a small amount with the boiling water. Hazard, Blaze, and Empress took turns, again bending low over the comatose man, dripping small spoonfuls of the yarrow tea through the funnel-reed apparatus. It had to be accomplished very slowly, so Trey wouldn't choke or accidentally draw some into his lungs.

Through the night their ministrations continued: fresh rosehip tea to bring him strength; a monkshood brew in a minute carefully modulated amount (it was poisonous) to reduce the chance of fever; another portion of sleeproot in the rich, chilled eggnog.

"Don't ask me how it works," Empress told them once, "but my mother saved a man once who was ravaged by gangrene with her eggnog. It makes new tissue, she says, and heals the old." Then, a half hour later, another serving of yarrow tea, which slowed the flow of blood, sedated the nerves, and served also as an anesthetic.

Afterward the poultice on Trey's back was exchanged for an application of monarda oil, an antiseptic.

Then a brew of araica to reduce swelling and the chance of infection.

And so it went.

They spelled each other routinely, hardly speaking, weary with fatigue, but bound by their determination to keep Trey from slipping away.

Hazard often talked to his son in a low murmur, altering occasionally into a quiet, melodic chanting that twice caused a faint eye movement beneath Trey's closed lids.

They all noticed the almost imperceptible reaction, for each in their own way were watching Trey with vigilance. Hazard looked up at Blaze both times. "It was always his favorite," he said the first time with a sad smile, and when it occurred again very near morning, he murmured, "The People are watching over him. I can feel it." Hazard went off by himself shortly afterward to a darkened corner of the large room, sat on the floor, closed his eyes, and remained motionless, as if in a trance.

"He's praying to his spirits," Blaze explained. "He sees them and hears them. I wish I had his faith; it gives him infinite strength. He talks to them with reverence, and they to him. It is the mind that leads a man to power, he always says, not strength of body."

When Hazard returned to Trey's bedside, he took a thin gold chain with a small bit of rough stone wrapped in fine gold wire from around his neck and carefully placed it around Trey's. It was the most important spirit medicine in his life, his talisman, which had always kept him safe. And now, in his son's greatest extremity, he gave it up to save him. *"Ah-badt-dadt-deah,* he is in Your hands," the Absarokee name meaning "The one who made all things."

Empress and Blaze were near exhaustion, and at Hazard's insistence they lay down on cots set up near Trey's bed. Hazard didn't sleep but sat in a chair close to Trey and watched the faint rise and fall of his son's irregular breathing. He had already made all the promises and offerings to the spirits, and now he sat silently and willed his son to live.

Empress woke first, her sleep fitful and light, her subconscious brain racing over the remedies and potions, racking her memory for anything that would help Trey survive. He must live! her mind insisted, an emotional response so powerful that she sat bolt-upright on her narrow cot and opened her eyes to find herself already half out of bed. She owed him her life, she thought, still dimly enveloped in sleep although both her feet were on the floor, sensitive to the softness of the carpet. She would repay him by saving his life. Her eyes finally focused on the electric light over the bureau mirror. Electric lights! She hadn't noticed in the frenzy of the past hours. Hadn't expected them on the isolated prairie. But why not? the logical part of her brain reminded her. Helena prided itself on its technological progress; their first streetlights went into operation in '82, and the mines had used generators before that. The Braddock-Blacks had everything else, why shouldn't they have electricity, and the lights were dismissed although the phenomenon was startling so far up-mountain. Single-minded, Empress's only concern was that Trey must live, and that purpose overwhelmed even minor miracles of technology.

Trey's silvery eyes continued to haunt her even though she'd not caught the slightest glimpse of them locked tightly away behind his shuttered lids. She could still see their luminous beauty, the humor and heated passion that had shone lambently from their depths. Complex emotions surrounded her practical, debt-ridden fight to save his life, Byzantine reasons that also dwelt on a man's tenderness, the quirked curve of his mouth when he smiled, the arrogant assurance that he would find her flowers in January snowed-in mountain country.

Hazard had risen when Empress woke and gone to the windows facing east. He lifted the dark drapery aside. The first gray light of dawn was rimming the snowy mountain landscape, coloring the darkness of the sky with a fringed, pale border. "It's morning," he said quietly, throwing back the heavy material.

His voice woke Blaze and, silently walking to his side, she leaned her head into the solidity of his shoulder.

Empress echoed the softly spoken words in her own mind with a rush of hope.

Each of them, in their own way, saw victory in the light.

Trey Braddock-Black had not died during the night.

It was a triumph.

Very early, Blue and Fox came in to help while Empress, Hazard, and Blaze left briefly to wash and change.

Empress was shown into a bedroom suite larger than her entire cabin home, with sunlight streaming through large windows facing the mountain view. Golden light also illuminated, through stained glass windows, the adjoining bathroom where she had the luxury of a bathtub large enough for her to stretch out in. But the room's decor received only a cursory glance as she hurriedly bathed and dressed. Her bedroll had been carried in and set out on the bed, her second pair of worn trousers and shirt hung in the grand armoire, a silk robe thoughtfully added to the emptiness of the wardrobe interior. The three garments looked woefully insignificant in the cavernous mahogany closet. A search of the several bureau drawers eventually located her change of underclothes. She was dressed in minutes, her feet slipped into her old comfortable boots, dried now and polished to a burnished sheen. Her newly washed hair would take too long to dry, although a warm fire burned in the fireplace, so she toweled it dry and combed it with an ivory comb set conveniently on the dresser top next to a matching brush and hand mirror. Then, drawing it back from her temples, she held its shiny length in place with two tortoiseshell combs found near the toilette set. Fingering the gilded ornament on the small combs briefly, a sudden nostalgia for her former life inundated her senses. Then, resolutely, she shook away the melancholy images, recalling with a demonstrable lift of her chin her brothers and sisters back home, needing her, and jabbed the combs into place. Without another glance into the mirror she strode out of the room.

In all the terror and apprehension of the long night nursing Trey, she had momentarily lost sight of her reasons for being here. He had to live, not just for the personal satisfaction saving him would bring but because her bank draft must be honored if her family was to survive. Trey's father had said last night: "Whatever I have is yours if he lives." She wasn't greedy; gold in the amount of her bank draft would be more than sufficient reward.

Now to see that Trey Braddock-Black continued to breathe through another day. And then another night.

If infection could be curtailed, if gangrene could be thwarted, if his temperature could be kept down—any number of problems could still arise. He'd lived through the night, but the battle for his life was far from over. But it was, Empress thought, striding down the hall, allowing herself the smallest smile, a very propitious beginning.

By evening, Trey could swallow from a spoon; at midnight he opened his eyes for the first time and said faintly, "Mama," to his mother, who was standing beside him. His glance moved the short distance to where his father stood. "Papa." His mouth turned up in a small smile. Then his gaze drifted to Empress, and his eyes widened in an abrupt reflex of startlement. "Hello," he murmured. A hasty, scanning look assured him he was in his room, in his bed. "You've met my parents." It was more a statement than a question, and under ordinary circumstances he would have been embarrassed as hell to find his latest paramour and his parents in his bedroom at the same time. But his memory had quickly recalled the reality of Flo's shattered face, and he knew he was lucky to be opening his eyes at all. Parents, lovers, and bedrooms be damned. Not that it took a scrape with death for Trey to be audacious. But he'd always tried in the past to keep his amorous escapades out of his parents' direct lines of vision.

Empress was blushing.

"This wonderful girl saved your life." His mother was beaming.

"I think," Hazard declared with feeling, "a bottle of Cliquot is in order." And soon the room was filled with well-wishers toasting Trey's health.

It was Empress who ordered them all out after a decent interval, although her courteous *"S'il vous plait"* softened the command. Trey was far from out of danger yet, and she didn't want his celebration party to cause a setback. The regimen of fresh eggnog, medicines, and poultices was repeated through the second night, and by morning Empress knew that the risk of infection was over. The wounds were clean, with no drainage developing. Trey's forehead was cool to her touch, and he was conscientiously drinking his eggnog. Although after a long period of untroubled sleep, near dawn, he'd awakened and grumbled about wanting real food.

"Another day," Empress answered, but she ordered broth and pudding for his lunch.

By the third day, everyone's routine was nearly back to normal. Hazard and Blaze helped in the sickroom whenever Empress needed them, Blue and Fox were underfoot, and every servant on the ranch wanted to stop by and visit. Visitors, too, had been calling, offering consolation, but had been kept from the sickroom on Empress's orders. "After a few more days," she'd declared, "when he's stronger."

Empress still slept on the cot to be near if problems arose, but Trey generally slept through the night.

On day four Trey announced, "I'm getting out of this bed." He was feeling increasingly fit after two days of solid food: the steaks, potatoes, and Bessie's pies that he loved. "I'm well."

For a brief moment Empress debated defying his announcement but thought better of it when his eyes met hers. Determined eyes. "Haven't I followed your orders contritely for days?" There was the faintest edge to his voice although his smile was pleasant.

So she helped him cross the short distance to the chair by the window and refrained from saying "I told you so" when his jaw set hard to keep back the gasp of pain as he slowly lowered himself into a sitting position.

"You're a peach," he murmured a moment later, his face drained of color, a thin beading of sweat on his forehead.

Empress's brow rose questioningly.

"For not saying 'I told you so.'"

"I haven't known you long," she replied genially, gratified that he'd recognized her reluctance, "but long enough to know better than to argue with you."

He smiled. "An astute woman." He gingerly relaxed against the chair, his color returning, his grin boyish.

She smiled back. "I like to think so."

He was suddenly starkly masculine in his severely tailored nightshirt; or maybe in contrast to the pale blue striped linen, his dark skin and hair and the solid play of muscle revealed by the open neck was more compellingly male. His bronzed hands, grasping the chair arms, were strong and large. He seemed, in the short moments since leaving his sickbed, to have changed in dimension and presence.

His potent energy disquieting, Empress drew back, leaned against the windowsill, and grasped it with both hands behind her back. Maybe it was his smile, she thought abruptly; his smile was part wolfish and enticing. Did someone practice to perfect such devastating charm, or was it a natural extension of his perfect, charmed life? Rich beyond measure, if rumor was true, endowed with a physical beauty that startled at first glance. The kind that required a second careful look to assure one that one's eyes weren't playing tricks on one. Insulated by both, she thought. Except for the enemies, she reminded herself. Every paradise apparently had its serpent.

"And talented," he was saying. His tone was ambiguous, and for a moment she wasn't sure what he meant, her own thoughts distracting. His eyes were grave, she noted, as her glance rested on his. "I owe you my life, I'm told." Clarification was instant then.

"And you, mine," she responded sincerely.

"That was only money," he remarked with a shrug.

"More generous than needed," she quietly pointed out.

His eyes sparkled suddenly. He had an aversion to solemnity and touching scenes. "Should I"—he grinned—"retract a portion of my payment?"

She liked his grin even more than his smile and, after the last six months of struggle and despair, was whimsically partial to drollery. "You could try," she responded with her own grin, patting the bank draft she kept close in her shirt pocket.

"Tempting," he murmured, the fullness of her breast apparent under the soft flannel pocket. "Very tempting . . ."

She flushed under his drawling scrutiny and belatedly recalled the substance of their agreement.

"What day is it?" he asked quietly, and she knew his thoughts were in the nature of hers.

Empress stammered twice before blurting out, "It's the fifth day," in an altogether uncalled-for phrasing. She should have just said Tuesday, or January 25, or anything else but her gauche reference to their three-week arrangement.

"You never did get your clothes." It was a simple declarative, yet infused somehow with a sense of future.

"I don't need them. Really," she added as his gaze swept her from the toes of her newly polished boots, past the frayed trousers and faded shirt to the tip of her wild, tawny mane of hair.

"Mother must have something."

"No."

"Why don't I talk to her," he went on, ignoring her negative reply.

"I like my own clothes."

"Do you ever wear dresses?" The question was a casual inquiry.

"Sometime." She couldn't tell him she'd outgrown her

last dress a year ago and hadn't had the heart to remake any of her mother's.

"Maybe you could just borrow one." Empress began to protest, and he hurriedly finished, "For the visitors. Mama says they're beating down the door, and how would it look for the enchanting healer who saved my life to be clothed like one of the hired hands?"

Empress's lower lip trembled, and she looked away so he wouldn't see the wetness in her eyes. Did he think, for heaven's sake, that she wanted to look ragged? It was only that Guy, Emilie, Genevieve, and Eduard required clothes as well, and there hadn't been any money.

"Oh, Lord, I've said it all wrong," Trey said, apologizing. Reaching out, he caught a corner of her belt loop and tugged her closer. Taking her hand in his, he smoothed her slender fingers with his thumb. "You look wonderful. It's only . . . oh, hell, you know how provincial some females can be. You saved my life. I'm extremely grateful. My parents are grateful—*extremely*," he emphasized softly. "You should be shown off as an angel of mercy." He grinned. "God knows people have been saying for years that I need one. What do you say to Mama lending you a few gowns to—ah, stem the flow of gossip?"

Her eyes swiveled around instantly and held his in a deliberate peremptory glance.

"You will," Trey declared calmly, "be introduced as the nurse who saved my life. No one will dare ask more."

"How much do people know?" she asked with a cautious emphasis.

He didn't answer immediately, weighing the nuance and substance of his reply. "You don't live around here, do you?"

She shook her head no.

"I would have remembered if I'd seen you before," Trey said softly, more to himself than to her. "Everyone knows everyone," he went on.

Her green eyes were expressionless.

"And Lily's caters to—well, many of my father's friends and acquaintances, and some of mine too." Expelling a small sigh, he continued, "Fifty thousand is—I guess you'd say—over the usual amount for Chu's—ah, particular line of trade. That's to say . . ." He paused, uncertain how to go on.

"Nearly everyone in Helena knows about you and me and

the fifty thousand dollars,'' Empress finished bluntly, and pulled her hand away.

Trey raked his fingers through his hair, a nervous gesture that only after the fact made him wince in pain and hastily drop his hand. "I don't know exactly how many.''

Empress's glance was challenging.

He met it solidly. "What the hell did you expect? Bold as you are, sweetheart,'' he said with a small smile, "you must realize that sort of thing is not business as usual.''

She ignored his rebuttal. "Then why do I have to meet anyone at all?''

He didn't say she was the absolute center of attention in this shooting, discounting his own role and the provenance of the deed. He didn't say he had no intention of letting her leave before her three weeks were up. He didn't say he was seriously considering not letting her leave *at all*. The latter, however, was going to be slightly more difficult to arrange until he was more mobile and out from under his mother's and father's watchful eyes. He said instead with a casual blandness, "Don't you know about stonewalling?''

She looked perplexed.

"It mustn't be a French term,'' he murmured, shrugging negligently, and added, "It's a way of life for the Braddock-Blacks. You simply pretend nothing happened. How else do you suppose anyone survives a life of scandal?''

Her brows rose a fraction.

Was it a mild affront or inquiry? He wasn't sure, but he opted for politeness. "So you haven't lived a life of scandal.''

"Of course not.''

Ah, he was right. It was an affront from a woman selling herself at Lily's. Amazingly flexible standards, he cheerfully decided. "To this point.'' He couldn't resist responding with a wicked grin.

"And maybe I won't,'' she retorted pertly.

Now that was a shade too flexible, even for his amiable assessment of social realities. "Too late, pet, I'd venture to say. At least in Helena. Montana's a big territory, though.''

"Oh?'' Her voice was fringing on coolness.

"I suppose you could return my check,'' he remarked lightly, "and we could pretend that none of this happened, discounting the holes in my back, which would be difficult to ignore.''

Her temper flared suddenly. "You owe me, damn you.''

Trey realized immediately that he'd gone too far in his teasing. "Absolutely right. A thousand pardons," he said, quickly apologizing. He didn't care about the money, and good God, he could care less about society's scruples or what people thought. For some unknown reason he only wanted her to stay. So he quickly soothed and appeased and diluted her anger. And before he returned to bed, he'd extracted a promise from her to consider trying on a dress or two. Step one accomplished.

He was politeness itself, circumspect in his remarks, flattering, generous, kind. He was very good at endearing himself to women. Too damn good, various disgruntled fathers in the neighborhood had been known to remark. He ate particularly well that afternoon and took all his medicine without complaint in order not to offend his nurse. He also wanted all his strength for step two.

It must be a sign of returning health, he decided. All he could think of was welcoming Empress back into his bed.

Six

———————————————————

WHEN BLUE AND Fox came in to visit later, Empress took the opportunity to go down and talk to Hazard. Now that Trey was on the mend, she would like to discuss the money with him.

In Empress's absence, Trey asked his cousins about Jake Poltrain for the first time.

Blue told him Hazard was having the shooting checked out, had the sheriff investigating, was dealing with private inquiries on his own.

"How sure is everyone that it was Poltrain?" Trey inquired.

"Probably one of his men, more like," Fox said. "Poltrain doesn't do his dirty work himself."

"What about Flo?"

"She was buried yesterday."

"I want to do something for her. Does she have a family?"

"No one seems to know."

"Have Lily look into it." Trey closed his eyes briefly and saw the bloody sight again. "If my head had been where hers was," he said, shaking away the terrible image, "I wouldn't be here today."

"It's fate," Blue declared.

"The People are watching over me."

"They always have," Fox said. Everyone knew Hazard and Trey had powerful medicine.

"Thank God it was a shotgun instead of a rifle. I'll be out riding soon."

"Does the woman stay?" Blue asked. It was a great curiosity to everyone.

Trey gave a man's answer to his cousin. "I paid for her, didn't I?"

Empress sat facing Hazard across the large, polished surface of his desk. The library was small and cozy, a fire blazing in the stone fireplace, the floor-to-ceiling shelves glass-doored and glistening in the late-afternoon twilight, the room smelling familiarly of old leather, like her father's library had. Who would have thought five years ago that she, Comte Jean-Louis Charles Maximilian Jordan's daughter, would be discussing the business of her indenture in the remote mountains of Montana? She rarely allowed herself the luxury of self-pity. It wasn't a commodity that served any good purpose, like putting food on the table or clothes on the children's backs, so she brushed the small twinge of lamentation aside.

"You realize how indebted we are to you, Miss Jordan," Hazard began. "Deeply indebted," he added very softly, leaning back in the graceful Sheraton armchair and looking at her from under his heavy, dark brows. "As preface, I want you to know that, and also know I mean every word I said the night Trey was brought home." He was being gracious, trying to make it easier for her, aware of the unusual circumstances surrounding her relationship with his son. He paused, giving her an opportunity to speak.

With her hands clasped tightly in her lap, Empress's brain raced over various possibilities of wording. How precisely do you ask the father of the man who bought you in a brothel to give you $37,500 in gold?

"Is there something I could help you with?" Hazard prompted. A sudden fearful thought struck him. "Is Trey worse?" he inquired swiftly, leaning forward anxiously, his brows drawn together in a frown.

"He's fine," Empress quickly assured him. "Remarkably fine considering how recently—well, everything happened," she stammered, then, taking a deep breath, plunged on. "The reason I wished to speak with you, Mr. Black," Empress said hurriedly, before she lost her nerve entirely, "is . . . well . . . it's about . . ." She hesitated.

"Money?" Hazard interposed helpfully, taking pity on the nervous young woman.

"Oh, yes, I mean . . . this is terribly unconventional. . . ."

"I heard about the arrangement at Lily's," Hazard interjected, trying to make this all a bit easier for the painfully uncomfortable young woman sitting before him in clothes he wouldn't ask his lowliest groom to wear. "And I've—er, been helping my son out of scrapes like this—" He was going to say "endlessly" but decided instead on the more benign "occasionally."

"You mean, he's bought a woman before?" Empress exclaimed.

Hazard smiled, and Empress saw where Trey had inherited his devastating smile. "No, actually," he said kindly, "you're the first."

It was so damned embarrassing to be here, so damned awkward to have to ask for money. "I don't want you to think I go around doing things like—"

"Miss Jordan," Hazard interrupted gently, "let me assure you, no one is making any judgments. I don't know how long you've been in Montana, but social etiquette out here only requires that you give your first name. Beyond that, you need offer no further enlightenment. There are no questions west of the Red River."[3]

He really was a wonderfully understanding man, with some of the same gentleness she'd seen in Trey. Her gaze was direct, her voice only marginally nervous when she spoke. "I wouldn't even have to ask you about the money, but you see, I have certain responsibilities"—she paused—"back where I come from, and well . . . I don't know exactly how fast Trey will mend, and just in case it takes longer than . . . ah . . . the time I've allowed myself to be gone"—she finished in a rush—"I'd rather have the money now."

Without hesitation, without inquisition, with only the blandest expression, Hazard said mildly, "How much do you want?"

"Only what Trey owes me, sir," Empress replied quickly, reaching in her shirt pocket for the bank draft and handing it to him. "It's more than enough. Actually, it's terribly generous, and if my circumstances allowed, sir, I'd not expect you to honor anything near that high, but—" She ran out of breath and boldness and suddenly felt very much alone in this strange house, importuning this virtual stranger for a staggering amount of money. The tears started welling up in the back of her throat, and clenching her hands together until the pain distracted her thoughts, she managed to avoid embarrassing herself by weeping before this powerful, influential man who owned a great deal of Montana.

Glancing at the scrap of paper, Hazard sequentially thought it was a high price to pay for this pretty thing's time and a low price to pay for his son's life. "I offered you considerably more than this, Miss Jordan. Don't be bashful." And he waited for her answer. A man of his word, he was also curious about Miss Jordan's motives.

There was relief apparent in her abruptly altered posture; her hands unclenched, the stiffness of her spine relaxed, and her nervous expression melted away. "That will be more than sufficient, Mr. Black," she responded with a noticeable exhalation of breath. "And just as soon as Trey's better," she went on with a politeness that reminded him of a young child recalling the required courtesies, "I'll be out of your way."

"Nonsense," Hazard replied with both politeness and sincerity. "My wife and I both extend the hospitality of our home for as long as you like." For a brief moment his gaze dropped to his own hands, clasped in front of him on the highly polished desk, and when his dark glance lifted again, his eyes were bright with unshed tears. "We are forever in your debt." His deep voice was low and level with self-control. "If there's anything we can ever do for you, Miss Jordan," he said very softly, "you need only ask. To us Trey's life is beyond price."

Empress understood all that was in his heart, for in only the fleeting time she'd known Trey, she, too, had fallen under his spell.

Hazard cleared his throat and went on in a more normal tone. "I'll have the gold packed for you immediately and brought to your room. Are saddlebags suitable?"

Empress nodded. "Yes, thank you." And she thought of the new boots she'd bring home for everyone, and the food. There'd even be enough for Christmas presents for the children, for the Christmases past, celebrated so frugally that it had tugged at her heartstrings. They had all been so brave and understanding, it had made her cry. She smiled suddenly at her new wealth and at the large, dark-haired man who was as kind as his son. "Thank you *very much*," she added.

*   *   *

It was discussed first between Hazard and Blaze—the numerous visitors who were turned away daily from seeing Trey. It was discussed next with Trey—whether he felt up to receiving company. But ultimately it was left to Empress, in charge of the patient and the sickroom. The final decision was hers.

She listened while Blaze listed all the people who had been to call. She watched Trey, whose reactions varied from bright-eyed interest when some of his friends were mentioned, to unmistakable groans when a long tally of ladies from Helena were announced.

"Couldn't we be selective about this?" he demanded cheerfully. "Even healthy, some of those people would blight one's good humor and wish to live. Surely, as an invalid, I'm entitled to special prerogatives."

"For instance?" Blaze inquired.

"For instance, all those insipid young women who sent me embroidered handkerchiefs. Have pity."

"I don't know, dear," Blaze replied slowly, looking to Hazard for support. "I'm rather of the opinion that you either have to let everyone in, however briefly, or keep everyone out."

Trey moaned. "Why do I have the feeling that I'm going to lose on this?"

"They don't have to stay long, and it *is* a bit of a trip out here every day for nothing."

"Can Trey's condition withstand an hour or so of visitors a day?" Hazard asked Empress.

Empress had seen Trey walk to the chair that morning with a quiet determination she knew would be fully capable of dealing with a visitor or two. "If it wouldn't be for too long, I'm sure his health won't suffer. A limited time, though," she cautioned.

"*Very* limited," Trey repeated. "Spare me Arabella McGinnis and Fanny Dixon, and for pity's sake, *not* their mothers!"

"Don't be rude, Trey. Your father and I have to deal with these people," Blaze reminded him, and although her voice was mild, it was a tone that brooked no further argument.

Hazard grinned. "I'll run interference with Miriam Dixon. Maybe she's too much to ask of anyone, darling," he said to his wife. "Even well, it's an affliction to have to listen to her pious quotations."

"That's because she's partial to you, dear, and feels you are well worth saving. I always keep a watchful eye on you when she has you cornered, so she won't steal you away." Blaze's grin was mischievous.

Hazard's eyes widened in surprise. "Good God, you can't mean it!" It wasn't that he was unaware he attracted women's attention, but *Miriam Dixon?* He'd never actually considered her as a woman. She seemed more like a wind up machine with an appropriate, trite maxim for any occasion.

"Now you know what it's like, Papa," Trey said, "and Fanny's no better, although she does have an edge on her Mama's looks," he finished with a wide grin.

"Your father knows very well what it's like, and has long before you were ever born, dear," Blaze said calmly, "but to make it easier on everyone, we'll see that the horrid ones don't stay too long. How would that be?"

"Promise?" Trey asked warily.

"My word on it," Blaze said pleasantly.

"In that case . . . send them up. No one can manipulate a social occasion better than Mama," Trey explained to Empress. "She's a master of crowd control."

"It comes from having to control your unmanageable father all these years," Blaze retorted with a gaminlike lift of her brows. "After that, the rest of the world is easy."

"I feel it my duty," Hazard replied mildly, his eyes amused, "to see that your life remains eventful."

"How kind," Blaze murmured, and she and Hazard exchanged affectionate glances.

"Just remember," Trey warned, "Miriam Dixon isn't allowed up here without a full complement of family to save me from her preaching."

"Agreed," Blaze said. "Now, is ten o'clock too early?" She looked to Empress for confirmation.

"Ten o'clock is fine."

Seven

DUNCAN STEWART, BUTTERING his toast with crisp precision, was speaking to his daughter in a sharp tone. "If you insist on keeping company with"—he paused, spread the butter carefully into each corner, looked up at his beautiful daughter with deliberation, his cool, disdainful eyes the prototype of her and derisively went on—"ineligible men, I suggest you find someone with enough money to support you, should it come to that."

"But, Daddy, you've plenty of money for us both," Valerie Stewart replied uncontritely, dropping a teaspoonful of sugar into her teacup and negligently lifting her lacy black lashes to gaze unconcernedly back at her father.

"Just like your mother!" he said, exasperated, and took a neat bite of his toast. "You don't understand a thing about money."

"Actually . . . I'm just like you, Daddy. Poor Mama thought money was sent in the mail on some regular schedule. I know better. I know how you make your money. The question is, since you're in this sharp-set mood this morning, did one of your business transactions with the Indian agents go awry?" And the lovely young woman with dark ringlets artfully arranged atop her perfectly shaped head scrutinized her father with baby-blue eyes, predator's eyes, as cool as ice. When he gave that level of attention to buttering his toast, he was irritated. She smiled then and soothingly coaxed, "Tell me. Is there someone who could be pleasantly—er—talked into something?"

"No, dammit," her father grumbled. "I wish it were that easy. They're talking about another investigation in Washington. Hell and damnation, a few Indians die[4] and you'd think it was everyone's favorite grandmother."

"Daddy, don't take it so hard. You know very well, the hue and cry will die down in no time. A few headlines in the papers always gets the do-gooders motivated, but never for long. By the time the investigation gets sifted down all the bureaucratic levels, no one will care anymore." Even before her mother had died, Valerie had already stepped into the role of confidante to her father. Priscilla Wyndham Stewart had never understood her dashing, volatile husband. But he was one of the youngest colonels ever to be commissioned in the Civil War, and he'd swept her off her feet when he'd come back to Ohio on leave. It was the uniform, she'd always fondly recalled. Her father, Judge Wyndham, had never quite approved, but he'd continued to send money to his only daughter until her death three years ago. Her health had always been frail, the doctor had said. Personally, Valerie thought the laudanum her mother took for her genteel "nerves" had finally done her in after twenty years.

Duncan Stewart wasn't wasteful with his wife's money, and in truth, he had amassed a modest fortune in his business transactions. The problem was, he always wanted more. He sat in occasionally on the poker games at the Montana Club. But he wasn't comfortable writing a check for six figures every night of the week, and if you couldn't, you didn't get invited into the inner circle.

Helena, Montana, had more millionaires per capita than any other city in the world. Over fifty millionaires lived in the small mountain capital. And some of the millionaires were bringing in a million a month from a single one of their mines. Hundreds of English remittance men, younger sons in some form of disgrace, had also settled in Helena until such a time as the scandal died down and their families called them home. Society was very blue and very extravagant. It was also fluid.

One society hostess remarked, she was always cautiously

polite to her servants, for one never knew if they might be a member of society a week hence. There were still overnight fortunes to be made in mining gold, silver, copper, and coal. In timber. In railway construction. In land development. Across the world, it was the time of the robber-baron philosophy. J. P. Morgan had just cornered control of the steel industry and eastern railroads. It was a time of open, brash manipulation.

Duncan Stewart and his daughter, Valerie, were on track, in good company, and infinitely sure in the logical assessment of things that their personal gain was all that mattered.

"And as far as a husband, I've already picked one out."

Her father stopped his grumbling and glanced up in surprise. Setting aside his fork, he curiously asked, "Anyone I know—or care to know?" he added, well aware of his daughter's inclination toward transient liaisons with unsuitable men. His choice had been the Duke of Sutherland's youngest son, but Valerie said he was fat and wouldn't be civil to him.

"Trey," she replied sweetly. "Does that sound eligible enough to you?" Her smile was a slow upcurving of her lush mouth.

"He won't," Duncan retorted bluntly. "There's bets at the club that boy will never marry. That young stud shares his special skill freely, but not his name."

"I intend to have him."

Duncan Stewart thought, not for the first time, that his daughter was bold as brass tacks. But competent as hell, too, he admitted. "How?" he asked, imminently curious.

"He'll marry me when I tell him I'm carrying his child."

"No he won't."

"He'll marry me when you tell him that."

"No he won't. Even Carl Morse's shotgun wouldn't budge him. Or Blair Williard's. The Braddock-Blacks don't step back when they're pushed. They stand firm and reach for their own guns. Rumor has it, anyway, he wasn't the first with Carl's daughter or any of them. Prefers it that way, I hear. Less complications. They paid off Carl Morse and Blair Williard, and God knows who else. Talk's been rampant since that young Turk's been back from school for good. He's out to set records, some say. So think of a better angle than that, darling, if you want a wedding band from Trey Braddock-Black."

"How about . . ." She paused, then slowly went on, a touch of affectation for effect and a small smug smile on her face. "Perhaps he'll marry me when you tell his father that Gray Eagle and Buffalo Hunter are going to hang for raping me."

Duncan hesitated, but a moment later he shook his head. "Not good enough. Not with Hazard. *Are* you having his child?" he asked as the realization finally dawned on him.

"No."

"Thank God."

"Not his."

"Jesus! Whose?"

She shrugged. "I'm not sure."

Her father slammed both palms on the table and exploded. "How can you be so damned unconcerned!"

"Because I intend to marry Trey," she replied confidently. "With your help, of course," she added softly.

"It might take a helluva lot more than just my help," her father muttered. "Hazard Black doesn't negotiate to lose."

"Daddy, he wouldn't be losing," she answered with a complacent smile. "He'd be gaining a loving daughter-in-law, he'll be saving the necks of two of his nephews from the hangman's noose, and he'll be a proud grandfather in the bargain."

"You may have forgotten one small item in this ideal scene of yours. What if Trey doesn't survive his wounds?"

"The reports are gratifying, Daddy. He's on the mend. And really, now, don't tell me you wouldn't like to be related to that fortune. Much as you hate the thought of an Indian like Hazard Black having millions, you'd be a fool to ignore that. And the political power—they say Hazard knows half the congressmen in Washington. We can do it, Daddy. Don't be so negative."

When Duncan considered it, Valerie's plan had its merits. Yes, decidedly it did. And she was right about Hazard's concern for his tribesmen. He'd been their advocate in numerous controversies over the years, often single-handedly stepping in, paying their way out if necessary. Additionally, Duncan had influential friends in two of the local judgeships. If they could get an indictment against the two Indians, or even have the jurisdiction transferred to Judge Clancy's court, hell, it just might be possible. "When," he asked with the faintest of smiles, "does this all begin to develop?"

"There's no rush, Daddy. Let's give Trey another week or so to recuperate; the legislative session begins next week, anyway. Maybe when Hazard comes in to lobby, you'll have an opportunity to talk to him. It wouldn't hurt to approach Livingstone at *The Mountain Daily,* either. You know his attitude toward Indians. Why don't I plan on stopping by to see him.''

"And when I'm having lunch with Judge Clancy, I can broach the subject with him. Since Hazard saw that his son was dismissed from his post as Indian Agent, Joe Clancy's been out for blood, preferably Hazard Black's.'' And Duncan began twirling the fob on his watch chain like he did when he was contemplating some new scheme.

"Be discreet, Father,'' Valerie cautioned, that familiar habit prompting a touch of anxiety, for Duncan's intrigues occasionally outstripped his intelligence. "We don't want any warning to reach Hazard.''

Her father's fingers stilled, resting on the ample proportions of his embroidered waistcoat, and he sighed, suddenly struck by the enormity of the task. "With or without warning, this idea of yours may not succeed.''

"Don't be so pessimistic,'' Valerie replied mildly, plotting being second nature to her. "By the time we engage Livingstone's blatant prejudice and see that Judge Clancy knows he has an opportunity to humble Hazard Black, we have every chance of succeeding.''

Duncan snorted like he always did when at a loss for words. "What if you're wrong?'' he grumbled. "What do you intend to do about the child?''

"Marry someone else''—she lowered her dark lashes slightly—"perhaps. More likely, take an extended vacation to Europe. For a trifling sum a child can be sent out to be cared for in the French countryside . . . or the English. More coffee, Daddy?''

Eight

———————————————————

THAT MORNING EMPRESS overslept, waking finally to the low resonance of conversation coming from Trey's bedroom. She was sleeping in the dressing room now that the crisis was over, still adjacent to his room if needed, but more comfortable on the soft couch than on the cot. The room was small, mirrored, a narrow, elongated area like a widened passageway between his bedroom and the modern bathroom with the luxurious bliss of hot and cold running water. It was a stark contrast to her home in the mountains. The huge gas generator running the electric plant that serviced the ranch could be heard in the early-morning quiet, droning away on the mountainside behind the stables.

With a sinking feeling she recalled that this was the day visitors were going to be allowed upstairs. Would it be possible simply to stay in this cozy room, out of sight, away from curious eyes? Her appearance with Chu that night at Lily's may have seemed brazen, but instead, it was an act of desperation, totally out of character. And while Trey may have led a life immune to opinion, having perfected stone walling to a fine art, she had not. Having to face inquisitive visitors was going to be painful.

Maybe tomorrow, she cowardly decided, and burrowed

deeper under the blankets. But she couldn't sleep anymore, she decided long minutes later and, glancing at the clock, saw that it was only nine. It was still too early for the voices outside the door to be company. Trey must be visiting with his family. In that case she could dress, see to Trey, and be back hidden in this room by the time the first visitor arrived.

When she rose to dress, she noticed several gowns laid out on the window seat, simple day dresses in wool and velvet. She walked by them first like a poor child might walk by a candy store, wistfully, but not stopping. The colors glowed at her, enticing her, and she slowly walked back and touched the richness of a green velvet gown. She stroked it gently, the sensation of luxury touching her senses. Temptation was too irresistible, and a moment later she was holding it up to her body while she looked at herself in the mirror. The deep green set off the shimmering paleness of her hair, accented the golden tones of her skin, flowed in luscious folds over her bare feet. Facing her image in the mirror, she recalled child-hood days when playing dress-up held this same kind of tantalizing allure. The opulent dress reminded her of the same winsome pleasure, the same strange delight she was feeling today, where one could become a fantasy person for a fleeting time. It wouldn't be playing grown-up anymore, though perhaps the reverse to a young woman forced to be grown-up too soon. The dress was offering her a chance to be young and frivolous again.

Empress hesitated, conscious that she wasn't a child any-more, conscious of a saner side to her feelings that reminded her it didn't matter what one wore but what a person was inside. But then she smiled, a bright, buoyant light in her eyes, and decided to discard saner emotions temporarily. How would she look in an extravagant gown? It had been so long.

Tossing her borrowed nightgown aside, she slipped the gown over her head, the heavy fabric sliding over her nude body, silk on silk. The material smelled faintly of rose scent, like Trey's mother. Slipping her arms into the long sleeves, she adjusted the skirt on her hips and began buttoning the numerous covered buttons that ran from hip to neck. It but-toned easily over her trim hips and slender waist, but the fullness of her breasts resisted attempts to close the buttons further, no matter how she tugged. The bodice was made for a smaller woman; in length, too, the dress was designed for lesser height. In bare feet, however, it would serve. The revealing bodice, open halfway down to her waist, on the other hand, wouldn't do at all. Perhaps another dress in another style less fitted would suit. She was in the process of deciding whether to try on the Prussian-blue wool or the mauve faille when Trey shouted, "Empress! *Empress!* Come here!" His voice was agitated, and a stab of panic pierced her stomach. Had everything gone too easily? she thought nervously. Should he *not* have gotten up yesterday, was the appearance of healing masking some poisonous infection . . . dear God, was he *hemorrhaging*?

In a flurry of rippling velvet she ran toward the door, stumbled in the abundant fabric twisting around her legs, swore softly, and gathered up the skirt in one hand even as she reached for the doorknob with the other. Wrenching the door open, she rushed into Trey's bedroom.

There was a horrified gasp, a small squeal, and two steps into the room Empress froze, her bare feet and legs exposed, her rounded breasts almost spilling out of the partially closed bodice. Simultaneously dropping the skirt and clutching the bodice together, her glance frantically searched for Trey, the only known in this room, this house of strangers.

He was there—in his bed, looking rested, healthy, not tragically in pain or harmed, his wide shoulders resting against a cushion of pillows. Very much unhurt, she noted with spontaneous relief, a welcoming smile on his handsome face. And when their eyes met, she knew her panic-stricken alarm had been unnecessary, for his pale eyes smoldered with that same heated look she'd seen as she'd stepped out of Lily's tub on that snowy night in Helena. For a pulse beat she felt his hot desire lick at her senses, and then his gaze slid slowly downward to the mounded swell of her breasts.

Wrenching her eyes away from the passionate attraction in Trey's unreserved glance, plain-spoken in its need, she took in the other occupants of the room with a disquietude provoked not only by her unsuitable attire but freshened suddenly by the unfettered appeal of Trey's wild, luminous eyes.

A corpulent woman stuffed into a tight corset and a black dress had her hands clasped tightly to her ample bosom and was staring at Empress, wide-eyed and appalled. A diminutive young woman dressed in pale pink that didn't suit her white complexion looked as though she were going to faint.

Hazard, leaning against the bedpost, was controlling his impulse to smile while Blaze was calmly pouring coffee.

Lord, she was a beauty, Trey decided, not only carnally stirred but enchanted. He'd never seen Empress in a dress. The lush green velvet accented her vivid eyes, her sun-kissed skin, the rosy blush on her cheeks, the pure satin of her rounded breasts, teasingly revealed. How soon he could clear everyone out of the room was his first selfish thought.

Blaze spoke first into the fascinated silence. "Empress, dear," she said with meticulous courtesy, "come and meet Mrs. Bradford Dixon and her daughter, Fanny." It was important that the Braddock-Black position be immediately apparent. Rumor and gossip was to be stopped now. The girl had saved Trey's life. Nothing else mattered. They owed her everything.

Empress advanced a short distance, her cheeks feeling red-hot, her heart thudding wildly, but the scathing look in Miriam Dixon's eyes brought ten generations of Jordan arrogance to the fore, and lifting her straight nose a trifle in the air, she stepped barefoot over the carpet to within a yard of the seated women.

"Miriam and Fanny, I'd like you to meet Empress Jordan, the wonderful nurse who saved Trey's life," Blaze pronounced, as though she were presenting Empress to Queen Victoria in full court dress, not half undress, as was the case. "We are, as I'm sure you understand," she stressed softly, "grateful beyond measure."

Miriam nodded her head briefly in Empress's direction, opened her grim mouth sufficiently to utter, "Good morning," and snapped it shut again. Fanny's gaze swiveled skittishly between her mother and Empress before she murmured an almost inaudible "Good morning," then dropped her gaze to her tightly clasped hands.

"The dress, I see," Blaze remarked with a sunny smile, "needs some alterations." Turning to the two ladies opposite her, she casually explained, "Miss Jordan, you see, is temporarily without her luggage, and we are making do." She could have said as well, "She fell from the moon yesterday," and no one would have disagreed.

Without her luggage indeed, Miriam Dixon thought hotly. The little tramp is cool as a cucumber too. The events of the scandalous night at Lily's were common knowledge, discussed in Helena, with varying degrees of affront or interest. *How dare she look down her nose at me*, the haughty woman thought, fuming. But the Braddock-Blacks were a power one didn't openly offend. A semblance of a smile appeared across her tightly drawn mouth, and she said with biting courtesy, "Winter travel does create its share of problems." Her eyes were hostile. "Do you plan on returning home soon?"

Trey's emphatic "No!" clashed with Empress's "Yes."

He didn't care what the Miriam Dixons of the world thought. He never had. And if Empress was inexperienced in unconventional social occasions like this, he was not. He could protect her. But before he could continue, his father stepped in.

"That is," Hazard interjected smoothly, his eyes cheerfully blank, "when Trey is fully recovered, Miss Jordan will return to her home. As you see, Miss Jordan is optimistic about our son's full recovery. She is a marvel"—his glance touched both Trey and his wife—"we all agree."

Trey smiled at everyone, his expression affable. Absolutely a marvel, he thought, in and out of bed. Now, if he could convince all these people to leave, perhaps he could test his recovery with a very slow and leisurely appraisal of Miss Jordan's marvels.

What was a marvel, Miriam Dixon thought scathingly, was that the tart hadn't completely fallen out of that dress, while Fanny only sat wide-eyed, rooted to her chair.

"Would you like a cup of coffee, my dear?" Blaze inquired into the silence greeting Hazard's remarks, smiling at Empress.

"No thank you."

"A scone?"

"Thank you, no."

Miriam Dixon's expression was one of intense dislike, and when she began to open her mouth to speak, Trey decided to forgo any possible unpleasantness. "*Oh,*" he cried, loudly enough to cause a reverberating echo, "I feel a sharp, stabbing pain!" And then, with utter disregard for realism, he moaned theatrically and clutched his chest.

Empress shot him a startled look. The man was completely without shame. His silvery eyes cheerfully met hers, and he groaned again, noisily.

Standing immediately, Blaze informed her guests with a perfectly straight face that the poor boy was occasionally seized by these painful spasms. "Please excuse us, and thank you for coming to visit." Shepherding the two women to the door, she ushered them through with further words of appreciation. Shutting the door on them, she leaned back against the dark wood and said, "Trey Braddock-Black, you are thoroughly without scruples."

"And the world's worst actor," his father added tranquilly.

"Got rid of them, didn't I?" Trey replied angelically.

"Miriam did look damned near to detonating, darling," Hazard said, and then allowed the laughter he'd been suppressing to escape.

"She was," Blaze said with a chuckle, "the image of every dowager bitch I've ever met. How are we going to get through this with a straight face?" she said, finishing with a sigh.

"Papa and I will take charge," Trey replied with a grin. "We're much more ruthless than you."

"Don't you dare terrify me with that prospect," Blaze admonished smilingly. "One deathbed scene a day is enough, thank you."

And they all laughed.

Empress felt left out for a moment as parents and son enjoyed their warm camaraderie. Their relationship was special somehow, untamed and enchanting. In the next instant Blaze included her in the bantering group. "Forgive us, dear," she said, "but Miriam Dixon is such a trial, we all feel like children let out of school whenever she leaves. She's terribly unpleasant at times, but one feels so sorry for poor Fanny; you tolerate Miriam for her sake. Thank you for suffering her presence so graciously. She's really quite mean-spirited. And now we must do something about dresses for you. I'll have Mabel sent for, and she'll set everything to rights."

"Don't go to any trouble," Empress replied, uncomfortable as the object of scrutiny, gripping the green velvet across her breasts more tightly. "That is—some—of the others might fit," she said, stammering, and embarrassed.

"In the meantime, Mother," Trey interposed smoothly, "why not wait to usher up further visitors until Empress's clothes are . . . altered." Trey's eyes hadn't left Empress since she'd first burst into the room, and ulterior motives completely to the fore, his primary interest at the moment was getting Empress alone. It was like being an adolescent again; he hadn't had to deal with lack of privacy for years.

"I'm not getting involved in this visitor argument again," Hazard said with masculine disregard for any of the nuances of social etiquette. "I leave it to your discretion, my love. You look fetching, Empress. Ignore Miriam. She's living proof of 'The good die young.' And don't take advantage of your mother's sympathy," he said to his son in gentle re-proof, his smile warm. Walking to the door, he quietly said, "I'll be out in the stables with Blue and the mare that's about to foal, if I'm needed. Anything less than a national crisis, please handle it without me." He smiled and left.

"I'm feeling extremely tired, Mama," Trey lied blatantly, the minute his father left the room.

"Oh, dear," Blaze responded with motherly alarm, "I suppose Miriam and Fanny were too much. This entire issue of visitors is ridiculous," his mother abruptly decided, her sudden fear invoked by Trey's declaration obliterating all sense of polite social courtesies. "They will be kept down-stairs, and that's that," she firmly stated. "Now, dear, you rest and I will handle any visitors."

"Thank you, Mother," Trey replied meekly, his voice a shade wispy, and Empress thought he reminded her exactly of her young brother, Eduard, when he was trying to inveigle a favor out of her. "Could Mabel wait?" he murmured in a breathy, sinking tone, sliding down under the covers.

Good God, he was unprincipled, Empress mused exasperatedly.

"Of course, dear," his mother replied hastily, coming over to put her hand on his forehead. "Are you feeling warm, sweetheart?"

"A little," he responded weakly. Hot, really, hot, he thought, burning with fever for Empress, who was standing in the middle of the room casting him a narrow-eyed look of knowing scrutiny.

"Empress," Blaze inquired worriedly, "what do you think it could be?"

Self-indulgence, Empress reflected, along with too much practice at having his own spoiled way. "I'll mix up some-thing for a fever," she said briskly, deciding Trey needed a touch of restraint.

"Not some more of that vile-tasting, brackish stuff." Trey reacted instantly, his tone quite normal.

"You want to get better, don't you?" Empress purred.

"I'd also prefer keeping my breakfast down," Trey muttered.

"If you *have* a fever, you need it," Empress retorted pleasantly, a challenging light in her eyes.

"Really, dear," his mother said, "it's for your own good.

Now do what Empress thinks best, and I'll leave you to rest.''

Trey smiled then, a broad, satisfied smile, his mood altering abruptly. ''You're right, Mama,'' he agreed genially, his expression maddeningly virtuous. ''A good rest will relieve this fever, I'm sure.'' At last the solitude he wanted, with Empress all to himself. He never questioned his ability to lure her into his bed. That was a confident certainty. Glancing quickly at the clock, he gauged the time before lunch, saw it was more than sufficient, and added, ''See that no one disturbs me until noon.''

''That's very sensible,'' Blaze agreed, her expression approving. ''Isn't he an obedient patient?'' she inquired of Empress, sure of a shared endorsement of her parental pride.

Trey was lounging against the mounded pillows, his pale eyes innocent, waiting with amusement for Empress's answer. Perceiving her skeptical reaction to his performance, he was enjoying her predicament. Would she disagree with his mother or politely concur? Would she dare to call his bluff? Would she melt around him with or without resistance? Or more aptly, how long would it take before she joined him in his sickbed?

''If Trey promises to take his fever medicine, I couldn't ask for more,'' Empress replied, malice sweet in her tone.

''Of course, he will, won't you, dear?'' Blaze returned immediately, pleasantly assured her darling boy would be accommodating.

''I'll do whatever makes me improve,'' Trey answered ambiguously, his own notion of what would improve his present health perhaps not exactly what his mother or Empress had in mind.

Empress was instantly suspicious. His tone was too amiable, his eyes too confident, his answer much too vague.

''In that case I'll leave you in Empress's capable hands.'' Blaze kissed him lightly and left.

A prominent silence filled the room.

They wouldn't be disturbed until noon.

With a hunter's sense of situation, Trey slowly appraised the lavish velvet-clad woman standing before him, her extravagant breasts prominent in her state of half dress, succulent baroque luxury against the deep green framing them, very white in contrast to the forest-green fabric. ''Come here,'' he said. It was a low, throaty command. There was no other word for it. It was pleasant, unhurried, softly rich in timbre, but it was the tone of a man comfortable with authority.

Empress stood very still, her posture tense, feeling his raking eyes perusing her with languor. Much against her will, a pulsing began deep inside her, an inexplicable yearning responding to his heated gaze and the casual command. It was madness that a look and two words could cause such sudden spiraling warmth, and she deliberately shook away the incomprehensible longing.

It was like coaxing a reluctant filly closer, Trey thought, so when he spoke again, his husky voice was tranquil and soothing. "Everyone's gone. You needn't clutch that top together. To me it's only a dress that doesn't fit, not some issue of prudish decorum. As a matter of fact," he added in a soft, hushed drift of words, "you look very lovely." Sliding up from his lounging posture, he sat up very straight in bed, an image of virile strength, very much not an invalid.

She tried not to notice how broad and hard his forearms were below the rolled-up sleeves of his nightshirt; she tried not to notice how his heavy, dark hair slashed carelessly across his strong brow, how his white nightshirt was open almost to his waist, the bandages wound around his chest emphasizing his powerful physique rather than accentuating his infirmity. His vital presence assailed her senses, his ardent desire overt and tangible. But he was setting her at ease with a consummate gallantry she reluctantly admired. How many times did one practice in how many boudoirs, how many women did it take to perfect that exact degree of faultless charm?

His was an effective approach; as she continued to hold her bodice together, the prudishness would be hers, a silly and negative word in the privacy of this room between two people who'd experienced the ultimate intimacy. And at base, she was grateful for his flattery, a kindness after Miriam Dixon, to restore her shaken confidence. Her fingers uncurled from the velvet and her hand dropped.

Trey's glance was immediately appreciative. The deep vee of the bodice now slashed from throat to waist, only the outside curve of her breasts covered by the soft velvet. He remembered the feel of her heavy breasts, remembered their taste, the way she moaned in sighing surrender when he gently caressed each begging peak. Her bare feet peeped out below the crushed folds of her velvet skirt, adding a waifish quality to the implicit opulence of her body.

"You're not strong enough," she softly said into the heated silence.

"Stronger than you."

She shivered at the implied assertion, and the small flame in the pit of her stomach flared. "You could hurt yourself." Her warning was low-pitched, a concession made to conscience without the necessary conviction in her soft, breathy tone.

"I hurt already," he replied in the same quiet resonance, his arousal pulsing and erect. "That's why I want you"—he paused, carefully choosing his words—"to come here and help me."

In any other circumstances the innocuous words could have had any number of meanings, but the hushed demand was alive with clarity in that sunlit room, restless, impatient, heated.

It took her a moment to respond, contemplating a means to save him from what he wanted, to save him from possible injury, even though her own desire was flustering her sense of duty, poignant with its own longings. "If you take your medicine first," she declared, decisive in her role of nurse, forcing her emotions aside.

"Hurry." His voice was deep-pitched, on the verge of a whisper.

Was it an answer? She wasn't sure. "Will you?" she asked again.

He nodded, the bargain made.

Not out of malevolence but rather out of consideration, Empress mixed a sleeping potion. Trey was too newly recovered; what he wanted could be dangerous to his health. And while he may not understand the consequences, she did.

She gave him the medicine in a small cup, and he smiled warmly when he took it from her. "Would you mind taking off that dress yourself," he asked in a civil, conversational way, "to save my strength?"

"You drink that and I'll go and take this off," she replied. "Should I shut some of the drapes?" Moving toward the windows, she reached for the pull cord, deciding he'd sleep better in a darkened room.

"I don't care." Lifting the cup to his mouth, he queried, "Do you like it in the dark?" Soft amusement tinged the words.

Spinning around, she cast him a glowering look. "Has anyone ever told you you're a spoiled, pampered brat?"

"Not since you last did," he replied cheerfully, and tipped the liquid into his mouth.

Sniffing softly, Empress returned to the remaining windows and soon had the room shut off from the morning sun.

"No more stalling, darling. Take the dress off and come join me."

Swiftly checking to see that there was a discarded cup on the bedside table, she replied amiably, "I'll be back in a minute." Entering the dressing room, she shut the door and glanced at the small clock on the dresser. She'd give the medicine five minutes to work.

Leisurely she unbuttoned the dress, slid her arms out of the sleeves, the gown slithered to the floor, and she stepped out of it. Picking it up, she carefully shook the beautiful material free of wrinkles. It was exquisitely made, all lined in silk, sewed with stitches so small, they were barely visible. Mama had had a riding habit in this same forest-green velvet. She'd looked so smart in it when she and Papa rode. That seemed a lifetime ago. The riding habit had been made into a quilt cover three winters back and now kept Guy and Eduard warm in their loft bed.

Opening one of the mirrored panels, she hung the dress up in a row of pressed shirts, neatly arranged by color. Out of curiosity she unlatched all the mirrored doors lining the walls of the dressing room. Suits, topcoats, jackets, trousers, more shirts, and shelves of shoes, boots, and sweaters. A dozen silk robes, some quilted for winter. Silk cravats in every shade of the rainbow. She saw before her a very complete wardrobe, tailored, she noticed, checking the discreetly initialed labels, primarily in England. Off to the side, there was a larger door, which she pulled open last and gazed in amazement at its splendid contents. Leather—fringed, beaded, quilled, decorated with ermine and wolf tails, the most exquisite leather clothing she'd ever seen. She touched the colored quillwork, smooth as satin, intricate in design. Her fingers slipped through the long fringes, gently curled around the fluffy wolf tails, slid luxuriously over the pure white ermine. A different world required clothes like these, and though she was aware of Trey's heritage, she'd never seen him except as a wealthy young man. The way he dressed, this house, the scores of servants, how did he fit into his Indian world? How different he'd seemed, dressed in these clothes.

She lifted out one decorated shirt, a creme leather with

bands of lapis blue beading, and held it against her shoulders. The leather was like satin on her skin. She gazed at herself in the mirror with the garment held in front of her, its fringed bottom hanging almost to her knees. A pattern of green quillwork swept down both sleeves, geometric in design, very male and powerful. Dare she try it on? How much significance did these clothes hold for Trey? Would she be overstepping into a private, spiritual world?

But she'd never seen anything so richly embellished; it was like a work of art, and Trey was sleeping by now, she rationalized, so wouldn't be aware of what she'd done. She'd just quickly slip it on and then as quickly return it to its place in the wardrobe. Then she'd check on her patient to see he was covered, and when he woke, she'd apologize for the deception with the sleeping potion. The medicine was for his own good, she quite righteously reflected, and whether he agreed or not, she knew what was best for his health.

Carefully lifting the heavy shirt over her head, she slid it down, adjusted it on her shoulders, and was admiring the garment in the mirror when a voice behind her said quietly, "There's a bear-claw necklace in the third drawer down you might want to try with it."

She spun around.

Trey lounged in the shadowed doorway, one shoulder braced negligently against the jamb.

"You're supposed . . . why aren't you—" She stopped, aware suddenly how defensive she sounded. "You should be sleeping," she calmly went on, but the size of him dwarfed the portal, and her voice was more calm than her state of mind. Wearing a gray silk robe and framed in the darkened doorway, he looked like an apparition from some Stygian gloom. His voice, though, when he spoke, was the opposite of his mysterious appearance. It was light and unclouded, sunny almost. "I had other plans," he said, and smiled.

That smile had always been his greatest asset. It was unexpected, as he was, and dazzling. Dizzy with its impact, Empress forced the caught breath out of her lungs. "The medicine," she half whispered.

He lifted his fingers in a vague gesture. "Back in the cup, I'm afraid."

"You didn't trust me." She had found her voice.

"Should I have?" he inquired mildly, pushed away from the jamb, and stepped into the light-filled room. The outside wall, broken by French windows, allowed the morning sun to stream in, brilliant and sparkling. Carefully shutting the door into the bedroom, Trey closed the first of the mirrored doors, advancing slowly around the perimeter of the small room, gently pushing shut each closet door Empress had opened until he stood near the last wardrobe, still open, the one with his Absarokee clothes. "If you like, you may have that," he said, indicating the elegant leather shirt Empress wore. "It's much more attractive on you than on me."

"I couldn't—it's too valuable," she replied, uncomfortably aware of being caught rummaging in another person's belongings, aware also of Trey's potent nearness, fascinated inexplicably by the pearl-gray Chinese shantung of his robe, an alluring foil for his blatant masculinity and deep bronze skin. He was never ordinary, always extraordinary, in his startling physical beauty.

Was it normal to want to run your hands up the gray silk of his sleeve and feel the muscled strength of his arms beneath? Was it customary to find one's eyes drawn to a carelessly tied silk belt around his lean waist? Forcing her gaze away, Empress's eyes lifted to Trey's handsome face, perfection modeled in sharp-cut planes. He smiled.

Bathed in the warmth of that soul-stopping smile, the overwhelming feeling of wanting to reach out and touch him, she abruptly decided, was orthodox and habitual with Trey Braddock-Black. And he knew it.

"I should make you pay," he said softly, breaking into her thoughts. When her eyes widened in startled response to the ominous words, he went on casually, his expression pleasant, "Because of the deception." The sunlight sheened his long, dark hair with ornamental shadows, tipped his thick lashes with gold.

"It was for your own good," Empress instantly responded. "You're too weak."

"If I faint," he retorted softly, advancing another step closer, a small smile on his face, "ring for the servants to carry me back to bed."

"Are you always so . . . single-minded, and damn the consequences?"

"Rarely." The word was murmured, mild and uninflected.

She was surprised, and it showed in her eyes. "I wouldn't have guessed. All I've seen is Trey Braddock-Black getting what he wants."

His brows rose slightly in inquiry. "Does it offend you?"

"Not particularly . . . I've known many men like—" Just in time, Empress remembered: The details of her background were to remain concealed. She had been about to say that most of her cousin Claude's friends, and Claude as well, were as selfishly bent on pleasure as Trey. And if the duel her father had been involved in six years ago hadn't come to trial in the wrong province, she'd still be living in that same splendid world. So she was very much aware of pleasure-bent young men. But as provincial courts were by definition parochial, and the man her father killed had been the son of a local duke more powerful than the counts of Jordan, he'd been convicted and her world had changed.

Grandmama had kept the channels of appeal open for almost a year until she died because Grandmama had favors to call in from a lifetime. But when she died, the obligations of old friends were less staunch toward her son, who had, after all, killed the Duc de Rochefort's only son. An old and bitter rivalry originally had begun over Mama, and when the slur had been cast at Mama that day at the races, everyone knew Papa must respond.

Mama had come to Paris in the British ambassador's entourage, engaged to the ambassador's son, and her astonishing beauty had instantly attracted every man in Paris. She was La Belle Anglaise that season, idolized and feted. At a ball given by Empress Eugenie, she and Papa had fallen in love—the scandal of the season. Disowned by her family, she and Papa had retired to the estate in Chantilly and lived a quiet, happy life. Until the duel.

Trey's eyes narrowed at the astonishing answer that had ended so precipitously. "Tell me, have you known many men?" he asked, a slight edge to his voice. "I'd like to know." He understood, of course, that she'd been a virgin that night at Lily's, but he was also aware of some men's fetishes. She *could* have known men—a slight scowl drew his brows together—in other ways. If anything, Trey's experience in vice was extensive. Not that he'd necessarily engaged in the unconventional inequities, but he knew men who did. He knew men who used women in any but the conventional ways; he knew men—and suddenly a flare of anger surfaced. He wondered if he'd been taken in by an innocent-appearing young woman who was the very opposite of innocent, who perhaps knew ways to please a man he hadn't thought of.

Restraining his mercurial temper with a dispassionate reminder that this beautiful young woman standing before him in a tumble of tawny hair, in his leather shirt and nothing more, *had* saved his life. Visibly tamping his bristling irritation, he told himself to be reasonable. And he was for three seconds more.

Taking umbrage at Trey's restrained fierceness, feeling quite rightly, she reasoned, that her past was none of his business, Empress replied in an even, level tone, "You don't have to know."

"I paid enough," he said bluntly, "to have my questions answered."

Empress stood a bit straighter, twin patches of angry red color appearing on both cheeks. "Your money didn't buy my past," she retorted curtly, "or my future."

"You're not going to answer?"

"No."

"Then I'll have to find out for myself what you've learned from all those men you've known," Trey threatened. "We didn't have much time that night at Lily's to explore"—he paused, discarding the crude word that came to mind—"the *variety* of our experience." He smiled wolfishly. "I look forward to the education."

"And if it kills you," Empress snapped, annoyed at his presumptions, resenting his all too ready inclination to think the worst of her.

"I'm intrigued," Trey drawled, deliberately misconstruing her response. "I never realized your fascinating taste for excess. Shall we begin?"

"You're mad!" She moved back a step.

His voice was composed, gentle in its temperance. "Hardly," he murmured. "But pleasantly expectant, I admit." And he closed the distance over which she had retreated.

Empress withdrew another step and found herself against the cool, mirrored wall.

"How charming," Trey breathed softly, scanning her frightened expression with a negligent gaze. "The enterprising young lady who sold herself at Lily's has a flair for drama. Tell me," he drawled languidly, reaching out to slide his fingers through the pale curls lying on her shoulder, "is that look of fear a particular favorite of the many men in your past?"

"Damn you," Empress retorted bitterly. "Think what you like, but you don't own me."

"I know," Trey replied mildly, slowly rubbing her golden hair between his thumb and fingers. "I can't own you for only fifty thousand dollars. Your skin's too white. But I paid to *use* you"—he deliberately emphasized the verb—"for three weeks. Are we agreed on that?" His fingers tightened on the fall of hair, and he tugged.

Empress winced, debated whether to resist, and for a confusing variety of reasons, many of which were muddled by the smoldering heat that seemed to emanate from the tall man towering above her, she moved forward until the tugging ceased and she was pressed up against gray silk shantung and a powerfully muscled body. "You're wrong, you know," she declared quietly, lifting her face to look into Trey's cynical eyes.

"It isn't three weeks," he said sarcastically, but his mouth was already lowering to hers, and when his lips lightly brushed the fullness of her mouth, he murmured, "We'll argue numbers later."

She bit his lip in angry retaliation, and he grunted at the sudden pain, but his hands only tightened on her shoulders, and for a badly injured man his strength was formidable. His mouth closed fiercely on hers and with bruising force, reciprocating for her biting him until a few moments later she felt him quicken against her and his mouth gentled.

It was madness to react, she told herself, insanity to feel a heat curling blissfully downward, intemperant to have this irresistible impulse to melt into his body. But then his tongue slid across the inner surface of her upper lip, lightly skimmed the smoothness of her teeth, and probed with delicate inquisition until her tongue met his and he drew hers slowly into his mouth. Her low moan escaped in a breathy, feathery exhalation, and his hands relaxed on her shoulders.

Leisurely his hips moved in a languid rhythm against the softness of her body, his arousal delicately, skillfully assertive, reminding her of all he could make her feel, reminding her of the pleasure he could give. *No*, she thought, *I won't be seduced by a man so cynical and arrogant*. No, and never, and then her disloyal senses noted the warm tip of his tongue sliding up her cheek to her ear, recognized the blatant offering of ecstasy hard against her stomach, remembered exactly how long he could make the pleasure last until her whole body trembled. His touch was magic, his heated words whispered into her ear an invitation to his own special paradise, and she shivered in sudden anticipation, shivered away the no and never, twined her arms around his back, and spread her hands lightly over the Chinese silk.

Whatever she was, Trey thought with a practicality conditioned by his impatient libido, she was exquisite and passionate. She may talk resistance, and maybe that, too, was one of her games. And effective. For when he'd felt her arms lightly embrace him and heard that soft, melting sigh, whatever she was doing worked. He didn't care what her reasons for being here were; he only knew he must have her, and soon, or he'd embarrass himself like a callow schoolboy before he even entered her.

She was docile when he said, "Take the shirt off." And while she did, he discarded his robe with only a brief, wincing pain. He couldn't lift his arms too high or move too fast or bend any distance, but his legs were fine; his arms, at mid-height, were competent; and the wild, pulsing erection lying flat against his belly was splendidly healthy.

A moment later Empress stood naked before him, her cheeks flushed, a pink glow suffusing her throat and breasts; her breathing, he noted with the authority of experience, was erratic. He reached out and softly touched her cheek with his fingertips, then her mouth, throat, and with delicacy brushed downward until his palm caressed her taut nipples slowly, feeling their hardness spring to life, watching, as his hand moved back and forth, the pleasure on her face. Her hand came up, closed around his wrist, and without a word she pulled him closer. Her timing was perfection because he'd been too long without a woman and was about to take her with or without her permission. Kissing her lightly, he murmured, "Heal me, fierce kitten," and, pressing her up against the mirrored wall, bent his legs so he could enter her and slid upward into her hot, silky sweetness with a violent, thrusting need that he felt to the tips of his toes.

The rhythm of his desire was feverish, intense, and powerful, and Empress lay against the cool mirror and let her pleasure build in rushing, dark torrents that flooded her senses, let the peaking, hot spirals of passion spread outward from the imperious hardness that filled her. That impaled her with pleasure, and then withdrew until she felt Trey's hands tighten on her shoulders and she waited again for the delicious penetration that touched her so deeply and powerfully that she understood with clarity how one could die for love.

Her body was lifted the next moment, and a wildness raced through her blood. Then the velvety heat began to elude her, just when she needed it most, and involuntarily she cried, "No!" her hands tightening on Trey's back to pull him closer. His eyes shut with the sudden agony as her strong grip closed on his bandaged back, his smothered grunt of pain barely audible.

But Empress realized in an instant what she'd done. "I'm sorry . . . I'm sorry," she cried softly, her hands dropping away as if burned. "Oh, God, are you all right?"

Trey's eyes opened, he nodded and smiled, the more exquisite sensations drumming through his lower body, submerging the brief, racking torment. "I wouldn't want to faint, though," he murmured, his eyes heavy-lidded, his smile languid, "in the next few minutes." Gripping her wrists, he placed her hands low at the base of his spine, whispering, "There . . . hold on tight, darling." And the passionate invasion continued, forcing her open to accommodate his size, gliding expertly higher that extra small distance where they both lost control of their minds and bodies and rapture abundant and copious heedlessly held sway.

Into this prodigal sensual excess beating at the limits of their sensibility intruded a jarring sound.

"Trey, Trey . . . where are you?"

A shuddering pause to absorb the incredible.

It was his mother's voice, and she was in his bedroom next door.

While his mind was receptive to the sensitive situation, his feelings were feverishly unimpressed. There could have been a gun to his head at that moment and he wouldn't have stopped. An ungovernable passion was irrepressibly peaking, and he could feel the pleasure about to explode. Trey felt rather than heard Empress's soft cry of alarm, and his arms only strengthened their hold. Bending his head low, his lips brushed her cheek, slid around to her ear, and he breathed, "Ignore her," just a pulse beat before he surged upward, pouring a throbbing white-hot orgasm into the frightened woman in his embrace, tense with nerves.

A moment later a second call. "Trey, are you in there?"

And Trey, quicksilver-mutable with his orgasm passed, withdrew and, after a deep inhalation to refill his lungs, answered in a calm, controlled voice, "I'll be right there, Mother."

Empress was shaking in his arms, her own pleasure unsatisfied, capricious desire still volatile and burning. Trey's
withdrawal was too staggeringly abrupt, as if the unexpected
suspension was an ice-cold current of air. But if her skin was
cold where contact with Trey had disappeared, inside, her fire
of wanting flamed. Unreasoning feeling impelled her, and
though she knew better, she whispered, "Don't go."

He hesitated briefly as he reached for his dressing gown on
the floor, glanced up at her with a quick, measuring look,
then, straightening, his voice liquid and smooth, said, "Don't
move. I'll be right back."

Slipping his arms into the sleeves, he pulled it up onto his
shoulders with a small grimace of pain and, while striding
quickly toward the door, tied the belt with expeditious economy of motion.

Through the warm, pulsing rapture that throbbed undiminished through Empress's senses, she saw Trey put a warding
hand up as he opened the door and said, "Empress fell
asleep, Mama. She's been working too hard. No, she's fine.
I just covered her." And serviced her, he thought, and will
again just as soon as you, dear Mother, are convinced to
leave.

In two minutes, perhaps, no more than three, he was back,
an excitement flaring through his senses. Empress hadn't
moved. Not because of Trey's softly spoken order but for
lack of wanting. This was all very new to her, the brilliant,
heated glory of wanting, the hurtling sense of pleasure that
was like flamboyant excess, rich and luxurious, the feeling
that made one weak with lust. She had never realized a
sensation like that existed—where everything fell away, where
nothing mattered but Trey's touch, where delight and excitement and insensate frenzy fused into a hot glow that suffused
one's body and burned away reason.

She watched him enter the room and lock the door, the
quiet sound of the key turning in the lock sending shivers of
anticipation up her spine. Their eyes met across the sparkling,
sunlit room, and Trey asked in a hushed whisper, "Are you
ready?"

She stood exactly where he'd left her, her hands at her
sides, her back against the beveled mirror, flushed a heightened rosy pink from her arousal, from the arousal that still
kept her breasts tingling and the sticky wetness between her
legs throbbing in a hard, steady rhythm. His sperm traced

shiny rivulets down the smooth flesh of her inner thighs. He could see the pearly glisten inside her left thigh from where he stood, and inside her right thigh, reflected in the mirrored wall opposite him. Her form was in profile, too, in those ranked mirrors, repeated in varying angles down the length of the narrow wall. Her breasts were large and firm, youthfully high with jutting nipples, pale and pink and jewel-hard. She was peaking still, his experience told him, uncon-summated, her eyes half shut against the sensations, taut and flushed and wetly ready for whatever he wanted to do.

Her obvious passion reminded him again of his misgivings apropos her previous experience. Was she a novice as she professed, or a practiced virtuoso skilled enough to portray that fugitive innocence with a rare talent? It would be, he thought, untying the belt to his robe, fascinating to discover the answer.

The door was locked, she was clearly ready, she was also, after all, his purchase, so the manner in which he assuaged his carnal appetite and discovered the answers to her previous sexual history were unobstructed.

Empress's eyes followed him as he approached, discarded his robe, and came to stop short inches from her. Tumbled waves of fair hair framed the expectant face she raised to him and her eyes, meeting his, were magnetic with longing. "For-give me," he said softly, "for leaving you"—his bronzed hand reached out delicately to stroke one turgid nipple; she shivered uncontrollably—"unsatisfied," he finished in a whisper. A novel excitement stirred his senses. She was prime and primed, and so near to orgasm that it was tantalizingly provocative. He was hard again in one racing moment.

"Look in the mirror," he said, cupping her chin gently and turning it toward the reflecting wall. "Would you like that inside you?" His erection was magnificent, poised quivering only inches away from her own shuddering need. A tiny gasp escaped her, and he turned her face back, his fingers warm on her skin. "You sound interested," he whispered. "What would you do to have that inside you?"

Her eyes came up passion-hazed, but she fought for com-mand of her senses. "That's not fair," she declared in a small, hushed voice.

"Aren't you used to games, darling? After all, if you've known many men, there had to have been games. And if you

were a virgin . . . the games must have been *interesting.*"
The accusation was low, husky, tinged with distaste.

"You're wrong," Empress said, but her voice wouldn't
argue, for her senses were still in thrall to the lush mysteries of
passion coursing through her body.

"Tell me how I'm wrong," Trey insisted in a hard, brusque
murmur.

"I can't . . . touch me," she replied in one uninterrupted
rush of words. "You must," she finished in a rich, throaty
imperative that bespoke her years of wealth and position.

It stopped him for a moment—the sureness, the authority,
incongruous somehow in the trembling, sexually aroused woman
he held, with his long fingers securing her jaw. He forced her
chin up a fraction higher, an imperious gesture of his own.
"And if I don't?"

Empress reached down and touched him, her small fingers
curving around the pulsing crest of his rigid manhood. With
an economy of motion she slid her curled fingers slowly
down, and then up again, the pressure strong and sure, and
with an equal economy of words she said, "Maybe you will
now," as he released her from his grip.

He let the exquisite surge of pleasure subside, then laughed
softly, charmed by the swift, adept altering of vassalage.

"Now that I have your attention," Empress purred sweetly,
"if we set our minds to it, I think we can both help each
other. I take orders so damned poorly." She drew an imagi-
nary line in the air midway between them. "Meet me halfway," she murmured, her voice delicious with suggestion,
"and I'll take you to paradise. . . ."

He chuckled. A low, rich sound of pleasure. "A charming
proposition," he whispered, the words like velvet on her
skin. "How can I refuse?" His eyes lazily gauged the distance between them, and he bent his head a small, measured
extent, his silvery eyes amused yet curiously alert. It was a
quiet engagement of wills, and then—

She smiled.

He smiled.

And their lips met precisely, exactly, equidistant between
vassalage and command. An agreeable position for two personalities well grounded in pride.

They kissed leisurely, letting the raw emotions, the hard,
rough disagreement subside, letting the beauty of minute
sensation unveil slowly. It was so endlessly blissful with

him—was it so with every man? Empress briefly considered
old Chu and Jake Poltrain and, though inexperienced, instantly decided Trey was special, that what he was making
her feel was special.

Trey didn't question his feelings, although he recognized the
exquisite arousal experienced with Empress as unique. But
introspection was a thousand priorities down the list at the
moment. Rather, he was wondering if his back would tolerate
lying down with Empress riding him. Why not try? he resolved venturesomely and, nibbling at her lips, murmured
"Come." Taking her hand, he led her to the chaise.

Her thighs were slippery with sperm, sliding against each
other sleekly when she walked. "It's very decadent," she
breathed, wanting him to feel what she was feeling, wanting
him to understand the intensity, and when he turned slightly
to wonder at her statement, she pointed down to the lustrous
glaze spread now with the movement of her legs to a glossy
satin.

"Is decadence pleasant?" he asked, soft and knowing.

When she nodded, he said, "I can give you more. . . . I
can fill you with . . . decadence." Pulling her close, he ran
his hands leisurely up her body from the damp juncture of her
thighs, up her trim stomach, slowly lingering a moment later
to caress gently the round softness of her breasts, sliding at
last to the graceful curve of her throat. Heat had risen in
Empress's body like the temperature of a desert afternoon as
Trey's hands traveled upward. She closed her eyes, drowning
in the rising flame, luxuriating in the delicious bliss, until he
softly ordered, "Look at me."

Her heavily lashed lids lifted languidly as she returned to
reality from her own private enchantment.

"I'll fill you," he said in a low, husky murmur, "saturate,
gorge you"—one finger slid softly across her throat—"to
here."

For a body throbbing with unfulfilled desire, for a passion
only incompletely assuaged, it was an irresistible promise.
"How nice," Empress whispered, reaching up on tiptoe to
lick a warm, wet path up his throat.

It was enormously more than nice, Empress thought a
moment later, lying on the chaise, Trey's tongue unhurriedly
licking the sleek flesh of her thighs, moving upward with a
piquant slowness that prolonged the building ecstasy; beyond
words; so near paradise, she forgot momentarily who and

where she was. She slid her fingers through the heavy, dark waves of his hair, scented with an elusive, exotic fragrance that brought to mind caravans under great open skies, accommodatingly eased her legs apart when Trey's palms pressed outward, and shivered as his tongue slipped over her dewy wetness.

He licked and nibbled and sucked until she begged. It was beyond her comprehension at first. *I won't*, she thought. *I'll wait*. But she was running wet with desire, adding her own passionate fluids to the residue of Trey's, and her heart was beating now with an intensity that sent her heated blood racing to every peaked nerve in her body.

But then Trey raised his head and effortlessly lifted her upward, settling her slightly higher against the chaise back so that she was half reclining, her thighs spread like a trained and obedient houri. He settled comfortably between her welcoming thighs, but casually, as though she weren't dying, weren't mad with desire. And he stroked her stimulated, sensitive breasts with gentle fingers, smoothly circling each nipple, cupping the heaviness in his large palms, lifting them until she felt a streaking, stabbing desire race downward to the throbbing center of her being. With her breasts raised high and mounded in his hands, he touched the nipples teasingly with his mouth, little tugging bites; soft, light sucks; brushing his cheek against the elevated, swelling prominence of her large breasts until she capitulated and begged, "It's torture," she whispered.

His dark-lashed eyes lifted in mild inquiry.

"Please," she breathed.

"Wait," he whispered.

"No!" It was a sharp, emphatic demand.

"No?" His tone was softly blasé.

"Damn you," she threatened, low and heated, "I'll give you poison."

"That sounds serious," he responded in mock alarm. But then his expression changed, as well as his voice. "Maybe," he said evenly, "you'd like to tell me about the many men."

She hesitated for a moment at the blatant blackmail but was stretched so taut with longing, her resistance crumbled. "There aren't any."

"Then why the comment?"

"My cousin, damn you. I was talking about my cousin and his friends. I'd grown up with them and knew how they acted."

"Sure?" Trey slowly rubbed her nipple, a trembling need shuddering through her with each leisurely stroke.

"Poison," she whispered threateningly.

He scrutinized her for one brief moment more and, satisfied, said, "That won't be necessary, fierce kitten. I'll be glad to accommodate you."

When he entered her swift seconds later, she began to climax before he had fully penetrated, and as he drove in deeply, he felt the little fluttering convulsions along his entire length, heard her soft cry of release, held her in his strong arms until with a small sob, she lay replete. "Thank you," she breathed, her cheek resting on his solid shoulder.

Trey looked down at her, warm and satiated in his embrace, and murmured, "Thank me later"—his grin was sudden and boyish—"when I deserve it." He was rigid inside her and had every intention of seeing that the lady was satisfied in a much greater and more lengthy variety of ways. He smiled to himself. He was alive, he gratefully reflected, and moved then just a fraction to gauge the extent of blissful living. He was on the mend, his pain at very manageable levels. It was a beautiful, sunny winter morning—his eyes came up to check the bureau clock—and he had another hour and a half before lunch. Empress was soft beneath him, her body warmly welcoming. Smiling down at her, he said gently, "Now tell me, darling, can you feel me better here"—he moved up into her hot, slippery interior and was gratified to hear her hushed little moan—"or does the feeling peak more intensely when I do this?" His hands slid under her bottom, and he lifted her to meet the full, hard length of his arousal.

"Oh, God!" She gasped, the violent intoxication too mercilessly fierce, and when he rotated his hips slightly to touch all the quivering surfaces of her pulsing lushness, she groaned. "Not yet . . . it's too soon . . . I can't." She pressed against his bandaged chest, her hands trembling.

He wouldn't listen. "It's never too soon," he whispered low, and moved inside her with a gentleness that soothed, a slow, lazy, tactile movement that before too long caused her hands to relinquish their pressure and slide up his chest. Her hand caught briefly on his gold pendant, suspended between them, but in a swift, clean motion he tucked it away under his bandage, and her hands continued upward to rest docilely on his shoulders. "See," he said as her slender hips arched up slightly, "you can . . . after all."

She screamed that time when she climaxed, a long, low, irrepressible cry that echoed around the small room and justified Trey Braddock-Black's reputation for finesse.

The following hour or so was both extravagant and excessive, exciting in the newness of sensation, lush with playfulness, embellished by vivid, mirrored images of carnal lust and teasing dalliance. Empress's initial astonishment at Trey's stamina gave way to an ingenuous acceptance, and finally to an unreserved, eager demand that he found artlessly charming.

He was, however, not in the peak of health and pleasantly exhausted, sprawled on the floor, his head pillowed on Empress's legs. He placidly reminded her that he could stand a short rest.

Empress was instantly contrite, then shamefaced and apologetic.

At which point he smiled at her and said, "Sweetheart, if I had more energy, I'd roll over and kiss your toes. Do not even *consider* apologizing." And then, teasingly, he did just that, causing Empress to cry sharply in alarm, "Trey, my God, your back's bleeding!"

"It's nothing," he replied, feeling deliciously content. But she wouldn't be satisfied until she had him soaking in the tub, filled high with steaming hot water.

He lay with his head back against the travertine marble, considering himself an extremely lucky man, blissfully satiated, anticipating the next time his beautiful companion nurse would wrap her sweet arms around him.

"Are you sure you feel all right?" Empress inquired nervously.

"Great," he murmured.

"No pain?"

His eyes opened, half-lidded and amused. "Are you kidding? I've never felt better."

"It does look as though the bleeding is only superficial," she hastily assured him.

"Good," he replied blandly, unconcerned with the bleeding, worry-free in his utter contentment, and he slid deeper into the water.

"I think it would be therapeutic"—the syllables were softly pronounced with Gallic emphasis—"if you soaked in the tub every day now that you're feeling better."

He looked at her cheerfully, his dark hair clinging silkily to his shoulders. "I'll consider it."

"Don't be obstructive." It was the nurse tone of command, accompanied by a stubborn pout of her lush bottom lip.

"On one condition," he replied casually, undeterred by commanding tones.

"I won't respond," she said a bit huffily, knowing what he was about to say.

"In another few days I'll be able to carry you, and then what can you do?"

"Think what your parents will say."

"They're leaving for Helena tomorrow. The legislative session began yesterday, and the only reason they stayed home this long was because they were worried about me. So what do you say to that? I'd say, you lose."

A sudden, stupefying flare of excitement raced through her senses. No, losing was not exactly the word to describe her sensations. Heaven on earth, rain after a five-year drought. That was closer to the feeling. Trey's gentle hands on her body, his mouth soft and warm on hers, the excruciatingly glorious pleasure when their bodies joined. But all transient, she abruptly recalled. A rich young man's momentary bauble. So she replied in a composed reasonable way, "I don't suppose I could realistically fight you off."

"Extremely sensible, since I outweigh you by several score."

"You're a bully."

"You should talk. Who's been cramming vile concoctions down my throat for days now?"

"It's for your own good."

"So is what I have in mind." There was a smile in his voice.

She reached down to splash him in retaliation, but his hand caught hers in midair, gave it a quick tug, and tumbled her into the water.

They discussed the relative merits of water therapy at close range and in increasingly murmured cryptic phrases.

He was most convincing.

Nine

———————◆———————

HAZARD AND BLAZE left the next morning for their home in Helena. The territorial legislature was a hotbed of selfish manipulation, the lobbying blatant and crudely mercenary. Hazard brought a good supply of money to influence those who could help his cause.[5]

For years attempts had been made to diminish the Indian reservations, and last year the Blackfoot reservation in northern Montana had been reduced from 21,651,200 acres to 4,073,600 acres, because the cattle interests were desperate for more grazing land.[6]

A bill was being introduced again that year to reduce the Absarokee reservation, and Hazard was committed to staving off passage. In 1879, 1882, and 1884, similar bills had been introduced and, through dint of tremendous pressure and money, had been defeated, thanks very much to Hazard's personal fortune and influence. He was on familiar terms with congressmen in Washington, as well as bureaucrats in the Department of the Interior. When necessary, he and Blaze opened their Washington home and actively worked to defeat those bills detrimental to his tribe's interests.

Until now the Absarokee reservation had remained untouched, but each year the pressures mounted by cattlemen, railroads, lumber interests, and this year the lobbying efforts were intense. The Braddock-Black acreage and mineral holdings were extensive and more than sufficient for their clan, which had prospered in the last twenty years. But the other clans on the reservation had need of additional support, and Hazard and Blaze generally spent the months of the legislative session in Helena.

There was nothing democratic about Montana politics; the men with the most money and influence had their legislation approved. The only restraint was the occasional repudiation by Congress in Washington, the final judge of territorial government. But federal interference in territorial politics was rare and relegated to other than local issues. So the legislative sessions in Helena were nepotistic, venal, and rife with monopolistic intent.

This mercenary attitude toward government was not unique to Montana but practiced with cavalier shamelessness by every robber baron of American industry. These were the decades of J. P. Morgan, Carnegie, Rockefeller, Forbes, a time of unregulated industrial growth and a social Darwinist policy of "the ends justifies the means." These capitalists would mouth platitudinous phrases on the marvels of laissez-faire free enterprise while signing a monopolization agreement negating these very principles. And Standard Oil was beginning to buy up all of Butte, Montana, so they could set prices worldwide on copper.

So in the broad context of capitalism's theory of "the public be damned," Hazard's fight in Montana to save what he could for the Absarokee was just one very small battle in an enormous losing campaign. But decidedly, it was still money that mattered. Money bought votes, money bought land to protect one's borders, money bought stock in companies and, with that stock, influence. So they left on their private train, promising to be back at the end of the week.

Valerie dropped by to see Hiriam Livingstone that morning on the pretext of placing an ad in his paper for the church auxiliary's annual bazaar. Knowing his interest in women and his disinterest in his wife, she dressed in a violet velvet walking suit trimmed in ermine. The violet brought out the best in her eyes, and she'd always felt the ermine encouraged the impulse to touch the soft fur.

Hiriam was suitably taken with Valerie's judgment in clothes and told her so as he ushered her into his office. "That ermine makes you look like a queen, my dear," he said in lieu of his more lecherous thoughts, which gravitated toward Valerie's perception of touching.

With a flirtatious smile she thanked him in a little-girl voice that worked every time with these old roués. Over tea that a clerk brought in they discussed the church-bazaar ad. But when Valerie said, "I'd love one," to his offer of a tea cake, and held his eyes a moment longer than necessary, Hiriam Livingstone began to consider other than business with the ravishing Miss Stewart. Although well over sixty, Hiriam was sturdily built and, like his father before him, intended to live until ninety. And like his father before him, who'd sired children with a third wife well into his seventies, the editor and owner of *The Mountain Daily* enjoyed a healthy sexual appetite. Luckily Lily's was available because his wife of forty years hadn't held any attraction for him in decades. Abigail was fat, prone to discussions of a spiritual nature, and zealously doctored her various ailments, which left little time for anything else. They had four maids, a housekeeper, two gardeners, and three grooms; she was well taken care of. And his leisure time was his own.

"You were saying, my dear, that you lacked any culinary talents to make pretty tea cakes like these. Frankly I find it extraordinary you should feel you need them."

"Why, sir, doesn't every young woman have to be able to care for her future husband?" Valerie's eyes lifted on the word *care*, exuding a visible sensuality.

Leaning forward across the small tea table, Hiriam patted her hand, lying like an open invitation on the Portuguese lace cloth. "Miss Stewart," he said, innuendo evident beneath the gravel of his voice, "I'm sure there's not a man alive who intends your care of him to include domestic skills."

Sliding her hand out from under his with a lingering slowness, Valerie settled back in her chair and smiled demurely. "How sweet of you to say that, Mr. Livingstone." Her voice dropped into a low, breathy hush. "But Mama always taught me that the way to a man's heart is through his stomach."

Hiriam had to swallow once before his breathing returned to normal, since the visual image that came to mind at her breathy words was far removed from allusions to food. "Mamas don't always understand, my dear," he replied gruffly, "what men want."

"And what is that, Mr. Livingstone?" Valerie asked coyly.

He cleared his throat before he answered. "Why don't we discuss it at the box social." And although an elder at the Presbyterian church, he smiled a lecher's smile, promising to outbid everyone for her box lunch at the bazaar auction.

"I'll look forward to that, Mr. Livingstone," Valerie cooed, "although I do declare, what will Mrs. Livingstone say?"

"It's for a good cause, my dear," he assured her with avuncular heartiness, but his glance was perversely nonavuncular. "And Abigail's been feeling poorly lately, so won't be attending."

"How Christian of you, sir, to represent the family at the bazaar."

"We try, young lady, to perform our Presbyterian duty."

"How unselfish," Valerie purred.

"Consider me completely and unselfishly at your disposal, my dear." Hopefully very soon, he thought.

"How splendidly chivalrous, Mr. Livingstone, and it brings to mind a *small* problem I recently encountered. Perhaps you could advise me on the proper course of action . . . I mean, to whom I might refer the complaint." She lowered her eyes shyly and said, "I'm afraid it's slightly embarrassing." But then her chin came up, and her mouth trembled faintly in what she hoped was touching apprehension. "Although it was very frightening, too, sir."

"What is it, my child?" Livingstone immediately responded. "If I can be of any help . . ."

"Well, you see, sir," and she touched the top button of her suit jacket as though checking to see that she was fully protected, "I was walking past the livery stable on Syracuse when an Indian stepped out in front of me; he seemed to appear from nowhere—out of the alley running between the livery and Bonner's Mortuary . . . and . . . and he accosted me," she went on in a trembling tone. "He touched my breast . . ." And she faltered then, to let the full impact of the shocking attack be absorbed.

Livingstone's face flushed red. "We'll hang him!" he thundered. "Would you recognize him again?" Hiriam Livingstone's Christian charity didn't extend to Indians, Negroes, or Orientals, although it did include the female minority, encompassing, among others, Miss Rogers, the choir director who met him Wednesday afternoons at the apartment he kept downtown.

Valerie sighed softly and delicately stroked the appliqué work on the linen napkin arranged on her lap. "I'm afraid not, sir. It all happened so swiftly . . . I mean, I screamed and ran. I think my scream frightened him off . . . and I didn't stop running until I reached home."

"Your father must find out the dastardly culprit's name, and justice will be done!" *The Mountain Daily* was only one of many Western papers advocating the "final" solution to the Indian problem in blaring headlines and flaming editorials.

"Oh, no, sir, please, I haven't mentioned the incident to Papa. He's quite opposed to Indians outside the reservation."

"With justification, the dirty savages!" Livingstone exclaimed, his expression livid with rage. "He must be punished. Hung! If these savages aren't taught a lesson, they'll continue to threaten innocent white women with impunity!"

"Oh, sir, I didn't mean to bring the scandal out in public view. Please, Hiriam," and her deliberate use of his Christian name suggested an intimacy he could almost taste, "I would be so terribly embarrassed to have the story racketed about town. Please . . . it was *my* breast he touched, Hiriam . . ." She left the sentence hanging between them, suggestive and inviting.

"The scoundrel must pay," he growled. "This is not the time for tender hearts; the damn savages have to be taught their place," he went on heatedly. "Filthy heathens!"

"I beg of you, Hiriam," Valerie pleaded prettily, adding a little catch to her breath, "you must promise not to allow this to become public." She allowed a single tear to slide down her cheek. "I'm . . . I'm sorry I confided in you . . . only, you see, I thought perhaps you might know some authority I could discreetly lodge a complaint with." Wiping away the tear with her knuckles like a small child might, she ran the tip of her tongue hesitantly over her upper lip. "Please . . ." she murmured.

Livingstone responded to that sensual innocence like a wolf to the fold. "Of course, Valerie"—he took the liberty of using her Christian name, as she had with his—"if you wish this to remain confidential, it shall." Reaching into his pocket, he took out his handkerchief and handed it to her. "Your servant, my dear."

"You're so understanding," Valerie replied softly, dabbing her eyes with his handkerchief. Smiling perkily a moment later, she said, "I feel so much better having spoken of this sordid affair. With your gracious kindness," she went on, deliberately placing his handkerchief into her reticule as though she were offering a future assignation to return it, "you must be inundated with women beseeching your gentle counsel."

"None as lovely as you, my dear," Livingstone replied gallantly, mentally counting the days until the church bazaar. "Consider me your champion in all things." And what a satisfying combination of events, he thought: Having Miss Stewart in his bed and hanging a worthless savage in the bargain.

"How very sweet," Valerie returned, rising in a flurry of scented velvet. "And I hold you to your promise to bid for my lunch at the box social," she finished with a dazzling smile.

"You can be assured of that, my dear."

She allowed him to guide her out through the offices to the main door, his hand on her elbow, and when she turned to bid him good-bye at the door, she made certain her breast brushed his hand.

Later that afternoon over sherry, Valerie and her father compared the success of their initial interviews.

"Hiriam Livingstone is suitably primed," Valerie said with a trilling laugh. "Good God, Papa, he was practically salivating . . . not only over me but at the prospect of hanging an Indian. In fact," she went on, one dark brow arching drolly, "I don't know if he was obliged to make a choice between my pleasant company and the spectacle of hanging a savage that he wouldn't choose the latter."

Duncan lifted his glass in salute to his daughter, feeling more confident about the success of their venture for the first time since Valerie had broached the startling proposal, entertaining the possibility they might just pull it off. Hazard's millions glittered like a gold strike. "My compliments. He's on our side, then."

"Not only on our side but anxious to take the initiative and lead the way. I only restrained him from immediately printing screaming headlines about ravished white women with a tearful reminder of the embarrassment it would cause me. But. . ."

Duncan relaxed against the sofa. "But . . . ?" he prompted with a smile.

"But . . . I could, under extenuating circumstances, such

as a brutal rape by two Indians," she replied with a cheerful
smile, "be convinced to set aside my personal embarrassment
in the interest of saving future defenseless females from
barbaric Indian assaults. And Hiriam would be in the van-
guard, agitating for a lynch mob."

"Hiriam?" Her father lifted his eyebrows speculatively.

"We're on a first-name basis, Daddy."

"He's an old rogue," he grumbled.

"But a useful old rogue . . . a useful old rogue with a
hatred for Indians a mile wide and the means to broadcast that
hatred for our benefit."

"Do you ever think, daughter of mine," Duncan mused
contemplatively, "in counterpoint to the apparent ease with
which Livingstone has been manipulated that Trey, even
should your scheme come to fruition, might not docilely
assume the role of husband?"

"Now *that*, Daddy, is my special department." Valerie
had every confidence in her ability to hold Trey's interest, an
overconfidence, perhaps, considering Trey's child-of-fortune
mentality. She'd always gotten what she wanted in the world
and didn't anticipate any problem once Trey was securely
hers. That assurance was a mistake based on her vast empiri-
cal experience, which, however, had not to date run up
against an adamant Trey Braddock-Black. "Don't worry your
head about Trey," she said confidently. "Tell me about your
lunch with Judge Clancy. Was it as productive as my
interview?"

"Luckily for us, Joe has an abiding hatred for Indians in
general, and Hazard Black in particular. In addition to his
son's loss of an extremely lucrative post, the judge's decisions have been overruled a dozen times when Hazard's
appealed them to higher courts."

"So he'll be amenable then to an indictment should the
need arise."

Duncan patted the inside pocket of his suit coat. "He did
one better; he wrote a warrant for their arrest, leaving the
names blank so we just have to fill them in. Say those two
men you're thinking of naming hightail it for the mountains,
well . . . two other names will do as easily."

"How ingenious . . . like a lettre de cachet."

"In a manner of speaking—except, of course, we can't jail
them indefinitely."

"That's not likely to transpire with two Indians jailed on

rape charges, anyway, is it? The *indefinitely,* I mean." Her
smile was cool as she thought of the seven Indians recently
hung with summary justice on the Musselshell. "I'd say,"
Valerie went on contentedly, "we're in a very good position."

"Not bad," her father replied, less certain than his daughter, but he'd dealt with Hazard before. And quite frankly he
gave a thought to his life. Hazard, especially in his younger
days, had a reputation for violence.

"Not bad! Daddy, we're covered and protected and primed
to move! Really, Daddy, all you have to do now is talk to
Hazard."

"It's still a gamble." And Duncan Stewart had a sudden
vision of Hazard putting a bullet in his head in angry reply.

"Daddy, Daddy . . . Daddy," Valerie chided softly. "It's
not a gamble *at all.*"

"He's a killer, Valerie," Duncan said in a low, flat voice,
"and don't you forget it."

The following days alone were idyllic for Trey and Empress. Each day he became stronger and devoted himself with
joy and energy to entertaining her.

On waking one morning, Empress found the bedroom awash
in forsythia, as freshly scented as spring, pale golden blossoms that brought flooding back youthful memories of Chantilly. Tears sprang to her eyes and to the beautiful man
leaning on one elbow in bed smiling at her she whispered,
"You remembered."

"Do you like it?" he only said, used to remembering what
women liked, familiar with lavish gestures, happy that she
was happy.

"Oh, yes," and she wished she could say how it reminded
her of Mama's grotto glade with the waterfall and warm
spring afternoons in the sun. "It's like a spring bower," she
happily declared, the phrasing general enough, yet very spe-
cific to her.

"There's more in the dressing room."

Her eyes widened, and she looked very young with white
eyelet on her nightgown and a rosy blush to her cheeks. She
swallowed very hard and said softly, "Thank you." The
gesture was thoughtful and extravagant, and no one had
offered this sweet luxury to her—ever.

"I think the ones in the bathtub are going to sprout," he
declared teasingly.

And like the young child she so resembled that morning, she sprang from the bed and flew into the adjoining rooms. When she returned, he was lounging against the graceful headboard, all elegant bronzed skin and wildly handsome looks. "They're beautiful!" she breathed.

"Like you," he replied softly.

"How did you?" she asked, astonished at the logistics in the dead of winter.

"A boxcar, tons of sawdust, and a fast train," Trey replied casually, "so my fierce kitten is happy."

"You'll spoil me," she said winsomely.

"I intend to," he replied.

Although Blaze had left instructions for Mabel to alter the dresses, it was put off, for Trey much preferred Empress without clothes. The servants gossiped, of course, about Trey and his lovely nurse, who never stepped foot outside the bedroom suite, who had all their meals sent up, and only had servants in to change the linens and clean briefly once a day. Blue and Fox had accompanied Hazard and Blaze to Helena, so the lovers were quite alone in their own private paradise.

They slept late and then played in bed, waking slowly in a sensual touching and feeling and wanting. And when they wished for variety, they made love in the mirrored dressing room or in the large marble tub.

Empress blossomed like a summer flower under the ardent devotion she found in Trey's arms. There were times when she chastised herself for succumbing so readily to the shamelessness of Trey's charming demands, but the die had been cast, she reminded herself, that night at Lily's. The sacrifice had been made for her family; the money was secure in her saddlebags. And it would serve no purpose to pretend that Trey's enchantment was wicked. On the contrary, she had never been so happy. Pampered, cosseted, loved, it was a respite in a five-year life of hardship, and she'd be a fool to repudiate the dizzying joy.

They were reminded by a note from Blaze that company was expected for the weekend, so reluctantly on Thursday, Mabel was sent for, to see some dresses for Empress. Trey lounged on the window seat in the dressing room, long-limbed and vivid, while an embarrassed Empress stood dutifully still, letting Mabel tuck and pin and talk of letting out darts and taking down hems. Blaze, understanding how vague men could be about clothing, had sent out several new gowns with her note. It was simply a matter now of seeing they fit properly.

Gratefully Trey was well behaved in front of Mabel, but he kept casting her appreciative glances over Mabel's head with teasing smiles, and Empress nervously feared he'd make one of his personal remarks that would glaringly indicate her immodest position. But he was gallant to Empress and gracious to Mabel, tactfully discussing trivial matters of weather or ranch life, complimenting Mabel on her skill.

He commented only once on the gowns when Empress tried on a cashmere plaid with a white Peter Pan collar and a large taffeta bow. Her honey-colored hair was loose, hanging in ringlets down her back, her face touched with rosy highlights. "You look thirteen," he said. "Almost," he added softly, his eyes on the stretched fabric across her breasts. "Mabel, get Mama's cameo, will you, and we'll see how it looks with this dress."

When Mabel left the room, Trey said, "You look as innocent as a schoolgirl in that."

"And you look as lecherous as the devil, sprawled in the sun, all dark hair, dark skin, and black silk." Trey was robed in an exotic-patterned brocade that accented the severity of his features.

"How appropriate. I've this devilish urge to play school with you. Do you think we have time before Mabel gets back?" And he half raised himself on one elbow.

"Don't you dare embarrass me!"

"I'll just lock the door."

"Trey! She's coming back in a minute!"

"If you promise to play school with me, I won't lock the door."

Empress glowered at him, his languid elegance and dark beauty juxtaposed to amused pale eyes, an overindulged young man she had no intention of humoring.

Mabel appeared in the next moment.

Trey's glance met Empress's, and he said, "Well?"

When he started to rise, she quickly replied, "Very well."

He smiled, then turned to Mabel, and with an expression full of effervescent charm, said, "Thank you, Mabel. Let's try that brooch a touch below the collar."

They all admired the effect, agreed it was very nice with

the unusual lavender-and-moss plaid. "Although," Mabel said, "if the lady wants to wear this dress tomorrow when company comes, I'll have to get started on the alterations right now."

"Why not the chamois wool for tea tomorrow," Trey suggested, "and the emerald panné for dinner?"

Inexplicably it annoyed Empress that he understood perfectly the suitable gowns for both occasions. And panné? How many men knew the distinction between types of velvet? Evidently this was not the first occasion Trey had participated in a dress fitting. And when he asked Mabel, "Where did Mama find the moiré Doucet?" her temper escalated. She supposed he was in the habit of purchasing expensive gowns for women a dozen times a week. Damn him.

Mabel went into a long explanation of how Elizabeth Darlington's daughter's trousseau had been partially misplaced in Chicago on her honeymoon trip to Europe, and by the time the trunks had been returned to Montana, new gowns had been purchased in New York so Barbara wouldn't suffer any deprivation on her trip abroad, leaving Elizabeth Darlington with sixty thousand dollars worth of gowns that would be outdated by the time Babs came back from her year in Europe. And, in any case, it was more than likely, everyone breathlessly hoped, that Babs would be with child by then, a young baronet or lady-to-be, in which case the gowns would be doubly useless to her, for everyone knows what childbearing does to a young matron's figure. Trey listened to this all with well-mannered attention, said "How fascinating" when Mabel eventually rambled to an end, and then cordially issued instructions for the dresses. "The chamois wool and panné for Friday, the black moiré and Creed's emerald serge for Saturday. We'll decide later on the rest, thank you very much." He said it all with efficiency and practiced charm. Mabel was dismissed.

"Apparently you've done this before," Empress remarked rather coolly as the door closed on Mabel.

"Never," he replied, his smile wonderfully sunny.

"Panné, moiré, the usual male vocabulary?"

"My tailor is loquacious."

"Do you wear panné velvet often?"

"I have successfully resisted his efforts to date—with the exception of my scarlet dressing gown." He had no intention of getting into an argument about the women in his past.

"I don't believe you." Empress jealously resisted all attempts at suppression.

"I'm crushed," he replied teasingly.

"Umph!" Empress sniffed, looking at the tall, handsome man who was unfamiliar with the sensation of being "crushed." "Now help me off with this. It's too tight."

He smiled and remained in his sprawl on the window seat. "I thought we had an agreement."

"I have no intention," Empress took great pleasure in saying, "of playing games with you. Are you going to help unbutton this?"

Against the brilliant sun, the silhouette of his powerful body was potently dynamic, the dark angel in a blaze of sunlight. His pale eyes were shadowed by his heavy brow. "I don't think so," he quietly said.

"Very well," Empress responded impatiently, "I'll do it myself." Flouncing off, she entered the bedroom next door. The first problem she had was with the cameo brooch. It was a Roman original, set in a modern setting, but because of its extreme value, the safety clasp was infinitely complex. Additionally it was too close under her chin to be seen when looking down, and trying to unclasp it in the reverse image of the mirror proved unsuccessful. The safety clasp consisted of a delicate chain attached to a screw mechanism, and after several minutes of muttered frustration, she turned to find Trey standing in the doorway, silently observing her fruitless attempts.

"Need some help?" he offered pleasantly.

She refused to answer.

He slowly walked closer and repeated softly, "Would you like some help?"

"As you can see, I can't get this off." That was ambiguous enough; it was not asking for help.

"I need a kiss first."

"Oh, very well," and she raised her mouth like Lady Bountiful bestowing a favor on an underling.

Trey kissed her very gently, his hands on the soft cashmere of her waist. It was a slow, leisurely kiss, a daytime kiss that roused in a tingling, languid way—the kind where time stretched limitlessly and one could nibble at passion's edges without haste.

Tiny, sparking flutters flashed down Empress's spine, very tiny flutters. "You feel good," Empress murmured, her hands running up the black silk of his back, her pique vanished.

"You feel small," Trey whispered, his fingers spanning her narrow waist.

"It's the boning in this dress," Empress complained softly. "It's too tight."

Setting her slightly away, his hands on her arms, Trey slowly scrutinized her. The sewn-in boning was like a corset in construction, from hip to breast compressing her figure in the acceptable wasp-waisted style that accented womanly curves. In turn, the boning pushed her breasts up and out, straining the soft cashmere fabric of the bodice. "Is it too tight here?" he asked gently, brushing his fingers over her nipples, which were pressing prominently through the clinging cashmere.

"Umm," Empress murmured, the rush of pleasure intensified by the elevated exaggeration of her breasts above the tight-fitting corset.

"You look like a schoolgirl in a dress you've outgrown," he whispered, his fingers softly tugging at her nipples until the peaks were distended and hard. "This material is sheer," he murmured, stroking back and forth across her conspicuous nipples. The fabric was so fine, it hid nothing, the swelling roundness of her breasts as visible as if unclothed. "If you were a schoolgirl in this dress and I were your tutor, I'd think you were teasing me. You shouldn't be allowed out of your room in a dress this tight," he whispered, bending to touch her half-open lips. He continued caressing her hard, peaking crests until her face was flushed, until her mouth parted in small, panting breaths. His tongue slowly entered her mouth and entwined with hers, forced its way deep into her throat. She reached out to hold him, a streaking heat shuddering through her. But he didn't embrace her, his hands on her tingling nipples, his mouth forcing hers wider, his tongue penetrating until she moaned deep in her throat.

His mouth lifted, and he whispered, "It's not proper for a schoolgirl to kiss her tutor."

She didn't answer, only reached up for another kiss, pulling his head down to hers.

His hands moved finally from her breasts and, holding her firmly by the arms, looked at her in mock severity. "Are you trying to tease your tutor?"

She murmured, "No," very low, and tried to move closer.

"Then why are you making improper advances toward me? You're flagrantly throwing yourself at me and may reap the consequences. Do you understand what that means?" His voice was husky, teasing, warm against her cheek as he brushed a kiss across her jaw.

"Trey, please, this dress is too tight, and Lord, I want you . . ."

"Do you want this tight dress off?" His palms brushed over her straining breasts.

"Oh, yes, please. It hurts."

"You must do as you're told, then, sweetheart."

"Anything," she agreed breathlessly, sensation accentuated by the captivity of her body in the binding corset and overtight gown, as if coercion sensitized her skin and her constrained breasts enhanced desire.

"I'll take the cameo off first," he said in a moderate tone.

"Hurry!"

"Patience, dear," and he unclasped the brooch with deliberate care, then, setting it aside, turned her slowly and undid the top two buttons in back, loosening the constrained neckline and small, lace-trimmed collar. "Is that better?" he asked tranquilly.

"No."

"No?" Placing his hands delicately on her shoulders, he turned her back to face him. "You're not very grateful," he admonished mildly.

"I'm sorry. Oh, Trey, I'm dying for you," and she reached to feel him, wanted to touch his arousal.

Brushing her hands away, he held them loosely. "We should discuss this, my dear"—his voice took on a feigned prudishness—"this unusual preciosity. Your behavior is quite inappropriate. Come sit on my lap and we'll analyze this want of principle in you. Would you like that?" And when she nodded yes, he led her to a chair near the window and, sitting, pulled her down on his lap.

She could feel his arousal through the silk of his robe and the fine cashmere of her gown, and moved lightly to touch her throbbing bottom to his obvious hardness.

"Shameless, my dear." He held her hips, constraining her movement. "You must suppress such unnatural desires, or you'll stray from the path of virtue. You must sit still." His faint smile was very untutorial. It was knowing and experienced. And wolfish.

Empress was single-minded, beyond reason or teasing words. She could feel Trey's erection, hard and long and ready; her breasts were swollen and hotly sensitized from Trey's attentions. She could only think of how he'd feel when he plunged into her, how his splendid arousal would fill her, put an end to the restless, hot longing.

"Since I'm your tutor," she heard him murmur low near her ear, his fingers sliding through the golden silk of her hair, pushing the heavy coils behind her ears, smoothing the tumbled waves down her back, "we'll recite our lessons now. If I begin very slowly, you'll be able to keep up, and if you recite your lessons perfectly, I'll give you a prize." His large hands cupped one breast and gently squeezed, drawing out the soft, swollen flesh to a peaked point, and when his fingers rubbed the tip in a slow, lazy rhythm, he asked very quietly, "Would you like a prize?"

Empress lifted her face, and he bent to kiss her lips. "You know what the prize is, don't you," he murmured before their lips met, and when she whispered, "Yes," into the softness of his mouth, he kissed her lightly—an abrupt, teasing kiss, and added, "But you must be very good."

"I will," she said, the throbbing deep inside her pronounced and insistent, her dampness explicit and pulsing.

"Repeat after me, then. 'Virtue is its own reward.' " He turned her head with a crooked finger under her chin so she was looking at him.

" 'Virtue is its own reward,' " she said softly.

" 'Be thou as chaste as ice, as pure as snow.' "

She repeated the phrase, her eyes on his, the heat of her desire capable of melting the polar ice cap, her voice throaty with passion.

"Very good, you're a dutiful student." And he kissed her then, an intrusive, heated kiss in response to her purring, suggestive reply. "Have you ever lain with a man?"

"Yes."

"Disgraceful, shameless." His pale eyes narrowed so that he was scrutinizing her through his heavy, dark lashes. "Did you like it?"

"Yes."

His brows rose as an astounded young man's might when stunned. "And did he"—the question was a slow, meditative conjecture, his hand slipping under her petticoats—"touch you here? You aren't wearing drawers." His tone was a perfect blend of fascination and amazement. "How naughty. Are you waiting for me to touch you?" His fingers brushed against her honeyed sweetness, slid in easily, and as her eyes closed in ecstasy he said, "Answer."

"Yes," Empress breathed, a long, drawn-out sigh, and arched fiercely upward. "Oh, yes."

"And does it feel good when a man makes love to you?" His fingers were stroking, sliding in as far as they'd reach, then sliding out again, in a slow, bewitching rhythm.

"Oh, yes," she whispered, her eyes shut.

"Look at me." Dutifully her eyes opened. "Do you like to make love to a man?"

"Yes."

"Say it."

She whispered, "I like to make love to a man."

"That's a good girl. Would you like a kiss?" And when she nodded and lifted her mouth, he kissed her, a hard, bruising kiss, and his fingers continued their caresses. When he withdrew his fingers a moment later, she cried out softly.

"You must obey your tutor," Trey said very low, "or I won't allow you to take this confining dress off and give you your prize. Now say, 'I want to make love to my tutor.' "

And she did.

" 'And I won't make love to any other man.' "

She repeated it quietly, reaching for him again.

"And who's your tutor in everything?" It was a man's question, no sophistry allowed.

"You are," she breathed.

He smiled, satisfied. "You've been so respectful a student, you can sit on me for a short moment."

At his low, quiet words Empress could feel the pulsing increase, as though he were inside her already.

Trey pulled up the petticoats and billowing yards of skirt, pushed them aside, and lifting her, settled her slowly on his rigid manhood, seating her sideways across his lap, both her legs pressed close together. "Can you feel that?" he murmured, and surged slightly upward.

The penetration was rapturous, and Empress, moving slightly to experience the staggering pleasure, turned to put her arms around Trey.

"No," he said, taking her arms down from his shoulders. "You must sit perfectly still. If you move, you won't be allowed to keep the prize."

She became very still.

"Your report card is going to be excellent, Miss Jordan,"

Trey said, stroking her jutting breasts, pressed high above the restrictive corset. "Tell me if you can feel this." And he tugged firmly on her nipples. She gasped as the glorious spasms raced downward and shifted slightly at the heightened pleasure.

"Don't move," he warned curtly, and the next time he caressed her breasts, she sat immobile while the delectable lushness washed over her. "Your cheeks are flushed, Miss Jordan," Trey whispered. "Are you warm?"

"Yes," she murmured, drifting in her own blissful enchantment, insulated by hot waves of passion, reason superseded by feeling.

"Yes, who?"

She hesitated.

"Yes, my tutor," and he waited till she said it.

"Would you like this tight dress loosened?" His hands smoothed over the plump fullness of her breasts, bound repressively by the fabric, and squeezed slightly as he swelled upward into her clinging heat.

She stifled a low moan of pleasure and whispered, "Yes, oh, yes," careful not to move as instructed, careful to do exactly as she was told so she didn't lose his magnificent fullness, buried deep inside her.

He slowly unbuttoned several inches of pearl buttons down her back, easing some of the tightness across her shoulders. "Is that better?" he asked quietly.

"Some," she replied softly.

"Is it still too restrictive?" His splayed fingers ran down the trimness of her waist and smoothed over her hips, the light boning sewed into the seams, tactile beneath his brushing fingers, compressing her waist and hips, sharpening her posture, pushing her breasts upward in a magnificent exaggeration of their rounded abundance. They were suspended like a bounteous sensual offering above the rigid framework imprisoning her form.

"A little."

"That's all I can do until our next lesson, but if you follow directions properly, I'll let your breasts free. Do they hurt, lifted so high and bound so tightly?"

"Slightly."

"I think if you stand up, you'll be more comfortable."

She didn't move.

"Stand up," he repeated.

"I don't want to," she whispered softly.

"Does your lascivious little bottom want to stay filled?"

She nodded dreamily.

"But you must obey, Miss Jordan, or you'll never feel me again. Do you understand? You must be compliant and submissive." And he lifted her off his lap and placed her standing before him. "An assertive young lady is inexcusable," he went on in prudish irony. "You must learn obedience, Miss Jordan, and then you'll always be able to make me ready for you. Would you like to have me always ready for you?"

Empress's gaze was bewitched by Trey's upthrusting manhood, framed by the elegantly patterned black brocade. It was splendidly formed, capable of bringing her incredible pleasure. He stood, held her by her shoulders, and bending low, kissed her gently. "You're nicely docile, Miss Jordan, an asset in a young lady." His fingers brushed across her shoulders and slid up her throat until he held her face lightly in his hands. "Do you feel empty inside, Miss Jordan? Would you like me to satisfy your luxuriant needs? Would you like to have a very proper tutor allow you gratification?" His words were like rich promise, meltingly warm, husky, a foretaste of lavish sensuality.

Placing his hands on her shoulders, he murmured, "Kneel," and eased her down in front of him. When she looked up at him, her pale hair fell in luxuriant profusion down her back. "If you perform this properly, I'll supply the fulfillment your heated body longs for. But you must do it right. Take hold of me, Miss Jordan, and open your mouth; you'll be able to taste your sticky sweetness on me." His hands lay lightly on her hair, and she did as instructed, sliding the hard length of him into her mouth, her thighs pressed tightly together as the pulsing wetness between her legs flowed with the flame of desire. "Now you must move very slowly, so it goes in all the way to the back of your throat and then out again until your lips nearly lose hold. If you execute my orders diligently, I'll let you feel me inside you. If you don't, all that hot longing will be unresolved. Do you understand?"

She nodded, running her tongue over the swollen crest of his manhood, and felt him swell against her lips. He felt solid and hot and so very large; the promise to feel him inside brought her senses trembling to a quivering peak of violent need. She must have him or die, and if she could so easily bring him to such enormous length, it was searing pleasure to anticipate his offer.

Trey's eyes closed against the rush of electrifying sensation, and he stood very still while Empress's soft lips and playful tongue moved over and around and rhythmically against him, slowly as he'd commanded. The excruciating delight was almost more than he could endure, and after a moment more, before it was too late, he reached down and pulled her up. "Are you ready?" His voice was deep and hushed, the inquiry an offer of repletion.

Empress's eyes were half closed in passion, her full lips wet with the taste and feel of him, her legs closed tightly beneath the petticoats and gathered skirt, so the ripe sensations building with each pulse beat were irresistible. She nodded in answer to his question, swaying her hips in invitation, promoting a heated, spiraling bliss that caused a breathy whimper.

"Do you think you're wet enough, Miss Jordan? Ease your legs apart, Miss Jordan, and let me verify your readiness." She didn't want to because she'd lose the splendid pleasure, but he scowled, said, "Obey," and reluctantly she did. He lifted her skirt then, so she was naked from the waist down, her slender legs slightly separated, the straight-laced dress bodice contrasting erotically with her nakedness offered for view. "You seem moderately aroused, Miss Jordan. Is this normal for you . . . this lavish profusion of compelling need?" Wetness was evident inside her thighs. He slid two fingers forcibly inside her, widening the entrance to accommodate his large, long-boned fingers, stretching the delicate flesh to oblige the addition of a third finger. And then he pressed upward and said, "You must be a too familiar young lady. Are you?" His tone was stiffly indictive, a mixture of moody lust and decorum.

"Oh, no," she murmured, "never," and moved against the thrust of his fingers, impaling her with false propriety.

"Ah, that's a proper, virtuous answer," he said in better humor, mock ethics assuaged. Brushing his fingers up the milky liquid dripping down her thighs, he lightly stroked the swollen, distended entrance to pleasure. "Does it feel wet enough to you?"

She sighed and nodded, too absorbed in the shuddering ecstasy to respond more actively.

Withdrawing his hand, he dropped her skirt and petticoats,

covering her once again, and his damp fingers lifted her chin, the odor of wanton need warm in her nostrils. "Say 'Yes, sir,' " he insisted, pressing her to respond past the focus of pleasure inundating her brain.

Forcibly bringing herself back to reality, she whispered, "Yes, sir."

"And you feel you're wet enough to accommodate me now that you've made me hard with your dutiful mouth?"

"Oh, yes," she breathed, feeling a drop of fluid ooze down her thigh.

His brows rose slightly, and she quickly corrected herself. "Yes, sir."

"Do you want your dress unbuttoned first so your breasts are free?"

"Please, sir."

He reached around her and unbuttoned a dozen more buttons, slid the dress off her shoulders, and eased the fabric down over her breasts. They quivered softly, free above the stiff boning of the dress that supported the underside of her voluptuous breasts. "You must say 'Thank you.' "

"Thank you, sir," she whispered gratefully.

"Your breasts are presented very invitingly, Miss Jordan. Are you shamelessly trying to attract my attention?"

"Oh, no, sir, I would never be so forward, sir. That would be brazen."

Trey touched one distended nipple softly, and her breath caught in her throat. Every nerve in her body was trembling, a heartbeat away from consummation, every flame-hot inch of her flesh ripe for the taking, her mounded breasts pink with arousal, elevated like ready candidates for caressing. "You have a very cordial nature, Miss Jordan. Your nipples are eager for my touch."

"Oh, sir, if you wished to, but I would never dare to suggest it." And her full bottom lip pushed out invitingly, like a compliant coquette.

"Perhaps another lesson in obedience would enrich your character. Offer your nipples up for me, Miss Jordan." Placing her hands under her lavish breasts, he raised them high, the hard, peaked pink crests angled upward toward his mouth. And when he lightly bit on the closest tantalizing peak, her knees trembled briefly with the stabbing pleasure.

"If you let men caress your breasts, Miss Jordan, suck on your engorged nipples, some might say you're lacking in propriety. It's not seemly behavior for a young lady. You shouldn't let any man suck on your nipples. Your large breasts will never squeeze back into your schoolgirl frocks if you let men stimulate them so. Your eagerness is very improper. You understand, if anyone knew what you were allowing me to tutor you in, I'd have to deny everything. I have my reputation to consider, Miss Jordan. I have a position in the community. And though I'm willing to see to your education zealously, your propensity for physical stimulation is really quite immodest. Now say, 'Suck on my breasts, sir,' and I'll see that you not only get an *A* in deportment but my unstinting attention to your education.''

It was a passion-hot, teasing dalliance where paradox met morality and pleasure scorned convention, where two adults pressed the perimeters of rapture and, upon reaching those limits, leapt the barriers.

"And if you give me an *A, sir,*" Empress purred a moment later, her voice so ardently heated, the sound vibrated in the quiet room, "I'll see that you never forget this winter day as long as you live. . . ." The lust in her eyes matched his, and the teasing game was over. But the unforgettable morning had just begun.

The dress was discarded, along with the brocade robe, and in a mutual, unrestricted giving, they made the morning memorable. And irrevocably ruined the velvet covering on the chaise.

The following afternoon, the house began filling with guests, and Trey and Empress no longer occupied their private Elysium. Trey was carried downstairs for dinner, dressed casually in dark trousers and a loose silk shirt. Empress accompanied him, attired in the emerald panné, suitably altered to fit. They sat near each other but couldn't touch. Sensual vibrations from their heavenly week of privacy still remained in their consciousness, and one look would rekindle the sweetness. With effort they smiled and chatted and parlayed questions neither cared to answer. It was torture to have to share each other with dozens of other people, all bent on intruding into their very private thoughts.

Much was made of Trey's rapid recovery, and Empress, as his savior, was forced to accept kudos from everywhere. All modestly and shyly acknowledged. She didn't know any of these people, knew less what they were thinking. Cared very little what their reasons were for appearing. The conversation was all political. Heated conversations continued in the parlor after dinner, and with thankful blessing Empress heard Trey plead fatigue at ten. Blue and Fox carried him upstairs in one of the armchairs—a precaution, perhaps, since he walked well. But Blaze was worried about her son overdoing.

She was unaware, of course, that anyone with stamina enough to make love several hours every day was strong enough to navigate the stairs. But those explanations not forthcoming, Trey didn't argue when his mother insisted he be assisted upstairs to bed.

Empress was green-eyed with jealousy after watching the three young ladies who'd accompanied their parents for the weekend visit spend their entire evening making flirtatious advances toward Trey. Since Empress had been introduced as Trey's nurse, and common knowledge had added another sobriquet to her identity, she'd been dismissed as unimportant by the wealthy young ladies. It was galling to be talked around and over and through for an entire evening, and while Hazard and Blaze were warm in their cordiality, setting the expected tone for the other guests, the spoiled young ladies had only sullenly responded to their parents' warning glances.

"Are those the kind of bitches you spend time with?" Empress exploded as the door closed behind Blue and Fox.

"Ignore them," Trey responded dismissively, unbuttoning his silk shirt. "Women like Arabella and Lucy and Fanny are too uninteresting to dwell on."

"They were rude," Empress retorted, hot with resentment.

"Really?" Trey looked at her cryptically for a moment. "I'm sorry, I hadn't noticed."

"You hadn't *noticed*?" Empress repeated heatedly. "Good God! I've never met such supercilious snobs!"

"They're just rich young ladies. It's normal for them." One must forgive Trey's unfortunate remark because he was, of course, unaware of Empress's background. After all, he'd only seen her in her cowhand garb, without money or family. And all the rich young ladies he knew were empty-headed snobs. It was a natural mistake to assume wealthy young ladies would be an oddity to her.

"*Normal! Normal* to be *rude*?" Empress was responding more to her evening's worth of being disregarded by the parvenu young women than to Trey's remarks.

"Lord, Empress," Trey said, standing with his shirt half off, "it's not my fault they're bitches."

"Do you socialize with women like that?" she asked pettishly, the thought of Trey being the recipient of all that sugary adoration jealousy-provoking.

"What do you mean, socialize," he inquired cautiously, aware that he had an angry woman on his hands and not altogether sure why.

"I mean, take them out, dance with them at parties, take them to plays, the opera, whatever the hell you do in this frontier country."

With relief he listened to her explanation. He was in the habit of socializing in more sensual, unconventional ways, too, and he wasn't certain in the mood she was in at present that he cared to admit it. "Occasionally," he blandly replied, this man who was the most eligible bachelor in Montana and had been since he was eighteen.

"How do you stand it!"

"Poorly," he replied with a smile and, dropping his shirt on the floor, opened his arms and said, "Come here, sweet, forget them. They don't have an ounce of brains between the three of them."

Mollified by his reply, she walked into his arms and, womanlike, asked for verification. "Truly?"

"Word of honor. I don't like them."

"Well, they surely like you," Empress reluctantly murmured into his chest, feeling alone suddenly after the crowd of strangers downstairs, and the women angling after Trey, and the lavish display of wealth that was casually accepted by Trey's family. She remembered suddenly her own poor home and the children waiting for her. Trey was out of danger now, but her contracted time wasn't up yet. With the gold in her saddlebags, she was obliged to honor their agreement. But she didn't delude herself that it was a burden. Trey had seen to that.

"It's not important," he replied with graceful evasion. "Now let's ring for a maid and have some of that meringue torte brought up. I'd like to eat it off your tummy."

She looked up at him with a pouty enchantment. "You're scandalous," she murmured with a smile.

"But entertaining," he said with a grin and, bending low, kissed her inviting mouth.

They were left alone until teatime the next afternoon, when

they appeared in the west parlor. Blaze was presiding over tea and more substantial refreshment for the men. A large portion of Montana was settled by Southerners lured by the gold in '63 and driven from their original homes by the Civil War. They favored bourbon or whiskey, with or without branch water, and voted Democrat. The liquor had been flowing for some time when Trey and Empress appeared, and the dissection of local Republican politicos was sharp and vociferous.

"If Saunders thinks he can push through Carlyle for Attorney General next fall when we become a state, he's deluding himself and spending a lot more money than he'll ever realize in political favors."

"What do you think, Trey, of Carlyle's chances if we have Doyle on the ballot?" and Trey was drawn off to sit with the group of men around the fireplace.

Blaze immediately rescued Empress and, after complimenting her on Creed's tailored serge that brought the green of her eyes to the fore, brought her over to join the tea-drinking ladies who were seated on the embroidered chairs she'd brought back from their last trip to Paris. The matched ensemble had originally been made for Marie Antoinette by Avril and was a masterpiece of inlaid wood and gilding. Empress politely drank her tea and listened to the women's talk, which was primarily related to clothes and shopping. Casting Empress an apologetic glance, Blaze pleasantly replied to Mrs. McGinnis's question concerning Worth's new interiors. Much discussion ensued over the outré green silk walls and whether it wasn't terribly exciting to be dressed by a couturier who clothed the royalty of Europe.

Occasionally Empress was drawn into the conversation by Blaze, in an attempt to make her feel comfortable, but the three young ladies refused to direct a word of conversation in Empress's direction. Their mothers, since they had a better grasp on the importance of the Braddock-Blacks to their husbands' livelihoods, participated in the conversation with Empress, but with feigned enthusiasm.

Aware of Empress's predicament in being seated in the midst of the uncharitable young ladies, Trey suggested after no more than a half hour that it was time for his medicine again. Owen Farrell intercepted his attempt to leave with Empress by saying with garrulous good cheer, "Hell, Trey, have the little lady bring the medicine down. We're going to

play a game of billiards, and that ain't too strenuous for you
to set there and watch.''

Trey looked to his father for support, but Hazard was
engaged in explaining the reservation boundaries near the
Roaring River that must remain inviolable and hadn't heard
Owen's reply. "I can wait," Trey said casually, planning to
escape with Empress once the men began to move to the
billiard room.

"Nonsense, son, you need your medicine to get better.
Hey, little lady," he shouted across the room.

Trey swore under his breath.

All the women looked up, and Owen waved his whiskey
glass in Empress's direction. "Little Angel of Mercy there in
green, Trey here needs his medicine, he says. You're the boss
lady on that score. Mebbe you'd tell one of the maids what
y'all need.''

Trey's face was expressionless as everyone's glance focused
on him. "Really, Owen, it can wait.''

"No way, boy, got to get you well." Owen, after two
drinks, was a runaway train when his mind took hold of
something, and the drink he was sloshing in Empress's direction was his fourth.

Trey shrugged, abandoning his subterfuge to quit the room,
and smiled resignedly at Empress.

Empress understood Trey's attempt and decided to take
advantage of the opportunity to slip away for a time. "I'll
fetch it myself," she replied quickly, thankful for an excuse
to take leave, however briefly, of the vacuous conversation.
And before any protest could materialize from the inebriated
Owen, she was on her feet. "I'll be right back," she said
with a charming smile.

She stayed upstairs much longer than necessary, reluctant
to join the tepid young ladies and their boring mothers. She
understood the necessity for the Braddock-Blacks' political
socializing, but she'd prefer not being involved. When it
reached a point where her absence might be remarked, she
put a small amount of the fortifying rose-hip liquid in a glass
and, taking a bracing breath, left her refuge to face the cool
female visitors from Helena.

"Empress Jordan—it sounds like a dance-hall queen.''

The voice paralyzed her for a moment—and the high-
pitched sneer—and she stopped in her tracks, fascinated and
repelled. Her hand on the polished stair rail, she stood mo-

tionless on the first-floor landing, recognizing the speaker. Another voice, soft and lispy, said, "Hush, Arabella, someone might hear."

"Hush, yourself, Fanny. The men are in the billiard room, and our mamas are with Mrs. Braddock-Black starting their third cup of tea. You always were a little mouse."

"For pity's sake, Arabella, mind your manners. Although you don't have any to mind," a third person replied. By process of elimination, Empress knew it was Lucy.

"Don't talk to me about manners, Lucy Rogers. You're the one who unceremoniously dragged us out of the parlor to see your new dress. As if we didn't know what you wanted to see!"

"Well, you want to see him, too, so don't make any bones about it."

"He's handsome as a Greek god," Fanny said in breathless awe.

"Handsomer," Arabella firmly declared. "And he knows it." Everyone at one time or another had watched the dazzling good looks used so charmingly.

"He's not vain at all, Arabella. He's the sweetest—"

"Spare us your girlish vapors, Fanny. We're agreed. And he's accessible."

"If you can get through the usual crowd of women," Lucy pointed out.

"At least tonight there aren't any," Arabella said in a matter-of-fact tone that suggested a practical woman.

"Now who's going to be the first to barge into the men's billiard room?" Lucy asked with a tinge of trepidation. "I, for one, know my daddy will scowl something fierce."

"*I'll* do it for land sakes. All you scaredy-cats can follow me."

"Maybe he won't even talk to us," Lucy declared fearfully. "He doesn't seem to have any time for anyone but his *nurse*." There was a pregnant pause before the denigrating pronunciation of *nurse*.

"Everyone knows about Trey and women. It's no secret," Arabella said. "His reputation's notorious. You know men like Trey always have women. And what did you expect, when he paid fifty thousand dollars for her? *Of course* he'll pay attention to her."

"You don't think it's serious, then?" It was Fanny's lisp. "He does look at her—well—differently."

"Don't be ridiculous," Arabella snapped. "It's just the same old Trey. He only plays. He doesn't get serious. Especially with sluts."

"Fifty thousand dollars could be the beginning of serious, I heard Daddy tell Mama."

"Fifty thousand isn't anything to Trey. He loses that much in a card game."

"I don't know," Fanny's timid voice interposed. "I saw him look at her up in his bedroom one day last week when we were visiting, and Mama said it just went to show that he was fast as ever, even in his sickbed, and that look he gave her could have boiled every coffeepot in Montana for a month, she told me."

"Then your Mama hasn't seen Trey look at women much. Those silver eyes are famous for their scorching power. They say he's never had a refusal. Now stop all your worrying over nothin'," Arabella declared. "The day Trey Braddock-Black wants anything more than sex from a little tart he buys in a brothel will be a cold day, as they say."

"That's what my daddy said," Lucy firmly agreed, feeling better now that the possibility of Trey's involvement had been thoroughly put to rest.

"I don't know." Fanny persisted stubbornly. "If you could have seen that look—"

"Hush your mouth, you twit. If you ever grow up, you'll know that looks like that happen all the time, but it's nothing more than a man's lust. Now, are you coming in with us, or are you going to stand here and debate the future of some paid-for hussy?"

"You're not the only one who wants to see him," Fanny retorted boldly, the disagreement having altered her normal placidity.

"What would you do with him if you managed to catch his interest, Fanny? You'd die of fear."

"I would not, Arabella McGinnis. Don't think you're the only woman who knows what to say to a man."

"If you two can stop scrapping over Trey's damaged body," Lucy drawled sweetly, "we all could go into the billiard room and see the darling in person. And arguing over various approaches or scintillating dialogue is totally unnecessary when it comes to Trey, since it's common knowledge in this part of Montana that the only word you have to know to get along beautifully with Trey is *yes*."

"That's provided," Arabella said concisely, "he notices you in the first place."

"I'll throw myself at him," Fanny said.

"Get in line, it's been done before. He's credited with never restricting his performance, and that's why the line's so long."

"I'll have his baby. He'll marry me then, and we'll live happily ever after." Fanny's eyes were alight with the romantic fantasy.

"Ask Charlotte Tangen or Louisa or Mae or any of the hasty marriages in the last few years with paid-for bridegrooms about that likelihood transpiring." Arabella was after effect. She chose not to mention that none of the cited women were virtuous. But chaste or not, Trey's liability had been defined in terms of prodigal sums of money rather than marriage. In this businesslike manner no censure occurred, and geniality was restored.

"No!" Fanny gasped.

"Yes, a very emphatic yes. You should still be in the nursery, Fanny. Lord, you're naïve. He's *not* the marrying kind." Arabella's tone was smug.

"Well, then, smarty pants," Fanny replied heatedly, "how do you propose to get him? You've been after him for years."

"My daddy will suggest a business merger when the time is right. Our marriage will be profitable and advantageous" —she touched her blond ringlets—"for the Braddock-Blacks and for us. Don't you know how these things work? It's not romance, you ninny. It's money. And my daddy has almost as much as Trey's daddy. So you see how convenient—"

"In the meantime," Lucy said sarcastically, "I'm going into the billiard room. I think he's still available, since I don't see an engagement ring on your finger, Arabella."

And the voices drifted off down the hall.

Empress was numb with a chill realization. All she'd overheard was not a startling revealed discovery as much as a substantiation, verifying with bone-cold clarity what she'd not allowed herself to contemplate consciously. In the lushness of Trey's embrace, when silken caresses and trembling desire inundated her senses, when Trey's extraordinarily gentle kindness fascinated and charmed, it was easy to ignore the cold, hard facts. She'd deluded herself, allowed romantic notions to overcome her more prosaic nature, preferred to accept the gilded dream.

But stark reality faced her now. Unvarnished truth, unembellished by bewitching sensations. She was bought and paid for. And according to the world at large, that placed her in a certain class. Whatever her personal reasons, the public image was fixed. She had understood the consequences, of course, from the beginning.

It had been Trey, his smile, his warmth, his gently offered journeys into paradise that had made her disregard the image. Beautiful Trey, who never forgot anything she liked, even her favorite flower, although she'd only mentioned it once. Charming Trey, who always was kind. Always. And so handsome, she wanted to touch him a thousand times a day. But then, so did every other female who saw him. And just looking at him could ignite physical desire. The brutal conversation she'd overheard echoed through her mind—"slut . . . fifty thousand dollars—scorching looks from silvery eyes."

It was all a familiar game with him—not a miracle of love and passion like it was for her, a dream come true. For Trey it was only casual lust and another willing woman. A thousand excuses might explain away rumor after rumor, woman after woman. That's what her unhappy mind would like to do.

But disclaim, deny, forgive, absolve—underneath it all, he enjoyed it. Or he'd stop.

Her first impulse, immediate and uncurbed, was to flee. But then her conscience overcame the first powerful feelings, and she distractedly tried to determine the numbered days remaining of her servitude. Was it five or six? Was it less? It seemed at once a mere passing moment and a lifetime. Then more rational thoughts intervened. If she fled now, would she be missed? Would she be pursued? By whom and to what purpose?

Confusion and questions tumbled through her mind until she forced herself to deal with this logically. She couldn't leave now, not with a houseful of guests. And if pursuit was a possibility, her leaving would be noticed immediately. Since Trey's parents and their guests were returning to Helena late Sunday afternoon, if she were to leave after Trey fell asleep Sunday night, she wouldn't be missed until Monday morning, giving her a six- or seven-hour lead on any pursuit. Trey wasn't strong enough to sustain any length of time in the saddle, she decided, and with Blue and Fox returning to

Helena with Hazard and Blaze, anyone with any authority for
action, excluding Trey, would be in Helena. She would have
adequate time to outdistance pursuit—if it materialized.

She had momentary qualms about taking the gold without
fulfilling her entire obligation, but she rationalized the misgivings away with the remembered offer from Hazard the
night Trey had been brought home dying. Surely the money
she was taking home to her brothers and sisters was much less
than Hazard would have paid.

It made it easier—the resolution and the rationalization—to
enter the billiard room a few moments later. Trey drank his
medicine without demur, grinned when he handed the glass
back to her, and murmured, "It almost worked."

The smile Empress returned was forced but, in the buzz of
conversation and the haze of cigar smoke, not readily apparent to a man who considered his companion pleasantly content. The last week had been a halcyon idyll of sweetness and
pleasure, unique even in the sensual activities of a profligate
sybarite. How could he imagine that a sudden vicissitude had,
chameleonlike, altered the fascinating pleasure.

He did not.

And Empress consciously played her role, pleasant when
spoken to, vivacious even in the company of the spiteful
women, a fact Trey noted with satisfaction. Once when Arabella
attempted a less than friendly remark, she'd been curtly put
down by her father. Undeterred by the moral strictures of the
visiting ladies, the men were all charmed by the lovely Miss
Jordan.

Somehow Empress managed to survive dinner that night.
Somehow she managed to lie in Trey's arms that night without crying bittersweet tears. Somehow Sunday progressed
through a tortured lunch and teatime. With relief she watched
the royal-blue and gilt parlor car pull away from the small
private depot.

With relief and trepidation, for now she was alone with
Trey. Her role-playing uncushioned by busy conversation and
numerous guests. Through dinner her nerves showed, and
when she'd answered an innocuous question about some choice
of food in a long, convoluted, totally irrational overabun-
dance of words, Trey looked across the small table set near
the fireplace in his suite upstairs and said, "Is something
wrong?"

"No," she replied too quickly, too breathlessly, and he stared at her intently.

"Are you sure?" he asked gravely, then added, "You mustn't let any of the people out here this weekend make the slightest difference to you. And if an apology would take away the stupidity of those blasted women, consider it offered." He smiled. "Again. In triplicate." Reaching across the crisp white linen cloth, he took her hand in his. "If the legislature wasn't in session, and if I wasn't still ill, they would never have been out here. Tell me you understand."

It took all her strength to keep the tears from spilling over. How could he be so sweet? No wonder all the women loved him. It was that thought that suppressed the welling sadness. She was, after all, only the latest in a long line of adoring women. She managed to smile then with a credible magnitude, and said, "Oh, I understand perfectly. I haven't given them a thought of any consequence. Really. And nothing's wrong. I probably had too much wine. I talk too much and too fast when I drink. Do you think it'll snow tonight?"

Trey answered politely, even though her sudden change of subject was as restless as her nervous chatter. It was probably the overlong weekend, he decided.

He made love to her with an added tenderness that night, conscious of her disquietude. And when he held her in his arms later, as they fell asleep, he didn't notice the tears glistening wetly on her lashes.

Ten

EMPRESS WAITED UNTIL midnight before she carefully slid out of bed and dressed. Her leave-taking was simple, for after she'd put on her old clothes, she only had the saddlebags to carry downstairs. Taking the servants' stairway down, she slipped out the kitchen door.

The cold struck her like an icy curtain when she stepped out on the porch. The night was clear with a full moon, so the temperature was well below zero. But thankfully there was little wind. The wind would freeze you faster than the cold.

Not wishing to call attention to herself with lights, she stood for a long time in the dark barn before her eyes became accustomed to the gloom. Clover was pleased to see her, repeatedly nudging her with her nose like a puppy while Empress saddled her and tied on the saddlebags. She debated briefly before saddling a second horse. It wasn't stealing, she told herself, only borrowing. If she was going to bring supplies home for the rest of the winter, she needed a packhorse.

Ten minutes later Empress carefully led the horses out of the barn and, with extra precaution, walked them a good half mile before mounting Clover. She walked and rode by turns during the night to keep her feet from freezing and by morning found herself within an hour's ride of Cresswell's crossroad. It wasn't exactly a road, more like a heavily traveled trail, but the river forked there, and years ago the traders had set up a post. Now it was the closest store for the farmers who'd settled in the rich mountain valleys.

Cresswell's was far enough away from their mountain cabin that she'd never gone there with her father, but she knew its location and intended to shop for her family. The gold would buy the necessities: the flour, sugar, coffee, tea, bacon, dried apples, and canned milk. And boots for the children and clothes. Plus the Christmas presents none of them had received because all the money was gone.

It was still half dark when she woke Cresswell with her knocking. He attempted several inquisitive forays as she selected her merchandise, in an effort to determine who this young woman was buying with a careful frugality. This woman dressed in worn men's clothes paying with gold. This woman who had to have ridden all night to appear here at this hour of the morning. But Empress chose not to answer except in the briefest way, and Ed Cresswell had been in business long enough in this remote valley to know that most of his customers didn't care to talk about themselves.

The horses were carefully packed, each precious bundle tightly tied into place, and when Empress left, she deliberately headed northeast. Ed Cresswell watched her until she was lost in the shrub pine lining the creek.

Once out of sight of the store, Empress swung Clover sharply and rode northwest to the hidden mountain valley that was home.

Thoughts of Trey intruded, were pushed aside, suppressed, then stealthily stole back into her consciousness, more sharply set than before. She remembered how he woke in the morning with first a smile for her and then a kiss; how he looked seated across the breakfast table from her, dark-skinned and relaxed, eating with an appetite she teased him about. She remembered how it felt to slide her fingers through his silky black hair when he'd be bending over her; it was thick and heavy, and he'd always smile. With a deep sigh she realized how much she'd begun to care for him. A futile exercise up against Trey's casual view of women. A futile exercise considering the numbers of other females who cared for him.

Overhearing the disagreeable conversation was for the best, she decided. Otherwise the temptation to stay would have become stronger every day. And the temptation to be drawn into Trey's enchantment ultimately would have been heart-breaking. He'd loved too many women. He'd loved too many women. Better a small, wrenching sadness now than a humiliating heartache later. She silently congratulated herself on the merit of her rational judgment. Trey Braddock-Black was not interested in permanence.

But her mental soliloquy didn't quash the longing or dispel the sadness at leaving. Her chest ached with the pain of it.

As Empress was passing just north of Cresswell's store, Trey was roundly cursing, alternating with shouted orders as he tucked his wool shirt into the heavy worsted pants he wore. He had on two pair of woolen socks inside his fur-lined, knee-high moccasins, and one of the upstairs servants was now scurrying to bring him his buffalo coat.

The alarm that had the house in a state of panic had sounded at about eight-thirty, when Trey had leisurely rolled over in his large bed and encountered cool sheets rather than Empress's warm body. His roar had brought every servant in the house to attention, and the braver ones ran upstairs to see what had caused his angry displeasure.

It took only two crisp questions and a servant's lightning-quick trip to the stables to ascertain that his pleasant interlude was abruptly over. No one argued with Trey, although most would have liked to point out that he still wasn't fully recuperated, and a precipitous chase across the winter mountains might be beyond his physical endurance. But since they valued their heads, in his present storming rage, instead they surreptitiously called Helena with the news. Hazard would send instructions when he and Blaze returned home, they were told. "Find him!" Timms had snapped and hung up.

Ten minutes later Trey was mounted, his gun belt buckled on over his heavy coat, his Winchester ready in the scabbard of his saddle, his expression dangerous. Empress had several hours head start on him, but the tracks in the sunlit snow were like a blazing trail.

He didn't want company, he'd curtly snapped. He wanted to be alone when he caught her; he wanted *her* alone, he thought savagely as he turned to check the bindings on his packhorse one last time. An unrestrained ferocity burned through his brain. She'd left! Ill-tempered and moody, all he knew was that he wanted her back! The reasons were incomplete and subliminal, and at present he was in no state to intellectualize them. But he wanted no witnesses at their meeting. So he brushed off the offers of help, told them lies. Told them she only lived twenty miles up the mountain and he'd be there in three hours. Told them in a polite, but coldly controlled voice, that no one dared challenge.

He was at Cresswell's store at one-thirty, having pushed his paint at a steady canter all the way. He saw that Rally was fed and watered while he questioned the store owner. He discovered when Empress had arrived, what she'd purchased. Trey paid for Cresswell's answers with gold but refused his inquiries. And with the Colts that looked worn from use strapped on the rider's hips and a fierce anger in his voice, Cresswell only asked the questions once.

It took Trey less than ten minutes to find where she'd backtracked and headed upcountry.

At the base of the Elbow Pass, Empress reached down for the tenth time to check that Genevieve's doll was still unbroken in the small package tied to her saddlebow. And a happy smile crossed her ruddy-cheeked face. The children would be ecstatic with their Christmas presents. Genevieve was eight and hadn't had a real doll for as long as she could remember. Empress recalled her own array of porcelain-faced mademoiselles, left behind in haste when her family had fled the château.

The last appeal had been abruptly lost, and Papa was to be sent to prison for shooting Rochefort's son. They'd left with very little: what money they could gather at short notice; a few prized possessions hurriedly packed; Mama's jewelry. All gone now after five years of flight . . . the first two in Montreal, and then when word reached them that Rochefort's detectives had been asking for the Comte de Jordan in Montreal, they fled west to the raw frontier where a man could hide for life. As a precaution, they moved over the border into Montana and, with their much depleted funds, bought the mountain homestead two years ago. The site was beautiful, majestic, and wild, but none of them were familiar with hard work, none were skilled in farming, and although Papa tried, he never acquired the necessary talents.

With the gold in her saddlebags, she'd have money to buy the extra horses they needed for the spring plowing. One horse wasn't enough to plow the sod, and they'd all had to help push the plow with only Clover in harness. With all of them pushing and Clover pulling, they'd broken six acres the previous spring and seeded it. But in a country where four- or six-horse teams were the rule, their attempts at plowing were pathetic. And six acres would never keep them alive.

The money in her saddlebags would do more than simply buy enough horses. It would give them back their life. "Thank you, Trey," she murmured into the bracing air. "For everything," she added gently. Then, pushing away the too sweet memories, she sternly set her mind on the future. Nudging Clover with her heels, she looked at the cloud banks coming in from the west. They were too high for snow, and if the drifts weren't too deep in the intervening valleys, she would be home by dark.

They had seen her when she crested the narrow mountain defile, for Guy had set up watches during the last two days with a systematic logic he'd inherited from his father. He'd had to man the watch a great deal of the time himself, though, since the younger children were disinclined to sit still for more than a few minutes. The screams of delight filled the tiny cabin, and the two windows facing the valley framed happily chattering children watching their older sister returning home.

Guy came out alone to greet her, wearing Papa's large boots and clasping Clover's bridle, his eyes bright with tears although he tried hard to appear the man. There was only Papa's boots left, and they were shared, so the other children crowded barefoot in the doorway, calling and shouting their welcome. "You're back! You're back!" Emilie and Genevieve screamed, dancing up and down in their excitement, while Eduard clung to Emilie's skirt calling, "Pressy! Pressy!" in a shrieking squeal that caused the chickens to begin squawking.

Empress noted the sound of the chickens with relief. Their food must have lasted. She'd given instructions, to kill the chickens if they had to. But only as a last resort, because they could live on the eggs longer.

Sliding off Clover, Empress gave Guy a big hug, then ran to the cabin door and crushed Emilie and Genevieve in her arms. Genevieve began to cry. "You didn't forget us."

Empress took her small face in her hands. "Hush, darling, I'd never forget you. I'll always take care of you. Look, I've brought you a present." She received a hiccuping smile then, and bent to swing a clamoring Eduard up in her arms. Her own tears of homecoming streamed down her cheeks while Eduard clapped his hands together and shouted into her ear, "Presents! Present! Me too!" He was still solidly chunky in her arms, and for the first time since she'd abruptly left Trey, she knew she'd done the right thing. She'd always taken care of them. The children needed her, the elder sister who comforted, teased, scolded, and loved them. They needed the food she was bringing home several days earlier than expected, and if she'd left Trey Braddock-Black a few days shy of her agreed three weeks, he could afford it a whole lot more easily than her young family out here in the wilderness. She closed her eyes for a moment and hugged her plump little brother. *Good-bye, Trey,* she said silently. *For all the joy you gave me, you were hard to leave.*

A smacking, wet kiss intruded, and she opened her eyes, sweeping aside the memories. "I have presents!" she cried cheerfully, and the level of squealing rocketed skyward. The chickens, deciding that some calamity was about to transpire, added their squawking to the merry din.

"Hush, they won't lay," Guy warned sternly, their depleted food supplies a constant source of worry to him.

"Let them cackle all night," Empress replied joyfully, giving Eduard another kiss, which was sloppily returned an instant later. "It's all right now. I brought food."

A sudden silence settled over the small, jubilant group, and it made all she'd gone through to get the money a thousand times worthwhile. But it saddened her, too, to realize how important simple food had become to these young children.

Handing Eduard to Genevieve, she turned to Guy. "We'll unload the horses. Emilie, set the table and take out Mama's silver candlestick." It was the only thing of value they hadn't sold; the only reminder the family had of Mama. The candlestick had become their reliquary of hope for better times, their symbol of celebration, a remembrance of their former life. Only little Eduard was too young to have no memories of the château near Chantilly.

Empress carefully untied the gold-ladened saddlebags herself, and placed them under her bed, then she and Guy carried everything else into the cabin. While Guy took the horses to the barn to wipe them down and feed them, Empress unpacked the food. Almost reverently the children helped her put it away, arranging the bundles and packages on the open shelves near the stove and dry sink. Then, washing their hands, Empress and Emilie set to cooking while Genevieve entertained Eduard with a story from the much-used book of fairy tales. They were singsonging their way through a silly rhyme, the smells of bacon and biscuits, stewed apples and creamed potatoes, wafting through the room when Guy tramped in from the barn with a warm bucket of milk.

In short order they were eating amid much chattering and laughter, each trying to describe the events of the intervening days to their sister.

"Guy was bossy," Genevieve complained, and before Guy could utter the reply he'd opened his mouth to express, in the next breath Genevieve said, "May I have more applesauce?"

Empress smiled at her eight-year-old sister, whose mop of black curls, so like Papa's, suited her gaminlike face and turned-up nose. "You may have all the applesauce you want. And there's oranges for dessert, too, and chocolates."

"Chocolates!" they all exclaimed in a clamor of astonishment.

"With a pink bow on the box."

"Show me," Emilie demanded impatiently, closer to Empress in looks with the same tawny hair.

"Has everyone had enough supper?" Empress asked calmly while four pair of eyes watched her intently.

"What's orange?" Eduard asked, standing on his chair. "Me see orange."

So they all ate oranges and exclaimed over the beauty of the chocolates, before they slowly ate the treat with much discussion of everyone's favorite flavors.

Later they sat on the floor around the fireplace while Empress handed out the presents. Shoes or boots for everyone, and new coats and mittens, the necessities they'd all gone without. Empress brushed a swift hand across her eyes and swallowed the lump in her throat when she heard their happy cries of delight. And then the special gifts: a clown with movable arms and legs for Eduard; the doll with real hair and a painted porcelain face for Genevieve; a mirror, comb, and brush set in silver gilt for Emilie. Guy couldn't hold back his tears when he opened the package with the Colt revolver. Papa's gun collection had been left in his study at Chantilly, and only the utilitarian rifle had been purchased on the frontier. "The handle's carved," Guy whispered, running his fingers lightly over the polished wood.

"You must promise to be careful," Empress warned, only

to be treated to a scornful, sixteen-year-old glance for her effort.

"I can shoot," was all he said, sounding very grown-up. Guy had stretched out a startling number of inches the last year and towered over Empress now. It was time, she thought, struck by his resemblance to Papa, to consider going back to establish Guy's claim to Papa's title and property. Now that Papa was dead, the threat of prison was over. And had their finances permitted, she might have taken the family back to France after Mama and Papa died. With the gold in her saddlebags, maybe they should consider it now. Or perhaps it would be more sensible to stay another few years in this peaceful valley, where Guy could grow to manhood before attempting to reclaim his title of Comte de Jordan.

Her reflections were cut short by Eduard tugging on her arm and wanting his new shoes untied. "Tight," he pronounced emphatically, sitting next to her on the floor. "Pressy, shoes tight."

Empress smiled at her baby brother, who'd run barefoot all his life, and decided she should have bought him something more practical for his feet, like moccasins. The thought of moccasins, of course, brought vivid images to mind of a tall, bronze-skinned man with long black hair like satin, and with a shiver she turned to Emilie and quickly asked, "Are there any chocolates left?"

Much later, when the younger children were all tucked into their beds with their new presents clutched in their hands, Guy and Empress sat near the fire, relaxing after the hectic, noisy evening. Guy had checked the animals an hour before, to see that they had food for the night. "It's going to be cold tonight," he'd said, stamping in with his new boots. "The sky's clear, with brilliant northern lights. It's at least twenty below right now. Going to be worse by morning."

If the moon hadn't been nearly full, he wouldn't have been able to follow the track at night at the speed he'd been traveling. She hadn't been cautious at all, except around Cresswell's store, her track open and easy to see after that, with the heavily loaded horses.

The cold was dry and windless, the kind of night the temperatures would drop into the bottom reaches and you wouldn't notice your face freezing until it was too late. If he didn't come upon her destination soon, he'd have to find some shelter for Rally or lose him. In his buffalo coat over the Hudson Bay capote and his fur-lined moccasins, he could handle any temperature, but the journey was beginning to tell on his paint; frost clung to his nostrils where his breath froze. Luckily Empress's two horses had broken trail through the snow, but in places it had drifted over—on the high ridges where the winds always blew.

Trey wouldn't admit to his own exhaustion, rancor sustaining his fatigued body. How many times in the last hours had he talked himself into an acceptance of her actions—of her sneaking off in the middle of the night like a thief? Empress had some good reason, he'd told himself. Of course she did. But then the niggling doubts intruded. Why hadn't she told him? And next, the litany that had been repeating itself without discrimination or disclaim resumed: A woman who'd sell herself in a brothel can't be trusted . . . can't be trusted . . . can't be trusted.

But his anger generated from purely selfish motives. He had been deprived of something he wanted. A novel experience in a young man's life that had been, to date, exceptionally favored.

Rally stumbled, caught himself, and Trey swore. Damn Empress, there was no reason they should be out in the middle of the mountains in the dead of a winter night, freezing, fatigued, his fingers numb since five miles back. He chose to ignore the fact that no one forced him to follow her.

His mood was foul when the trail reached the crest of the next rise, foul and hot-tempered and inclined to blame first, then ask questions later. He saw the lights of the small cabin nestled in the bowl of the narrow mountain valley. His mount sidled as his gloved hand crushed tightly on the reins. "Eureka," he said with a quiet grimness, his eyes narrowed against the gleaming, moonlit snow. There was no doubt in his mind that he'd found his quarry. Reaching forward, he rubbed Rally soothingly between the ears in apology for his inadvertent reaction. The beaded black-cougar design on his fur-lined gloves flashed in the moonlight. Raising his hand, he briefly touched the glistening talisman to his lips. "We have her," he said.

Trey carefully surveyed the homestead, taking his time like he'd been taught as a scout, checking the contour of the land, listening for the sound of a watchdog, trying to determine whether this was a ranch with armed men. Sliding his Colts from their holsters, he checked to see that the chambers were turning easily in the intense cold. He lifted his rifle from its scabbard and broke it open to check the full magazine. Then his heels touched Rally lightly, and they started down into the valley.

Guy had just asked Empress where she'd gotten all the money. He'd wanted to ask any number of times since she'd returned with the lavish array of presents and food, but when she'd not offered an explanation, he'd been fearful of inquiring . . . she had left with such somber determination.

Empress gazed at Guy, seated opposite her and near the fireplace in one of the sturdy chairs Mama had brought halfway around the world, and paused before answering, even though she'd rehearsed the answer a hundred times on the way home. He'd blurted out the question, an embarrassed flush burning his cheeks. "I was going to hire myself out in Helena to earn enough money for food and seed," she began, telling half the truth, not mentioning where she had planned on hiring herself out, "when a man was shot. I happened to be near at the time . . ." Another half-truth. No need to explain how near and in what state. ". . . and was able to help him live. His family is wealthy. They gave me the money as payment for saving his life."

"How was he shot? Was it a shoot-out?" Guy was still young enough to be fascinated with the drama of gunslingers.

"Nothing so honorable," Empress replied, remembering the brutal, bloody sight of Trey and Flo that night. "He was shot in the back."

"That's cowardly!" Guy exclaimed in disgust, youthful idealism still prominent in his convictions. "Did they catch the skunk," he asked in the next breath, "and string him up?"

"Really, Guy, don't be so bloodthirsty," Empress chastised teasingly, her brother wide-eyed with sensational interest. "And, no, they didn't catch him, as a matter of fact. But they will."

"How can you be sure? If he got away, they may never find him."

Empress thought about the conversation she'd heard one morning when Blue, Fox, Hazard, and Trey had discussed Jake Poltrain and the possibility of legally indicting him for the shooting. The consensus had been that if legal means weren't adequate, they would handle it their own way, in their own time. There had been no equivocation or doubt as to their "handling" of the problem. Jake Poltrain would pay, one way or another. What had shocked her most about the conversation was not the discussion of vengeance but the quiet assurance that revenge on Jake Poltrain was inevitable. Hazard's voice had been eerily soft when he'd said, "I don't believe in vigilante justice, so we'll give the courts their chance first. This is supposed to be a civilized country. However, if the courts fail to hang Jake Poltrain . . ." The implication left unsaid was absolute in its certainty.

"This family," Empress explained, "are half-blooded, and they're very good"—she searched for a suitable word—"trackers."

"Real Indians!" Guy exclaimed, enchanted by the notion of savage revenge. "Will they scalp him when they catch up to him?"

"Good God, Guy, you're fiendish. People don't scalp anymore."

"The Blackfeet still do. Papa told me once. He told me he'd heard it down the valley."

"That's just a rumor. No one scalps," she lied. She knew better; Trey had told her bounties were still paid for Indian scalps, although it was covert. In Deadwood, South Dakota, he'd said, not too many years ago, Indian scalps were worth two hundred dollars; and women's were most prized. And then the image came to mind of the four men in Trey's bedroom that morning, their hair shoulder-length, their sculpted cheekbones exhibiting classic perfection, their softly spoken discussion centering on Jake Poltrain's death. That image put the lie to her bland assurance.

"Papa said they leave the reservations for hunts, and he'd seen a whole party along the ridge one time. But they'd ridden on. Papa said they like to raid horses."

"I don't know anything about Indians—and you don't, either, except gossip—and we've never been bothered in two years. Not once. So I think we can assume there aren't any Indians interested in Clover."

"And the other horse . . . the good-looking paint." Guy's voice rose half an octave. "Is that an Indian horse? Did you get that from the half-blood family?"

"It should go back. I just borrowed it for a packhorse."

"When will you take it back? Can I go with you?"

How pleasant it would be to ride back next summer and

return the paint and say, "Thank you." She could see Trey
again. But then all those women's voices reminded her of
what she meant to Trey. It was over. She could never go
back. And after a few days he would forget her in some other
woman's arms. It was worse than she thought it would be. He
was always in her thoughts. "I don't know," she said with
soft finality. "We'll probably never take it back." And it was
the truth. Although she used the word *borrowed* advisedly,
she had no idea how she could possibly return it.

While Trey was checking the barn for the number of horses
at the ranch, and Empress and Guy moved on to a topic less
fraught with angst, Duncan Stewart returned from a gala
hosted by the Montana Improvement Association, a group of
greedy men intent on cutting every stand of timber in the
territory and willing to entertain the legislators for that privilege.

"Your *intended* has disappeared," Duncan declared, walking forcefully over to the liquor table and taking the stopper
off a decanter of bourbon. Splashing some liquor into a glass,
he took a large drink before he turned to look at his daughter,
who had declined to rise to the bait. She was lounging on a
silver satin sofa, dressed in full evening array, only recently
arrived home herself from a small dinner party. Taking a sip
of champagne, she carefully set her glass on the table at her
side before she quietly met her father's sharp glance and
mildly said, "The news is about town."

"No concern?"

She shrugged, and the violet tulle barely covering her
décolletage bristled delicately. "Would it do any good?" she
asked calmly.

"You're the cool one."

"There's no great need for haste."

"What if he freezes out there? The man's barely out of his
deathbed."

"Really, Daddy, think. He's half Indian. He knows how to
survive in the"—she gracefully waved her slender, perfectly
manicured hand—"out-of-doors."

"They say he went after the woman."

"They also say the woman sold herself at Lily's. Do you
consider that marriage competition? I rather think not. And
surely, Daddy, being a man, you must understand the
difference."

Her father nodded once, cleared his throat, and silently

wondered, as he did so often, at his daughter's cynical grasp on the realities of life. "They're out looking for him, in any event."

"And I'm sure they'll find him," Valerie replied tranquilly. "Now, then, what do you say to a talk with Hazard, perhaps in a week or so? Obviously Trey is past death's door sufficiently to take a wife. I think you should offer our little proposal to Trey's father and give him some time to grow accustomed to the idea. He'll have to check our story out with Gray Eagle and Buffalo Hunter, of course."

"If Hazard Black wasn't so protective of his clan, this idea would never work, you know."

"If Hazard Black wasn't so protective of his clan, we'd have to think of another idea, then, wouldn't we? But he is. Which is the point. And I'm very good at playing the outraged maiden in court. You and I both know how justice serves the Indians out here. They just hung four of them last month in Missoula. And those seven on the Musselshell. Was it over someone's cattle?"

"Horses."

"You see how easy it's going to be, Daddy?" She raised her champagne glass to him.

The kerosene lamp on the mantel flickered first, and then the cool draft of air struck them. Empress and Guy both turned at the same moment.

A swirl of snow swept into the room and eddied in tiny gusts across the plank floor. Trey filled the narrow entry, dark and massive in the open doorway, his head brushing the low lintel, the heavy buffalo coat augmenting his large frame. His capote hood was tossed back, frost-covered like his lashes.

He was here. Why was it that she had this overwhelming feeling her life had begun again? Unconsciously Empress rose to meet him.

He stepped inside, his moccasin-shod feet silent on the wooden floor, and pushed the door shut with a casual sweep of his arm. "You owe me six days," he said.

Empress's heart was thumping wildly from the sight of him. The suddenness. From the low, husky, deliberately pronounced sentence.

Guy was out of his chair. "Who's this, Pressy? Who's he? What six days?"

Trey glanced at the young boy as if seeing him for the first time, then his gaze returned to Empress. "Should I tell him?" he threatened softly, his silver eyes in the next second cautiously sweeping the small interior of the cabin. He'd already checked the barn and had looked into the lamplit cabin before entering. It appeared that they were alone, but it never hurt to be careful.

"What, Pressy?" Guy blurted out. "Tell me what?"

Trey's eyes swept back to Empress, and he raised his dark brows in mild inquiry.

"No," Empress murmured in a breathless rush, her own eyes pleading. "Guy, I'd like you to meet the man I told you about."

Trey's eyes opened appreciably in faint surprise.

"The man whose life I saved," she declared firmly.

"With unbelievable expertise," Trey interjected softly.

"The man whose family rewarded me with all that money. For saving his life," Empress added with challenging emphasis.

Trey's smile was instant and lavish; his arms opened in a languid gesture. "In the flesh," he drawled lazily.

Empress shot him an exasperated look. His effrontery never ceased to amaze. "Guy," she went on, mildly snappish, "this is Trey Braddock-Black. Trey, this is my brother, Guy."

Walking over, Trey winked delicately at Empress, put his hand out to Guy, and said gravely, "My pleasure."

"Good—good—evening, sir," Guy said, stammering, hastily recalling his manners, his eyes transfixed by the enormous man with twin six-guns strapped low on his hips. "You're the half-blood," he declared maladroitly, then colored instantly at his faux pas and began stammering an apology.

Trey cut him short. "Never mind, Guy," he said with a smile. "I'm used to it. As a matter of fact, I favor my father's side of the family."

"Pressy says you're going to hunt down the man who shot you. Will you shoot him, hang him, or stake him to the ground with ants and everything?"

Trey looked amused, cast a cheerful glance at Empress, and said, "Your sister told you that?"

"Oh, no, sir." Guy quickly came to Empress's defense. "I just thought, well . . . being half Indian and all."

"I like the idea of ants," Trey agreed playfully. "Would you like to help if I ever find the scoundrel?"

Guy's eyes opened wide, and he gasped aloud.

"Trey, that's enough," Empress admonished. "And, Guy, don't embarrass Mr. Braddock-Black with any more of your outlandish ideas."

"Are your six-guns Colts?" Guy asked, undeterred by his sister's chastisement. He had never seen a man who looked so much like a gunfighter.

Trey nodded.

"Custom?"

"Yes."

"Pressy brought home a Colt for me, but it's not custom."

"Any Colt's a damn fine weapon."

"Would you let me look at one of yours?" Guy's eyes were riveted on the pearl-handled revolvers, touches of niello barely visible at the top of the holster.

"Sure, here, try them on." And Trey unbuckled his gun belt and handed it to the young boy.

"I hate to interrupt this masculine discussion," Empress said resentfully, Trey's ready charm annoying her. Everyone liked him instantly. It was galling. Not only women. *Anyone.* "But perhaps you'd tell me what you're doing here, Trey."

"I already did," he drawled softly, his glance direct and warm.

"Trey, look, it fits." Guy had buckled the belt on its last notch, and the heavy holsters framed his slim hips. "Can I shoot them?" he asked, excitement in his voice and expression.

"Not right now," Empress said tersely, and turning back to Trey, repeated in a hard, staccato cadence, "I want to know your plans."

"Please!" Guy implored.

"Guy!"

"Later, Guy," Trey said quietly. "We'll go out later. The moon's nearly full. If you'll excuse us for a minute now, I'd like to talk to your sister."

"Huh!" Guy looked at Empress's pursed lips and heated glance. "Oh, sure, I'll go put your horse in the barn."

"He's already there, but you could feed him and bring in my bedroll." He'd packed swiftly and efficiently, a habit he'd learned from his father on the summer hunts. A change of clothes, extra moccasins, the ammunition he'd need, all wrapped in his bedroll. "And I wouldn't mind eating, either," Trey said with a smile.

"Oh, we have *food* now, don't we, Pressy?" Guy swiftly answered. "Pressy will fix you something, and I'll help when

I get the horse done. I'm a pretty fair cook when there's food," he added, "but until Pressy came back, we were eating oatmeal three times a day. With eggs," he quickly explained. "It wasn't so bad, but Eduard didn't understand. Pressy sure was a sight to see coming down the valley. Did I show you my new boots?" Guy breathlessly rushed on while Empress died of embarrassment.

"I'm sure Mr. Braddock-Black's not interested in your new boots," Empress said, already too late, since Guy had hitched up his pant legs and was showing off his shiny new boots.

"They look very nice," Trey said, struck with the sudden realization that he'd never had to consider not having new boots.

"We only had an old pair of Papa's after he died, and well . . . it was hard when everyone wanted to go—" Guy stopped abruptly, having finally noticed his sister's glare. "I'd better see to your horse," Guy muttered, edging away.

"He talks too much," Empress said into the silence after the door shut behind her brother.

"All children do." Trey smiled. "It's one of their charms."

"He doesn't see himself as a child. I'm afraid he feels very grown-up since . . ." She hesitated.

"Since your father died?"

"Yes."

"And your mother?" Trey asked, looking at the twin portraits over the small sideboard.

"She died three days after Papa."

"When was that?"

"Last summer."

"I'm sorry. And that's why I found you at Lily's."

She nodded. "And that's why I wouldn't let you renege on our agreement."

"I wouldn't have. You could have had the money." There was sympathy in his expression and voice.

"I wasn't sure."

"Lucky for me." His smile was lush and inviting. "And since we're on the subject, perhaps we could discuss exactly how we're going to arrange—er—the remaining days you owe me with Guy and Eduard around." His anger was gone now that he'd found her, the days only a bargaining ploy if one was required, if she needed moral justification for her actions. Empress wasn't in the habit of sleeping with men, and her precipitous departure may have had something to do with conscience or morality. If she needed an excuse, he'd give her one.

"Don't forget Emilie and Genevieve," Empress added with her own smile, smugly brilliant.

"There's more?" Shock, frank and explicit, colored his voice, but single-minded and resourceful, his composure was restored in the next moment and he said calmly, "That's right, you said you had sisters, too, that night at Lily's." He wasn't in the habit of dealing with children, was totally unfamiliar with children as an accessory to seduction. This would, he reflected, require a certain subtlety.

Empress had seen the shock, the instant transformation a moment later, and gave him high marks. His poise was as impeccable as his charm, but their positions were reversed now that Trey was on her territory, the situation entirely different from the ranch where Trey had the advantage of family and servants who allowed him anything. With her four brothers and sisters and very cramped living quarters, ordering the world to his perfection may elude him this time. Not that she was disposed to harbor hatred for Trey, or for his inclination to authority rather than deference. She'd found it impossible even on her long, cold journey home to hate him, and now, in his presence, it was out of the question. In fact, she had an overwhelming impulse to throw herself into his arms, an impulse she ruthlessly suppressed. Enough inner monologues and agonized musing had ensued in the last few days for a very realistic perception to manifest itself apropos her place in Trey's very full and busy life. Love or otherwise.

"Four, total. Brothers and sisters," Empress clarified. "I'm afraid your trip might have been a waste of time." Even as she uttered the words, her pulse rate spurted forcibly, for Trey was unbuttoning his buffalo coat. His dark lashes came up, and the glint that so often reminded her of moonlight flashed up at her.

"I damned near killed my horse to get here, so four brothers and sisters or forty . . ." He opened the Hudson Bay capote he wore under his coat and, with a lift of his heavy brows, left the sentence deliberately unfinished. "It's just a matter of"—he grinned with a quick, boyish warmth—"arranging things." Shrugging off his coat and capote, he handed it to her, only to immediately pluck her upright as the sudden weight of the coat buckled her knees.

"Good Lord, you wear that?" Empress exclaimed, a throaty gasp of surprise following her startled cry. "You must be stronger than I thought."

"And you weaker," he replied softly, his strong hands under her arms. "A pleasant combination, if I remember . . ."

"Hush, Trey, the children might hear," Empress warned, her gaze lifting toward the loft floor, her nerves tremblingly on edge. When he'd walked in from the winter darkness, inexplicably it seemed as if her life had begun again, and now, with his hands supporting her effortlessly, his physical presence engulfed her senses, like being wrapped in the eye of a hurricane.

"Give me a kiss, fierce kitten," he whispered. "That's quiet enough." And lifting her off the floor, buffalo coat and all, he brought her face level and kissed her, his lips still slightly cool from the outdoors.

"No," she protested as he put her down, "you mustn't," as if saying the words would still the familiar desire Trey's kisses always provoked. As if simply saying no would deter the leaping need based on lush memories and his warm, demanding kiss. "You shouldn't have come," she said in answer to his kiss.

Taking his coat from her, he tossed it on a chair with one hand, as if she might discard a children's blouse. "You shouldn't have left me," he replied, turning back to her, his voice soft and deep. The wool shirt he wore was a brilliant crimson and so smooth in texture that it must be cashmere and silk, the warmest combination against the cold. She felt shabby in comparison, the contrast in their lives, even with her new wealth, too disparate. Even with her father's comfortable income as the Comte de Jordan, she had never envisioned resources and affluence on the scale Trey was used to. Maybe more than anything, it was his self-assurance based on that personal empire that was the obstacle to their relationship. The privilege and fortune made him what he was, and it clashed with her own wishes for the future.

"I had to," she replied, knowing he could never be hers. "You shouldn't have followed." And she backed away.

"*I* had to," he said so low, the words were a husky resonance, his moccasins silent on the wooden floor as he advanced the step she'd retreated. He was much too close, she thought with alarm, trapped between the sideboard and the bookshelf, her back against the wall.

The scent of him filled her nostrils as his hands came up and settled solidly, palms down, on either side of her shoulders. He never had understood no, she thought as his dark head bent down toward hers. She looked as opulent as he remembered, he thought, delicate, soft, her eyes wanting him even as she refused his advances. Thinking ahead, he wondered where they could find some privacy in this crowded cabin; there was hardly room to turn around. Their lips touched, Empress's half open in the artless surrender he always found so tantalizing, and his arousal stretched the soft wool of his trousers. She felt it hard against her stomach and moaned unconsciously, her small tongue reaching for his when Guy's tuneless whistle sounded clearly outside the door.

Empress broke away, sliding quickly under Trey's arm, and was halfway into the kitchen area when her brother walked in the door.

"Trey, what's your paint's name?" Guy inquired, stamping snow off his boots. "He's a real beauty!" He was the picture of youthful enthusiasm, standing just inside the door, his grin wide, Trey's bedroll balanced on one shoulder.

Trey swallowed once to bring his voice back to normal and to still the raging desire so abruptly curtailed before he turned a half-step to face Guy. "His name's Rally," he answered. "He won the time trials at Helena as a one-year-old and has beaten every racer west of Sheridan in the last two years. You might like to try riding him tomorrow," he graciously offered.

"Yippee, you've got a deal! Where do you want your bedroll? Can we shoot now?" Guy had a veritable Western hero here in his own home, and he wanted to get him settled in just as soon as possible, so he'd be sure to stay.

Trey knew exactly where he wanted his bedroll, but this boy was too young to understand, so he said instead, "We should help your sister with the food." Empress had been opening and shutting containers with a nervous agitation that looked potentially explosive. Knowing her temper, he was all for soothing concession. "Besides," he quietly said to Guy, "we can shoot tomorrow. I'll be staying a while, if you don't mind."

"If we *mind*?" Guy repeated in awe. "You hear that, Pressy? Trey's staying! Isn't that grand! He's going to let me shoot his custom revolvers and ride his paint and—Pressy, isn't it *wonderful*?'' Guy was at the impressionable age where masculine accomplishments and feats of derring-do were significant and exciting.

It was heaven, Empress thought; it was everything she'd dared not dream. Paradise within her reach. Trey smiling at her and touching her, kissing her, weaving his seductive spell around her so there was bliss so profound, it obliterated her reluctance. The most beautiful man on six continents wanted her.

It was going to be a living hell. Because nothing had changed in the real world—the one outside the charmed circle that seemed to close around her when Trey held her. In that world—the real one—she was disposable. In that world Trey played at love. In that world a broken heart was all she'd ever get from loving Trey. Tempered by the baffling frustration that wouldn't conveniently arrange for both loving and happiness, Empress's voice was more sharp than she intended. "It's wonderful. Now, you'd better help me with those potatoes.''

"Sure, Pressy, sure," Guy quickly agreed, his voice happy enough for both of them. "You watch me peel. I've gotten real good while you've been gone.''

When Trey offered to help, Empress's refusal was less strident than her answer to Guy as she guiltily regained her composure. Guy was so happy with a man's company, surely she couldn't deny him that pleasure. It hadn't been any easier for him to leave their comfortable world and at the age of eleven take on duties and responsibilities beyond his capabilities. In some ways he and Empress had adapted better than their parents, more resilient in their youth to the unfamiliar tasks and manual labor.

Trey recognized the hard, clean line of her jaw when she'd said no to his offer, and he didn't press her, wanting to avoid any further disagreements. The sensation of her soft mouth under his and the richness of her small body pressed against his was vivid, and the last thing he wanted was discord. He waited for supper in the chair by the fire and in minutes had fallen asleep. Sheer willpower had sustained him on the trail, but he was exhausted, his partially healed body pushed to its limit. As though his indomitable will understood that he'd reached haven at last, that he was where he most wanted to be and could at last relax its vigilance, he slept.

"Hush," Empress chided Guy once when he spoke too loudly. "Let Trey sleep." And there was tenderness in her glance when she dwelled on the sight of him sleeping in front of her fireplace. She knew what an effort it must have been for him to follow her into the mountains, what stubborn courage it took to ride seventy miles in subzero cold with the fragile state of his health. Damn the unknown future, she thought spontaneously, and damn little bitches like Arabella McGinnis! She wanted him, and maybe the test of a seventy-mile ride through winter mountains meant he wanted her more than the Arabellas and Lucys of the world. In the tenderness of the moment, his tall, lean body sprawled on Mama's sturdy chair, maybe nothing mattered but his being here. She let him sleep for almost an hour before waking him, and he smiled first when he saw her, as she'd remembered, then rubbed his eyes like a young child waking from a nap. "I'm glad I found you," he murmured, and her heart swelled with happiness.

Supper was quietly cozy, the kerosene lamp casting its soft golden light across the table and over the faces of the three young people. It almost seemed as though they were entirely alone in the world, isolated high up-mountain in the blackness of the night. Relaxed in a lounging content, Empress watched Trey eat systematically like he always did, with relish, and beamed along with Guy when Trey complimented the chefs. He ate two servings of everything, said, "Yes, please," with an intimate smile for her when she asked if he wanted more hot chocolate. Why can't the world disappear, she thought briefly, returning his smile, and we could all stay here forever?

Guy had been warned by Empress, while Trey slept, not to be too inquisitive and demanding of their guest, so he stifled the impulse to talk Trey's ear off and only asked a modest number of questions about Indians and scalps and bloody revenge. All of which Trey courteously answered with a grave sincerity. It was agreed that they'd do some target shooting in the morning.

"If the blizzard hasn't hit by then," Trey said.

"Do you really think so?" Empress queried. "The sky's so clear."

"The wind was picking up and changing direction when I rode in. It smelled like snow to me."

"Maybe if we're lucky," Guy declared with childish enthusiasm, "we'll be snowed in!"

"Might," Trey said, stirring cream into his applesauce.

"Oh, *no*," Empress responded, her feelings an ambiguous confusion of wanting and not wanting, of reasoning and feeling at war. "We were snowed in the first winter we were here for over two months!" In the current state of her mind, how could she possibly deal with the thought of enforced detention with Trey?

"It doesn't matter this time, Pressy," Guy agreeably reminded her, "you brought home plenty of food." Immune to the sexual undercurrents disturbing his sister's peace of mind, the thought of a winter in Trey's company was delightful.

"But snowed in . . . you can't possibly stay that long," she blurted out, then, realizing how rude she sounded, added, "I mean—your family will worry," she said, stammering.

"I don't mind being snowed in," Trey said, his smile as warm as a summer day. "And my family knows where I am." Now, that wasn't exactly the truth, but they knew where he was going, if not the precise destination. And while his mother might worry, his father understood that he was capable of taking care of himself.

"Hear that, Pressy? Trey doesn't mind!" Guy's face was alive with joy. "Will you teach me to shoot a bow and arrow? Do you know how to shoot a bow and arrow? I'll bet you know how to shoot a bow and arrow," he said, answering his own question in breathless excitement.

"We'll have time to do lots of things," Trey replied calmly. "The first thing we should do if the storm hits is to make some snowshoes. Do you have snowshoes?" He'd seen the panic in Empress's eyes at the talk of being snowed in, and took pity on her anxiety.

"No, we don't," she answered. "Papa tried once, but—"

"Why don't we make some, and then the snow won't matter. You won't have to worry about being snowed in. How does that sound?" he asked with kindness.

"I'd like that," Empress said quietly, knowing in the short time Trey had been in her home that any lengthy stay would be disastrous to her emotions. He was vivid happiness and affection, with a natural warmth that lit her soul like a votive offering. He already meant far too much to her. They were going to have to seriously discuss his staying. Later, when Guy was sleeping.

But Trey fell asleep in the chair near the fire before Guy, the strenuous twelve-hour ride having depleted his reserves of strength. She covered him, and after Guy had gone to bed, she sat for a long time watching the lean, bronze-skinned man, the complex man who'd followed her home for what appeared to be utterly simplistic reasons. It would never pay, she reflected, staring at the perfect planes of his face in repose, to become too involved with the richest, most eligible confirmed bachelor in Montana; it would be the height of foolishness to become enamored of a man so handsome, if he wasn't wealthy, he could make his way in the world on his looks alone; it was absurd to harbor the same simplistic attachment for him, as his was for her, an attachment based on purely sensual pleasure, which was incompatible with all her idealistic conceptions. Everything about their relationship, from their initial encounter as purchaser and purchased, was imprudent and absurd. Why was it, then, that she found her heart filled with limitless affection; why was it, then, that she softly whispered, "Don't stay too long on Winter Mountain . . . or I might never let you go."

A moment later she smiled at her own presumption. As if she could ever cage a man like Trey!

In the morning Trey woke stiff, but rested. He looked across the small room to where Empress stood adding wood to the cook stove and said softly, "Good morning."

She turned around and smiled.

His smile leapt back across the room.

Lifting both hands, he laced them on top of his head and, leaning back comfortably, asked, "Where did you sleep?"

"Over there," she replied, pointing to the bed built into the dark corner under the loft, neatly made already with a colorful quilt covering.

Stretching his back slowly, he removed his hands, his smile widening. "I don't think I'll sleep in the chair tonight."

"You can share a bed with Guy." Empress gestured over her shoulder to the opposite wall. "It's Mama and Papa's bed, and large enough for you two tall men."

Lowering his voice when Trey saw Guy sleeping in a tumble of disarranged blankets, he flexed the stiffness from his arms and murmured, "He seems to be a sound sleeper."

Empress faced him across the small distance, dressed in her

familiar costume of trousers and flannel shirt, looking fresh
and young. "Don't get any ideas, Trey."

"I have them already, darling." His pale gaze slowly
traveled up her slender legs and curved body to her brilliant
green eyes. "It's too late."

"This little cabin has four other people in it besides you
and me, all with big ears and wide-eyed curiosity. Keep that
in mind."

"I promise," he said with a genial smile, "to be discreet."
Laying the quilt aside, he stood, ran his hands through his
tousled hair and, arms upraised, looked at her in an intimate,
assessing way. "I missed you," he said softly.

"You tell that to all the ladies," Empress replied calmly,
making a serious attempt that morning to keep Trey at a
distance. She had decided in the cold light of morning to:
first, not be dazzled by Trey's beauty and charm (easy to say
when not in his presence); second, try to maintain a cool
detachment (equally hard when he smiled like that); and third,
send him on his way as soon as possible, for he would only
complicate her life. Unbelievably.

"Never," he said very low. "You're the first."

His deep, husky voice, his startling reply, sent a flutter
down her spine, and all Empress's carefully crafted plans
blurred. It took a full moment for cooler reason to prevail
over the swift, flashing response. "Pardon me if I find that
difficult to believe," she declared firmly. The overheard
conversation, the sound of Arabella's snide aspersion, came
hurtling back to remind her . . . any man that popular with
the ladies had to know all the charming phrases.

Trey moved toward her, past the rough-hewn table with its
mismatched chairs, knowing he could make her believe when
he was holding her close. Her reserve, her shyness, changed
once he kissed her or whispered sweet love words or managed
to get by the barriers she kept reconstructing whenever he
allowed her.

There was no reason for all the reserve or barricades anymore. Her shadowy past was revealed—the brothers and sisters, the dire poverty with its poignant remnants of a genteel
respectability, like the family portraits, the lone silver candlestick, and the officer's dress sword hanging over the mantel.
What more was there to hide? In Montana Territory—anywhere
in the West—were countless families who had moved to the
frontier to repair their fortunes. Why the cool detachment

now? And he mentioned it gently, before he reached out to touch her. "Why the restraint, sweetheart? I meant what I said. I missed you." But when his hand went out to grasp hers, she moved away and took three steps aside, so the table separated them again.

How do you respond to a man whose bedroom is larger than your entire home, with your brother possibly listening only a few feet away, or the other children overhearing, so near that Trey could reach up his hand and touch them? How do you say, "I'm not a tart, and although I was at Lily's, I'm not for sale—not inside my soul"? And how do you tell someone as accomplished with women as Trey, "I'm not capable of simply playing the game"? According to Arabella and Lucy, dalliance for Trey was normal and frequent; perhaps *habitual* was the more suitable word.

Her feelings for Trey were too disastrously involved already to allow even the mildest game to begin again. She must be strong. She had been and could be, she knew, for she'd taken on the full burden of her young family when her parents died. So she chose to give Trey the bland answer that wouldn't reveal her feelings, or embarrass her if the children were listening, and would also serve as protection. "There's no privacy; be practical." But her emotions were not so easily quelled, and much against her will, she heard herself say, "I've missed you too."

"I will *arrange* the children," Trey said very low, watching the rapid pulse beat under the fine skin of her throat, remembering how it felt to kiss the pale golden flesh near her ear, knowing she was feeling precisely what he was feeling. "You and I are going to be alone."

"No," she protested, his words causing a pink blush to creep up her cheeks, her disloyal senses too receptive to his assault. "You can't."

"Yes," he said, very, very softly, "I can."

He didn't attempt to touch her again, but his words were as potent as if he'd stripped her naked where she stood. She shivered. He smiled.

"Would you like help with breakfast?"

Trey was the model of respectability that day, although his pale eyes would stray to hers circumspectly when the children were busy, and Empress was sure the thudding of her heart was audible clear to Helena. He was on his very best behavior, and from the first moment that morning when Trey said to the silent, wide-eyed young children who had just wakened to find a strange man in their home, "Let's have cake for breakfast," he was universally adored. Empress hadn't realized he could cook, and when she said as much, she was accorded an arrogant, arched brow and a conversely feigned humility. "Why shouldn't I?" he said, which didn't explain a thing and made her want to shake him and ask where he'd learned to cook anything as complex as apple-sauce cake (from memory, no less) when she'd never seen him lift a finger at the ranch other than to ring for a servant. After the children had cheerfully assisted in the cake baking and eating, Trey suggested everyone dress warmly and he'd take them out sledding.

He instantly became a combination of paragon, idol, and best friend, a remarkable feat considering the gender and age difference among the children he was bewitching. "I'm hoping the children will want me to stay," he said casually as he ushered the last one out the door and turned to take leave of Empress. His smile was ironic, his luminous eyes aglow with amusement.

"Can I throw something at you?" Eyes narrowed, she glared at the self-assured man.

The sunlight streaming through the window defined the stark bone structure of his face, the perfect, straight nose and severe cheekbones, illuminated the teasing light in his eyes. "Have I ever refused you anything, darling?" he said, his arms open wide.

But his reflexes were superb. He was outside, the door already slammed shut when the kettle Empress flung at him hit the door.

He seemed as much a child as they, Empress thought, watching them frolic in the snow, and she briefly wondered who was having more fun. Later she was coaxed out for the building of the snow forts, and although Trey's side lost (he told Guy and Eduard that a gentleman always lets a lady win, which lesson they resignedly accepted), he had whispered to Empress that he'd really won, since he intended to steal a kiss from her during the surrender ceremonies.

That kiss had shaken them both. It was the merest brushing kiss, bestowed and received in a clamorous, shouting frenzy of children's voices and brilliant winter sunshine. But it was like touching through prison bars or greeting a lover in full view of a spouse. They were both flushed and warmed from the furious snowball warfare, and unexpectedly experienced the singular sensation of wind-chilled flesh meeting in a kiss. Hypersensitive detonation, riveting magic. Trey turned and walked away abruptly. Empress leaned her cheek against the ice-block fortress wall and trembled.

That afternoon they all became involved in snowshoe construction, and after having seen her mother and father so incompetent in the wilderness, Trey's casual expertise was astonishing. His long-fingered hands bent and molded the steamed wood, tied and wove the rawhide, and glued with smooth, even strokes, despite the frequent interruptions to help struggling, chubby fingers and willing, but inept, apprentices, all cheerfully involved in "helping" him. He was kind and benevolent, quick to praise small successes, indulgent with the numerous blunders. He fixed, repaired, adjusted, so each one's project bore a reasonable resemblance to its ultimate goal. But his eyes met Empress's occasionally over the children's heads, and Trey's gaze sent desire racing through her blood. He'd smile then in that slow, lazy way she remembered, and another shiver of pleasure would course through her. It was only a matter of time, that lazy smile was saying as clearly as though the words were spoken aloud.

And when the wind started howling as evening fell, Trey said, "Now here's the storm that was brewing last night."

Eleven

BY MORNING, THE mountain valley was snowed in, and Trey's clansmen, forty miles away, still out searching for some sign of him, gave up. His tracks had almost disappeared that first day, and last night's storm had seen to the rest. The group trailing him was stranded at Cresswell's store three days, before the wind and snow abated. Twenty-two inches of snow fell in forty-eight hours, and when the winds picked up on the third day, the drifts were man-high in places.

In questioning Cresswell, Blue had discovered both Empress and Trey had gone through only hours apart, before the snow, a full day before the snow had even threatened. Aware of Trey's ability as a tracker, Blue was sure he'd found her. And if she'd reached her destination before Trey overtook her, Blue hoped that no interfering family had taken issue with his pursuit. If Trey had overtaken her on the trail, they may be holed up in some shelter from the storm. That, too, Trey was capable of finding; survival techniques were honed to a fine edge in Hazard's heir.

But now that the storm was over, their search would go on. Blue sent men back to the ranch to bring additional horses and supplies while he and Fox began questioning the ranch owners around Cresswell's to determine the direction Trey had taken. No one had seen him.

While the hunt for Trey went on, Jake Poltrain spent more and more time at Li Sing Koo's Pleasure Palace. He'd plan his revenge on the Braddock-Blacks, and in his opium dreams he was never thwarted; he always won. It was opium's major appeal, the convincing triumph and the sense of euphoria at besting Hazard Black at last. And in his dreams he never had to back down like he did in reality. Like the last time, when the fences he'd put up protecting his water rights had been leveled, Hazard standing there larger than life, with his damn son and damn private posse. With his hands loose at his side, the Colts with as big a reputation as their owner slung low on his hips, Hazard was just hoping Jake would make a move for his gun. Damned arrogant Indian. He knew no one had ever outdrawn him. And his son, as insolent as the devil, the spitting image of the old man, with more flash, it was said, than the cold-blooded calmness of Hazard's gun-play, in his own handling of a Colt. And out to match his father's record, it was rumored. Hazard had said in that deadly quiet voice of his, "You're on Absarokee land. We don't allow fences on Absarokee land. The water rights are ours."[7] He could have been God himself for all his humility. Jake drew in another breath of opium smoke, and the tower-ing resentment dissolved like the outer ripples of a pond splash. One inhalation more and the much more pleasant dream of triumph was restored.

Jake had coldly shot the man he'd paid to kill Trey at Lily's. On the night the Texan had met him for the second half of his payment, Trey was at death's door and, had the killer but known, so was he. Jake was no fool, understanding with the ruthlessness of a predator that witnesses were by definition expendable. The derringer concealed in his gloved hand was a surprise even to the gunfighter from Texas, who'd learned to be wary at a young age. His frozen body was found by a homesteader out looking for a stray a week later. No one knew his name, although Jake Poltrain's bunkhouse crew, with whom he'd stayed the past month, said he called himself Waco.

Another suspicious set of circumstances was laid at Jake's door.

A week after Trey had left in pursuit of Empress, Hazard and his lawyer left the sheriff's office in Helena.

"It doesn't look too hopeful," his attorney said to Hazard. The sheriff had just informed them that the evidence against Jake Poltrain was all circumstantial. Nothing concrete enough to file charges. Hazard had scowled, and the sheriff had quickly said, "We're continuing the investigation."

"He owes me," Hazard grumbled, moving through the ornate portals of the courthouse and out into the sunlit winter day. The cold wind rippled his dark hair over the fur collar of his topcoat, and he stopped to button his coat. Why, he wondered, was he allowing himself to be so civilized about this shooting? Just put a bullet in Jake Poltrain and be done with it, was his first reaction. When he was growing up, he'd been taught to take vengeance on his enemies. He sighed into the gusting wind.

"Martin's trying," his lawyer said, reading the sigh correctly. "But there's no witnesses." The judicial voice was pleading the sheriff's cause with a reasonableness that was typical. "No one was out in the hall at Lily's that night to see the killer either arrive or leave."

"Do I detect a touch of defense for Martin? He's a nice enough young fellow, if you like conservative procedures. Good-looking fellow too. Do you want him? I could—"

"Don't you dare say he owes me a favor, Father," his daughter said levelly, her large, dark eyes serious. Hazard's daughter, Daisy, born before he met Blaze, drew herself up to her full height. "Can't I make a sound statement about the legal process without having it misconstrued as some silly female crush on a man? There is not suitable evidence for conviction, Father, whether you like it or not."

"Relax, Daisy." Hazard smiled, but Daisy didn't smile back, her expression adversarial, the arch of her brow, which matched his in contour and sweeping line, raised high in disdain. "I wasn't questioning your judgment on the legalities," he apologized gracefully, reflecting that the years at Vassar and the highest score on the bar exams ever recorded in Chicago, where she'd studied law,[8] lent a certain haughtiness to his daughter. He was very proud of her. "It's only that I prefer a bit more expeditiousness."

"You can't put a bullet in everyone who disagrees with you, Father." The words were contentious, but her smile was not. She had a beautiful smile, with a touch of sensuousness, which was what had attracted him to her mother.

"I'll try to be more civilized. Would you like that?"

"Don't put on noble-savage airs with me. You know damned well you're more civilized than most anyone in Montana."

"Well, what do you say to being civilized, then, and inviting Martin over for dinner? Would that be amenable to your punctilious sense of etiquette?" Hazard asked, grinning down at her.

"Don't embarrass me, Father."

"Don't call me Father. It sounds like we just met two days ago."

"Very well," Daisy said, deleting the form of address altogether because Dad, Daddy, or Papa were much too informal for her staid, earnest soul. Even when she was very little, she'd been gravely solemn, looking out on the world with a thoughtful concentration, slow to express her opinion until she'd weighed all possible alternatives, an ideally suited personality for the profession she'd chosen.

Conceding to her careful omission, Hazard said, "I'll settle for Father, rather than that judicious blank," and with a quick grin he ruffled the feathers on her plum velvet bonnet.

Ducking away swiftly, she ran a smoothing palm over the expensive feathers and then, in her slow, attentive way, returned his smile. She was dressed by a Paris couturier, her Virot hat lavishly feminine, and while she'd inherited her height and her opulent eyes from her father, Daisy Black was lovely, like her mother. "Don't worry, Father, I won't go through life an old maid."

Not likely, Hazard thought, with his experienced eye for female beauty, but his reply was tactful and mindful of Daisy's views on women's rights. "I don't care if you do, Daisy, if that's what you want, but damn, if you want Martin Soderberg, let's do something about it."

"*Us* is not the operative word, Father. I'll take care of it in my own way." She reached out conciliatorily and slipped her small gloved hand in his.

And Hazard was reminded of the frightened twelve-year-old who had just lost her mother and stepfather in a hunting accident and was waiting for him in his study long years ago. She'd seemed so quiet and grave, he didn't know if she'd understood all he'd said to her, but when he'd put his hand out and said, "Come, Daisy, I want you to see if your room looks the same,'' she'd slipped her hand in his and had become a permanent part of his life, not just a summer visitor.

So Hazard shrugged, smiled, and let the topic drop.

But when they arrived home at the town house on the hill, he sought out Blaze at her desk in the library. ''Next dinner party, love,'' he said, ''invite Martin Soderberg for Daisy.''

Blaze looked up from her letter writing, her glance mildly surprised. Hazard hadn't completely crossed the threshold before he'd spoken. This, apparently, was serious.

''Surprised the hell out of me, too, but that's the way it looks.'' He pulled the silk scarf from around his neck with one swift tug and tossed it on a chair. ''Make it a big party, though, so it's all very tactful and Daisy doesn't get suspicious. She made it plain that I wasn't to interfere.''

''I see you're following orders in your usual fashion.'' The startling blue of her eyes was as provocative as her tone.

''Don't follow orders at all, *bia*, as you well know.'' And he walked over and bent to kiss her gently on the cheek. ''With one exception,'' he murmured, his breath warm on her cheek, his voice teasing. Straightening, he looked down at her with a boyish grin. ''You know I do everything you tell me to.''

Blaze smiled up at him as he shrugged out of his coat, thinking he looked as wonderful as he had the first day she'd met him all those years ago. And she knew under the cutaway coat and dark trousers that his lean body was as fit as ever. It came from the horse training he always casually maintained; it kept every muscle toned. She replied with her own mocking amusement to his teasing. ''You may do as I say, Jon, but only if I beat you into submission first.''

Hazard's glance was cheerful as he lounged on a corner of the desk, one long leg idly swinging. ''And you're the only one who can.'' Checking the hour on the desk clock, he grinned. ''Is there time before dinner?'' His wife's raised eyebrows brought forth a full-throated chuckle.

''Not unless you can set new records, darling,'' she said. ''And you know, I've never been interested in speed. However,'' she went on in the lush, suggestive tone he always adored, ''once we get rid of all those tedious politicians, I would be happy to share the remainder of the evening with you.''

''A bottle of Cliquot and a roaring fire?'' Hazard proposed.

"With the curtains open so we can see the stars."

"*Our* stars, like the lodge in the mountains." Each year Hazard and Blaze went back to the place where Trey had been born the first winter of their marriage, and stayed for as many days as they could arrange. It was a time of peace for them, away from the demands of the world. "We don't have to go back, do we?" Blaze would always ask when the time for their departure drew near. And Hazard would say no, and hold her tight. It was a barefaced lie they delighted in, like children shutting out the demons with a litany of nonsense.

"A very poor second to the lodge in the mountains but the best we can do here in town. Say eleven o'clock?" Her smile was open.

"You're on, *bia cara*. This is going to be the shortest dinner party in the history of Helena."

"Oh, dear," Blaze said nervously, "you won't be obvious, will you?" Hazard had a tendency to overlook the subtleties of etiquette on occasion.

"Now, sweetheart, you know how easy I am to get along with." He ran a fingertip over the irregular, downy arch of her brow. "You've till ten-thirty to see them all out the door—with my help, of course. After that, I can't guarantee any civilized manners."

"You're incorrigible, Jon, but I adore incorrigible men."

"Keep that singular, love, so I don't have to kill anyone." His dark eyes were affectionate, and he thought how lucky he was to have found the only woman in the world he'd love till he died. Which brought to mind Daisy's affections. "What do you think of Martin?" he asked, loosening his cravat and vest buttons.

"He seems very pleasant. If he meets Daisy's standards, he must be even nicer than he looks. She's *very* particular."

"With a remark like that, I don't know if I should take offense. Meaning you're not?" he inquired teasingly.

"Heavens, no," Blaze replied with a quick grin. "I'm not particular at all. The only thing I ask is that a man love me more than anything else in the whole world."

"That must be why we get along," Hazard said with an easy charm.

"If I ever catch you saying anything that smooth to another woman, I'll kill *you*." Blaze's smile was wide, but her heart was touched by their love, undiminished by the years.

"Knowing how well you shoot," Hazard replied, amusement rich in his voice, "I'll be careful."

Shortly afterward, as Blaze and Hazard were dressing for dinner, Fox was announced and immediately admitted.

"Did you find him?" Blaze asked, worry evident in her voice and expression and in the anxious way she reached out for Hazard's hand.

Fox filled them in on the quest, ending so far at Cresswell's store; answered Hazard's brisk questions about timing, supplies, and the amount of snow, and left with further orders from Hazard to relay to Blue when he returned up-mountain the next day.

Blaze was more concerned than Hazard. Hazard had every confidence in Trey's ability to survive on the trail. Trey had plenty of supplies, he'd assured Blaze, but her apprehension was with her son's health. Mothers, Hazard thought, were always prone to overlook little things, like the reports he'd heard about Trey and Empress's hermitage in Trey's room while everyone had been gone the previous week. Not exactly, he'd decided on hearing the gossip, the conduct of a weak young man. So Hazard wasn't worried about Trey's health, but if Blaze wanted to overlook those activities, which she'd heard of as well as he, that was her motherly prerogative. And he wasn't foolish enough to point out the error of her thinking.

Twelve

TREY WAS, WITH cheerful vigor, shoveling a wider path to the barn. It was after midnight, the moon shining brightly down on him once again after the storm, and everyone in the snug cabin was fast asleep.

The past days with the children had been genial and pleasant. The snowshoes were finished, they'd begun bows and arrows, and before supper that night everyone had made snow angels in the fluffy, drifted whiteness. He and Guy had carried in dozens of pails of water so everyone could bathe; both the boilers had been put on top of the cook stove and filled; a makeshift curtain had been hung in front of the stove; and each person in turn washed in the large tub, on the floor.

During supper, with everyone's skin scrubbed clean and shining, the array of faces around the table reminded one of an idyllic image of wholesome health. With the children, Trey sang round songs in French and English he'd never heard until that night, and when Empress whispered, "Thank you," to him before she herded the little ones upstairs, he'd wanted to say, "The pleasure was mine." But it sounded too glib, and she was disturbingly suspicious of his warmth. At times it bothered him to see her obviously enjoying herself and then abruptly withdraw from the easy gaiety, as if she'd let herself go too far in her enjoyment. She was very different in those instances from the captivating, spontaneous Empress he remembered from his home, and all he could credit the curious retiring disparity to was the fact that the children were present.

So . . . that night he was cheerfully shoveling because he intended to talk to Empress alone, with no children. He'd already made a warm bed for them in the hayloft, with two heavy quilts burrowed deep in the sweet-smelling hay.

It was a dream, her slumbering mind lazily noted, and Empress murmured a low, purring sound deep in her throat. Unconsciously lifting her chin a scant, drowsy distance, she reached for the elusive, cool mouth on hers. She found it and felt the heated rush of feeling, sharp and splendid, like melted gold sliding into hidden corners. The texture of pleasure took on tenuous substance, surprisingly cool on her lips, her cheeks, stroking down the delicate skin of her throat. And she purred again, a contented, feline vibration, answered fine-grained and exact, graphically, like a flare deep in the pit of her stomach. And lower.

Her arms responded like flagrant wantons to that flaring glitter of feeling, and when they rested lightly, then twined around a strong, solid neck, an answering sound, male and relevant, brought the small fevers precipitously to combustion.

Anyone who had watched the young couple during the previous days could have foretold the speed of their arousal; hot youth and passion burn still and, if repressed, flare higher when released. And all the foreplay, seductive assault and withdrawal, perceptible, unmistakable, even though silent, veiled from children's eyes was material now. Palpably, tangibly material.

She woke when he lifted her into his arms but hardly felt the chill when he carried her outside, so heated were her senses. Wrapped in blankets and his arms, she tasted his earlobes in little nibbling caresses as he strode down his newly widened path to their haven in the hayloft.

With swift efficiency he lay her in the soft bed, slipped her nightgown off, and covered her with the heavy weight of the quilt. She watched him quickly undress with a high-strung impatience and felt as though some inexplicable sorcery were in motion that night, and it was her right to possess the magnificent body revealed before her.

Sitting back on his heels, he was gazing at her, his muscled form like some pagan god, broad-shouldered, powerfully built, his silver eyes like jewels.

When the silence had lengthened, her sovereign need blindly ordained, she spoke his name: "Trey." The tone was not diffident or hesitant; it wasn't the voice of the woman who had been retreating from his affection or kindness or warmth. The woman he'd met at Lily's was back, the bewitching woman from the ranch.

He held his hands out then, and she saw that they were trembling. "I'm like a young boy. You affect me that way." He smiled a crooked, rueful smile. "I'm not used to this." He placed his hands solidly, carefully, on the taut muscles of his thighs and inhaled deeply. "You mustn't leave me again." His handsome face grimaced.

Empress couldn't answer in a way that would please him, for at base, they wanted different things, but this night, at this moment, she only wanted him. They were in accord.

Sliding her hand out from under the quilt, she held it out to Trey, and in the short seconds before his lifted, it seemed as though they'd never touched before. As though the passion were achingly new. That feeling of newness was a novelty to the large man kneeling in the fragrant hay, like turning back time or holding the moon in your hands.

"Come, you must be cold," Empress whispered, her eyes taking in the athletic, strong arms and chest, Trey's elegant long-boned hands lying atop his hard thighs. It was winter and he was nude.

"I'm not cold," he murmured. "I'm hot." The sensation was like stepping out from a sweat lodge into a chilly night: You never felt the cold. But it was more, he knew, even if she didn't understand. His body was heated from within. "See," he said, and his hand stretched out toward hers, the gem-cut seal on his ring flashing.

Empress waited as if she'd waited a lifetime to know his touch, saw his lean-fingered hand move toward hers, and wondered how wanting could fill your entire body like this until the fierceness of it poured over in suffocating waves. Her lips still tingled from his kisses that had wakened her. And physical desire, suppressed and contained in the small, crowded cabin during the past days, was peaking like a storm out of control, reckless, heedless now of the self-denial she exercised.

Trey's fingertips touched hers and then slid down, interlacing smoothly until their hands touched, palm against palm, his long fingers curled around hers. His skin was hot. So hot, her first thought was, *He'll warm me.*

"You're cold," he whispered. "Are you afraid?"

Terrified, she wanted to say, *that you'll engulf me with the flaming passion you give away so lightly.* "I'm not afraid of anything," she said, and his teeth flashed white in the dimness of the loft.

His grip tightened on her small hand, and the smile in his voice was tinged with soft suggestion. "I'd forgotten how exciting you are. I can discard the sonnets, then; my fierce kitten is in form."

Her upper lip slowly curved, and her eyes half closed. "I'll eat you alive," she murmured.

A flicker of surprise glinted in his eyes before he drew her hand to his mouth and, opening her fingers, pressed her palm to his lips.

She shivered, stabbing pleasure tearing through her senses.

Lifting his mouth, Trey responded in a husky growl that was vehement, not with anger but with excitement. "We'll have to see who does what to whom. If I recall," he whispered, his tongue tracing leisurely over the soft pad of flesh rising toward her thumb, "we're rather evenly matched." And it all came back in a rush—searing memories that had been obscured in the previous days of tender glances and stolen kisses, of childish games and children underfoot. He'd forgotten that she'd confidently forced the pace as often as he, that she had initiated unguarded pleasure in equal measure. He had forgotten in all the dulcet domesticity that when Empress Jordan was hot, she took his breath away.

A moment later he was lying lightly above her, braced on his elbows, the feel of her body soft beneath him, cushioned by the padded quilt separating them. Trey's mouth hovered above hers and he smiled. "Let me know," he said, his grin full of mischief and affection, "when you're warm enough to move the quilt away." His eyes shone with lazy amusement. "And then I'll decide whether"—there was a considering pause—"when," he finished in a quiet, intense voice.

That night, with the gentle animal sounds below them, the glistening moonlight and stars above them, the summer-sweet scent of pasture rich in their nostrils, minute by minute, with tempestuous joy, with sureness and delicacy, they gave to each other their gift of love.

The following week was the stuff of fairy tales. The children adored Trey, and the days were spent *en famille*, Empress happier than she thought possible. She had everyone she loved near, and the joy the children experienced in Trey's company was a tangible happiness.

Emilie preened under Trey's teasing compliments, while Genevieve simply viewed him as her personal Roland. In the courtly world she avidly followed in the medieval tales of knightly deeds, the paladin who saved France at Roncevaux had always been her hero. The melding of folklore and reality was complete in Trey, as far as she was concerned.

Guy treated Trey as a loved older brother, and Eduard spent every waking moment in Trey's arms, on his lap, or perched on his shoulders. Even as Empress apologized for the imposition, she knew that short of tying her baby brother down, Eduard's behavior was fixed. Trey only smiled and said, "We get along great, don't we, Eddie?" For which he received a sticky, warm hug.

"He misses Papa and Mama," Empress explained. "He was so young when they died, he couldn't understand."

"Two brothers and two sisters younger than I died. I know how terrifying death is when you're young. He's no problem. I like sticky hugs." His smile was mischievous.

Empress blushed, recalling their heated lovemaking at night when the children were sleeping. They'd christened their sweet-scented hayloft bed the Nest, because of its balmy perfumed security and bliss, and Trey's look made all Empress's lush memories crest.

A week passed in their isolated mountain cabin, halcyon and rich with sweet emotion. They talked of the days ahead and the weeks ahead, and Empress dared for the first time to consider Trey in more permanent terms. Each night in their enchanting hideaway he whispered that he loved her, and each day he worked on the farm, helping Guy build and repair, setting the fences and outbuildings to rights. "When spring comes," he said, looking out on the snow-covered valley, "we'll get some more horses up here and put in the crops properly."

Empress's heart filled with contentment. He spoke of the future—their future.

"And when spring comes," he murmured in a husky, warm voice that night when he held her close, "I'll show you where the crocus first peaks through the snow, and I'll make you a bed of alpine trillium and lay you in it. . . ."

When Empress's fever began, she brushed it off as just the initial stages of a cold. But by evening she was burning up, and when she started vomiting, Trey panicked.

He knew nothing of medicine and could only follow her instructions, mixing some hot spirit teas to soothe her stomach and take down the fever. By morning she was worse, not better, and Trey was terrified. People died every year of the winter fevers. His own family had been decimated by illnesses that had begun as innocuously. And they were seventy miles from the nearest doctor. If Empress weakened, it would be too late in another day or two to take her out.

He woke the children early while Empress fitfully dozed, his mind made up. Whispering instructions to them all to dress and pack, he told them that they were going out on snowshoes. He wanted a doctor for Empress. With the children's help, he made oatmeal and toast and saw that they all ate and dressed warmly. He lifted Eduard down from the homemade high chair, wrapped him in his outer clothes and a large blanket, and stood him in the packsack while the girls put on their caps and mufflers.

Guy left enough hay in the small corral for the horses and the cow; the chicken feed was left open and available. While everyone stood dressed and ready, Trey bundled Empress in a quilt, then buttoned her into his buffalo coat. "We're going back to the ranch," he said when she protested the additional warmth. "I'll have you outside in a minute." She was flushed with fever, her eyes brilliant with illness, and a dark fear, with him since childhood, crept back. What if she didn't get better? Even the doctors hadn't been able to help his brothers and sisters. He shut his eyes briefly and said a silent prayer to his spirits, *Listen to me, Ah-badt-dadt-deah, she cannot die. Do you hear me? Give her strength.* It was neither meek nor submissive. Trey wasn't a humble man; the plea was as powerful as the man who uttered it, simple and unreserved in its request.

Picking up Eduard in the packsack, he put it on his shoulders, adjusting the Hudson Bay capote under the straps, settled the headband across his forehead, and walked over to Empress's bed. He took her in his arms, walked out of the cabin, and saw that all the children were ready. Stepping into his snow-shoes last, he smiled, said, "Hang on, Eddie," and in the lead started across the snow-drifted valley. They had forty miles to walk to the nearest cabin. From there Trey could send for help.

The children were awkward at first on the snowshoes, although there had been some practice after they were completed and their progress was slow. Even with Trey breaking trail, he had to travel slowly with the children, stopping often to rest, and at midday pausing to eat. Trey cleared a space of ground, using the net shoe to shovel away the snow, and built a fire. He cut fir boughs and made a bed to lay Empress on, near the fire. While the children ate the food they'd carried in their small packs, Trey tried to feed Empress. He begged her to eat, but she had weakened since morning and would only swallow a little.

At the speed they were traveling, Trey knew they wouldn't reach Swenson's that night, as he'd hoped. The children couldn't travel as fast as he. They'd just have to keep going through the night. Empress had drifted into a kind of stupor from which it was difficult to rouse her. They'd keep going until they came to Swenson's. There was no other choice.

By late afternoon it was necessary to rest more frequently; the children were trying to keep up, but Trey was walking slower and slower, and they were still falling behind. So he would stop, make a small fire, and let everyone rest for a time, then cajole and encourage them to go on. Every muscle in his body screamed, and only the utmost exertion of will kept his own feet moving. The parts of his body that didn't ache from overuse were numb from the cold and the burden of carrying Empress and Eduard both. Luckily Eduard had fallen asleep a short time ago, so the pack on his back no longer moved; it was only dead weight now. He'd almost fallen twice when Eduard abruptly shifted his position without telling him.

Darkness was no more than fifteen minutes away, and it was evident that the children were near exhaustion. Genevieve was only eight, and for the last hour Guy had been pulling her along, his jaw set hard with the effort. But his thin face was white with fatigue, and he wouldn't last much longer. Genevieve had begun crying once during the afternoon and was immediately silenced by her brother and sister. "Pressy's sick," Guy had said, "and we *have* to keep walking. When you can't anymore, I'll carry you on my back." Emilie had coaxed, "Be strong, Genny, because Trey is already carrying Eduard and Pressy. Don't cry, and I'll give you my book about Roland." Genevieve gulped, sniffed, and trudged on.

Trey felt like crying himself at the daunting journey still before them; at the fear he felt every time he looked down at Empress, so still in his arms, her breathing ragged and irregular; at the poignant courage of the three young children behind him who had gone through so much in their brief lifetimes and were endeavoring to conceal Genny's tears from him to relieve him of an added burden. But crying, of course, wasn't a practical option. There were very *few* options. The children could go no farther. They couldn't be left alone in the wilderness. Empress had barely roused since midday, and he would have preferred going on. But they would have to camp and let the children sleep, then start very early in the morning—and pray Empress was still alive.

"We'll go on until dark," he told the children. "Only another fifteen minutes. Can you manage?"

Trey received three plucky smiles and a hoarse, tired affirmative from Guy. He swallowed the lump in his throat.

A heavy growth of cedar, black-green in the dimming light, bordered the open ground they were crossing. In all the whiteness, distances were deceiving; it wasn't as close as it looked, but it would be their camp that night. Stolidly he set his gaze on the dark margin of the upland pasture; wearily he set one foot in front of the other. With heartache he contemplated the cedar grove as their night camp. Perhaps it would be Empress's dying place. He wanted to scream in rage at his helplessness.

Blue and six men came riding out of the shadowy cedar, their horses laboriously advancing through the high snow. At the sight of Trey and his small party, Blue whipped his paint forward. Trey stopped dead in his tracks.

There *was* a God, watching over him.

Having seen the torture of Trey's progress, Blue hastened to take Empress from his cramped arms when he reached his side. Quickly sliding the band off his wet forehead, Trey swung the sleeping Eduard into his arms and handed him up to another rider. Since the search party was well equipped, Blue suggested they camp for the night. Trey refused.

White and strained with fatigue, he said, "You stay with the children. I'll take Empress to the doctor."

It was unthinkable in his condition. He'd carried Empress for ten hours.[9]

So everyone stayed in the saddle, Empress cradled across Trey's lap. He talked to her as they rode, but she didn't answer him, not even in the faint whisper with which she'd responded before. She'd been failing all day. Hadn't eaten. Only drank sparingly, although Trey had pleaded. "Let me sleep," she'd murmured last. But that had been three hours ago, and Trey was afraid.

It was two in the morning when they rode into the ranch yard. Outriders had raced ahead to see to preparations, so the entire household was out to greet the weary party.

Trey issued instructions for the children's care, then introduced Guy, the only one of Empress's family still awake. Eduard, Emilie, and Genevieve were sleeping, wrapped in buffalo robes and carried by three of the search party. They were carried into the house and put to bed in the nursery. Guy followed Trey upstairs in the wake of the doctor, who had quickly ordered Empress inside.

Hazard and Blaze had been summoned home when the outriders reached the ranch and had been waiting since midnight.

After Empress had been put to bed and the doctors and nurses brought up from Helena were watching over her, Trey helped Guy settle in for the night. "She'll be fine now," Trey said, having to reassure the young boy, terrified he might lose his sister, although the awful dread was starkly prominent in Trey's own mind. She hadn't responded to his voice as she lay in his large bed; she was too white and too still, and it took every ounce of self-control he possessed to appear calm in the presence of the young boy.

His first reaction had been to grab the doctors by the shoulders and demand they cure her. His second reaction had been to threaten them. "I'll kill you," he wanted to say, "if she dies." Only tight-leased restraint kept him from losing control. But to the servants familiar with him, his voice had been too quiet, the set of his jaw alarming. And to the officious doctor who had addressed him last, only the servants realized how close he'd come to violence. "I'll be back," he had gritted out to the doctor, who suggested he leave everything to them, and Trey turned away abruptly, his hands clenching and unclenching at his sides. Blue had gently urged him out of the room. "Guy is dead on his feet, Trey. You'd better help the boy to bed."

And in more diplomatic terms Blue discussed with the doctors the approach less likely to offend his cousin. They were reasonable men; Hazard paid splendidly for their time.

A late supper had been set in the library, and when Trey came down after seeing Guy to bed, his parents asked the questions that could be politely asked. Trey was obviously worried about Empress, exhausted, dark shadows under his eyes, the strain of his journey out manifest in every line of his lean body, now slumped in the chair opposite them. He was high-strung with nerves, his voice fluctuating from agitation to weary lassitude. They didn't have the heart to bring up the unsettling visit Hazard had had yesterday from Duncan Stewart. Trey had enough ominous uncertainty in his life at the moment without burdening him with Duncan's oppressive news.

They all sat up that night, since Trey wouldn't think of sleeping, restlessly coming down at intervals for coffee, spending most of the night at Empress's bedside. The doctors worked feverishly all night, bringing Empress's temperature down with ice packs, fearful of convulsions with her elevated readings.

Trey sat at her bedside, gimlet-eyed when watching the doctors, like a literal dark spirit of vengeance. The quality of her care under that dangerous stare was first-rate, and toward morning Empress's breathing became less labored; her temperature had dropped. Trey fell asleep in his chair, his hand curled around Empress's.

"What are we going to do?" Blaze asked Hazard wearily, snuggled under his arm on the sofa near the fire. "Trey cares about Empress. It's plain to see. Blue said he almost threatened the doctors upstairs. How sure was Duncan about—" Her words ceased uneasily. The fact that Valerie was naming Trey the father of her coming child was still too unsettling to put into words.

"It doesn't matter, *bia*, whether anyone's sure or not." And Hazard had immediately gone to the village to inquire into the other allegations Stewart had brought up—the possible rape charges leveled against Gray Eagle and Buffalo Hunter if Trey didn't agree to marry Valerie. Both men had been intimate with Valerie, but there had been no coercion. On the contrary, Valerie Stewart was provocatively aggressive. Not that any of that mattered, as Hazard had already known. If a white woman accused an Indian man of rape, there wasn't a chance in hell he'd be acquitted. The men could disappear, of course, but Duncan and Valerie had presciently considered that contingency. Duncan had informed Hazard, in a perfectly modulated voice, unembarrassed by his flagrant blackmail, that should the correspondents disappear, Valerie would simply name some other man in the clan. It made no difference to them. Hazard stroked Blaze's shoulder, a gentle, soothing pressure that eased the tension in the back of her neck. "Don't worry, love, there'll be a way out." But the words chilled like a lie, even as he spoke them.

An hour later Trey came bounding into the room, buoyant with cheer. "I'm going to shave and clean up," he declared. "Empress opened her eyes. I think she knows where she is. I told her the children were all sleeping, and she smiled. She looks terrible, but she looks wonderful!" His statements were ecstatic, as though these mundane pronouncements were measured profundities, universal and cogent. "Gotta go." He waved a lighthearted good-bye and bounded back out of the room.

His parents smiled nostalgically at each other. "That's love if I ever saw it," Hazard said. "The boy was damn near ready for a doctor himself a few hours ago. I've never seen him so tired. And now—" His smile disappeared like the ending of his sentence, and he sighed. "I think we've got trouble on our hands."

"You have to do something, Jon. He's never going to agree to Duncan Stewart's demands. This is just like Carl's threats again. You know what Trey said about that. He wasn't the first or the only one. Charlotte Tangen had other lovers too. Her child may or may not have been his. You see, it's the same all over again."

"You don't have to convince me, darling. I've heard it all before." In fact, he'd heard it many times before, although Blaze was unaware of any but Charlotte. The situation had upset her so, Hazard had shielded her from the others. And occasionally, if bits of gossip reached her ears, he'd discounted them as small-town rumor. "Now don't fret, *bia*. I'll do everything I can."

"I want him to be happy."

"I don't think you have to worry about that, love," Hazard said dryly. "He's been pursuing happiness rather diligently for years." He knew how much Trey meant to Blaze. Their only child. And he loved Trey as much as she. But Blaze was his touchstone, his life, and it grieved him to see her unhappy. "Leave it to me," he said gently, bending his head to give her a kiss. "We'll work this out." Somehow, he thought morosely. "Let's get Empress well first," he went on, "then Trey can concentrate on another problem. I can put Stewart off for a few days. No one knows Trey's back yet. If I give orders, we can keep the news from spreading for at least a day or so." Hazard was realistic about secrecy in a household with several dozen servants. He'd give it two days on the outside before all of Helena, Montana, knew Trey was back.

Thirteen

———————•◆•———————

THE CHILDREN WERE all perfectly behaved at breakfast, with the exception of Eduard, who blithely ignored Genevieve's whispered commands and repeated in his high, piping voice, "Pee pee inside, pee pee inside." Trey interpreted Eduard's new enthusiasm toward his parents as childish fascination with the indoor plumbing. He had, in fact, spent the previous hour flushing the toilet in the nursery, embarrassing his older sisters half to death. And all three older children were pink now with the disconcerting direction of Eduard's conversation at breakfast. Hazard and Blaze put everyone at ease with interested questions of the children's farm up-mountain, and once Eduard was distracted by the sight of frosted cinnamon rolls, his conversation took a more socially acceptable turn.

After breakfast everyone trooped upstairs to see Empress, who although weak, was much improved. Her temperature had decreased dramatically, and she'd managed to keep down some chicken soup, but she was very pale, her delicacy emphasized by the size of Trey's bed.

Trey's parents were pleased to have her back, and pleased, they told her, to have the opportunity to meet her family. More vulnerable in her frailty, Empress almost broke into tears at their kindness but was diverted by Eduard's pithily significant announcements on the state-of-the-art plumbing. Empress giggled; Genevieve said, "Really, Eduard, you're such a child!"; and Trey cordially pointed out they had at least a month's worth of entertainment in the house for Eduard with ten bathrooms.

After several more minutes one of the three nurses in the room began clearing her throat with pointed glances at her watch. Blaze suggested the children go to the nursery with her and Hazard and see if any of the toys were still in repair. The room was cleared in under a minute. Even Guy and Emilie, who on occasion saw themselves as adults, had been awestruck at the array of toys neatly shelved on the nursery walls. In a minute more, an explicit glance from Trey sent the nurses from the room.

"Do you mind?" he asked, pulling up a chair near the bed. "I wanted to be alone with you. And those three nurses, I'm sure they are wonderfully competent, but they look like they should be on the pediments of Notre Dame. They'd scare me into getting well, I'll tell you." Trey gently touched Empress's hand, then twined his fingers in hers and smiled. "It worked, right? You're feeling better."

Empress smiled back at the tall, powerful man who was holding her hand as though it were rare Ming porcelain. "Much better, and my hand won't break."

Just to show he could be objective about the state of her health, he gave her hand a squeeze that wouldn't have ruffled the down on a chick. "I know, dear. You had me worried, though."

"I'm afraid I was a tremendous trouble to you, although apparently the children see it all as a great adventure, now that it's over. If you hadn't made those snowshoes . . ."

"We would have thought of something else."

Although he'd politely used we, Empress knew that without Trey at their farm, none of them would have been able to leave in the deep snow. And while the fever may have run its course without incident, she was grateful to Trey for taking the burden off Guy. He was too young at fourteen to have such adult concerns. "I'm in your debt," she said with a quiet gravity.

"I think I like the sound of that," Trey replied with a grin. "You're rarely so docile."

"It must be the fever," Empress answered, her smile lighting up the green of her eyes.

"Whatever it is," Trey said, his tone once again serious. "I'm glad you're feeling better. I've never felt so . . . help-less. I didn't know what to do."

"*You* should be careful. This fever is what killed Mama and Papa last summer, and it hasn't been so long since you've recuperated."

Trey shrugged. "I never get sick." And it was true. With the exception of the shooting at Lily's and the occasional cold as a child, he'd been remarkably healthy.

"Don't sound so smug," Empress chastised. "I used to say that, too, and look at me now."

"You were run-down after nursing me, then the long trip home. It was too much. Now you mustn't think of doing a thing. Just eat, sleep, and rest. Leave the children to me." He grinned. "You may have noticed, we get along—tolerably well."

"The man has a modest bone in his body, after all." Delight was in her eyes and voice, a touch of color defining the gentle curve of her cheek.

"I'm hurt," Trey mocked, elegant in soft kid boots, navy wool trousers, and a foulard shirt in tones of navy and wine. "Don't I simply exude modesty?"

"Never in memory." And she wondered suddenly what he'd looked like as a child, or an adolescent, before the insouciant sophistication.

"You're not exactly unassuming, yourself, Countess." Trey knew of Empress's aristocratic family, had heard the story of her father's duel, their flight, the hard years following in Canada and Montana.

"If I were unassuming, you'd be bored to tears."

"True," Trey replied with a ready grin, aware he'd never been so happy, aware Empress had become immeasurably important in his life, conscious during the long trek back when he feared she'd die that his life would be desolate without her. "Have you ever considered . . ." He paused, realizing with sudden shock that he was about to express him-self in a way he'd been prudently avoiding for years. "I mean . . ." He detoured once again, caught off-guard by new emotions, years of experience putting up a last resistance. "We get along"—his glance was warmly amorous—"fam-ously."

"Agreed," Empress said, her own glance affectionate. Always independent in her thinking, she'd accepted her newly discovered sexuality as a wonderful added pleasure to her life.

"So then . . ." Trey cleared his throat, and for the first time Empress realized that this conversation was not frivolous banter. Her heart skipped a beat. Was it possible Trey's feelings were as intense as hers? Was it possible the most eligible bachelor west of the Red River had stopped playing games? "I was thinking . . ." he went on.

She could have made it easier for him, but if she was mistaken, the embarrassment would be terrible, so she remained silent, although her pulse rate was peaking.

"You really need help with the children," he said. His statement was circumlocutional, but Empress didn't know, and she thanked her stars she hadn't blurted out her passionate feelings for him.

"And I appreciate your help," she replied politely, melancholy overwhelming her. Trey Braddock-Black was a womanizer, and she was a fool to forget it. He adored females but not on a permanent basis, and only silly tyros thought otherwise.

He caught the coolness in her tone. "I didn't mean that," he said, only adding to the vague confusion.

"Really, Trey, you don't have to help. I don't expect you to feel any obligation to my—"

"Oh, hell," he said tersely, dropping her hand and standing abruptly. Striding over to the window, he braced his palms on the oak molding and moodily stared out at the winter landscape.

"I appreciate everything you've done for me and my family," Empress said quietly. "But you mustn't feel any responsibility, and just as soon as I'm feeling better, we'll go back up to Winter Mountain."

"It's not responsibility I feel," Trey said, his back rigid, disturbed by the knowledge that Empress could walk out of his life the next day.

"And you shouldn't." Empress curbed her pain, forcing out the required courtesies. She was a dreamer to think she was any different from the scores of amorously devoted women in Trey's past. "I'll be back on my feet in a few days, then we'll no longer abuse your hospitality."

Pushing away from the window, Trey turned back to her in an abrupt, restless motion. "Damn, I'm not good at this," he said curtly.

Oh, God. How could this be happening, her wanting him

so, when every word he spoke was coolly opposite from her own feelings? Gazing at the severity of his expression, the tense conformation of his figure silhouetted against the window, she called on her reserves of pride and calmly answered, "I understand. No one expects you to—"

"I've never even thought of this before," he said as if she hadn't spoken. "In fact, I've seriously avoided it."

Empress didn't want to hear any more. Whatever he was about to say was going to hurt her. "Trey, really, you needn't—"

"And it doesn't have anything to do with the children," he went on, seemingly oblivious to her response, a slightly forbidding quality to his tone. "Although," he added quickly, as if his words were being played back with a three-second time lag and he'd only realized the austerity of his voice, "I like them very much," he finished with a kind civility. He seemed to come back from an interior focus, and in the next moment he saw the panic in her eyes. "Are you all right?" Instantly fearful, he was at her side in a few swift strides, memories of her stillness the last hours before reaching the ranch vividly recalled. Sitting beside her with a haste that echoed his apprehension, he quickly touched his palm to her forehead. "Should I call the doctors? Do you feel warm?"

"I'm fine." Like someone about to walk off the end of the earth was fine.

"Are you sure?"

"A little tired," she said, wanting him to leave, wanting this unhappy conversation terminated.

"I'll take care of you," Trey said very softly, his fingers lightly brushing her pale hair off her shoulders.

"You don't have to. I mean it. We've all imposed too much already." Empress thought of the enormous sum of money he'd given her, enough to allow her family a new start in life, how he'd devoted himself to the children, how he'd brought them all out safely in her illness. The debt was becoming too large. And the sooner she stopped adding to it, the better it would be.

"I *want* to take care of you."

"I can take care of myself," Empress replied a trifle brusquely, her shattered feelings contributing to her curtness.

"Don't be so touchy."

"I'll be touchy if I please."

"Suit yourself," he said pleasantly.

"Thank you," she replied in an ungracious tone that wasn't thankful at all.

"Certainly." His smile was benign. "I know how a fever can make one irritable."

"Dammit, Trey, don't be so insufferably understanding."

"I'm always understanding."

"And I'm the Queen of the Nile. Now, if you don't mind, I'd like to rest." *And cry my eyes out,* she thought.

"I guess I've no other choice."

"Well, you could stay and watch me sleep, but I'm sure you've better things to do."

"I'll just have to flat out ask you," Trey went on, curiously unresponsive to Empress's replies.

"No, not now, I've a headache," Empress retorted, sweetly malicious, her resentment of Trey's libertine life-style having overcome her melancholy.

"Will you marry me?"

Yes! was her instant reaction, a screaming, shrieking yes from the world's highest mountaintop. Unequivocal, without hesitation. "Are you coming down with my fever?" she said instead.

"Answer my question," Trey said. He wanted the answer he wanted. Trey Braddock-Black, scion of wealth and power, wanted assent. "Answer," he repeated quietly, encircling her wrists with his slender fingers. He didn't want her to leave him.

"Are you sure?" Empress inquired, his question so abrupt, so without endearments and gallantry, Trey's fingers clamped like shackles on her wrists. It was not the dream young girls dream; it was not a fairy-tale proposal.

He hesitated a bare fraction of a moment before he answered, "Yes."

Still no ardent words of love, only the cryptic pause and single word. And if Empress Jordan had been a practical woman, she would have replied in the affirmative without further ado. She was, however, not. She was impractical enough to want at least the minimum words of love. "Do you love me?" she asked simply, her large eyes inquisitive. Her background, the early years of privilege and wealth, never completely altered by the more recent years of hardship, may have prompted the question. Her passions said yes, but where another woman may have unhesitatingly accepted Trey for his position and fortune alone, Empress wanted her love returned.

Trey looked at her, at the delicate beauty of her face, the

willful lift of her chin, her eyes regarding him with unreserved candor. He smiled, suddenly positive, in the tumult and refractory images of freedom curtailed, of one thing at least. "I love you," he said. "I love you very much."

She smiled back, an assured, dazzling glow. "Don't you want to know if I love you?"

The thought hadn't occurred to him, with female worship commonplace in his experience, that she would not love him. But he was less arrogant than he appeared, so he apologized with charm and waited to hear her answer.

"I love you," she said with a sweet, fey air, "more than Clover."

"What more," he replied graciously, his dark head dipping gracefully with a courtier's fluent ease, "could any man want?" And he released her wrists with smooth finesse, as though with the bargain completed, the threat of compulsion was no longer necessary. "Is tomorrow too soon, or would you like a large wedding?" The teasing tone was nicely prominent once again.

"Are you always so presumptuous?"

"Years of practice." Exuberance, now, in his voice.

"Is there a rush?"

That heartbeat again, before he answered, that unnerving hesitation, the locked innermost door. *Yes, marry me before I panic and change my mind. I've never done this before, swore I never would, at least not for another decade; marry me tomorrow before all the logic takes hold again.* His feelings were all too novel, the habit of avoiding matrimony still powerful. It was like overcoming a built-in prejudice. "No, of course not," he said.

"I'd like to wait, then, until I'm stronger. So I can stand for my wedding."

"I don't want to wait," he said, his voice low. "But I understand." He drew in a deep breath, of apprehension or relief, she couldn't tell. . . . But his pale eyes were fervent; of that at least, she was always sure. "Next week will be fine," he agreed. "Should I tell the children, or would you like to?"

"We'll both tell them. They're going to be ecstatic."

"The feeling is mutual," Trey replied charmingly, thinking how lucky he was to have found her for now and all the joyful, sweeping tomorrows.

The bright morning light accentuated Empress's paleness,

her eyes dark like pine forests and enormous against the fairness of her skin. She was resting white on white: her batiste gown stark chalk, the pillows and sheets shimmering pearl, the soft blanket touched with glimpses of ivory in the luxurious wool. Only her hair held color, gilded crocus and lemon, in melodramatic disarray. It had frizzed around her face from her fever, delicate tendrils brushed back from her ears and temples, resting on the Irish lace of her nightgown collar.

On all the whiteness of the bed, against the delicacy of Empress's small form, Trey's dark power contrasted starkly. He was lean, muscled strength and bronzed skin that seemed to bring in the outdoors, and when he slowly reached out to recapture her hands, his large hands completely engulfed hers, his long fingers curling so that her hands fit into his palms. He had almost lost her, he thought with a stab of fear. Death had almost sprung the trap, and his mouth went dry at the remembrance. A feeling of protection washed over him, novel in its impulse and impact. Until Empress, he had never considered taking care of another person, and he understood for the first time his father's fierce protection of his mother.

How many times had he heard his father say, "I won't have your mother unhappy," when one of his escapades came to light, "and your behavior is very likely to cause her unhappiness"? Hazard's reprimands were delivered in a moderate voice, never issued as an order, but the message was clear: Trey was to restrain himself on the point in question.

"Next week, then, we'll be married." There was that touch of impatience again in his voice. "Is that all right?" he added, remembering his manners.

Empress smiled. "Next week is fine."

"Good," he said with finality, and he brushed a light kiss down the bridge of her nose. "I'll have Mabel bring up materials for your wedding gown. She'll have to begin sewing immediately if—"

"Trey," Empress interrupted, "I don't want a large wedding. I don't need a special gown." She wanted something simple, intimate, not a grand, staged spectacular.

"Nonsense." The word was surety from a man familiar with ordering the world to his perfection. "You're my Empress and should be dressed accordingly. You should have a train, diamonds—or would you prefer sapphires? Our Black

Lode Mine produces some of the finest . . . they're touched
with lavender.''

Pulling her hands free, Empress lifted her chin so her eyes
softly challenged his. "Trey, I don't *need* that.'' Her voice
was quietly hushed. "I only want *you*.''

Swiftly his hands closed on her shoulders, and his dark
head bent low so that their faces were level. "Hey . . . hey,''
he whispered, "I'm sorry . . . really. Whatever you want.
And you have me''—his gentle, pale eyes held hers, and she
saw deep inside grace and caring and overwhelming desire—
"forever.''

To know true happiness, she thought, it would have been
enough to have him for a single moment . . . and he was
hers—forever. "I love you,'' she murmured, tears glistening
in her eyes, and the world was suddenly too small to hold her
happiness. She had gained her heart's desire in the few
moments past, and her joy spilled out into the universe.

Trey's hands slid up her shoulders, drifted fingertip-light
across her throat, and gently cupped her face in his hands.
"Don't cry. I'll take care of you,'' he said softly, "and the
children. You're my life.'' His mouth brushed hers in a light
caress of self-control, for she was still frail with illness.
"Later,'' he said with teasing warmth as he straightened and
looked down at her, "when you're stronger, you can kiss me
back.''

"And I will,'' Empress replied, more happy than she
thought possible, "in our lifetime ahead.''

It gave him enormous pleasure to see her happy. "In that
lifetime now,'' he said with a resolute dispatch she'd never
heard before—the kind no doubt used at the legislature when
he saw to it that things were gone, "if you want to regain
Guy's title, we'll hire the best lawyers in France. Or if you
want to stay on Winter Mountain, we'll build a new home
and a better barn, plant orchards, bring up equipment to really
farm. Or if you choose,'' he went on, a faint smile lifting his
beautiful mouth, "to live under a palm tree in Tahiti, we'll do
it. Whatever you want,'' he said, quietly determined, "I'll
give you.''

Tears welled up in her eyes. To have Trey help with the
overwhelming responsibility of the children, to be able to lean
on him and rely on his strength, to have this beautiful man
she loved beyond anything in the world—hers. It was orchid
bowers and perpetual springtime. "You don't have to give

me things," she said, and her lush lower lip trembled with
the intensity of her feelings.

She was still so pale, Trey thought, her hair unkempt, faint
blue hollows under her eyes, and . . . so precious to him. She
carried delight in her body that completely disarmed him and
so much more, he'd realized, not only in the harrowing hours
of her illness but again this morning. He wanted to give her
everything; he wanted to dress her and feed her and brush her
hair in the mornings. He wanted to give her the world's
treasures and eternal happiness. He wanted to give her children. He was young and in love for the first time in his life,
and if he didn't have her beside him, he knew his life would
be unutterably empty.

With a light fingertip he brushed the tears from her lashes.

"I *want* to give you everything. I want you to know every
happiness. But most of all," he said, this vastly favored
young man, "I want you to be *mine.*"

"I am, I am, I am," Empress replied joyfully, the scent
and touch and feel of paradise enveloping her like a perfumed
dream. "But if I love you," she went on, her voice fragrant
with playfulness, "you must love me back as much."

He smiled, thinking how often and with what variety he'd
show her he loved her once she was well again. "I'm more
than willing," he replied, his smile lighting his eyes, "to
love you back until the seas run dry."

"Good," Empress declared, her answering smile winsomely
ingenuous with that paradoxical hint of seductive invitation
Trey always found so intriguing. "Because I'm not at all the
kind of woman you can take for granted."

His smile, she thought, could bathe the world in shimmering glory. "I would never be so foolish," Trey responded
softly. "In fact, after finding you for sale at Lily's and half
killing Rally and myself tracking you back to Winter Mountain, I'd be the last man in the world to take you for granted.
You're not exactly the stay-at-home type a man could get
complacent about." The teasing light in his eyes compared
favorably with radiant sunbeams.

"There are complacent women by the bushel," Empress
retorted with a tiny, denigrating sniff. Count Jordan's daughter had not been raised to defer; there were those back in
France who would have said deference had been bred out of
the Jordans long before the Crusades. The family motto was

"Stand aside," and their escutcheon motif, of sword and lightning, dramatized a tradition of aggressive impulses.

Trey groaned faintly, recalling all the pursuing women. "True," he replied with a rueful grin, "literally by the bushel."

"*I* shall never be complacent." Although the words were pointed, the opulent resonance of her voice, underscored by the piquant glance she cast him from beneath half-lowered lashes, intimated auxiliary meanings.

No, he thought, recalling the numerous occasions when she reminded him of living, breathing flames. "My good fortune, sweetheart," he murmured pleasantly.

"And one more thing," Empress declared, vivacious, her eyes brilliant with joy, "you must love me forever and ever and ever."

"Your servant, ma'am," Trey replied in a low, husky murmur and pulled Empress into his arms.

Into this elysium of bliss, a knock intruded.

Trey only tightened his embrace. "Go away," he shouted.

"Your father wishes to speak to you, sir." It was Timms. Trey's brows rose fractionally. Unusual. Why wasn't a footman sent up, Charlie or George . . . Timms didn't deliver messages.

"Must be a royal command," Trey murmured ironically, setting Empress back against the pillows. "I'll be back in a minute."

"Don't go . . . I want to tell you how much I love you," she teased, reaching out to run her finger lightly down his straight, perfect nose.

"And you shall for eternity, darling, as soon as I return," he replied smilingly. Leaning over, he brushed her mouth with a kiss. "Don't go away," he whispered.

When Trey opened the door, he saw Timms waiting at attention in the hallway. Blowing Empress a kiss, he pulled the door shut behind him and raised his eyebrows in inquiry. "Is this an execution, Timms?" he joked.

"Your father didn't take me into his confidence, sir." But Timms understood, too, that under normal circumstances an underservant would have been sent for by Hazard to deliver a message. And it was unmistakably clear that Mrs. Braddock-Black had been crying.

Fourteen

"IT'S OUT OF the question!" Trey exploded furiously. "*Absolutely* out of the question!"

Hazard looked across his desk at Trey, who'd come to his feet, infuriated, and was standing bristling with anger and affront, his veins pulsing noticeably on his neck.

"You tell that bitch she can find some other scapegoat!" Trey exclaimed resentfully. "Better yet, I'll tell her myself!"

"They're threatening Gray Eagle and Buffalo Hunter or any other two Absarokee. Duncan made it perfectly clear that they were unconcerned about whom they accused," Hazard quietly reminded Trey, his heart heavy with despair. For two days Hazard had been trying to determine some way out; he'd made an added offer to Duncan Stewart just the previous day, an outrageous offer, enough money to stagger an ordinary blackmailer. But apparently they were holding out for a much larger amount. As Trey's wife, Hazard reflected with foreboding, Valerie would share all his wealth.

"There must be something we can do about that. Good Lord, she's the one who seduced *them*."

"She's white."

Trey began pacing, as well aware as his father of the

ominous implications in those two words. "There wouldn't even be a trial, would there?"

"The Indians hung on the Musselshell didn't have one."[10]

"She won't take money?"

"I already tried."

"Damn cunt. That's someone else's child she's having. Not mine." Contempt lashed through his words.

"Are you sure?" The inquiry was tactful, and the answer mattered less than simply knowing it. Hazard would support his son regardless of the circumstances, but it never hurt to be fully cognizant of the facts.

Trey stopped pacing and, facing his father, grimaced ruefully. "Look, I know what the general consensus presumes about my relationships with women, but contrary to popular belief, I am not prodigally reckless and rash; my capacity for liquor is excellent, and the last time I noticed, making love does not impair the senses. So I'm very much aware of what I do and where I am and . . . I haven't been with Valerie for four months. And even *that* night I fell asleep—so it's longer than four months. Give her credit for nerve!"

"I think we *all* agree on that."

Trey dropped back into the chair opposite his father, slid into a dejected slump, and, lifting his gaze, said, "I asked Empress to marry me."

Hazard's breath lodged with a suffocating sensation halfway up his throat, and it took him a moment to reply. "I'll go to see Judge Henry and Pepperell tomorrow morning. Maybe they can be persuaded."

"They won't," Trey replied quietly, their relationship with the judges strained, since the railway right-of-way case had been reversed in their favor at the appeal level. Henry and Pepperell had vested interests in that right-of-way and had lost a great deal of money.

"I'll try, anyway," Hazard said, his voice firm.

"And when they say no? With great satisfaction, I might add."

"We up the offer to Duncan."

"And if he says no?"

Hazard looked at his son. "We'll try something else."

"Fucking bitch," Trey growled, knowing there were limits to the options, knowing Valerie and her father had been aware of those limits. If anyone knew the dirty underside of political chicanery and social malevolence better than the Stewarts, he hadn't met them.

Hazard pushed the George III inkwell off-center, then restlessly slid it back again, reluctant to ask Trey the next question. He sighed twice, picked up the obelisk that had served for the sand, and twisting it, distastefully asked, "Will you marry Valerie if need be?"

"You know the answer," said Trey evenly. "Of course." He'd grown up with Gray Eagle and Buffalo Hunter. As young boys they'd learned to ride and hunt together, they'd gone on their vision quests at the same time, fasted, walked on the mountain together, seen the legendary beings in the night sky. They held a bond of brotherhood in their hearts. His first allegiance was to his clan. There was no need to remind him where his loyalties lay. "How long do I have to stay married to her?" was his next coldly practical question.

"Until the child is born. No longer than that."

"And the child?"

"I imagine the Stewarts will bargain for its right to inherit."

"Do we agree?"

"Frankly I don't see a choice at that point. We pay now, which they won't accept, or we pay later. At least the clan is safe. She will *not* be allowed near the village in future. We'll hire white guards if necessary."

"There's a possibility Valerie won't accept a divorce."

"I can persuade a judge to grant a divorce with the proper inducement. The divorce laws are tractable. Not hanging an Indian who raped a white woman is another story. At the worst, we can get a divorce somewhere else."

"Nothing's very sure."

"Nothing except Gray Eagle and Buffalo Hunter are sure to hang if you don't marry her. But we'll try the judges and more money first."

"I'm going to talk to her."

"It's worth a try."

"Could Valerie and her father just disappear—I don't mean permanently, although the temptation is keen, but say, a trip to Europe for a decade?"

"It would have been possible when I was young," Hazard said softly. "Retaliation on one's enemies was accepted. Expected. But she's a woman. Then, as now, it alters the circumstances; one doesn't make war on women and children." Leaning back in his chair, he wearily closed his eyes.

"We'll try," he murmured, "to deal with these people in the white man's way." His head came up, his eyes opened, and his voice took on the trenchant resolution that many men had come to fear. "I promise you, the marriage will be brief."

"And if the divorce can't be arranged amicably?" Trey was still sprawled in his chair, his father's terse voice not meant for him, the acid of discontent enervating his body and mind.

"Like Jake Poltrain, the Stewarts will be dealt with by Absarokee means. You understand—" Hazard rubbed his hand across his eyes, and a rueful sigh broke the silence of the room—"the decision is yours to make . . . this sacrifice for your clan. But once your duty is fulfilled, I promise you, on my warrior's oath, if the yellow-eyes methods don't work, the Absarokee ways will be used to rid you of an unwanted wife."

Trey understood his father wasn't forcing him to marry Valerie. He also understood that honor demanded it. Gray Eagle and Buffalo Hunter's lives were at stake. "Before I say anything to Empress, I'd like to see Valerie myself. Tomorrow morning. Maybe she'll change her mind." It was a mechanical, instinctive compulsion, separate from any reasonable motive. And fueled by an unpleasant hate. "Maybe I can *convince* her," he added, nothing moving in his lounging form except a flash of menace in his silver eyes, "to change her mind."

"I hope so," Hazard said, his voice suddenly threadbare with tiredness.

Valerie's reception was gracious and friendly when Trey was shown into the parlor early the following morning, as if none of the blackmail threats had been made. "You're up very early," she said in her low, sultry voice. "Have you eaten? Would you like coffee?"

Trey stood with his back against the door he'd firmly closed behind him. "I'd like your head on a silver tray, Valerie," he said in a deep growl. "Care to accommodate me?"

"Really, sweetheart, you always did have a macabre sense of humor," she chided in that sweet Southern belle voice she affected on occasion. "Come, sit down and tell me how you've been. It's plain to see you've recuperated superbly from the—ah—contretemps at Lily's." Her blue eyes slowly raked Trey's tall form. He was dressed in black except for the bottle-green silk of his vest lapels and the glittering gold of his neck charm. His long raven hair was pulled back behind his ears, accenting his high cheekbones and the harsh beauty of his face. His silver eyes were cold.

She ignored the menace in his stance and expression, secure in her position. She held all the cards.

He had come to her.

"Come, sit," she repeated, and delicately patted the aqua damask of the sofa she was disposed on with a careful eye to display. Her peach wool gown was effective, she thought, against the sleek blue-green. She was right; it made her appear almost naked.

Unfortunately, in Trey's present mood, the imaginative spectacle was lost on him. It was necessary he'd come, and necessary he carry this charade through to the end, he thought distastefully, even though he wasn't optimistic about his chances after his father's last substantial offer had been refused. But the effort had to be made, so he pushed away from the door, walked to a chair opposite Valerie, and sat.

"Coffee?" she inquired again. "Tea? Or perhaps something stronger?" she added in her perfect hostess voice.

She was slender still, he noted, his glance quickly ranging over the pastel gown she wore, and it made him feel better. The last time he'd been with her was four months ago. "No thank you," he said, and leaned back in tentative ease.

"No coffee, tea, no spirits? If not social, to what, then," she purred dulcetly, "do I owe this extremely early-morning visit?"

"It's been a while, Valerie. I thought I'd drop by and see how you're"—he paused—"looking."

"It's not been all that long, Trey, darling," Valerie replied with equanimity, her poise intact. "Remember last November?"

"I remember," he drawled. "More importantly, I particularly recall that nothing happened."

"How would you know?" she retorted archly, her hands composedly clasped in her lap. "You passed out."

"I fell asleep. There's a difference. I remember what happened, or rather, what didn't happen. And I haven't seen you since then, Valerie. That was four months ago. You and I both know this child isn't mine."

Her faint smile was undiminished by his blunt declaration. "It's your word against mine, sweet, isn't it?" she replied conversationally. "And everyone knows your—" her brows rose slightly—"fascinating reputation. In contrast," she went on, smoothing her skirt with a delicate gesture, "I'm the innocent Miss Stewart. I teach Sunday School, Trey, honey." Her eyes came up from the brief adjustment to the drapery of her skirt and met his with a practiced winsomeness.

"And also sleep around," Trey said pointedly, immune to the drama of her expression, "in your spare time. Buffalo Hunter, Gray Eagle, what—a dozen more? Dark skin excites you, doesn't it? Maybe we could compile a list of sworn affidavits from your Indian lovers."

"No one would believe them," she replied calmly. "They're Indians. My Lord, they live in the village in lodges."

Trey's eyes were chill. "But they're good enough to fuck."

She smiled. "Not quite as good as you, darling. But you've heard that before, haven't you?"

Ignoring her compliment, he said very quietly, "Why me, Valerie?"

She didn't pretend not to know what he was asking. Her beautiful face bore an ingenuousness he'd seen called into play before. "I love you, and I want to marry you, Trey. It's as simple as that."

"You don't know what love is, Valerie. All you want is to be Mrs. Braddock-Black."

"Is there a difference?"

He fought down an overwhelming impulse to slap her smug face. "How much, Valerie?" he said very softly, controlling himself . . . hard, "to find another father or take an extended vacation. Name your price."

Her full lips he remembered very well, pursed into an affronted moue. "You're a barbarian at times, Trey. And boorish to talk like some merchant."

"But still civil enough not to call you the names I'd like to, Valerie. I don't want to marry you."

"But I want to marry *you.*"

"You can have the money without me."

"All of it?" she said sweetly.

"Bitch," he whispered, his jaw clenched tight in anger.

"One you didn't mind making love to many times if you recall."

He stared at her, his anger visible. "Had I known the price was marriage, there wouldn't have been a first time."

"Life's been too easy for you, Trey, darling. Always

everything you wanted. Every woman you've wanted. Unlimited wealth.'' She looked at him from under half-lowered lashes and smiled faintly. "I thought I'd like to experience those sensations of surfeit myself. As your wife."

"You're a bold piece," Trey said grimly. "I'll give you that. But I'll find a way out."

"Dream on, sweetheart. You don't seriously think this proposal being offered you was a spontaneous impulse, do you? I rather think you'll discover that the ways out are nonexistent."

"Whose child is it?" he asked abruptly.

"I wouldn't tell you if I knew. For the record, it's yours, of course, darling." Cleopatra disclosing Marc Antony's imminent fatherhood couldn't have been more complacent.

"This can't be happening," Trey growled, his eyes like chips of ice.

"You're the richest, handsomest bachelor in Montana," Valerie declared with a smug certainty. "I'm the most beautiful woman. It's really quite perfect."

He looked at her and saw the beauty but also a cold, ruthless woman, as predatory as a tigress. "No!" he snapped.

"I'd like the wedding at Our Lady of the Hill . . . say, in three weeks. That should be sufficient time to get the invitations out. I'll have the announcement put in the paper. The bishop has to be contacted. I'll take care of that. Now, as far as the reception, perhaps the hotel isn't large enough . . . it will mean reserving Claudio's ballroom. Yes, Claudio's will be perfect."

"Never," Trey said rudely, abruptly rising, not sure he could control his urge to strike her if he stayed. He'd always known Valerie was without scruples. He'd never realized the relentless enormity of her intent.

"With French champagne . . ." he heard her say as he opened the door. He was out of the house in a half dozen strides, more angry than he'd ever been in his life.

Hazard's day with the judges wasn't any better. Although they weren't personally sympathetic to Trey's problem after the disagreements over right-of-way, both would have been practical about accepting a "campaign contribution" on a case other than rape. In fact, both were overtly desolate at having to turn down Hazard's generous offer. But if Valerie actually did bring rape charges into the open, the public outcry would far outweigh any judge's decision on an indictment or trial. The Indians probably wouldn't live out the week, and neither judge would ever be reelected again if they supported the Indians. Personal greed aside, there was nothing they could do for Hazard.

Father and son met for lunch in a private dining room at the Montana Club and compared their lack of success.

"They were all long shots," Trey admitted wearily, and drained the whiskey in his glass.

"If it were anything but rape," Hazard said with a sigh.

"And we weren't Indian," Trey added, cynicism softly prominent in his tone.

"There's lots of ifs," Hazard agreed. "If you weren't wealthy . . ."

"And if Valerie weren't greedy," Trey muttered. "She's talking about a wedding at Our Lady of the Hill."

"Good God!"

"My sentiments exactly. In three weeks, by the way."

Hazard looked at his son gloomily. "What about Empress?"

"I'll have to try to explain."

"I'm sorry," his father said. "You mother expects me to take care of this, you know."

"She's realistic, though. She knows that Gray Eagle and Buffalo Hunter, or whomever they accuse, don't have a chance in hell if Valerie presses charges."

"We could," Hazard said on a pensive exhalation of breath, "kidnap both Duncan and Valerie and keep them up in the mountains. A great hue and cry might rise at their disappearance, though, if anyone else is party to this bloody blackmail. At best all we'd be doing would be buying some time in the hopes of their reconsidering. A negligent hope, I think, considering their greed. Duncan's been cheating the government for years with his army contracts. He's not the kind of man to be reasonable."

"Valerie doesn't know what the word means. Look, the marriage would be at most six months, maybe less." Trey shrugged. "It's not as though we have a choice. Now, all I have to do is somehow explain this all to Empress." Trey slumped lower in his chair. "I need a drink."

His father reached across the table and refilled his son's glass. "In six months," he said, "I'll buy you a drink to celebrate your divorce."

Lifting his glass, Trey smiled grimly. "Providing I don't

strangle her before the six months are up. Now, then, let's go over all this one more time. Maybe we're forgetting something. Could the entire clan move out of Montana temporarily?'' Trey facetiously inquired, distaste laced through the words.

"I'm sure a migration of Indians and horse herds would be welcome anywhere in America,'' Hazard replied sarcastically. "The government particularly recommends farming in the desert areas.''

"What if we killed them?'' Trey said it for the first time in earnest.

"Duncan specifically warned against that suggestion,'' his father replied. "Keep in mind that survival has been a primary concern of Duncan for years now with all the reservation Indians he's starved. Later,'' Hazard promised quietly, "in extremity.''

"Can we rely on their word at all?'' Trey asked next, refilling his glass. "I mean, not having this threat repeated?''

"That insurance we have signed in triplicate,'' Hazard said with a great sigh of relief. "The document would stand up before the goddamn Supreme Court.''

Trey looked at his father over the rim of his glass. "There must be a but.''

"It's post-dated.''

"When?'' A brusque, curt inquiry into the length of his durance vile.

"Eight months from now, and even that required heated hours of negotiation,'' Hazard replied tersely. "They started with five years.''

"Congratulations,'' Trey said laconically, and emptied his glass.

"I reached for my Colts twice,'' his father explained with a wry smile, "and it seemed to help.''

"Duncan has never been known for the firmness of his spine, although his bitch of a daughter more than makes up for his lack.''

"She does have an unabashed brazenness,'' Hazard declared dryly. "When her father stepped out of the room briefly, she propositioned me.''

"I wouldn't,'' Trey replied sardonically, "linger in a room alone with her.''

"She seemed to take offense when I told her she was too old for my taste.''

Trey laughed. "That ingratitude probably cost you another million."

"There was a certain aggrievedness to her expression," Hazard said with a grin, "for the remainder of the negotiations."

"So, then," Trey drawled, "we can't lose them, kill them, or repudiate them. And while all men are created equal, some, in this year 1889," Trey went on cynically, "are more equal than others." Leaning back in his chair, he automatically reached for the brandy bottle and said, "I'm sold away for eight months tops." He carefully filled his glass brimhigh and lifted it to his father in salute. "Look at it this way . . . things could be worse. She could be the mother of my child."

"You're sure now she's not?" Hazard declared gently.

"It is the only certainty in this entire Machiavellian deceit," Trey said with a heartfelt sigh, "and all that saves my sanity."

Fifteen

———————————————

THE CHILDREN WERE all in Empress's room when Trey walked in, so he spent a torturous hour making polite conversation, listening to everyone's account of their activities that day, as well as listening to their myriad plans for their new future together, since Empress had ecstatically told them of their marriage plans. It was the very worst hour he'd ever experienced.

Recognizing his tenseness when the children's clamoring quieted, Empress thoughtfully sent them out of the room to ready themselves for supper.

Trey immediately stood and restlessly strode to the window and back.

"Your trip into Helena was unproductive?"

"You might say so," he murmured, lifting, then replacing, the hairbrush on the bureau top.

"Anything you care to talk about?"

"I'd rather not talk of it at all."

"I'm sorry," Empress apologized, Trey's brevity and agitation unusual. "I didn't mean to pry." Just when she thought she understood him, his mood would alter and he wasn't the Trey she knew.

Trey looked at the woman he'd only just realized he loved.

The only woman he'd *ever* acknowledged loving. She was rosy-cheeked today, her paleness gone for the first time since her illness. She looked fresh and wholesome, her tawny hair tumbled riotously on her shoulders, the crocheted lace on her nightgown and the ribbon-trimmed bodice making her appear very young. Her eyes were the vivid, clear green of a rain-washed meadow. And trusting.

The contrast with Valerie was sharp and abrasive.

"What I have to say . . ." Trey began in a deeply pained voice. He sighed and softly went on, ". . . has to be said."

Empress's stomach turned over with a lurch, and her fingers crushed the linen sheet. "I knew something was wrong."

"It has to do with us," Trey said, dropping into a chair near the bed. "Nothing that's your fault," he added quickly, seeing the dismay on her face. "It's partly my fault," he went on, sliding down in the chair and stretching his legs out in front of him. "And very much Valerie Stewart's fault. You don't know her"—he sighed again—"but I, unfortunately, *have* known her."

"Tell me," Empress said quietly, wanting to know where this was leading, although a crushing sense of doom engulfed her. Trey's dark handsomeness was marred with a harsh grimness, his mouth a thin, taut line.

"What would you say to a six-month delay in our marriage plans?" Trey asked, his tone expressionless.

"Is that all?" Empress replied with joyful relief. It wasn't so bad. It wasn't disastrous. Her desperate fear receded. "I don't mind. Summer's a wonderful time for a wedding." She smiled at Trey. "Don't be so gloomy. Our plans can be rearranged. I love you; whether we marry this week or in six months is hardly earth-shattering."

Trey wasn't smiling, and Empress realized there was more.

"I haven't told you the worst part," he said softly.

Her joyful reprieve had been grasping at straws, and one look at Trey's face told her to expect disaster.

"I have to marry Valerie Stewart."

It was a thousand times worse than she'd imagined. Annihilation of her dream, a blotting-out destruction of a happiness she'd only warily begun to accept. Several moments passed before Empress could find the breath to ask, "Why?"

"To save two of my cousins from hanging." And Empress listened, horrified and appalled, as the story unfolded, as her future with Trey fell into ruin. He was melancholy but ultimately more optimistic than she. Empress had a feeling women like Valerie Stewart wouldn't so easily be disposed of in six months' time. Anyone shrewd enough to hold the Braddock-Blacks hostage wouldn't be naïve about relinquishing that hold. Trey hadn't mentioned the Absarokee alternatives to be used in extremity, so Empress's reflections failed to take those into account. Disaster loomed.

"I don't know what to do . . . what more to say," Trey finished unhappily, feeling ill-fated, ill-starred, abandoned by his spirits of good fortune.

"You don't have a choice. Marry her. The children and I will go back to Winter Mountain, and you can come for us in the summer." Empress forced her voice to remain calm when she wanted to scream with pain. "I'll tell the children—" Her voice broke, she swallowed, then went on resolutely, her eyes filled with tears. "I don't know what to tell them." A crushing agony was swelling in her chest. "I think they love you more than I do."

Trey was on his feet the moment he saw the tears welling in her eyes. Lifting her in his arms, he carried her to the leather couch near the fire and, sitting down, held her in his lap, tucking the long flannel skirt of her nightgown around her bare feet. "It won't be forever," Trey whispered, despair shading his silvery eyes. His embrace tightened, the feel of her warm body solace to his troubled mind.

"Summer will be here before we know it," Empress replied softly, and although her words were sensible, tears were streaming down her face.

"Don't cry . . . don't cry," Trey pleaded, brushing away the tears with his fingers. "Oh, God," he whispered, wanting to offer her comfort, wishing there were some to confer, some magic deliverance from this hell. "And you mustn't go," he murmured tenderly, kissing her hair, her cheeks, the streaks of salty tears. "There's no reason for you to go back." The thought of losing her even for six months was unbearable.

"Don't ask me to stay. I can't," Empress replied, abject misery overwhelming her. "Not when you're married to someone else."

"It's just a wedding. It's not a marriage," Trey said quickly, harshly. "I'm not going to live with her."

"I still can't stay," Empress whispered in a small, sad voice. She couldn't explain that the thought of another woman married to the man she loved was not some casual arrangement to her. Somehow there was terrifying possession in the act, and a very firm commitment in a legal sense, however cavalierly Trey treated the matter. Valerie Stewart didn't sound like the kind of woman, either, who would placidly allow her husband to live with another woman. But say Trey was right and Valerie would agree to a divorce, there would be an end to his detention. If Empress could count the days until the six months were over, there was a possibility that she could contend with this devastating blow. But not here, not seeing Trey every day, not close enough to meet the Valerie who would be Mrs. Braddock-Black in her place. She wasn't that strong. "We'll go back home as soon as I can walk that last stretch on snowshoes."

"Very well," Trey agreed, because he wasn't going to argue with her now. But he wasn't going to let her go. One way or another he'd make her stay.

Circumstances came to Trey's rescue, and he didn't have to marshal any convincing arguments to make her stay. As it turned out, the children were all struck with the fever that had threatened Empress. Just as she was beginning to feel stronger, Genevieve complained of a sore throat. Five days later Guy was stricken, and so it went, until the house was like a small hospital ward. It was three weeks of mixing poultices and medicines, of soothing fretful children and walking Eduard when he screamed with the ear infection that had developed along with his fever. Trey did most of the walking, for Eduard slept best when Trey held him. But the long hours took their toll on everyone. In some ways it was a blessing, for the days prior to Trey's wedding passed, detached somehow from Empress's own small world of feverish children and sleepless nights, fighting death with every medicine at her disposal, with prayers and whispered assurances and love.

They all survived, and for that she gave thanks. Empress hardly noticed the day Trey left for his wedding. She had fallen into an exhausted sleep at dawn that morning, and Trey had quietly slipped away without waking her. It wasn't till late afternoon when she woke, the nurses having strict orders to let her sleep, that the unusual silence struck her. And she realized the reason for the quiet house.

Empress cried that evening despite a resolute attempt to stay her tears, and when Genevieve asked her what was wrong, she only said, "I'm tired and I want to go home."

There had been no simple way to explain the complicated
villainy of Valerie and her father, so Empress had simply told
the children they were going home as soon as everyone was
well, and Trey would follow in the summer when they would
marry. No mention was made of Trey's marriage to Valerie.
Trey hadn't openly disagreed with Empress when she spoke
to the children about the change in plans, but in his own way
he intended to persuade her to stay.

The church was filled to capacity, although the Braddock-
Black family was not out in force; in fact, most of the
relatives were conspicuous by their absence. But Valerie had
sent out invitations to half the town, and no one stayed away,
titillated with the spectacle of a speedy wedding between two
people who had not been in company together for quite some
time. Bets were taken on the reason Trey had finally succumbed or Valerie had finally accomplished the unaccomplish-
able, even while all those hazarding realized that the real
reason might never be known.

Two carloads of white roses had been brought in from
California, and the church resembled, above all, a heavenly
scented cloud, so bouffantly massed were the thousands of
blooms. Or a funeral parlor, the groom thought, depending on
your point of view. Valerie's eight bridesmaids, all in pink
organza, were fluffy counterpoint to the fragrant roses, while
the bride was magnificent—there was no other word for
it—in seeded pearl Venetian point lace with a twenty-foot
train. Trey felt a prisoner, and it showed.

The wedding dinner was singular for its luxury, with ten
French chefs responsible for its execution. French champagne
had been brought in, in quantity, and all the guests noted that
the groom was drinking his share. Immediately after dinner
the orchestra began playing, but the groom broke precedence
by declining to dance the first dance with his bride. He
preferred, he said, drinking to dancing.

The parents of the groom stayed only long enough at the
dinner to salve appearances. Hazard, rumor had it, was not
pleased with the match. Gossip suggested the bride was enceinte, and there was talk that the boy had been forced to
marry, but it was assumed that would eventually be the way
of it in Trey's case. With his record in the bedroom, it was
just a matter of time and pressure from the right family.

Would marriage settle the ladies' man in Trey? everyone

wondered with more curiosity than conviction. Any number of women who propositioned him at his wedding dance thought not. And then, of course, there was his newest purchase, ensconced at the ranch in the bosom of his family. He was a spoiled boy.

By the time the happy bride and difficult groom changed to their traveling clothes and left for their honeymoon, there was a distinct hint of menace in Trey's expression. One guest was heard to remark that Trey didn't look prepared for a life of domesticity. To which his companion replied, "Trey's never been adverse to domesticity but in small doses and with a variety of women. Valerie has her work cut out for her."

"That pretty thing he bought at Lily's," whispers passed from person to person, "is waiting at the ranch." Malicious eyes gleamed. Maybe he misses her.

Moodily Trey accompanied Valerie to the house she'd purchased with *his* money and stood silently just inside the drawing-room door while she gave up her velvet wrap to a maid and issued orders to the butler for a late supper. He was tired, and the champagne had given him a headache. Or maybe it was keeping the fury under control in front of all the guests that had given him the headache. Valerie's smug exuberance had done its share, too, toward the throbbing in his temples. Hypocritical bitch! She'd played the part of the glowing bride to the hilt.

After dismissing the servants, Valerie turned in a sweep of claret faille and airily gestured to Trey. "Darling, take off your coat and make yourself comfortable."

Although he'd married her, beyond that there were well-defined limits of what he would do for her. "I'm not staying," he said. He had no intention of touching her and taking the chance of being shackled to her in reality. This child wasn't his, but with different timing, it could have been. He meant to see that that would never happen.

Valerie was nonplussed for a moment. His refusal to stay was one contingency she hadn't considered. Having accomplished the marriage, she felt secure. "Of course you're staying," she said in aggrieved tones. "We're married. This is our home."

"This is your home," Trey rejoined, politely savage, "not mine. Let me know when the baby's born." And he turned to go.

She stared at him. At the tall, handsome man she'd schemed so to have. For one flashing moment she almost lost control and screamed and swore at him, but she hadn't gotten as far as she had by lapses in control. "What will I tell people?" she inquired calmly.

"I'm sure you'll think of something," Trey said from the open doorway. "Good night."

Empress heard the flurry of activity when Hazard and Blaze arrived home, but she stayed in her room and hoped neither would come in to visit. She wasn't sure she'd be able to carry on a conversation without breaking into sobs. The last hours had been painful; it was too quiet with the children in bed and nothing but her own company for diversion. Although she understood the necessity for Trey's wedding, a fearful sense of loss inundated all rational thought. What was he doing now? she reflected tearfully. Was he smiling at his new bride; was she smiling back at him? Did he hold her close when they danced? Did the guests favor the match; did Valerie look beautiful as a radiant bride? Why, Empress deliberated with gloomy despair, had her life been plagued with one disaster after another over the last five years? Was she being punished somehow for unknown infractions? How much more could she take; how many more burdens could her emotions bear before her spirit was broken?

She cried, then, alone and unhappy, and fell asleep with dreadful, crushing images of Trey and his bride on their honeymoon night.

Trey came back to the ranch late that night, brooding and moody and walking into his darkened bedroom; the man who had been coolly composed throughout the trying day slumped into a chair near the bed and shivered. Slowly his eyes grew accustomed to the dim light, and he silently watched Empress in her sleep. His duty had been done. Bitter at the prospect of the ensuing months, he dejectedly found comfort in simply looking at the woman he loved.

She was curled in a nest of quilts and pillows, diminutive in the expanse of the enormous bed, one hand thrown above her head like a young child, her pale hair gleaming like rivers of moonlight in the half-dark. Trey experienced a sudden, griping fear in this, the nadir hour of his unhappy wedding day, that Valerie and Duncan could somehow keep him from

having Empress. He shook off the grotesque demon of alarm
forcibly, telling himself it was the late hour, his dour mood,
the fatigue of banal pleasantries to a thousand guests. He
hadn't realized he'd sighed until Empress stirred. He watched
her eyes open slowly, then quickly when she saw his dark
form. She sat up immediately, the silk quilts falling away like
rippling water.

"Trey," she cried, a warm happiness in her voice, and
instinctively she leaned toward him until she remembered
what had happened that day. She held herself in check then,
wondering what he was doing here. And whether she could
live another moment without touching him. He was still
dressed in his outer clothes, his topcoat only unbuttoned, not
taken off, as if he'd been cold, his silk scarf still loosely
knotted under his chin.

"It's my wedding night," he said, feeling cold and empty,
desolation vivid in his deep, quiet voice.

A tear slid down Empress's cheek, followed quickly by
another. Are you more of a harlot when you love a married
man? Are you a harlot at all? She didn't know and in the next
moment did not care. She opened her arms.

"Thank you," Trey said softly, and went to her.

Wordlessly he held her, letting her small, warm body ease
the rancor and melt the icy fear, gently stroking her hair like
one might comfort a child. Her cheek lay against the velvet of
his lapel, her hands laced around his scarfed neck, and
neither spoke. It was enough that he had come and she had
welcomed him. Beyond that lay the terrifying future, and if
they walked too close to the edge, they might fall into the
abyss. So a very large, powerful man who had always faced
the world with a fearless intrepidness sat on an immense,
rumpled bed, silently, and tightly held a small golden-
haired women to keep the world from crashing down around
them. Dressed as he was in deepest charcoal, topcoat, suit,
the sleek sheen of his scarf, the woman looked as fragile as a
flower against a brooding storm cloud. But it was her slender
warmth, acutely felt beneath his large, strong hands, that
pervaded his soul and dissolved the bottomless chill.

The next morning, insinuating rumor floated delicately over
breakfast coffee, more robustly across clubrooms, wickedly at
Lily's, or in barrooms as the day progressed. The recalcitrant
groom had balked at his wedding night. And gone home to

the ranch. It just went to show you, one could depend on Lily's for prime merchandise.

Valerie's butler had had one ear to the door—the personnel on the Braddock-Black private train numbered ten—the only servant up when Trey had unexpectedly arrived home had wakened her cousin in town at six in the morning. News travels fast below stairs.

The malicious gossip reached Valerie before her luncheon was brought up. A phone call from an insincere friend who thought she'd like to know, "for her own good." Having had an entire night to fabricate a plausible explanation, Valerie prevaricated with ease. There had been an emergency at the ranch, she said, requiring Trey's attention. No, she didn't know exactly when he'd be back. It depended on the extent of the crisis. The type of crisis? Really, she hadn't paid much notice once Trey began talking about watts of energy and power plants. "Well, yes," she supposed, "he isn't the *only* one capable of handling the situation, but you know how responsible he is when it comes to family business. And, of course, I'm happy, Eunice. Wouldn't you be if you were married to Trey?"

It took only a few hours for Valerie to systematically analyze her rival's position, and another half day to develop a plan of action to counteract said rival. She had no intention of working this hard to land the biggest catch west of the Mississippi, only to find him a phantom husband. Granted, she had his money, her position as Mrs. Braddock-Black, but she wanted a husband too. And it wasn't for his wealth alone or to allay stupid gossip. Trey was, as she knew from considerable experience, the very best in bed, and it rankled her to think of him preferring some little slut to her.

Valerie considered herself an intelligent woman. And more importantly, a beautiful woman. With her beauty prominently displayed and her intelligence carefully concealed, she'd routinely achieved all her selfish whims. Even Trey, more difficult than most men to entice, had finally risen to the lure. That he hadn't stayed long within her sultry domain perhaps had been expected. He was not like other men. And she was smart enough to know it. She hadn't mentioned to her father that she'd planned all along to take Trey as her husband. (Her father was a ruthless man but not overly bright. She never confided in him.) And now that she had Trey for a husband, it was infuriating to see him slip away. Was it because of the woman? Or only his dislike of the marriage trap? She'd start with the woman.

It was interminable waiting another week before confronting this purchase of her husband's up at the ranch, but it was necessary. Valerie hired two men her father trusted to watch Trey's movements for a week, and four more to monitor those of his family. Her timing must be precise. She wanted to confront Trey's lover alone, with none of the Braddock-Blacks in attendance. Since the woman apparently never left the ranch, Valerie would have to go to her. It was a matter of selecting a time when Trey and his parents were in town for the legislative session.

Trey had almost convinced Empress during the past week that it was unnecessary for her and the children to return to Winter Mountain. His marriage was no more than the ceremony, and it wouldn't interfere with his life in any way. A business arrangement—no more. Besides, it was dangerous to think of returning to the snowed-in valley. Even if the trip back was uneventful, the possibility of further storms could put the family in jeopardy again. He didn't want to think of her alone, having to cope with some emergency. "Please," he had begged, this man who had never had to ask for anything, "stay."

Hesitant, emotionally dependent, torn with doubts, she had stayed. The children perhaps the deciding factor. "We love it here," they had cried. "Go back? All that way? In this cold?" Trey was standing aside from the family group, attempting an expression of pleasant, rather than tremulous, interest. "Leave Papa *Trey*?" Eduard squealed and ran to Trey's side, lifting his chubby arms to be held. Trey's smile was charmingly bland, only with effort. With Eduard's dark, ruffled head tucked into his shoulder, his own heart tripping with delight, Trey inquired tranquilly, "Is it settled, then?"

Their evenings that week, when Trey returned from town each night, were blissfully happy. And when the children went to bed, their hours alone were sheer heaven.

Sixteen

———————◆◆◆———————

ON MONDAY MORNING, after a weekend when Hazard and Blaze had entertained the children with a skating party and Trey had said once more, "See how happy the children are?" Empress gazed out the window at the bright winter day, contentment filling her heart.

Trey had left very early with his parents. A crucial vote was on the agenda for that afternoon, and wavering legislators required additional inspiration or exhortation, depending on the state of their consciences.

Empress and the children were still in the breakfast room when a thoroughly embarrassed Timms announced Mrs. Braddock-Black. Although the ranch was fully staffed, it was a casually run household, and Empress and her family had endeared themselves to the servants. Timms, the butler, was especially fond of Empress for her kindness to his wife, who was suffering from arthritis, and he'd attempted to halt Valerie at the main entrance. Without success.

She was hard on his heels and out to do damage. Valerie had had a seething, angry week, a week in which curious visitors had to be dealt with, each consumed with avid interest, all inquiring about her husband's whereabouts. It had been galling, a terrible week of sparring, rude inquiries, of

shrugging off impudent remarks. A horrid nightmare she had
never planned for but one she intended to remedy. She was
determined to see her husband under her roof one way or
another, and this interview with his paramour was only the
beginning.

Timms had barely finished pronouncing her name when
Valerie brushed past him, swept grandly into the cheery sunlit
room, her sable cape gliding majestically behind her and, her
steady blue eyes resting on Guy, said, "He can't be one of
Trey's. He's too old, although"—she purred sweetly—"the
coloring holds true." Her kohled eyes narrowed as her gaze
settled on Eduard. "Ah, the little one—he must be Trey's."
She turned so she and Empress were facing each other. "And
yours?" So that was it, Valerie thought with glee. An answer
to the inexplicable attraction. Trey had a child by this woman.
Apparently he had bought her that night in Lily's, not for the
novelty of the woman but as an act of possession. She had
never realized he was so fastidious about sharing, and if a
child made that much difference, a child by Trey would
certainly be indispensable to her marriage.

Empress had visibly stiffened at Valerie's rudeness, and
looking quickly to Timms, who was arrested in the doorway
in dismay, covering her own shock with a determination that
called on her full ten generations of nobility, she instructed,
"Please see the children out, Timms."

And the imperative tone, the air of command, altered
Valerie's preconceived notion of her husband's whore. This
pale-haired woman, much smaller than she expected, was not
the usual fare found at Lily's, although Lily prided herself on
quality. This woman everyone had talked about, not only
because she'd sold herself but also because she was dressed
like a cowboy, looked neither the whore nor the lowly hired
hand. And the trace of an accent that set her apart from the
ordinary also placed her at some elusively haughty level. Her
uncowed eyes enhanced that image.

With an internal shrug Valerie dismissed Empress's unusual attributes. The woman could look like some grand
queen for all she cared. She was a little farmgirl or ranch
hand who had sold herself at a brothel for all her fine airs.
Hardly the type of woman Valerie viewed as a threat. Valerie
was a product of her class, which acknowledged the inherent
superiority of the wealthy. Her uncharitable and selfish dispo-
sition reinforced society's assessment of her worth, and in her

eyes Empress was so beneath her station that she could be dismissed as a serious threat on principle. Since, however, Valerie disliked loose ends and further disliked gossip suggesting Trey was enamored of this lower-class female, a brief confrontation should send this woman on her way.

Empress stood as soon as the children left the room, placing her hands on the table to keep them from trembling. Her worst nightmare had come true; she was face-to-face with Trey's *wife*. "What," she said, nervously brusque, "do you want?"

Valerie discourteously stared at Empress. "I simply wanted to meet you, my dear. You needn't bristle so, it's not unusual for Trey's lovers to overlap." She shrugged, and the sable glistened with the movement. "He's always been much in demand; ask him to tell you the stories of the comings and goings at his apartment in town." Her smile was sweetly malevolent. "They're cozy little stories." She looks like a child, Valerie thought, in her pink wool dress, her hair tied back with a ribbon. A prick of irritation pierced her complacency at the ingenuous, nubile innocence of the woman, an unattainable posture for her own style of beauty, and when she spoke, pique colored the honeyed mendacity of her words. "We can all be friends," she said in dulcet tones, like a cat making the first teasing swat at an injured bird.

"I'm not interested in being friends, nor am I concerned with Trey's past. You're not welcome here," Empress said emphatically. "Please leave." She tried to keep her voice steady against the calm certainty in Valerie's tone, and her cool poise when speaking of Trey's attraction to women. She didn't need to be reminded of his reputation, not by this glamorous woman who had known him years longer than she.

"I'm not welcome in my husband's home?" Valerie retorted idly, although her rudeness was shiny bright. "You presume too much; I'm his wife." Her eyes held Empress's and she added softly, "I carry his child."

"I don't care to argue with you," Empress replied, the assurance in Valerie's voice disastrous to her peace of mind, "and Trey won't be back until dinner. If you'll excuse me . . ." She began to move around the table, intending to leave the room, her heart hammering in her chest, Valerie's smooth, confident words unnerving. Even if she told herself Trey loved *her*, even though she reminded herself of all he'd said about Valerie's mendacity and coercion, the terrible words

—"I'm carrying his child"—were startling in their simplicity. And the illusion to his amorous escapades in town and the casualness with which Valerie eluded to them caused another twinge of anxiety. Could Trey really give up his previous life-style? If she only knew him better . . . not better, simply longer.

"I don't think Trey will be back tonight," Valerie said as though she were delivering an incidental message. "He told *me* to expect him for dinner at eight." Her bold-faced bluff was designed to stop Empress from walking away.

It was effective.

"You're wrong," Empress replied sharply. "He won't see you." But the blow was devastating, and though she tried to conceal it, the spasm of pain showed. He couldn't be seeing her for dinner; why was she saying it? How could she lie, come all the way out here to lie?

"Really, dear, how naïve you are," Valerie purred, her smile wicked. "Does he tell you that?"

"It's the truth." But even as she was uttering the words, a creeping doubt overcame her, and her words were far from firm. Trey was so consummately smooth and practiced in amorous intrigue. Had he simply reverted to form, had all the endearing love words been only . . . words? Would this woman have such gall and poise otherwise?

Valerie's glance drifted out the window. "Out here in the country, I can see how easy it would be to deceive you." Her gleaming eyes swung back, and her expression was mocking. "Trey is a spoiled darling, you must know that; he wants us both, you see."

Fighting down her jealous qualms, forcing her voice to calmness, she said, "He hasn't seen you since the wedding." *These are all lies, you're a liar, he hasn't seen you,* she silently cried, but the skepticism and uncertainty grew under the relentless assurance in Valerie's pronouncements.

"Oh, dear, what a pity, child, that just isn't so." And she shook her head slowly in feigned commiseration. "He sees me every day." At the small gasp from Empress, Valerie went on to twist the knife. "It was really out of curiosity more than anything else that I decided to come and see you this morning." How easy it is, she thought, with a little farmgirl like this. No doubt she believes in God and eternal love and all the other beatific platitudes. "You know, of course," she went on in her carefully modulated voice, intent on edifying this incredibly naïve girl, "Trey's love life has always been scandalously full. Having known him for years, I understood this—ah—realistically, before we married. Men will be men, after all." She smiled, and the wickedness showed in her eyes for a flashing moment. "I'd suggest you see that he provides for your future now, when his passions are high, my dear. None of Trey's pets last very long, so you should be scrupulously practical. Although from the age of that young boy of yours, perhaps you know that better than I. I congratulate you on your longevity—a record, I'm sure, with Trey."

Stop it, Empress wanted to scream, It isn't true! None of the mocking words from the mocking woman were true. "Trey can't possibly be seeing you," Empress disputed, her heart in her eyes. "He's at the legislature with his parents during the day, and he's home every night."

Valerie delivered a pleasant, lilting laugh of disclaimer. "Really, dear, Trey's parents dote on him, everyone knows that. If he says he's with his parents, they'll agree. But instead of working at the legislature, he spends his days with me," she declared calmly, "and extremely enjoyably, I might add."

"You're lying!" Heart-sore and distraught, Empress threw the words at the beautiful, richly dressed woman.

It was gratifying to see the passionate outburst. Putting a studied finger to her chin, Valerie said, "Let's see, Trey was wearing his blue suit Friday with a gray striped shirt; on Thursday he had on range clothes, and he took a few hours for lunch with Judd Parker." The enumeration was softly triumphant.

Empress's heart plummeted. Trey had laughed about his lunch with Judd Parker and their discussion of Judd's unfortunate predisposition for poker—losing poker. Trey had told Empress with a teasing light in his eyes that he'd offered Judd some tutoring in the finer points of the game. Women weren't allowed in the Montana Club, so it couldn't have been accidental happenstance, her seeing him there.

"Would you like to hear more?" Valerie purred, sensing victory, her words spilling out now in exultant sweetness, the poor girl's face nearly drained of color. "Some soup stained his shirt Tuesday, or was it Wednesday? I forget," she went on with dramatic emphasis, the surge of power she always experienced when she dissembled particularly well, her tonalities colored with rich orchestration. "But the maid was properly scolded, you can be sure, for ruining his shirt when she blundered. It's quite impossible to get decent help anymore,'' she added with a mocking frown.

What more, Empress thought, the taste of bitterness in her mouth, can this confident woman disclose . . . the length of time they make love? She had teased Trey about the stain on his shirt, and he'd negligently dismissed it, like he'd no doubt dismiss whatever she accused him of. Was it possible, a tiny hopeful voice inquired past Valerie's smooth assurance, was it possible she was lying? In all the awful past moments, nothing was true. Confused and bewildered, Empress was forced to recognize that Trey had always lived an unrestrained, self-indulgent existence with women always about, besieging him, anxious to please him. Was she simply the latest, to be discarded eventually like all the others? Or was he sincere, and Valerie a terrible nightmare that would soon dissolve like a dream?

"If you don't believe me," Valerie said, her blue eyes shining, her voice flippant, tearing through the fiction of Empress's wanting this all to be a dream, "ask Trey, although he won't be back to the ranch for dinner, since he's dining with me." Valerie understood from her father that an addendum to the grazing-rights bill was to be introduced shortly before recess as a political maneuver, and there was a good possibility Trey would be forced to stay late if that occurred. Her ruse was a calculated risk, but she was more certain than not; Valerie prided herself on preparation . . . she had never been a risk-taker. "Oh, by the way, Trey forgot these," she added with rehearsed negligence, and slipped a pair of leather gloves from an inside pocket of her cape. With a delicate twist of her wrist she dropped them on the polished mahogany table, and the beaded black-cougar design embroidered on the fine leather caught the light like a flash of deceit.

If there was some possibility of explanation for all the rest, his gloves resisted efforts to ignore. Trey had worn them to town the day he was dressed in range clothes. Empress stared distraitly at the pale leather gloves, and then up at the exquisitely dressed woman who was calmly shattering her life to fragments. Trey's wife was more beautiful than she'd imagined, the contrast of her pure white skin and black hair striking, her full-bodied height stunning, her garnet gown and sable cape Paris couturier, the pearls at her neck flawless.

Trey's bounty, no doubt. He'd always casually dismissed Valerie as unimportant, but she wasn't the style of woman a man would overlook. And he hadn't, had he? she thought with disquietude. He'd admitted they'd been lovers, and with this dazzling woman standing before her she could see why. According to Valerie, they still were.

She was a liar, he'd said, spoiled and willful and out for his money, and Empress wanted to believe Trey. But powerful credence had to be given to *his wife* (excruciating words) and her intimate knowledge of Trey and his activities the previous week . . . damning knowledge. If she wanted to ignore all Valerie had said, call it all lies, believe Trey, even her aching heart couldn't overlook the gloves. They lay on the table like a tossed gauntlet, beautiful Indian gloves still shaped slightly in the fingers where his hands had been. Trey had forgotten them, Valerie said, like you might say, "Would you prefer to hang or be shot?"—with an insufferable self-assertion, and if it would do any good, if it would make Trey irrevocably and absolutely hers, she'd tear Valerie apart limb from limb. But it wouldn't make him love her or make him faithful, she thought numbly. It wouldn't help at all.

The frontier west was a world of expediency, blatantly acknowledged here on the raw fringes of civilization, and both Trey and Valerie apparently subscribed to a loose interpretation of ethics. A very thin line existed between a bad man and a good man, between right and wrong in a young country like this, and Valerie, with wifely pragmatism, agreed that "Men will be men." Trey, obviously, had always lived his life by that laissez-faire dictum.

Stricken and bewildered, Empress thought, *He asked me to marry him.* Could all those charming, endearing words be lies as well?

"I hope you don't think he was going to marry you," Valerie said carelessly, as though she could see behind the blank dumbness and read Empress's mind. She smiled benignly, like one would to a blundering, artless child. "Really, my dear, Trey is familiar with torrid devotion and adept at the play-love words, the seductive words. You mustn't think you're the first . . . and he's a heady experience, I won't deny. But he never would have married you."

Play-love words, Valerie called them. How appropriate for a man so practiced in playing at love. So he spent his days entertaining himself with his wife and his evenings with the gullible woman he'd bought at Lily's. She had been naïve, expecting him to perceive of her differently, and he was simply enjoying her in his own fashion, with a smooth charm that showed kindness to the children, casually extended the benefits of his unlimited wealth, soothed her with play-love words when her "torrid devotion" required mollification.

Dizzy with the lunacy of Valerie's arch, malicious words, Empress's first inherent impulse resisted the accounting, repudiated the innuendo and stark facts, wanted to believe Trey so her world wouldn't come tumbling down. But the gloves, pale and embellished against the dark wood of the table, kept drawing her eyes like a magnet. He was unfaithful. And then she silently marveled at her singular delusion . . . unfaithful to whom, or just unfaithful as always? Shame and wounded anger tingled across her skin at her misguided simplicity, her foolish naïveté. Experienced men like Trey frankly and naturally accepted the pleasure of women, simultaneously without scruple or permanence; even Valerie, Empress thought with satisfaction, might find her smugness altered eventually, for while Trey may enjoy her amorous company, he detested his matrimonial status. Or did he? Light-headed with the tangle of lies, she no longer knew whom or what to believe. *What a fool, what an infatuated fool,* echoed dizzily through her mind, and when she looked up, all she saw was Valerie's crimson mouth smiling at her simple-minded naïveté. Suddenly she felt like vomiting, and before she humiliated herself completely before this cool, decorative woman, Empress brushed by the smiling mouth and sable cape and fled the room.

Gazing after the small fleeing woman in strawberry wool, her long pale hair streaming in wispy tendrils behind her, Valerie, with a satisfied smile on her lightly rouged lips, murmured, "Good-bye, little farmgirl."

On the sleigh ride back to Helena, Valerie complacently congratulated herself on an effective round one, her pleasure a tangible thing, smiling on her mouth, shining from her eyes. The gloves were an unexpected stroke of luck; Trey had left them behind the day he and Judd Parker had lunch, and her man, following Trey, had pocketed them. Now it only remained to see how much opposition the fragile, terribly naïve woman would mount. Somehow, Valerie thought with a predator's instinct, she rather felt the opposition would be minimal.

The only consideration presenting the slightest misgiving was the very strong probability that the young boy was Trey's. In that case, an attachment beyond his usual transitory commitment might color the situation. Actually, the unusual sight of Trey's paramour surrounded by young children was startling. Somehow she'd never pictured Trey, the consummate man-about-town in that novel menage. Ever practical, a moment later she discarded needless speculation about Trey's image and concentrated on more pressing issues. She required a credible story concerning her visit to the ranch should Trey confront her. Like a game of chess, it always paid to plan several moves in advance of your opponent.

Reaching the privacy of the bedroom, Empress locked the door, walked distractedly into the middle of the large room, and stopped, trembling. He doesn't care, he doesn't care, repeated itself in her mind, and with each curt phrase her stomach tightened against her urge to vomit. Hadn't she expected a limit in the rational part of her mind; hadn't she *known* from the beginning that her joy was too intense to last? Hadn't she understood Trey's predisposition for amusement?

You'll live! she told herself sharply to still the trembling. *No one dies of unrequited love,* and she forced herself to walk over to a chair and sit. Placing her hands solidly on the chair arms, she held on tightly and fought for control over the sickening feeling in her stomach.

He'd left her for Valerie . . . he'd left her.

She couldn't stop shivering, her mind distrait, all thought processes reduced to a standstill, only loss, like a ferocious beast, tearing at her insides.

An hour later she was still in the same position. "It's over," she whispered. "All that beautiful feeling is over."

Trey hadn't come home for dinner, and the poignant hope that had persisted past the logic and distress was irrevocably crushed; he was dining with Valerie. Empress found it impossible to eat, although she heroically presented a calm facade to the children. They sensed her unhappiness, were shaken themselves by Valerie's visit, tentatively broached the subject of Mrs. Trey Braddock-Black. The startling revelation couldn't be casually explained away, although Empress related in a highly edited version the threat to Trey's clansmen and admit-

ted that Trey was indeed married to the woman who had
appeared in the breakfast room that morning.

Married for only a temporary period of time, she added
when their agitated questions exploded, in a voice that held
little conviction and less hope. And for the first time since
she'd met Trey, she brought up the possibility to the children
of returning to France to reclaim Guy's patrimony. "This
might be a good time during this temporary marriage of
Trey's to settle the question of Papa's estate," she forced
herself to say in a moderate tone, as though her world wasn't
disintegrating around her, as though an immediate trip to
France was the most sensible of plans.

The children were silent when she mentioned the trip, the
young ones having only known the wilderness, Guy and
Emilie indecisive when their own memories of France were
so dim. No one spoke of Trey, but he was in their thoughts,
important and influential.

"We'll think about it," Empress insisted into the silence,
the idea her lifeline to sanity. Thoughts that she had to leave,
had to get away, ran continuously through her brain, away
from this unorthodox situation, away from the deception. If
she had the luxury of only herself to consider, maybe she'd
contemplate staying to sort out her feelings, sort out the lies
and the pain. Maybe she could even think of staying until
Trey didn't want her anymore. But each day the children
became more attached to Trey, so she couldn't regard only
her own wanting; she had to plan for their future. They
deserved more than living in limbo in a household where their
sister was a rich man's paramour.

She had enough money now to return to France, thanks to
Trey. At least you couldn't fault him on generosity, although
she was only one of many, she was sure, when it came to
female recipients of his largesse. And then she thought wistfully,
like a young child might wish for a miracle, *If he does love
me, if all the shattering revelations were false, if Valerie by
some remarkable twist of fancy could be explained away, if
everything was some dreadful mistake . . . then he would
come for me.*

After the children were settled in bed, she sat alone, her
thoughts intentionally directed to planning her return to France.
The reasons all seemed sensible, practical; she shouldn't stay,
the children needed a secure future, but the hurt overwhelmed
the logic, the aching sadness brought tears to her eyes, and

she found herself about to burst into weeping at the slightest provocation.

If Trey did return home that night, she had every intention of calmly explaining to him that she and the children had decided to return to France, but by the time Trey walked in, it was very late, and her calm intentions had been slowly evolving in the course of the evening into a resentful anger. Images of Trey and Valerie had been superimposed over her initial hurt and sadness, and her mood had altered from a melancholy sense of loss to affront.

Trey was shedding his leather jacket as he walked toward her, a smile on his handsome face. "Missed you terribly," he said, and bending, kissed her lightly on the cheek.

Empress tried to smile, tried to appear normal, but all she could think of was the cozy evening he'd spent with Valerie. "It's late," she said tranquilly, but she really felt like screaming.

"The opposition brought in a surprise amendment at five o'clock, when most everyone had gone home or started home. They were hoping to pass it with their supporters on the floor, but we managed a delay and rounded up everyone again. They lost by two votes. It was damn close. They almost managed to lop off five hundred thousand acres of reservation." Flinging the jacket he held in his hand on the nearest chair, Trey collapsed on the bed, boots and all, and exhaled wearily. There were times when he felt the burden heavy on his shoulders. "We held them off," he said with the mocking irony of a man who had spent the day in heated debate and was not feeling his best, *"one more time."*

When one was cynically inclined, as Empress currently was, explanations like Trey's sounded too perfect, as though they'd been rehearsed.

"Valerie was here today," Empress said, and if Trey hadn't dashed by Timms in his hurry to see Empress, waving hello and good-bye in one casual gesture, he would have been informed of her visit downstairs.

He sat bolt-upright. "Making trouble, no doubt," he said gruffly.

"She had some interesting information about—"

"Don't believe anything she says," Trey interrupted. "She's a consummate liar. As I well know."

"She said you'd been over to . . ." Empress paused,

uncertain of her choice of words. ". . . visit," she finished, and felt the hot surge of her temper.

Trey frowned. Damn. Valerie was getting tiresome. "I haven't seen her since the wedding. I told you." More cruel and dangerous than he'd considered, Trey thought. He'd warn her off tomorrow.

"She says otherwise," Empress snapped, and both her tone and her words startled him.

Throwing his legs over the side of the bed, Trey rose. "Are you telling me," he said, his voice suddenly quiet with deliberate inquiry, "that there's some doubt in your mind?" Leaning against the massive carved bedpost, he watched Empress's face.

Empress sighed, confronted by Trey's soft challenge. "Her stories are very good." Her lashes lowered minutely in skepticism at the faint accusation in his expression. "She mentioned your lunch with Judd Parker," she said softly, wondering when and how he would refute the fact, or whether he would bother at all, "and the soup stain on your shirt. And she returned these . . ." Sliding the gloves that had been taunting her all evening closer to Trey, she watched his face.

Trey swiftly glanced at his gloves, lying on the small table beside Empress's chair. "Bloody hell!" he exclaimed softly, and Empress read the exhalation as exposure. Walking over to the table, he touched the colorful flowers surrounding the beaded black cougar. "At least the bitch brought them back," he murmured, his pantheistic reverence for his father's totem and his good-luck charm adverse to Valerie's contact. "She must have had someone following me."

"That sounds a bit farfetched." *Good God,* she wanted to shout, *can't you do better than* that? *Someone* following *you?* Her eyes traced the perfect symmetry of his dark, sweeping brows, the defined authority of his arrow-straight nose, the harsh, unmitigated strength of his jaw, then came to rest on the luminous beauty of his eyes and wondered whether the degree of passion he offered each woman varied.

"Nothing's farfetched for Valerie; the woman's unprincipled. Look," he said, genuinely tired after a long, fatiguing day, and suddenly weary of Valerie's continual machinations, "I lost those gloves somewhere last week. I haven't seen her since the wedding, and that's the truth." Picking up his gloves, he walked into the dressing room.

Somewhere, indeed, Empress thought, embittered, watching him stroll away, the subject closed, his infidelities disposed of with a casual disclaimer. Bristling with temper, she came to her feet and followed him into the dressing room. "Whatever the truth is," she said to his back as he stood inside one of the open mirrored doors, a sudden image of Valerie's smug expression flashing into her mind, "it really doesn't matter where you left your gloves."

He swung around with a suppressed violence. "What the hell is that supposed to mean?" he replied, his tone a shade too soft.

"I've been trying to tell you for weeks, I'm uncomfortable here," she said, thinking of the gloves, made, no doubt, by another devoted woman. "Your *wife*'s visit," she continued sullenly, "and her fascinated recital of your amorous history simply forced me to recognize exactly *how* uncomfortable."

"I didn't realize you were *uncomfortable*," Trey said sarcastically. "You could have fooled me. And I don't have a wife," he hotly contended, "I've eight months' insurance against a lynch mob in a society that measures the value of your life by the color of your skin. Damn," he said in the next rush of breath, his voice lowering perceptively, "don't listen to her version of my amorous history. I don't want to fight. You see, that's exactly what she wants. Let's not argue. All I have to do is last a few months and I'm rid of her."

His words suddenly sounded coldly selfish, as though nothing mattered but Trey's feelings, and in Empress's current frame of mind, where doubt predominated, she wondered whether Trey would be saying the same thing about her in a few months' time. For all she knew, six months ago he could have been telling Valerie it was she he adored. "I think the children and I will pass those six months elsewhere," Empress said quietly, her emotions volatile, unstable.

"I don't want you to." His expression was grim.

"But *I* do!"

Her ferocity surprised him. "Don't let her do this," Trey said quietly, his tone grave. "Please don't. It's what she wants."

Even those words held an ambiguous meaning tonight, as Empress listened, as if Valerie's words were right when she'd said, "He wants us both." Was it true? Was Trey only interested in his own pleasure and, like a child unable to choose between two treats, insists on them both?

She loved him, but every woman in his life loved him. Today, for the first time, Valerie's visit had underlined that fact. And the overheard conversation between the three young ladies, where Trey's reputation as a notorious womanizer had been discussed, reminded Empress of his taste for pleasure, for female pleasure. "It's what I want too," Empress said levelly, feeling as though she were going to break into a thousand pieces.

"Do you believe her?" His voice was flat.

Empress hesitated, and in that hesitation, Trey's temper flared. The entire episode with Valerie, his damn sacrifice for duty, his giving up of his freedom for his clan, the restraints necessary in the ensuing six months so *his dear wife* couldn't find some further coercion to control him, the overwhelming sense of being *trapped*—all suddenly exploded. "I see," he said almost inaudibly. Beneath his lips, his teeth were closed tightly.

"I don't know what to believe," Empress replied truthfully, and to a man momentarily frustrated past endurance, a cushioned lie would have been better.

"Fine," he said curtly, his nostrils flaring in an effort to keep his temper. "Believe some stranger you've never met before. A stranger, I might add, I've described in some detail as a cheat and a liar. Believe her, not me. Thank you, at least for your sudden"—his mouth twisted distastefully, as though the word were tainted—"honesty. I hadn't realized how superficial were your protestations of love. I thought you loved me."

"I do love you."

"And I you, ma'am," Trey replied with a curt, mocking bow. "Now that we've assured each other of our undying love, please excuse me if I retire for the night. It's been a long day," he said with restrained understatement, "and tomorrow promises an equally hard fight to keep greedy hands off the Indian lands. Although I forget," he murmured with a bitter smile, "that I was supposed to have spent the day dallying with my wife. Well, whatever—forgive my fatigue and good night."

Today had been one of the hardest, closest-won fights so far. Each year it became more difficult to save the reservation land from encroaching interests. Each year the long hours became longer, the old arguments less convincing. All anyone seemed to care about was money. Land was money. And the big tracts of reservation land were tempting prizes. Sometimes Trey felt as though the struggle were too much. Pointless. Never-ending. You win last year, this year, today, only to face a stronger attack tomorrow, next month. It seemed as though he and his father and their clan were trying to turn back the tide single-handedly. He was tired, cynically, bitterly tired, and now Valerie must be explained away. Again. And Empress must be comforted. Convinced of his love. Again. Tomorrow—he could face it all with renewed heart tomorrow.

Trey was awakened early. Now an attempt was being made on the Blackfeet Reserve. Good God. It never ended. Kissing Empress softly in the gray predawn light, he smiled at the tucked, childlike pose she held in sleep, then rose to dress hurriedly. He left a note of apology on the pillow near her head, telling her he loved her more than Rally and Clover *combined,* and tonight, when he returned from Helena, he would clear all her doubts about Valerie.

Trey ramrodded through a resounding defeat for those attempting to gain the Blackfeet land. And when Hazard congratulated him on his fierce energy and adroit maneuvering, Trey replied, "Had to. I've got to get home early tonight. No excuses. And I've got some shopping to do. See you tomorrow."

Shopping? Hazard thought, watching his son sprint down the marble staircase. Now that would be a first.

Trey arrived back at the ranch early, laden with gifts for Empress and the children, to be greeted by a surprised Timms. "They're gone, sir," he said. "Didn't they meet you in Helena? Miss Jordan and the children left at eleven to meet you in town. Did you miss her?"

Trey went still. He took a deep breath. "How did she get into Helena?" he asked tersely.

"The sleigh." Timms swallowed. His master's voice was much too quiet. "Rudy drove them."

"Is he back?" Clipped, bitten-off words like lethal weapons.

"Yes, sir." Sweat stood out on Timms's forehead. "He arrived back at four."

"Bring him to me," Trey said urgently, abruptly, and deposited the packages he was holding onto the foyer table.

The presents he'd selected himself instead of leaving it to
Timms, as he'd always done. Timms and Bolton, his father's
business manager, knew every eligible and not-so-eligible
female's address within a hundred miles. And prided themselves on their taste in jewelry. "Immediately," Trey added,
a scowl appearing as he glanced at his watch. "In the library."

He still wore his coat and gloves when the groom entered
the room five minutes later. Seated behind the desk, Trey's
posture was rigid, his gloved hands palm down on the desktop.
"Where did you take Miss Jordan?" he inquired swiftly. No
anger showed. His voice hadn't risen above a carefully modulated resonance. His face was expressionless.

"To Irwin's Department Store, Mr. Braddock-Black. She
said she was meeting you."

"What time?"

"When we got there?"

Trey nodded.

"About one-thirty, sir."

Unbidden, the disastrous thought struck his brain. Two-
twenty for the Union Pacific to Laramie. His next thought
refuted the first. She wouldn't. How long, he asked himself
in the next instant, would it take to discover her trail? There
was no need for her to leave. None at all, damn Valerie's
black soul. He was on his feet and halfway to the door before
he remembered Rudy. Checking in mid-stride, he turned
back. "Thank you," he said, "and tell the engineer I'll be
going back into Helena in ten minutes."

He took the stairs at a full-out run and threw the bedroom
door open with a crash, as though she might materialize
before his eyes with the violence. The room was utterly still,
strangely empty now that he was used to her presence. His
eyes scanned the untenanted vacancy, looking for some explanation, hoping there was some mundane reason for her
absence.

When he saw the note propped next to his on the pillow, a
sickening feeling washed over him. Walking over to the bed,
he only stared at it for long moments, delaying the expected
blow. He picked up his note first and turned it over to see that
it had been opened. It had. He dropped it and very slowly
reached for a similar white envelope with his name centered
on the textured surface.

It was not a brief note, nor an angry one. Empress's small
script told him of her decision to leave, words he'd already

heard last night, with added phrases to the effect that she felt it better for everyone if she waited for him elsewhere. With relief he read the sentence telling him of her love. "We're going back to France," she ended, "to see to Guy's inheritance. I'll send you our address when we're settled. All my love, Empress." In a postscript she asked him to care for Clover and the animals at the farm.

He went back into Helena, anyway, on some farfetched hope that she might still be in town. A phone call would have accomplished as much, but somehow he had to see for himself. He checked the railroad station first, and then there was no need to check the hotels. The ticket agent remembered the young lady with the four youngsters in tow. She'd bought tickets for New York. With gold.

The saddlebags with Empress's gold hadn't come back down-mountain with them because of their weight. Without horses, no one was strong enough to handle the two heavy bags. Trey had been burdened with Empress, and Eduard and Guy didn't have the strength for nearly a hundred pounds of gold. At his insistence Trey had replaced the gold for her last week, wanting Empress to feel independent of his family, with her new misgivings about staying and being beholden to him. More of a fool, he. A little less charitable benevolence and she'd still be here. He smiled ruefully at his touch of misanthropy and thought that at least he had the satisfaction of knowing that Empress had funds for her journey.

As he stood on the station platform, looking out into the evening gloom, a chill north wind buffeted him, a wind as bleak as his thoughts, and he damned Valerie to hell a thousand ways. For the first time in his life he felt like murdering someone, and if killing Valerie would have brought Empress back, he would have dispatched her cheerfully.

The stabbing cold eventually numbed his fingers and toes, forcing him to move, to go back to his carriage . . . to his life, which suddenly seemed utterly empty. Speaking softly into the blowing wind and black, silent night as he traversed the deserted platform, he murmured, "You're not gone forever . . . right, fierce kitten?" But no reassuring reply returned, only a wailing north wind and scattered snowflakes. Reaching the end of the long wooden platform, Trey paused at the corner of the building, drew a deep breath, overwhelmed by frustration, his spine tense, and slammed his fist into the solid, shingled wall. Swearing aloud at the pain, he

abruptly sprinted down the steps to his waiting carriage. After
indicating his parents' town house as his destination, he
slumped back into the cold leather and nursed his aching
hand.

During the legislative session his parents resided almost
entirely in Helena, and only Trey had entrained home each
evening to be with Empress. No need for that now, he
thought bitterly. And for a brief moment he considered going
after Empress and forcibly bringing her back or calling ahead
and having her taken off the train. In the next moment,
though, reason dismissed harsh emotion.

Maybe she was right to go if her feelings demanded it.
Empress was much more sensitive to society's shibboleths
than he; uncomfortable, she'd said, being his lover with all
the world knowing. He'd lived too long doing exactly as he
pleased to appreciate that sensitivity. With a sigh he alighted
at the mansion on Homer Street, thanked his driver, and
started up the swept granite steps. Snow was falling lightly,
and through the parlor windows he could see the party his
parents were hosting. Walking around to a side entrance, he
took the servants' stairs to his bedroom suite. Tonight he
wasn't in the mood to trade pleasantries with anyone.

Going directly to his desk, set in a bow window enclosure,
he picked up a brass-edged calendar and, walking over to the
bed, lay down. The snowflakes on his hair and shoulders
melted in the warmth of the room, and he felt sensation
coming back into his toes. The calendar balanced on his
chest, the heaviness of the brass sinking into the black beaver
of his coat, he flipped through the months, counting and
recounting, as if there were solace in seeing an end to his
misery. Six months. Six months until he saw Empress again.
He held up July and looked at August with a frown. *When* in
August? He'd never asked Valerie when her child was due. It
hadn't mattered before, but suddenly it did. Rising from the
bed, he retraced his steps to the desk and reached for the
phone.

Asking the operator for Mrs. Braddock-Black was an
unnerving experience; he'd avoided thinking of her in those
terms.

When the butler answered the phone, he was starkly reminded of the reality of his marriage. "The Braddock-Blacks',"
he intoned. "May I help you?"

Trey couldn't bring himself to use the formal address,

calling her Mrs. Braddock-Black. He asked for Valerie, and when the butler haughtily asked who was calling, it galled him to give his name.

He was put through immediately with sycophantic acknowledgment. *Why not?* Trey thought. *I'm paying his fucking salary.*

"Good evening, darling." Valerie's voice was replete with sweetness, and if he hadn't needed the piece of information he'd called for, he'd have hung up on the cloying treacle.

Without preamble he curtly inquired, "When is your child due?"

"Why, darling, how like you to have forgotten. But unless we want everyone in town to know," she said pointedly, aware that the operators at the central exchange knew everyone's business, "we shouldn't discuss this over the phone."

"Hell," he said softly, debating for a brief moment whether it mattered. But anything to do with this forced marriage was best kept in the family. He wanted no impediments to his divorce. "Right," was all he said, and hung up the receiver.

He swiftly walked the two blocks to Valerie's new home, a pink sandstone mansion in the same fashionable hill area, his wedding gift to her, she'd archly said when she'd selected it and asked for a check to pay for it.

The possibility she'd be entertaining hadn't occurred to him, with his mind almost exclusively occupied with thoughts of Empress. He should have known better. Valerie was the ultimate social butterfly, and now, with a house of her own and a generous allowance, she'd hardly become a recluse.

Refusing to be announced, he told the butler he wanted to see Valerie in the study. He paced while he waited—paced and watched the clock. Poured himself a whiskey, paced some more, and watched the clock. The bitch was true to form. She knew he wanted his information; she also knew he wasn't about to join her party.

Three drinks later the double doors opened, and she stood posed in the brilliant light from the hall chandelier. Her gown was cloth of gold, the fabric shimmered iridescently, diamonds sparkled in her ears, and he thought for a bitter moment that it was a shame all that beauty clothed such corruption. "How sweet of you to stop by, Trey," she cooed mendaciously.

"No sweetness is intended, Valerie." His face was set and still. "I came for the date."

Stepping into the room, she pushed the doors shut and, standing in the frame of gilded wood, ignored his statements and said, "I understand the woman and her family you've been *hosting*"— she languidly slurred over the word—"have left on the train for the East Coast. Did she tire of the mountain winter—or perhaps the isolation of the ranch?"

There was a short silence.

"You're a grade-A bitch, Valerie," Trey replied curtly, certain now that Valerie did have people watching him and the ranch. Although gossip traveled fast in a city this size, news of Empress's departure would not have reached her so precipitously.

"You always did have a wonderfully fiery temper, darling," she purred, reminded of some of their more physical moments making love. Valerie enjoyed teasing provocation and its sequential effects. And the consequences of physically provoking Trey were always tangibly erotic.

"A temper that's about reached its limits with you. In future, Valerie, I'd appreciate it if you'd refrain from visiting any of my friends."

"But we have so many mutual friends, darling, in this small city, I'm afraid that's impossible. But if you mean that little blond woman, I can't possibly visit her again, now can I?" The diamonds at her throat caught the light. They were enormous. How much, Trey wondered, violent death prominent in his thoughts, did those cost me? But handy for garroting, he decided.

"Valerie," he said very softly, "you don't know how close you're getting to being strangled."

"She wasn't your type, Trey," Valerie replied from her new position of strength, with her only serious rival on a train headed East. "She was much too docile. You would have been bored with her by spring."

"Someday," Trey growled, "I'll pay you back for interfering in my life."

"You should thank me, dear, for sending the tramp on her way."

"You're the only tramp I know."

"Darling, you forget, I've watched you cut a very wide path through the female population of Montana."

"I repeat," Trey said, his eyes as cold as ice.

"Really, sweetheart, I never knew you had this moralizing streak in you. You were always interested in pleasure without restrictions. Does it feel different with someone who's morally pure?"

"If I ever have the inclination to debate sexual morality with you"—his words were clipped and short—"I'll let you know. Now, if you'll kindly give me the information I called for, I'll leave."

"Judd Parker's here tonight, and Bo Talmadge. Why don't you take your coat off and stay for another drink?" Valerie was as cool as if they were discussing next week's menu. She had the advantage, of course, of having won very largely that day. She'd run Trey's newest girlfriend, the only live-in female he'd ever taken, had run her out of town with only one brief visit and a few well-chosen lies. Valerie was feeling cheerfully triumphant. Not only did she have Trey's name, she had a tidy sum of his money and the satisfaction of a clear field in the future. Miss Jordan was surprisingly easy to defeat. Trey would be more difficult to bring under control, but she was optimistic.

"You managed the marriage ceremony, Valerie, but you didn't get me. There are limits to my duty to the clan. I have no intention of joining your party. The child's birthdate if you please, and I won't keep you from your guests."

"Why," she asked bluntly, "do you want to know?" Suspicious by nature, resistance was her first impulse.

"I'm setting up my social calendar for the summer, pet, and want to be in residence to welcome the newest Braddock-Black into the world." His sarcasm was vicious.

"I don't know if I care to tell you," she replied, irritated by the naked hostility of the man she'd married.

Trey took a deep breath and ran his hands over the smooth fur of his coat, as if the movement would keep his booted feet anchored to the floor when a killing impulse was urging him to lunge. "Look, Valerie," he said with hard-leashed forbearance, his voice hushed, "this entire pregnancy has nothing to do with me, so there's no need for coyness at this late date. I have agreed, thanks to your blackmail, to be the father of this child. I don't care if it's a three-month pregnancy or a thirty-month pregnancy—the timing, the elusive father, none of that concerns me, except the damn due date. Now if you can see your way clear, I'm not trying to catch you out—*I just want to know*.'' The last sentence was forbidding in its plainness.

And for once Valerie Stewart understood the limits of bravado. ''September tenth,'' she answered in an uncharacteristically honest reply.

''Thank you. I'll see myself out.''

When she didn't move from the doorway, Trey hesitated briefly, controlling the violent urge to tear her to pieces. ''Dammit, Valerie,'' he ground out, his deep voice barely above a whisper. ''Don't push me. Get the hell out of my way.'' Reaching out, he put his hands around her waist and lifted her aside bodily. Thrusting the door open with a forceful, stiff-armed shove, he stepped out into the marble foyer, crossed its black polished floor in brisk strides, and nodding good night to the butler, passed through the held-open door.

September 10, he thought with weary relief, flexing his fingers, which had been unconsciously clenched. The snow was falling more heavily, great large flakes, drifting down gently, sparkling, like lacy crystals in the glow of the streetlamps, making the world pristine, dazzling. ''Not a lifetime, only September tenth,'' he breathed, then stuck out his tongue to catch a glistening snowflake, feeling better suddenly.

When he reached his room once again, he flipped forward the pages on the calendar to September and boldly circled the tenth. ''Freedom . . . and Empress,'' he whispered into the silence of the high-ceilinged room. Inexplicably, despite his melancholy over Empress's departure, he felt immensely relieved. There was an end. There was eventually a *goddamn* end to his servitude.

Seventeen

A LANDSCAPE EXISTED beyond the frost-tinged windows of their train compartment, but the blur of unshed tears in Empress's eyes curtailed the view. Confused, unhappy, hurt, she wished it was possible to be alone. Perhaps with solitude the vast sense of betrayal could be dealt with; she could neatly arrange all the doubts against the certainties, balance the inequities with the happiness, find some peace with her decision to leave. But she wasn't alone; the children's persistent inquiries required answers, answers unaccompanied by weeping sobs.

Why had they left, they'd ask, why was Guy's bid for the title undertaken, why did they want a title, why had they left without seeing Trey? And when Empress explained . . . again . . . only fresh queries would result: Exactly when would Trey arrive then, they wanted to know, and how would he find them in France? Was Empress sure he *could* find them? *How* was she sure? Forcing back the threatening flood of tears poised just beneath the surface of her control, she'd paraphrase the previous replies about the existence of letters and directions, Trey's busy schedule, extenuating circumstances that placed Trey at the Capitol when their train left.

"Guy's old enough now to take on the responsibility of the estates," Empress declared mildly, as if she hadn't uttered the identical reply scarcely ten minutes ago, "if the courts are willing to consider our case, and Trey's extremely involved at the moment with some boundaries on reservation land."

"Why couldn't we wait for him?" Genevieve asked again. "I don't see why we couldn't wait until Trey had time to leave too. Emilie said the other day that she didn't mind staying in Montana forever," and Genevieve looked to her older sister for support. Four years her senior, Emilie was mature enough to see beyond the moderation of Empress's replies and, cognizant of Empress's red-rimmed eyes, diplomatically kept silent.

"We shouldn't be going alone," Genevieve maintained morosely, ignoring her sister's lack of encouragement. "*You* said he would always be with us," she said, accusing Empress.

"Hush, Trey *can't* leave now," Empress quietly refuted for the umpteenth time, wanting to scream. "He simply *can't* with the legislature still in session." And it would be inconvenient now, she thought dispiritedly, for him to break away from his newly acquired wife.

Eduard, his face swollen from crying, suffered most obviously from Trey's absence, refusing to eat since they'd boarded the train, resentful and argumentative. Whenever Empress attempted to comfort him, he pushed her away, sobbing, "Me want Trey . . . go back . . . find Trey . . ."

"We're going on a splendid journey, Eduard," Empress cajoled, "like you've seen in the picture book with boats . . . and Guy will be a count. Do you know what a count is?"

"Don't care!" Eduard shouted, his little face puffy and reddened, "bout dounts. Want Trey!"

"When *will* we come back?" Emilie asked wistfully, her dark eyes reflecting her own unspoken fear at their sudden departure.

"I don't know," Empress said with a soft sigh, haunted by the possibility of "when" being boundless eternity if Trey's interest was indeed focused on his new wife. "Maybe—"

"Hate you!" Eduard shouted at Empress, single-minded in his grief, tears streaming down his face. "Dummy! Dummy, doodoo!"

And Guy, more perceptive of Empress's unhappy reasons for leaving, and with Valerie's humiliating visit still fresh in his mind, awkwardly tried to divert Eduard from his fretful misery. "You'll have a room of your own in our new house . . . a whole big room, not a loft you share with others."

"Trey's house bigger," Eduard retorted. "Want Trey!"

"You can have a pony all for yourself. You'd like that, wouldn't you?"

"Don't want pony," Eduard muttered sulkily, "want Trey."

Empress's stomach lurched as if in sympathy with Eduard's lament. *Don't we all want him*? she thought poignantly, the finality of their departure reinforced with each clicking revolution of the train wheels, and she clenched her hands in her lap against the yearning she felt.

"I'll buy you a candy at the next stop," Guy coaxed, but Eduard, kneeling on the pullman seat with his nose pressed to the window, only shook his head stubbornly. "I'll bet they'll have the purple-and-white taffy," Guy teased.

"Pink." Eduard's muffled response left condensation on the cold glass.

"Oh, is it pink-and-white taffy you like?" Guy replied with feigned surprise. "I wonder how many pennies I have here to buy pink-and-white taffy?" And he dug noisily in his pocket for his change. The lure of his favorite candy was irresistible, even to a heartsick little boy, and a moment later Eduard was snuggled in Guy's lap counting pennies.

Dear Guy, always helping, always comforting without censure; what would Empress do without him? Leaning her head back against the plush upholstery, she shut her eyes, fought back her tears, and prayed for fortitude to face the days ahead.

In addition to the emotional strain of Trey's loss and the children's unhappiness overwhelming her in the succeeding days, Empress was physically fatigued and plagued by frequent spells of nausea. She hadn't had an appetite since Valerie's visit, and the rocking rhythm of the train, she decided, aggravated her unsettled stomach. But once installed in a spacious stateroom aboard a steamship out of New York, she experienced no relief from her nausea. Food lost all appeal, her fair skin took on a greenish hue, and she assumed the cause this time was seasickness. Eight days later, however, lying in her hotel bed in Le Havre, solid ground beneath her, a tray of food untouched on the bedside table, her stomach gyrating uncomfortably, she realized with a sinking feeling of dismay that train sway or sea swells weren't the cause of her indisposition, nor was physical exhaustion or the emotional tumult subsequent to their leaving.

Rather, she was about to make Trey a father for the second

time that year. Or were there more beside Valerie and herself; how many enceinte lovers did that make now for Montana's most-in-demand bachelor? she wondered, both mortified and chagrined. He was certainly, if gossip was to be believed, in the way of setting some records, and her anger flared at his casual appropriating of all the willing females.

But as the day wore on, her resentment of Trey's heedless charm was mitigated by her own personal recollections of exactly how joyous and enchanting he had made her life. It wasn't all taking with Trey Braddock-Black, for he gave full measure of delight and laughter in return, and a warm affection she still held in her heart, in spite of all Valerie had said. So after the initial, staggering shock of her pregnancy subsided and she had run the fitful gamut of variable emotions from resentment to alarm to capricious cowardice, a small gladness took hold deep inside and, with warming reflection as the hours passed, intensified and heightened into whimsical triumph. She was carrying Trey's child, she thought, whispering the words to herself with wonder and a happiness she didn't try to understand. Growing inside her was his baby, who would remind her always of him. "Hello, little one," she breathed softly, welcome and tenderness in her greeting. He was with her after all . . . a part of her.

In addition to her own quiet happiness that she and Trey shared a child—a perfectly mindless and heedless reaction, she knew—a flood of disconcerting problems, less naïvely blissful, required immediate attention. Being single, of course, in her current condition, was most scandalously prominent, followed closely by the stark immediacy of her reentry into society. Hardly a propitious beginning for her new life in the fashionable circles her family had fled five years ago, she reflected with a flash of amusement. The Comtesse de Jordan had returned—young, single and pregnant.

Her present tangle was considerably less threatening than starving, which she and the children had faced the previous winter, she reminded herself pragmatically, and now with Trey's money and the application of a little energetic storytelling, the deficiencies in her persona could be rectified. After a short period of expedient rationalization and creative thought, Empress invented the necessary husband, his convenient death, and her sad bereavement, made less sad by the modest legacy he'd left her.

With a certain trepidation she informed the children of her

pregnancy and, with a combination of candor and omission, acquainted them with the reasons for a fictitious husband and past. Then, breath held nervously she waited for their reaction to the glaring unorthodoxy of her situation.

"Wow!" Guy joyfully exclaimed, beaming from ear to ear. "I'm going to have an Absarokee nephew. *I'm* going to be related to Trey!"

"It could be a girl, you know," Genevieve disputed instantly. "Pressy, I want a *niece.*"

And Empress, breaking into a smile, felt her nervousness disappear. "I'll do my best, sweetheart, but I can't guarantee a boy *or* a girl."

"See, *see,* Guy!" Genevieve jibed. *"There."*

"You can be a widow for now, but Trey's coming to marry you this summer, anyway," Emilie declared confidently, "so then everything will be perfectly fine." At fourteen Emilie perceived the intricacies of decorum. "And I want a girl, too, because Eduard always has sticky hands, and Guy does nothing but talk about guns and horses. A baby girl would be ever so much nicer."

"Trey's coming, Trey's coming, Trey, Trey, Trey . . ." Eduard said happily, attentive to the portion of the conversation having to do with Trey, unconcerned with talk of babies. "Me see Trey and get pony too," he went on cheerfully, certain that his fortune had changed.

Listening to Eduard's buoyant, humming tune, Empress wished that she had his optimism. Wouldn't it be wonderful, indeed, if Trey *did* come, if he left his wife, all the pursuing women, his family, his work, abandoned all to come halfway across the world after a woman he'd bought in a brothel one night on a whim? More aware of the profligacies in Trey's past, she didn't share Eduard's faith in Trey's arrival; the long line of women he'd loved and left was permanently etched in her brain—a thousand-foot-high barricade against optimism.

Without knowing what had become of her favorite cousin Adelaide, Empress sent her a telegram and then waited in Le Havre for a response. She understood much could have happened in five years; Adelaide may no longer even live in France if she had married one of their Hungarian cousins she was enamored of at fifteen, or could still be in Nice after Easter week, or possibly found it awkward to renew a friendship with a family that had left, some perhaps felt, under a shadow of disgrace. But early the following morning Adelaide's prompt answer arrived; she was still in Paris, was now Her Royal Highness as wife to Prince Valentin de Chantel, and was waiting with breathless anticipation to see them all again.

Amid hugs and kisses and dozens of excited questions, Adelaide, trailing an extravagant white fox stole, greeted them at the railway station, accompanied by a full retinue of servants, the stationmaster, and a host of obsequious officials. A smile here, a languid gesture there, and H.R.H. directed staff and officials whose briskly snapped orders saw them all quickly arranged into carriages and whisked away to what Adelaide described as their unpretentious bijou. Tucked intimately near Notre Dame on the Ile de la Cité, the precious little bijou, enriched with flamboyant tracery and ornament, was the perfect medieval setting for Adelaide and her husband's dilettante tastes as patrons of the arts. And all of the fifty-four perfectly decorated rooms were graciously offered as haven to Empress and her family.

Very late that night, when Empress and her cousin were alone for the first time, Adelaide, her voice breathy with anticipation, her dark curls dressed artistically rather than fashionably à la Grècque, quivering with her fluttering movements insistently said, "Now *tell me everything*. Valentin will see that all is restored to you, so don't worry for one moment about all the tiresome details," she added airily, waving her ringed fingers in dismissal. "Papa looked for you everywhere"—her gamin brows settled into a frown, her expression taking on a grave air as she digressed with her customary impetuosity—"but it was as if you'd disappeared off the face of the earth. But enough of the tragedy," she went on in her inimitable erratic delivery, as though the duel had never occurred and the terrible years of exile had never existed.

Seated across the fire from her cousin, Empress wondered briefly what she would have been doing now if the duel had never occurred, how insulated her life would have been, surrounded with advantage and privilege like Adelaide's. Where would she have been living now at twenty and with whom? —all indeterminate "what-ifs." And then she thought of the reverse side to the life of ease she would have enjoyed in France; what if she had never met Trey? No comparison was possible, she immediately decided; measured against Ade-

laide's frivolous life, Trey Braddock-Black was vital energy
and turbulent passion and a pleasure she never would have
known in the pampered cocoon of Adelaide's bijou.

"Tell me about your husband," Adelaide whispered, animated and vivacious. "Was he handsome like my Valentin?"
Her face sobered momentarily. "Oh, dear, it's too painful,"
she said consolingly, then, leaning forward conspiratorily like
she had so often during their childhood when they'd share
secrets late at night after their nannies were sleeping, she said
impishly, "But you *must* tell me, anyway."

Sitting in Adelaide's cozy boudoir sipping hot chocolate,
her legs tucked under her, listening to her cousin's staccato
inquiries in the same soft lisp that brought back flooding
memory, it seemed for a moment as though Empress had
never left. As though she'd never worried about food or cried
over her parents' graves, never stood in Lily's parlor or been
held in Trey's arms. She was fifteen again, and Adelaide was
saying irrepressibly, "Tell me everything."

Empress's heart lightened at the rush of remembrance and
the unconditional affection Adelaide offered. For the first
time since she'd met Trey, she could confide in someone, talk
of her ardent feelings and the indelible delight he'd brought
her. "After Mama and Papa died, I met a man quite by
accident. And yes," Empress added softly in response to
Adelaide's riveting attention, "he was very handsome . . .
more handsome than Roland."

"No!" Adelaide breathed, her dark eyes intent.

"Oh, yes, although his hair was jet-black."

Within the week, the Prince de Chantel, at his adored
wife's request, saw to it that Simoult, a lawyer of consequence, was retained to see to the restoration of Guy's estates, and one month later the Jordan suit was approved, not
particularly because Simoult was so brilliant but because the
influential and royal Prince de Chantel desired it. Of equal
importance was the fact the Duc de Rochefort had died that
past summer, taking his bitter hatred over the death of his son
with him to the grave. Five years ago, with grim malevolence, he had pushed the Comte de Jordan to trial, although
duels, even fatal duels, were commonplace in France, and
with unparalleled ferocity had seen that a conviction re-
sulted. In retrospect, every aspect of the case had been tainted
with corruption, and all Simoult had to do was see that the

Duc's bribery and unscrupulous dealings were brought to light.

A month of legal processing—of petitions approved and documents signed, affidavits assembled and judgments rescinded—was required, but justice was served at last, and the heirs of the Comte de Jordan were restored to their rightful position, fortune, and estates.

As the family was welcomed back, Empress, recently widowed and expecting her first child, was treated with great sympathy by all their former friends. And while she found a degree of solace in the kindnesses, the renewing of friendships satisfied only a small fraction of the void left by Trey. No matter how considerate or well-meaning her friends, she still wished many times a day that she were back with Trey.

But wishing and reality were continents apart, separated not only by physical distance but also by deception and betrayal and by a young woman's pride. Although Empress had promised to send her address once she was settled, her pregnancy checked that impulse. She had spent endless hours of internal debate over writing to Trey, but logic prevailed over impetuous feeling. Much as she wanted to write, "Come . . . come to me . . . this instant. I love you and nothing else matters," other things did matter, of course. Trey's feelings mattered considerably. And Trey Braddock-Black's feelings toward the women in his life were torrid but transient. For all she knew, he'd asked a dozen women to marry him in the heat of passion.

So a marriage proposal by a man known for his flagrant excesses was simply another of his intemperate impulses, like his extravagant offers of clothing and jewels. A liking, taste, or proclivity for Trey became as quickly an unguarded, impelling passion, but the delirium soon passed, as did all the women and all the compelling needs.

How could she possibly petition him as yet *another* enceinte lover? The rash, mercurial Trey Braddock-Black's response to women accusing him of fathering their children was common knowledge—he avoided them. And she would never forget his angry reaction to Valerie's pregnancy and subsequent blackmail. He'd felt trapped, irritated by the responsibility, stubbornly opposed to fatherhood, and while she may have once believed his denials of paternity apropos Valerie's child, after Valerie's visit, that belief was badly shaken and, on her worst day, mortally wounded.

How pointless it would be by all accounts, and how humiliating for her to write to him, informing him of her pregnancy. In any case, whether she wanted him to marry her or not was moot, since he was already married, with an iron-clad marriage contract. In retrospect, she didn't sometime wonder if Valerie was simply being foresighted with a husband of Trey's reputation; maybe marriage to Trey *required* an iron-clad marriage contract. Even newly married, he *had* been dividing his time between town and the ranch, involved with Empress at the same time he was enjoying his wife's bed.

However, with a wistful longing that disregarded wives, countless infidelities, and a penchant for walking away from enceinte lovers, Empress artlessly mused like some fairy-tale princess dwelling on an unassailable mountaintop. *If he truly loves me, he will come for me . . . against all odds, despite all complications, ignoring dragons and villains and contentious pride.* A highly romantic, unlikely occurrence, she logically concluded in the next moment, considering the man, his wife, and her own extremely brief sojourn in his busy life.

Although, she mused cynically, as brief as her interval was in his highly active love life, it was long enough to conceive his child. And what smarted most when she was angry was her injured pride—her inability to recognize his practiced, facile charm. She had been naïve enough to fall in love with the rogue. It annoyed her to succumb so easily; it annoyed her more to be one of a crowd.

So with resolution she intended to eject Trey from her thoughts and begin to reestablish her Jordan identity. That summer she kept busy with all the details of setting up their household, seeing that their town house was staffed with her own servants, arranging for her mother's rose garden to be replanted to its former glory, having the nursery redecorated for her child, escaping when she could to the estate at Chantilly for peace. No, not peace, not with memories of Trey resisting expulsion but quiet at least . . . and solitude.

With the International Exposition taking place in Paris that summer, feting the centenary of the revolution, the children wouldn't stay content in the country for long, a phenomenon typical of most rural citizens of France. The city was throned with visitors. The Eiffel Tower, raised at the cost of fifteen million uninflated francs, was condemned by many as a disfigurement to Paris, but it lured with affronting style and became famous overnight. Tourists visited it, artists painted it, newlyweds with happy faces were photographed beside it, suicides and inventors of flying machines jumped off it; there was no resisting its truculent stance as the first monument to modern engineering.

Scientific exhibits, pugnacious with the myth of progress, filled several buildings, including the colossal Hall of Industry. Gauguin showed his paintings at the Cafe Volponi, a Cairo street scene was constructed with imported Egyptians to live in it and perform the *danse du ventre*; the Javanese dancers became the rage of Paris. Thomas Edison visited his own pavilion, one of the largest on the grounds, and bought the allegorical statue entitled *The Fairy of Electricity* for his new West Orange laboratory. This winged woman, crouching on a dilapidated gas jet, surrounded by a Volta battery, telegraph key, and telephone, brandishing an incandescent bulb, all in the finest Carrara marble, perhaps best confirmed the flamboyant excess, the exuberant pageantry, of La Belle Epoque.

At first Empress partook of the festivities for the sake of the children, accepting the limitless daily invitations of friends, but by summer's end she was able to plead her condition as an excuse to avoid the unending round of activities: concerts, teas, dances, the races, and daily rides in the *Bois* all seemed empty, everything lacking that spark of enjoyment. She found herself thinking many times a day, Trey would laugh to see that, or scowl his displeasure at such pedantry, or say in his utterly charming way that something was delightful when he was bored to tears. She measured all her pleasures against his remembered tastes, then, outraged at her missah pining, would smile more determinedly at some vapid remark or say, "Really, how terribly interesting. Tell me more," at a discourse already tedious beyond belief because she would *not*, she heatedly reminded herself, remain hostage to a memory . . . no matter how seductive.

But it was an education to discover how one person in the entire world could so temper the warmth of the sun that she felt alone, like an alien in a chill inhospitable landscape, too far from the sun's warming rays.

And her sun was back in Montana.

Luckily, on the worst of her melancholy days, the children kept her irrevocably linked to the prosaic movements of life. They would not let her slip into her cloistered blue nunnery; she must see to their active, childish schedules of lessons, sports, and frivolity. And while they flourished in the resilient way of youth, she envied them their joie de vivre.

Trey regularly asked for his mail the first month after Empress left, but when no letters arrived, he abruptly ceased asking. Throwing himself into horse training after that, he rose early and worked the young bloodstock until late in the evening. With an unusual reticence, he spent long hours on the lunge, patiently took the new horses over the low learning jumps again and again, cajoled the belligerent young geldings into a semblance of obedience, mastered the stallions with gentleness rather than force . . . dusty, hot hours each day of intense concentrated schooling. But everyone close to him saw what effort it took for his reserve to remain intact: he was often preoccupied; rarely spoke; walked away from any questions about Empress; was miserably unhappy.

He hadn't had a drink in weeks, unusual for a man who'd congenially spent time in the bunkhouse over cards and bourbon. "Have to stay in training," he'd jest when he was coaxed by the men at the end of the day's work to sit in on a game, "until this young bloodstock gets off to market."

And he didn't even bother with an excuse when he was asked to join the expeditions to Lily's. "No thanks," he'd say, and his voice was so curt, his friends looked away, embarrassed by his grief.

On his own initiative, Guy mailed a letter to Trey in July, telling him he was now a *comte* (Pressy had taken care of everything, he wrote); that the Eiffel Tower was *magnifique*; and all the children sent their good wishes, each child adding a few lines to fill up the page with Eduard's rough scribble translated "I love you" at the bottom. Although Guy didn't fully comprehend Empress's express orders not to communicate with Trey, she'd not been the same since they'd left Montana, and his note was a surreptitious attempt to repair the friendship between his sister and Trey.

Unfortunately the letter had the opposite effect. At first sight of the postmark, Trey's heart leapt with joy, but the script was large, rounded, and childish in appearance, not small and neat like he'd expected on opening the envelope, and when he'd finished reading, he was gloomily reminded of Empress's words the previous winter: "I think they love you more than I." Certainly they missed him more than she;

Empress hadn't taken the time to write a single word. With bitterness he reflected on the ironic justice of a mocking fate: after all the relationships and women he'd politely evaded, he'd fallen in love with a woman capable of the same elusive withdrawal he'd perfected to a fine art.

For the first time in his life he pessimistically considered the possibility of heavenly retribution.

No more than ten minutes after reading Guy's letter, Trey saddled Rally and left for Helena. A mile down the road, he stopped and waited patiently in the hot sun for Blue and Fox to overtake him. When they rode up, he bluntly told them he wasn't interested in either bodyguards or friends. His eyes were chill ice, his mouth a grim slash. "I don't need taking care of," he said. "Jake Poltrain is at Li Sing Koo's and in no shape to threaten anyone." He sighed then, and the grimness mitigated. "Do me a favor," he went on with a rueful smile. "Give me a few days to go to hell in my own way. . . . I promise to send you a special invitation if I think you're missing anything fascinating."

"You're sure?" Blue said.

Trey nodded.

Blue and Fox looked at each other in brief silent communication, sympathy and understanding in their dark eyes. "If you need us . . ." Blue said softly.

"I'll call," Trey quietly finished, and raised his hand in salute. Wheeling Rally, he rode away, kicking up a haze of dust on the dry road.

In Helena, Li Sing Koo, discreet as always, personally ushered Trey into a large silk-draped room. "Would you like company?" he inquired politely, his face bland.

Trey looked at him blankly.

"Company. Would you like a woman?"

"No." A soft, abrupt refusal, then apparently a rapid rethinking, for Trey said, pulling his dusty shirt out of his buckskins, "Maybe later." He sat down on the opulent lacquered couch, the burnished wood a rich, deep scarlet, its scrolled and fretted carved canopy like an elaborately sculptured cavern. The silk-covered cushions were so heavily embroidered, the design gave the impression of three dimensions. Pulling his boots off, Trey lounged back against the embroidered silk flowers, riotous in scheme and color, the harsh darkness of his skin and hair offsetting the brilliant blooms, his fringed buckskins incongruously juxtaposed to the luxurious fabric. The gold chain of his cougar charm flashed as he moved to one elbow and reached out for the gilded pipe, his thoughts disarrayed and brooding, his eyes momentarily startled to see Koo still standing near the door. "Thank you, Koo," he said with an inbred, facile politeness.

It was a dismissal, however polite.

And when Koo quietly closed the door behind him, Trey's fingers curled around the lavishly engraved pipe on the low table beside him, and he let his morbid anger off its leash. For months now he'd controlled his exasperation and rage, tightly reined his impulse to strike out at Empress for the pain she'd caused him . . . was causing him; lived with a relentless, corrosive hurt. And he meant now to find some forgetfulness.

So in Li Sing Koo's luxurious private rooms Trey and Jake Poltrain both searched for an elusive peace or temporary respite from the caustic anger inside them. Jake Poltrain lived for his dream of Trey's death, while Trey struggled with his own black demons, cursing Empress as a fickle trollop interested only in his money. When Valerie had convinced her that there was no marriage in the immediate future, she'd left; it seemed quite plain in retrospect, and the only deductive conclusion for her not writing to him.

In the days ahead, together with the golden, tranquil dreams, existed alternate odious sensations urging him to punish Empress, rank and pernicious feelings, thin-skinned and violent, and he faced with perceptible horror the acute possibility that he'd enjoy the punishment. For the first time he was conscious of a dark side to his nature, a destructive, irrational impulse only wanting revenge. The opium always helped after it took hold, helped ease the rancorous malevolence and smother the battle lines between good and evil in his soul, smother them like a dense fog bank would terminate a day's fighting. But the drug never resolved the conflict, only disengaged the combatants until another day.

And a week passed in the hushed privacy of Helena's most lavish opium den.

Indulging his son's need for solitude, Hazard dispensed with Trey's usual bodyguards, but with Jake Poltrain at Koo's, his son required security. Li Sing Koo was to find replacements for Blue and Fox, and Trey was to be kept from harm; those were Hazard's explicit orders. And under normal circumstances a guard was constantly posted outside Trey's room.

But late one night in an altercation between two local Chinese warlords over a beautiful young prostitute, one of Koo's patrons sank a battle-ax into his adversary's head. The practiced blow, perfectly executed, sliced through the man's skull like it was butter, and the carnage drew everyone to the sight . . . including Trey's guard.

Day and night blended in the opulent, silk-hung room, and Trey, unconcerned whether it was day or night, had no perception of the frenzied activity one floor below him, insulated as he was by paneled walls and hazy dreams. He had lost weight in the past week, his hands were no longer steady, his pale eyes shone with a brilliant intensity, the dark shadows beneath his eyes accenting the leanness of his face. And he dozed between wakefulness and sleep on the soft cushions, his whipcord slender body clad sparely in black silk trousers. Only recently bathed by several of Koo's accommodating female servants, his dark hair lay coolly damp on his shoulders, the perfume of the bathwater still clinging to his skin. He was pleasantly quiescent, unruffled by black demons, his internal visions of a mountain landscape in early spring.

He stirred suddenly at dim sounds of shouting, his eyelids lifting indolently, a strange sensation intruding into his pastel and sunlit landscape. Listening intently for a moment, he heard nothing but felt more distinctly a hard, cold nudging infiltrating the tranquillity of his dream. Lazily sifting through numerous possibilities in a narrowing sequence of sensitivity, he thought himself very astute to ultimately distinguish the site. *My ear*, he casually reflected. And then his eyes opened fully to absorb the unusual sensation.

Shit.

Jake Poltrain towered above him, his close-set eyes virulent with hate, pressing a revolver into Trey's temple. This is, Trey ironically thought, a classic nightmare.

"You're going to die," Jake growled, the effort of holding his hand steady causing sweat to bead on his forehead, "and it's so easy," he murmured, his sense of euphoria animated in his voice. He'd simply walked through the unlocked door, crossed the carpeted room to the opium couch, and positioned the pistol barrel on Trey's temple, his first stroke of luck in dealing with the Braddock-Blacks. And he meant to take advantage of the opportunity. "I'm going to skin you afterward and make me a pair of boots."[11] Jake's smile was malevolently smug. "See if your daddy's millions will save you now, half-breed."

Trey laughed, a low, slow chuckle that shook his lean body, and his eyes drifted shut again. Irrationally the situation struck him as ludicrous, like some staged melodrama. All Jake needed was a thin waxed mustache and a leer, Trey speculated with amusement, although with those tiny pig eyes in all those folds of flesh, a leer wasn't a certainty. He chuckled again, a variation of a pig's face superimposed on Jake's, vivid in his mind.

Trembling with rage at Trey's casual indifference, Jake emphatically jabbed the pistol barrel roughly into Trey's flesh and growled, "Open your eyes, dammit."

Several moments passed before Trey ceased laughing and complied, moments in which Jake Poltrain cursed a torrent of vilifying invective having to do with degrees of skin color, and his wavering, unsteady hand clenched and unclenched on the pistol. He'd expected Trey to grovel and plead, a scenario he'd fantasized a thousand times in a thousand variations. Damn him for laughing, he thought, disordered by Trey's irregular response. He wasn't supposed to laugh; he was supposed to beg for his life, and Jake's opium-clouded brain failed to assess the boundaries of reality and fantasy.

When Trey's dark lashes eventually raised, his brilliant eyes indolently surveyed Jake's contorted face, vaguely felt the cold steel at his temple, and wondered briefly if there was pain with a shot in the head. He smiled then at the irrelevance and said, "Relax, Jake, it's not hard to shoot a man. You're taking this all too seriously. Take everything too damn serious, that's your problem," he murmured, his mind gliding lazily into more pleasant thoughts. "Now, Koo here knows how to take the seriousness out of life. Right, Jake?"

"Koo's scum, just like your kind redskin," Jake spat, his perception of social equality seriously defective.

"Now, Jake, that's no way to talk about your host," Trey admonished pleasantly. "Koo here's been supplying you with golden dreams and beautiful women for days now."

"Fuck you," Jake snarled.

"Sorry, you're not my type," Trey murmured, and his eyes half closed as a slow smile curved his mouth.

Jake failed to appreciate Trey's sense of humor, his hate so corrosive that it poisoned his mind sleeping or awake, drugged or not, until his only thought was killing Trey and ending the Braddock-Black succession. For too long they'd resisted expansion of his cattle range, for too long Hazard had stood unyielding and indestructible in his path; and if Hazard eluded death, his son was more susceptible, had always been, with a youthful, cavalier attitude toward death. Now . . . at last he had him in his sights. "I'm going to kill you," he muttered, "kill, kill, kill you . . ." The litany was unsullied by reason, implacable with spleen.

"Not if you don't stop shaking, Jake," Trey murmured, and rolled away onto his side as if drifting back to sleep.

A convulsive tremor shook Jake as he gazed at the tautly muscled back heedlessly turned to him. Why wouldn't the bastard beg for his life? Where was the pleasure and satisfaction if he wouldn't humiliate himself? And with sly cunning he thought of the woman, the one at Lily's, the one, rumor had it, who had walked out on Trey. Immune to fear, perhaps the arrogant Braddock-Black cub would respond to pricked vanity. "She wouldn't have left if I'd bought her," Jake said with an unpleasant smile. "I'd have locked her up right tight." His voice took on a goading satisfaction as he warmed to the subject. "Only a fool would give a whore freedom. You can't trust whores, you know . . . they'll fuck anything."

When Trey rolled back, Jake experienced a sudden galvanic glee. The pale, silvery eyes weren't lazily half lidded anymore, nor indolently unfocused or amused. They were, Jake noted, pleased with his strategy, anticipating his long-awaited revenge, malevolent with outrage. At last, he'd drawn blood. "I would have tied her to the bed and seen that she entertained me," he went on, twisting the knife in the wound. "You redskins are more stupid than I thought."

Adrenaline began pumping fiercely through Trey's body, and he saw the gun for the first time, really focused on it, only inches away. The violence of his feelings burned away the drowsy lethargy, and his mind came to a ragged attention. The pistol was wavering, he noted with brisk economy of thought, definitely. His glance swept the room, checking the door, Jake's swaying bulk, the tremor in Jake's gun hand, with a sudden, rapid alertness, as if he'd awakened from a ten-year sleep. Jake Poltrain had mistakenly stepped over the line, past Trey's sense of indulgence or neutrality and into restricted territory. His feelings for Empress, however inexplicable, were his personal property, and no one, particularly

Jake Poltrain, was allowed to infringe on his property. Emotion governed Trey's mind, not reason, and the thought of Jake Poltrain touching Empress, keeping her for himself, was intolerable. Trey's need for vengeance, the compelling impulse to punish he'd been struggling with for days, took on a new focus, and he hastily considered whether in his opium-induced languor he was capable of outmoving a bullet. Trey's gaze swung upward again to the trembling hand holding the Colt .45, and the faintest smile appeared on his lean, bronzed face. Damn good chance, he decided.

"So you couldn't make her stay," Jake taunted, his face flushed with vindictive triumph, his heavy breathing sonorous in the quiet room. "If I see her after you're dead, I'll give her a kiss someplace sweet in memory of you." And if it was possible to glow with success, Jake Poltrain would have illuminated the silk-hung interior.

Trey recognized what Jake was doing, was conscious of the irrational basis of his own anger, even understood in a brief moment of reflection that Jake's goading was all only words and could be ignored, if his emotions allowed.

But they didn't . . . because against all reason, she was still *his property*. "Pull the trigger, Jake," Trey said softly, "if you want her, because it's the only way you'll ever get close enough to touch her." And in the dimness of the room, Empress was suddenly between them, vividly real, a dream image, lush, smiling, waiting to be kissed. She took a step closer. "No-o-o-o," Trey screamed in an instinctive, roaring challenge and, rolling off the lacquered couch, lunged at Jake.

Jake Poltrain only dealt with sure things, and holding a revolver on an unarmed man a foot away offered the degree of security Jake preferred. Beyond that level of safety, he hadn't prepared. Confounded at Trey's audacity, his opium-dulled brain attempted to respond, but his reflexes were sluggish enough to allow Trey the half pulse beat he needed before Jake pulled the trigger.

As Trey's diving body struck Jake's legs, the pistol flashed, Jake staggered backward with the full impact of Trey's weight, and, off-balance, dropped the revolver. Jake scrambled for the weapon, which had skidded under a low, black-lacquered chair, but Trey ignored it, as he ignored the blood beginning to stream down the side of his face, indifferent to the weapon and his wound, intent only on one compelling need. Primordial and inherently uncivilized in resolve, he meant to make certain Jake Poltrain never touched Empress. Like a madman crazed with a single barbaric impulse, Trey threw himself on top of Jake, deterring him only inches away from the glistening pistol handle. Twisting violently, Jake turned to protect himself and, with heavy, flailing arms and booted feet, fought Trey off, outweighing him under normal conditions and measurably heavier now with Trey's weight loss. They rolled across the carpet, leaving a trail of blood, as Trey blocked Jake's fists and kicks or absorbed with grunts of pain the blows that connected. He was virtually unprotected, with only the silk pajama pants for clothing, and blood was impairing the vision in his left eye but single-mindedly Trey sought a grip on Jake's massive neck, reaching, always reaching, past the hammering fists and damaging boot blows.

Jake knocked his attacking assailant off, shoved him aside, plummeted him with vicious fists, fought for his life, but Trey's eyes were wild, his face harsh in its intent, his long-boned hands like powerful claws relentless on their prey. They closed finally, despite Jake's ferocious resistance, and would not be dislodged however frantically Jake struggled. Locked on like a machine set in motion, Trey's slender fingers squeezed with a fatal determination undeterred by human emotion. As Trey's blood dripped in a steady rhythm onto the wide-eyed face below, like some macabre accompaniment to death, Jake's face turned from red to blue to a hideous purple, his strangled, choking sounds muffled reverberations in the silken room. But Trey was detached from the sight and sounds, from the substance of humanity dying under his hands; only the slow, measured act of killing was real, the necessary silencing of Jake Poltrain, as if the action existed apart from the man.

He was no longer lucid, if he ever had been since the opium had taken effect, and light-headed now with the loss of blood, but implacably Trey maintained the pressure on Jake's throat until his arms screamed with pain. And even then he held firm, enduring the pain as he'd been taught, tenacious in his blind impulse, assuring himself that Jake would never touch Empress.

Perhaps some primal instinct triggered the causal directive to release his grip; perhaps, more prosaically, the drifting scent of incense from his brazier caught in his nostrils. Whatever the reason for the message to his brain, he relaxed his lethal embrace, rose to his feet slowly in a gradual uncoiling of rippling muscle and, stepping over Jake Poltrain's dead body, dropped gracefully onto his cushioned couch.

He lay against the heaped pillows until his dizziness passed, brushed the blood from his eyes with a portion of the drapery behind him and, clear-sighted now, thought briefly of walking to the mirror in order to assess the extent of his bleeding. On second thought he decided to see Empress smiling her welcome instead. Supported on one elbow, his breathing quiet once more, Trey slowly went through the procedure: the rolling of the sticky resin, careful placement into the small bowl, lighting, the first sweet inhalation from the long-stemmed pipe. He lay back on the silk cushions, let the drug work its magic, saw the familiar golden glow first, and then Empress was there, smiling at him. She was farther away this time, halfway up a snow-covered hill with crocus peeking through the frosty ice crystals, but she was smiling at him, calling his name. He reached for the pipe again to bring her closer.

Koo personally checked on all his important customers to see that they were satisfied, comfortable, adequately supplied with all their needs, and once the maimed body was carted away downstairs and order restored, he returned to his normal rounds. Appalled, he noted the unattended door as he neared Trey's room, viewed with alarm the half-open threshold, and began mentally packing in the event of catastrophe. His directives from Hazard were simple but clear: His son was to have anything he wished and *never* left unguarded.

How far did Hazard's vengeance reach? Koo reflected uneasily as he pushed the door open and eased into the room. At a glance it was apparent that Jake Poltrain was dead, and with trepidation he surveyed Trey's blood-smeared, reclining form. It took a moment to distinguish the slight rise and fall of his breathing in the dimly lit room, and with monumental relief Koo approached the couch. At least Trey was still alive. Quickly backing out of the room, he carefully shut the door and sent a servant running for a doctor.

An hour later, after Trey had been cleaned and bandaged and Koo had been reassured for the tenth time by the doctor that Trey's wound was a glancing trajectory, not in the least mortal, Koo had a message sent to Hazard . . . then personally guarded the room until he arrived.

*   *   *

Hazard, followed closely by Blue and Fox, came up the steps at a run. "How is he?" Hazard asked harshly, bracing himself for the worst after the garbled message he'd received from Koo's servant, which mentioned doctors, a gunfight, and Jake Poltrain.

"He's fine," Koo replied swiftly. "Just fine." His hasty reassurance was insurance against Hazard's savage scowl. "Jake Poltrain's in there dead, but no one's been in except the doctor and myself," he added quickly, after another look at Hazard's face. And Koo thanked his ancestors for guarding him from calamity. Hazard's fierce expression as he towered over him would have sent all the demons in hell running for safe haven.

Without a word, Hazard brushed by Koo and walked into the room, quietly closing the door behind him. He was wet from the rain outside, his tweed jacket smelling of Scottish moors, his hair sleek against his head, neck, and throat. Brushing it impatiently back, he narrowed his eyes in the gloom, his heart still pounding from the fear he'd lived with on the train ride in, the boiler plate red-hot by the time they'd reached Helena. Koo's words had stilled the terror—his son was not dead. And for that he said a silent prayer to Ah-badt-dadt-deah.

Trey's eyes came up at the slight sound of the door latch closing, and looking up at his father, he smiled. "Hello, Papa."

Hazard was momentarily shocked at Trey's appearance, but when he spoke, his voice revealed none of his anxiety. "How are you?" he said, ignoring the body in the middle of the floor, overwhelming relief that Trey lived quelling his initial shock at Trey's appearance. His son was noticeably thinner, the prominent bone structure of his face accenting the intensity of his eyes, brilliant in the glow of the brazier. But he lounged barefoot on the cushioned couch as though he hadn't recently defended his life, undisturbed by the dead man a yard away. "How are you?" Hazard repeated softly.

"I'm fine," Trey said, a faint smile lifting the corners of his mouth. "Would you like to try some of Koo's forgetfulness?"

Hazard didn't move, but he shook his head briefly in refusal, and his dark hair gleamed with the movement. "Your mother's waiting to see you. She's been worried." Hazard had been steadying Blaze's high-strung urge to interfere for days now. "She'd like you back home."

Rolling over with a languid grace, Trey reached for a paper lying beneath the lacquered couch. "I'm not beyond redemption, you know," he said, returning to his comfortable sprawl, his mouth quirked in a half-smile.

"I know," his father answered calmly, experienced and worldly. Opium dens of all descriptions from foul to fashionable catered to those interested in escape and pleasure. Hazard had been with the Prince of Wales's party last season in Paris when the night ended in a luxurious opium palace, a playful amusement for the wealthy all over the world. "Your mother's more anxious," he finished softly.

"Here," Trey said, holding out the page. "I'd given myself a week to indulge all the black demons." And to see Empress, he thought, in the opium dreams that made her so real, it seemed like he could feel the silk of her hair and the warmth of her skin. The sensations were a solace of sorts, juxtaposed and at war with the anger. "I was coming home tomorrow."

Taking the proffered page, Hazard glanced at the slashed lines across the squares and numbers before he dropped the sheet on a nearby table. "I think a day early would set your mother's mind at ease." There was authority beneath his quiet, deep voice, although his choice of words was diplomatic. "And," Hazard added, his dark eyes briefly flicking over Jake's body, "there's the immediate problem of . . . disposal."

"He drew on me first." The simple sentence was explanation and expiation.

"A mistake, apparently," Hazard said dryly.

"It does start the adrenaline pumping," Trey replied, and levering himself slowly into a sitting position, he flexed his long fingers. Looking up at his father, he said softly, "I didn't have any choice . . . he was out to kill me, plain and simple."

"I would have done the same, and probably with less provocation," Hazard answered, his dark eyes on his only child. Trey was alive, and for that he would have sold his soul and killed a dozen Jake Poltrains.

"I've never killed a man with my bare hands . . ." Trey's voice was almost a whisper now that it was over, now that the ferocious and jealous anger had passed.

Life was more ambiguous today, Hazard reflected philo-
sophically, hearing the hesitancy in Trey's voice, than when
he had been young. In those days, to exact vengeance when a
man like Jake Poltrain attacked was honorable. "Some men
live longer than they should," Hazard murmured softly, thinking the white man's laws sometimes allowed men to live who
didn't deserve it.

"He said things about Empress," Trey murmured, vi-
gnettes flashing vividly in his mind of Empress and Jake, and
he inhaled deeply to steady his nerves.

"You miss her." It wasn't a question.

Trey's mouth curved into a rueful smile. "More than I
expected. I've never *missed* a woman before."

Gazing at the ravages the week had produced, at the bandaged wound on one side of Trey's head, at the smeared blood
somehow forgotten on his bare feet, Hazard said very quietly,
"If you'd care for some fatherly advice . . ."

Trey shrugged, not insolently but with resignation. "Why
not? The last few days haven't exactly been a glowing success."

"You could go after her. I went after your mama."

"This isn't the same," Trey replied, shaking his head
briefly until the twinge of pain reminded him of the bandage.
"Mama left because she thought you were dead. That's un-
derstandable. Empress, on the other hand," he noted wryly,
"simply saw the Braddock-Black millions escape beyond her
reach. Hardly a love match, Papa."

"Valerie's a shrewd, vicious woman," Hazard reminded
him. "You've considered that, of course."

"Of course," Trey said tersely. "Along with a thousand
other possible explanations . . . none of which explains why
Empress didn't write. And she could have waited one day for
my return from the legislature. That wouldn't have been too
much to ask." He shrugged again. "She wanted the money.
What can I say? And Valerie made it clear she'd fight tooth
and nail to keep it. So Empress Jordan, consummate practical
woman, intent on restoring the family fortune, decided to
leave for greener pastures. Never underestimate," Trey said
with chill cynicism, "the nesting instincts of an empress." It
wasn't as though he were unfamiliar with women after his
money. Long ago he'd come to terms with the aphrodisiacal
power of a fortune in gold, only with Empress everything
had seemed different. Different from what? he thought grimly
in the next second. Hell, she needed money a lot more badly

than the wealthy young women he usually amused himself with. "Thanks, Papa," he acknowledged politely, yielding finally to the indisputable, "for the concern, but I've run this through my mind so many times." His sigh was visible in the drifting smoke from the brazier. "There's no other explanation for her silence."

Hazard's first impulse as a father was to say, "Do you want me to bring her back?" Abducting wives, after all, had always been an acceptable activity in the Absarokee culture. But he stifled the impulse as anachronistic, although as a man of action, the enterprise had decided merit. At least the question of her silence would be answered once and for all. Over the years, though, he reflected ruefully, he'd learned to make adjustments to "civilized" manners, and he supposed abduction might be frowned on as a form of courtship. And at base, he decided, he would be interfering beyond his fatherly prerogatives.

Moving forward, he stepped over Jake's body and, reaching his son, lay his hand on Trey's shoulder. "Come home," he said gently. "Your mother's waiting."

Trey was dressed in his buckskins and linen shirt when they emerged a few minutes later, and he courteously thanked Koo, who was waiting in the hall.

Hazard said, his eyes cool, his expression shuttered, "If you will be kind enough to see that everything is cleared up, I would be grateful."

Nodding deferentially, Koo understood that he could name his price and it wouldn't be questioned, but his silence would be expected. The soul of tact, he answered, "Consider it done, Mr. Black."

The following day, Trey left with his family for the summer encampment, and in the mountains surrounded by friends, urged and cajoled to join in the hunting, horse racing, all the conviviality of the summer, he was too busy to brood. After a week he fasted alone on Bear Mountain and asked the little people to help him forget and find comfort. By the third day, his visions were vivid, potent with imagery and symbolism; he saw the children riding on huge, red-tailed hawks that changed before his eyes into mountain ponies; Empress, dressed in her cowboy gear, was seated across the fire from him, but she wore sparkling diamonds in her ears, and when he reached over the flames to touch her, she disappeared, her image replaced by Valerie. The little people took his hand and soothed him when he screamed in rage, calmed his resent-ment, renewed his strength. In mystical guises they moved in and out of his dreams, reminding him of his heritage and faith, and with their slow dance of life he came to understand on Bear Mountain in the burning heat of day and the cold beauty of the starlit nights that the validity of a man came from within. And forgetting evolved slowly, the seasons of the heart an endless pattern like the seasons of the earth.

On the fifth day Trey came down from the mountain and into the bosom of his family, renewed, refreshed, attuned to his Absarokee heritage and, if not complacent about the ease of forgetting Empress, realistic about the remedy of time. He stayed that summer in the mountains, helping his two half-brothers manage their father's horse herds, which had been sent to the cooler pastures in the highlands. Stripped to his leggings, his long hair flying, he won all the races on Rally, as he did every summer, and there was pleasure in the victories. And while he spent more time with Rally than usual, his clan understood that he was heartsick over a woman and needed solitude.

By summer's end, there was no trace of his purgatory at Koo's; Trey was fit and deeply bronzed; ironically, he had never been in better physical form. To the outside world, young, handsome, wealthy, he had everything except the one thing he wanted most—the woman he'd asked to marry. And for reasons that eluded him still, she'd decided to leave him.

Eighteen

———————•———————

IN MID-SEPTEMBER Trey was precipitously called home when
Valerie delivered a daughter. The child was clearly a half-
blood, and at first sight Valerie refused to touch her, immediately called the ranch, and informed them she was having the
baby sent over. Several frantic phone calls located a wet
nurse, and by the time the unnamed child arrived, Blaze had
hastily outfitted the nursery.

The following day, when Trey rode in from the summer
camp and first looked at the tiny infant lying in the pink-
swathed cradle, he found himself instantly enchanted. Staring
up at him with enormous eyes, she gooed and gurgled wet
bubbles, and when she smiled a lopsided, erratic little smile,
Trey was struck by the potent magic in a baby's smiles.

"She's very bright," Blaze murmured proudly as she stood
beside Trey. "Most babies don't smile until much later."

"You sound like a doting Grandmama," Trey teased.

"She needs us," Blaze replied quietly, tacitly referring to
the Stewarts' abandonment.

"She's got me, I'll tell you. What a charmer." Trey
touched her tenderly on the top of her fuzzy head. "Does she
have a name?"

"Not yet . . . we thought we'd wait until you arrived."

"Didn't Valerie—"

Blaze shook her head.

"Fucking bitch," Trey murmured.

"There is a certain uncharitable quality to her personality," Blaze agreed sarcastically, and then swiftly smiled as the baby began smacking her rosebud lips like a tiny bird looking for food. "She's hungry again," his mother said. "Isn't that sweet?"

"Do you . . . I mean . . . how . . ." Trey faltered, baby care completely outside his realm of experience.

But in the ensuing days and weeks he spent hours each day in the nursery and learned to care for his infant foster-daughter.

She was named Belle because Hazard insisted.

"We're not agreeing only because you're an autocratic bully," Blaze had teased him when the name was first discussed.

"Of course we are, Mother," Trey had said with a smile. "You know how he sulks when he doesn't get his way."

"Very amusing," Hazard had replied in mock affront. "It's a perfect name."

"If you're a stage star," Blaze had said.

"Or a female rodeo rider," Trey added with a grin.

"You two can select a middle name," Hazard had said pleasantly, familiar with the teasing.

"Magnanimous," Trey said, his brows arched.

"One of your father's endearing traits."

But Hazard was indeed autocratic, and while his wife and son more than held their own as independent personalities, they didn't begrudge Hazard his preference. The name Belle was, in fact, dramatic yet fondly affectionate, and she was, in all their eyes, truly beautiful. So the unwanted child who had drastically affected Trey's life, Empress's future, and Valerie's bank account became the absolute center of attention at the ranch.

Hazard had a special fifty-piece baby-sized silver service engraved with her name and began training a sturdy little mountain pony for her first ride. Blaze completely redecorated the nursery and sent to Paris for a royal layette, while Trey found himself understanding the finer points of wheedling oatmeal gruel and stewed fruit into a baby's mouth.

And Belle Julia (Julia from Trey's favorite Herrick poem) thrived.

The eight months of his contracted conjugal duties were

over when Belle was one month old, and precisely on that day, Trey asked Valerie for a divorce.

He called on her late one afternoon, choosing the time after tea and before the evening's dinner engagement, when Valerie would most likely be home alone.

She was still in her tea gown, the pale rose chiffon edged with limpid yards of alençon lace, serving as a delicate foil to her dark good looks. She glanced up leisurely when Trey strode in, imperturbable in her usual fashion. "This must not be a social call," she murmured lazily, and tipped her head slightly to one side to gaze at him. Trey was dressed in dusty work clothes: leather jacket and vest over a sweat-drenched cotton shirt. His boots and trousers were covered with pale, gray grit.

"We're putting in a new crusher at the Tracyville Mine," he said, taking in her languorous pose on the damask settee. "Some people work for a living."

"And others don't," she replied with a luxurious smile.

"As usual, we're in agreement, I see," Trey retorted dryly. He was standing, restlessly, just slightly inside the drawing room, having no intention of staying any longer than necessary.

"You're always so bristly, Trey, darling. I know you can be altogether different . . . sit down and relax. We'll talk about old times," she murmured softly, and gracefully gestured to a nearby chair.

Her casual way of overlooking all the venal calamity she'd caused always grated on his nerves. "I want a divorce," he said bluntly, disinterested in any hypocritical socializing.

"No." Her voice was calm, her expression serene, and she reached for a glass of sherry, sparkling in the sunlight on a small marble table hideously shaped like a swan.

"No? Do you have a death wish?" he asked softly, thinking one powerful blow of that swan beak and his troubles would be over.

"I enjoy being Mrs. Braddock-Black." She took a sip of sherry and said with a composure he found irritating, "Would you like some? It's a very good Portuguese."

"I don't drink sherry, and if I *did* drink sherry, I wouldn't drink it with you," Trey replied in a voice taut with self-control. He hadn't expected this. "You signed an agreement." His words were arctic cold.

"I tore it up."

"Don't be simplistic," he snapped curtly. "We have a copy."

Her smile was classic innocence. "I'll argue that it's a forgery."

Good God, he thought with disgust. "You never give up, do you?"

Her smile changed, and her spleen showed for a moment. "But then . . . there's so much to give up, isn't there, darling?" she drawled. "So, no . . . I don't think I care to."

How satisfying it would be, he thought for a flashing moment, to wipe that smile from her face, and he felt his back stiffen under his sweaty shirt and leather jacket. "I always underestimate your avarice," he murmured, his silvery eyes glinting like ice.

"My advantage, then," she purred contentedly.

"This isn't a chess game, Valerie."

"But it is a game, isn't it, darling?" There was challenge in her throaty tone. Trey had always brought out the wildness in her, and his acute physical presence disturbed her in his alienation. He reminded her so often, and especially now, dust-grimed and leather-clad, of an animal—a great, dark predator. An exciting animal . . . no longer hers. And there was gratification in humbling him.

"If we're talking games, let's leave that to the lawyers," Trey said simply. "I'll check back with you when the preliminary rounds have been scored."

And he walked out.

Hazard spoke to Duncan Stewart the next day, reminding him that they had signed documents negotiated prior to the marriage.

Duncan was coy.

Irritating, Hazard thought, in a paunchy, middle-aged man. "I'm not going to take much of your time, Duncan," Hazard said. "Why don't you and your daughter decide what-all you need to, say, leave Montana. Run those numbers by our accountants and we'll get back to you."

The first rounds began.

Duncan and Valerie, greedily re-eyeing the Braddock-Black fortune, had decided they'd sold too cheaply the first time, and it never hurt to press a little. Hazard didn't want problems with Belle, so he accommodated the Stewarts . . . to a point.

*   *   *

"Kill them," Trey said one morning with disgust, and Hazard glanced up from the letter he'd been rereading; the letter suggesting Duncan be named legal guardian to Valerie's child. "Wishful thinking," Trey added with a sigh in response to his father's startled look. "It appears the negotiations may drag out for a time."

Leaning back in his leather chair, Hazard grimaced faintly. "I'm afraid so, but people like the Stewarts are for sale—it's only a matter of agreeing on price. I sympathize, though. I hate this haggling. How's Belle this morning?"

"Mother and I fought over who was going to feed her breakfast. I won," he said with a teasing grin. "Belle enjoyed her applesauce, resisted her oatmeal"—he sketched a brief arc over his stained shirt with his slender hand—"and liked my hot chocolate better than nursing. She's doing wonderfully." No matter his dark mood, Belle was sure to bring a smile to his face.

"I'm glad to hear that our Sarah Bernhardt is keeping you both entertained," Hazard replied, his own scowl replaced with a smile. "She's good for your mother . . . there hasn't been a baby around the house for a long time."

"I don't think we need the ballet slippers yet, though—or your mountain pony, for that matter," Trey noted mischievously, his silver eyes sparkling.

"Humor us," his father replied with a tranquil smile. "It's been so many years since we had a child this small to fuss over. When Daisy came to live with us after . . ." He paused, thinking of the two young daughters they'd lost and how you never really learned to live with the absence. His voice was softer when he continued. "She was almost grown-up."

Familiar with the desolation his father felt, his own childhood mourning never forgotten, the memory of seeing his father cry for the first time indelible in his mind, Trey's deep voice held a gentleness. "Mama's in complete charge and I only take orders," he said, "and I'm humoring her to the hilt, Papa, never fear. Although if it came to a knock-down drag-out fight," he added with a flashing grin, "I wouldn't bet on my chances of winning against Mama."

"Your Mama's willful spirit is one of her charming qualities," Hazard replied affectionately, "and I agree with you . . . she'd take on an army single-handedly."

"At least out of this turmoil and misery, having Belle has made it all worthwhile . . . not that I'd ever let Valerie know." Trey stretched, relaxing the tenseness in the back of his neck, his frustration easing as his thoughts centered on Belle. "Valerie doesn't realize she's added an entire new list of accomplishments to my repertoire," Trey said cheerfully, sliding comfortably low in the chair opposite his father. "Not only do I know how to change diapers and feed babies, but think of the expanded range of my polite conversation. Instead of simply saying, 'How are the children' and nodding at appropriate intervals, I'm now capable of comparing notes and offering advice." He grinned suddenly. "What do you think the Arabella McGinnises of the world would say to that?"

"What they say to every topic of conversation," Hazard said dryly. " 'How utterly fascinating. Do you like my new earrings?' "

"Or dress, or dressmaker, or hairdo . . . don't forget that . . . not that I ever really listened." He looked up at his father, seated behind his desk, from under the fringe of his lashes. "You and Mama really talk, don't you?"

"Always." Hazard's voice took on a gentleness. "She's my best friend."

"Unlike my wife," Trey returned sarcastically, "who understands friendship to mean a larger check and whose maternal feelings approach her father's concern for the reservation tribes. Remember, I want complete custody," he reminded his father, distaste prominent in his voice. "I don't care how much it costs."

"From the looks of it," Hazard said, his words collected rather than hostile, "they might take the whole of the Lost Creek Mine."

"A bullet would be cheaper," Trey said with a smile.

"It's a thought," his father replied, his dark eyebrows lifting.

As it turned out, someone with less scruples than they put an end to Duncan Stewart's ignominious life two weeks later. As an Indian contractor selling supplies to the agents for the reservations, he'd been accused along with his colleagues of vast, unscrupulous fraud, cheating white and Indian alike in reprehensible schemes. Fifty Indians had died of tainted food in July, and two hundred had starved to death the previous winter at the Black Earth Reserve for lack of adequate supplies, although government records indicated that the entire allotment of food had been paid for and delivered. It was common practice to charge the government full price for supplies and to deliver only a small portion of the goods to the Indians, leaving the major share to be resold for a tidy profit. Various reversals of policy had been attempted over the years to insure less corruption. Grant had sent out Quakers; other administrations had tried military authorities or missionaries of other denominations. While various agents and supply contractors had succeeded one another, regardless of the style of man, the enormous profits were too beguiling, too easy to attain, the punitive penalties too insignificant to overcome that common human failing when faced with the metaphorical unguarded room filled with gold.

When Duncan was found, he'd been scalped, his mouth stuffed with putrid meat. While on the surface his murder was made to appear as an Indian killing, both Hazard and Trey noted the ineptitude of the scalping and followed the investigation with more than casual interest. After a rudimentary inquiry the sheriff gave up the pretense of searching for the murderer, for life was still notoriously expendable on the frontier, and Duncan Stewart had made many enemies in his lifetime. Duncan was the kind of man who would cast away his cohorts to save his own skin, and with the new accusations extending beyond local jurisdiction this time, someone apparently was afraid they might be implicated if he talked.

From the varied list of Duncan Stewart's enemies, his killer must have been someone he trusted, the sheriff decided, since he'd been shot in the back of the head at close range. Out in the open country where the body had been discovered, no one could have approached undetected, and Duncan would never have allowed an Indian within rifle shot without leveling his gun at him. If nothing else, Duncan was a realist. The powder burns and shot from behind suggested a companion riding slightly to the rear.

On the pretext of extending condolences, Arabella McGinnis called on Valerie one afternoon shortly after the funeral. They had never been friends but rather rivals, both wealthy young women proud of their beauty and in contention for the same prized matrimonial candidate. Trey's renunciation of his marital duties only partially assuaged Arabella's covetous jeal-

ousy of Valerie's coup. To be Mrs. Trey Braddock-Black was
something Arabella would quite willingly kill for, and she
was over to apprise herself of what change, if any, Valerie's
father's death made in the status quo of Trey's marriage.

As Arabella advanced into the small back parlor that Valerie had with well-considered discourtesy chosen to receive
her in, she cooed, "What a charming room, Valerie. Your
stylish touch is so evident in the decor. Are those truly
blackamoor sculptures? How darling." She twirled theatrically in mock survey, the russet silk walking costume she
wore swishing softly over the carpet. "But are you alone,
dear, in your time of grief . . . without your husband by your
side. I should think you'd want Trey for comfort with your
dear father so recently departed." Her malice was palpable.

Valerie was not noticeably in mourning, nor grief-stricken,
nor was there any possibility that her husband would lend her
comfort—all circumstances both women fully understood. The
only unknown in the ensuing conversation was who would
draw blood first, and how savage the wound.

"At least I *have* a husband, darling," Valerie purred in
reply. "Have you brought any of your suitors to the mark
yet?"

"I'm much too young to think of marriage, Papa says,"
and Arabella tossed her golden curls in pert response. "Do
you find marriage satisfying?" she riposted cuttingly.

"I've discovered that marriage is delightfully"—Valerie
paused for effect—"lucrative. Would you like tea, or would
you prefer your usual bourbon," she inquired maliciously,
returning Arabella's thrust with smiling spite.

"Some of *Trey's* bourbon would be pleasant," Arabella
replied sweetly, when everyone in town knew Trey hadn't
spent more than twenty minutes with Valerie since the wedding.

"He drinks brandy."

"He always drank bourbon with me."

"Everyone drinks bourbon with you," Valerie declared,
ringing for a servant, "since that's all you have."

"Kentucky bourbon is *excellent*." Ross McGinnis was
proud of his Kentucky roots, and equally proud of his family's private-reserve bourbon.

"I'm sure I wouldn't know," Valerie countered disparagingly.
"Papa always imported his liquor." She then gestured to the
footman who had come into the room. "Bourbon for Miss
McGinnis and sherry for myself." And while the servant

poured their drinks, the two women sheathed their claws and spoke of trivialities concerning the weather, choir practice, the performance of *A Midsummer Night's Dream* put on by the Helena Thespians.

No sooner had the door shut on the footman's back then Arabella, casting a sneaking glance at the closed door, said, "What a fine-looking young man you've found to *wait* on you." The emphasis was unvarnished appraisal. "He doesn't look familiar. Is he new and imported as well?"

"He *is* new, but my butler does all the hiring," Valerie replied casually. "You'd have to ask him."

But Arabella had seen Valerie's glance slide slowly over the tall man's well-developed physique as he bowed and took his leave, although seated where she was she'd missed the more interesting response to Valerie's perusal. The handsome young auburn-haired footman who looked too tanned to have been a servant long had winked and smiled back. "What's his name?" Arabella's question was as casual as Valerie's bland disclaimer.

"Thomas."

"Does he have a last name?"

"I'm sure he must," Valerie said with a small shrug. "He answers to Tom as well," she added, her smile insinuating.

"He has beautiful large hands," Arabella murmured assessingly.

"Yes, doesn't he? I have to constantly remind him to be careful . . ." Valerie paused delicately. "With my china and crystal, I mean. Would you like me to call him back so you could—ah—have your drink refilled?"

"I'd like that," Arabella returned instantly, and decided in future to take an interest in her mother's selection of footmen.

When Thomas reentered the room, he performed his duties with a cheerful insolence; his smile bordered on impertinence, his bow was a touch elaborate, and when he said, "Ma'am," it was with an arrogance that was surprisingly charming.

"He *is* a bit cheeky," Arabella noted after he left.

"I prefer servants with a certain . . . vitality," Valerie purred, "and Tom is beautifully vital."

"How very convenient."

"Yes, isn't it?" Valerie said with an arch smile.

And Arabella received enough information from that arch smile to dine out on for a month.

Tom's entire name, by the way, was Thomas Kitredge Braddock; his tan had been acquired racing his yacht off

Nantucket, Australia, Macao, and Cowes, and Blaze Braddock-
Black had first met her unknown half-brother two weeks ago
when he'd been announced by Timms, walked up to her,
said, "Hi, Sis," and threw his large arms around her. Born
posthumously six months after Blaze's father's death, he'd
only recently learned that he had a half-sister. Billy Braddock's separate trust for his mistress had provided every
luxury for the son he never saw, and it wasn't until his
mother met him in San Francisco a month ago that she'd told
him the truth about his father.

"Call me Kit," he'd said, kissing Blaze warmly on the
cheek. "Everyone does." And he put his hand out to Hazard.
"I've never had a brother-in-law. I hope you don't mind."
And his smile, when he turned back to Blaze, brought tears to
her eyes; her father was smiling at her.

"You're my first as well," Hazard replied pleasantly.
"Welcome to the family."

And in the course of the hours-long get-acquainted conversation at the ranch that first evening, Kit had volunteered for
spy duty at Valerie's. "It'll be a lark," he'd said, this young
man out for adventure who had just returned from a leisurely
three years sailing around the world.

"The gambling and women in Macao," he told them,
"held my interest the longest." He'd stayed for six months.
"You never knew if you were going to leave the card game
alive with your winnings," he explained. "Keeps one keen,"
he added with a grin. "And pardon me, Sis," he apologized
"but that living on the edge"—his brows lifted swiftly—
"lends a certain piquancy to the later hours with the ladies."

"You needn't apologize to me," Blaze replied with a
smile, "after wondering all these years which irate father
would be putting a bullet into Trey. I'm afraid he subscribes
to your interest in reckless adventuring as well." Catching the
swift glance passing between Hazard and Trey, she sweetly
added, "Surely you two didn't think I believed all those
expurgated stories."

And Hazard and Trey both immediately wondered how
much she actually knew.

"So what's this wife of yours like?" Kit asked.

"If you like adventure . . ." Trey drawled.

"Sounds interesting. So all I have to do is keep an eye on
her until these negotiations are over."

"Don't feel you have to," Blaze interjected.

"Really, Kit," said Hazard from the depths of his favorite worn leather chair, the brandy glass he held catching the light. "Valerie will come up to the mark in a matter of time, anyway. You needn't involve yourself."

"Is she good-looking?"

Another glance passed between Hazard and Trey.

"Depends on your taste," Hazard replied neutrally.

"She's quite splendid," Blaze said. "You needn't be discreet for me, dear," she pointed out to Hazard. "I'm well aware of Valerie's type. I suppose she propositioned you," she finished briskly.

Hazard choked on his brandy.

"You see, Kit," Blaze said, "Valerie should be great fun."

Arabella's visit represented simply another small annoyance in dealing with her unconventional marriage to Trey, until Valerie found herself questioned about Thomas several times in the course of the following days, each inquiry accompanied by suggestive snickers. Her father's death had increased her incentive to finalize negotiations with the Braddock-Blacks, and now Arabella's vicious tongue-spreading innuendo hastened her inclination to settle.

She chastised herself briefly for not having more sense but almost instantly shrugged off her twinge of anxiety. Thomas certainly could be paid off to conveniently disappear should the need arise, and in the meantime—a small smile of satisfaction appeared—he certainly was a well-equipped young footman. Glancing at the clock, she decided it wouldn't hurt to be slightly late to Bruckhill's dinner that night, and she rang for Thomas.

An hour later her maid was dressing her hair, and she noticed her cheeks were still flushed a rosy hue from Thomas's sweet vitality. "No rouge tonight," she said briskly, "and if you pull my hair again, I'll have you dismissed without a character." While Valerie was a passionate woman, it never interfered with the practical side of her nature, and as she sat there watching the maid timidly comb each lock of hair into place, she decided she must be sensible about her future. With her father gone, her figure restored, her unwanted child disposed of, wider horizons beckoned. She began visualizing in minute detail her entrance into New York society. White egret feathers, she thought, would be striking in her dark hair, clasped with some of the Braddock-Black special sapphires. And then, of course, a gown in a matching shade of blue . . . blue always brought out the very best in her eyes. There was no rule against bringing a competent footman along, either.

Valerie insisted on negotiating directly with Trey—no lawyers, no intermediaries—wanting the sadistic pleasure of *seeing* him forced to accede to her demands. Curiously, what stung Valerie most was Trey's repudiation of his conjugal rights. Men had always been drawn to her beauty, and while Trey's refusal had initially challenged her, ultimately it had outraged her. The fault was his, of course, in the miscarriage of her plans, and the humiliations were to be paid for with a pound of flesh. The fact that Trey cared for her daughter didn't temper her vengeance. Without feeling or conscience, she'd dismissed the child from her life at the first sight of her dusky skin.

Trey had been raised in a functional ranch house, despite its large, sprawling size, with light, airy interiors decorated by Liberty of London with the occasional piece of his mother's favorite antique furniture added. Valerie's house always struck him as ostentatious . . . like its owner, he disgruntledly thought as he entered the sitting room.

Valerie was seated on a tufted and fringed brocade chair with her back to the lustrous daylight, muted by elaborate lace curtains. He had to walk around the clutter of heavy mahogany and overstuffed furniture scattered throughout the room, and skirt a ponderous claw-foot pedestal table with the requisite japonoise vase with peacock feathers. Tiger lilies arranged in a tall silver ewer near Valerie's chair were brilliant splashes of hot orange, reminding him of Valerie's predatory nature. Forewarned, he thought, although her pose today was of a demure ingenue in beribboned silk muslin.

She nodded, as did he, and he sat on one of her flamboyant chairs.

The negotiations began in an atmosphere of restrained coolness.

"The season in New York has only begun, so if we could come to some agreement today," Valerie said as though the entire insanity of events she'd initiated had never transpired, as though Trey weren't raising another man's child, as though he were concerned with her concerns, "I'll not miss too many of the festivities."

"Your daughter is healthy and well," Trey said mildly, dressed in unornamented buckskin today as if flaunting his Indian heritage in Valerie's overdecorated parlor.

"Children don't interest me."

"A pity you didn't think of that earlier," Trey retorted dryly.

"I'm sure the nursery at the ranch is capable of caring for a child."

"The nursery is not. Luckily my mother and the nannies are." He wouldn't give her the advantage of knowing how much Belle had come to mean to him. With Valerie it would be a further invitation to extortion, a pressure she could push to the limit. He was holding Kit in reserve against such an eventuality.

"If it makes you feel better," Valerie said, her tone implicitly denying her statement, "we can consider Belle my liability when we negotiate."

"Big of you, Valerie. Your generosity of spirit is touching." He lounged back in the overstuffed chair and stretched his legs out.

Her blue eyes narrowed at his insolence and his insouciant pose, as if these negotiations were of incidental interest to him, and her anger showed for the first time. "You should have acted the husband, Trey, darling."

"I'm not that good an actor, Valerie, darling," he replied with the same smooth malevolence that purred in her voice, only his eyebrows rising slightly in derision.

"Unfortunately," she said with spite and an instant resolve to go for the jugular, "that defect will cost you."

"Anything remotely having to do with you costs me." Trey smiled briefly. "I'm inured."

"Will you be racing after that woman you bought once you have your divorce?" she asked, feigned innocence concealing her resentment that Trey had apparently cared for the woman. He had eschewed female companionship since she'd gone, not only unusual but galling, for a woman like Valerie who had never had a refusal from a man. What did that little farmgirl have that she didn't have? Valerie had asked herself heatedly on more than one occasion. "There's talk she's unmanned you," Valerie murmured vindictively.

A muscle twitched along Trey's lean jaw, but his voice, when he responded, was impersonal. "You're not in the position to verify conjecture, I'd say, and I don't see it's anyone's business what I do after the divorce." His voice dropped to a murmur, and his pale eyes were implacable. "I might suggest, however, that after the divorce another part of the country might be healthier for you."

"Are you threatening me?"

"Would I threaten a woman? Notice," he added, lightly fingering the soft fringe on his sleeve, "I didn't say *lady*."

"Your reputation might not sustain two deaths in the Stewart family." There was no fear in her expression, only consideration. "And *you're* no gentleman."

"My reputation would be the least of your worries six feet under, Valerie." The hard line of his mouth was engraved with temper. "And I never said I was."

"Did you kill Daddy?" She asked it in a casual way, curious rather than distrait.

Seated opposite her, Trey gazed at Valerie for a moment to distinguish whether her expression was as bland as her tone. She could have been asking him if he found the temperature pleasant today, for all the feeling he saw on the porcelain perfection of her features. "I didn't have to," he replied. "Your father had 1,353 enemies ahead of me in line. He's been fucking over a lot of people for a lot of years. Now that we've completed the pleasantries," he said, suavely vitriolic, looking at her from under his dark lashes, "why don't you name your price and we can get this started."

A small shrug of muslin-ruffled shoulders, nothing more, and she replied, "I think we should begin by stipulating and defining the general principles of our situation. In matters of actual possession, like this house, in which the contract and deed are both in my name, title is clear."

"Valerie," Trey said, bemused, "we have twenty-four company lawyers. If I want to hear someone talk like a lawyer, all I have to do is go to the office . . . or listen to Daisy, my half-sister, at teatime. Let's get down to basics"—he quirked one dark eyebrow—"you know . . . money."

"I want a mansion on Park Avenue." Facile adaptation had always been her strongest suit.

"There you go. The Valerie we all know and love. I only hope," he went on with his familiar impertinence, "that these negotiations aren't going to require a working knowledge of blueprints and construction bids."

"I need a carriage and four with liveried grooms," she declared boldly, as rude as he was flippant. "A staff too."

"What style of furniture are we contemplating? Nothing too pricey, I hope," Trey said sarcastically, and then, sitting up suddenly in a single lithe movement, exclaimed exasperatedly, "Good God, Valerie, I don't care where you're going to live or how precious a life-style you envision. Quite frankly, at the moment, and if you're as clever as you seem, you'll take this as a warning, I don't care if you live at all. Name a goddamn price."

She gauged the threat deliberately, as she did everything, and decided to stand firm with the largest sum of money she'd ever contemplated. Offensive tactics were one of her specialties, and understanding those tactics, she'd begin with an unheard-of sum. Trey would counter with something ridiculously low. She'd come down marginally. He'd go up reluctantly, and eventually they'd settle somewhere in the middle. Taking a small breath, she named the sum.

Trey looked at her for a long, silent moment, his palms resting lightly on his knees, his expression unreadable. "That's a great deal of money," he said very quietly. "Am I supposed to beg?"

For a spinning moment her mind raced with the triumph of seeing just that—Trey on his knees before her. But practical motives immediately overcame unbusinesslike revenge, and instead she contemplated, How much should she come down? Should she remind him that she'd be gone from the city? Stand firm?

"Answer," he said, the words soft. "Do you want me to kiss your shoes for this divorce?" And Kit Braddock began moving center stage, out of the wings.

There was something deadly in the quiet menace of his voice, and Valerie looked at him, really looked at him for the first time since the bargaining had begun. "No," she said sensibly after seeing the expression on his face.

"That," he murmured, "was the right answer." And taking out a blank bank draft from his shirt pocket, he said, "You've got it, Valerie, but if you ever approach *anyone* in my family, I'll kill you. I mean it. In fact, I have a very strong desire to do exactly that right now. Think of the money I'd save." His pale eyes were so deadly cold, a frisson of fear briefly overset her previous triumph.

Without waiting for her reply, he finished the scrawl of numbers and words and slid the paper across the table toward her. Rising, he stood, the width of his shoulders under the smooth leather, startling from Valerie's vantage point. "I would have gone much higher," he said, a small smile creasing his handsome face. The money was secondary to him; he wanted her out of his life, without litigation and public squabbling. "*Bon voyage,* Valerie."

She had snatched up the check, and her thoughts were plain on her face.

"If you tear that up, you won't get another." In his voice sounded the absolutism of sixteen generations of chiefs; he had reached that point.

Valerie knew unconditional certainty when she heard it. Folding the check, she tucked it in her bodice. "I hope you never find her," she spat, striking back in her chafing resentment at being bested.

"And I hope New York has the good sense to pull up the drawbridge when they see you coming, honey."

He walked to the door feeling like a free man for the first time in months. "By the way," he said, turning back with a vivid smile on his face, " 'Tom' said you're the most accommodating woman he's ever known. I told him you would be."

Trey and Kit sat over brandy that night long after everyone had gone to bed, drinking toasts to Trey's emancipation. The divorce, Hazard had told them, would be expedited by friendly hands and processed within two weeks.

"To liberty and the pursuit of happiness," Kit declared convivially.

"To divorce," Trey murmured gently, "and wide open spaces." He had never had limits before Valerie, and silently he vowed that never again would he.

"There's wide open spaces in Macao . . . everything's wide open there. Twenty-four hours a day. You'd like it . . . for unchecked pleasure, and after Macao, I'll take you crocodile hunting in New Guinea."

"Is it as dangerous as bedding Valerie?" Trey drawled sardonically.

"Actually, no." Kit grinned. "You're allowed a gun while croc hunting. With Valerie you're in the arena bare-assed and"—his eyebrows rose—"she likes to give orders in bed."

"She tries," Trey said mildly.

"To amenable women, then," Kit toasted blithely.

"To divorce."

"Do I detect a slight bias tonight?" Kit inquired insouciantly, his green eyes sparkling.

"Like walking out of prison permanently affects your good humor."

But as the evening progressed, Trey's melancholy increased instead of diminishing.

"Shouldn't be brooding," Kit admonished, his smile kindly, "not tonight of all nights."

Trey shook himself out of the gloom pervading his mind. If Empress had been waiting for him, tonight would have been a joyous occasion. "Everything's anticlimactic," he replied so softly that Kit had to strain to hear him. "Have you noticed that anticipation often surpasses acquisition?" He shrugged, lifted his glass, and drained it.

"Hasn't a woman ever walked out on you before?" Although the question was blunt, Kit's voice was neutral, his lounging pose placid.

Trey's eyes drifted over Kit's sprawled form in the chair opposite him, and he thought a moment before answering. "No," he said, filling his glass again. "Have they you?"

"No."

Trey laughed. "You see, then." Sliding lower in his chair, he leaned his head back. "It's not the walking out," he said by way of explanation, "I'm not that egotistical. It's the woman who's plaguing me."

"Why?" Curiosity and sympathy blended in Kit's inquiry.

"If I knew I could put it to rest. She was . . ." Trey sighed softly. ". . . everything—hot and cold, soft and steel-sharp and so damned alive . . ." His voice trailed off, and his teeth flashed briefly in a grimace. "An adventuress to put even Valerie to shame."

"Valerie does have a certain talent," Kit acknowledged tranquilly, "you have to admit, but you haven't seen Macao yet. The women there are"—he grinned—"imaginative, even inspirational at times. You should come there with me. My yacht's in San Francisco. What better way to forget . . . what's her name?"

"Empress."

Kit's eyebrows rose. "Modest name."

"It fits her," Trey said. "The bitch."

Nineteen

———————————————

EMPRESS SPENT THE fall in Paris modestly secluded, at home to only her closest friends as she awaited the birth of her child. As her time drew near, her thoughts turned increasingly to Trey, natural, perhaps, for every mother, she told herself, to be emotionally susceptible to the father of one's child. She had struggled to obliterate images of a tall, dark-haired half-blood all summer, had purposefully partaken of society's frivolity, had smiled until her face hurt, determinedly attended luncheons and shopping, dinners and dances where men paid her enormous attention. Time and activity would gradually diminish her fierce longing, she reflected, distract her from the potent memories, divert her with new festivities, make Trey nothing more than a dim remembrance.

Wretched inequity—the maxim, time heals all, for despite the passing months, Trey was like a brooding treasure in her mind, stored away and precious, her first lesson in the power of love. However unforgettable the man, though, Empress was adamant that he shouldn't know of the baby she carried. He hadn't come. If he loved her, he would have, but he hadn't and she knew why. Restless, dissolute, and spoiled, he'd found someone else. Valerie's stately image rose in her mind, superimposed on an endless line of other females, all complaisant and adoring. He didn't deserve to know of his child, she fumed in a fit of pique, and then a worse thought, black and bitter, slid past the anger and wounded her: He wouldn't care, she had to admit, if he knew.

Sitting in the familiar rose garden of the Hotel Jordan under a warm autumn sun, just as she had so many times in the past, the scent of late roses sweet on the air, Empress wondered for a brief moment whether all the years of expatriation and adversity and the troubled memories of Trey were all some dream. Here on the carved stone bench crafted when the Sun King was expanding France's borders and the Comtes de Jordan had already served seven previous kings, it seemed as though she'd never left this secluded, walled garden with its playing fountain and carefully raked paths. As if Mama and Papa were only behind the drawing-room windows, and she had no cares beyond deciding on the most perfect shade of ribbon for her bonnet. Had everything been a quantum leap into an unreal fantasy and she'd wake to find herself fifteen again?

But in the next pulse of her heart the baby kicked and reality came surging back. She was no longer that young, naïve girl; she was no longer remotely like the young girl waiting for Mama and Papa to walk through the French doors. Responsibility for her family had abruptly curtailed her childhood, and Trey Braddock-Black had seen to her introduction into full-fledged womanhood. She should hate him, and she did, for not chasing after her like a heartsick lover, but she loved him, too, the love and hate coexisting, entwined like a convoluted, serpentine pattern with neither beginning nor end. And in all the months since her departure from Montana, she'd not been able to grasp the essential thread that would unravel the whole and bring her peace.

He hadn't cared enough to come for her, she thought with a small sigh that drifted away on the warm autumn air, and while she understood that it was naïve to think she was any different from the other women in his life, she had still hoped. Hoped he would find he couldn't live without her. The poetic phrase sounded ridiculous in the next instant, as if Trey Braddock-Black's life could come to a standstill because of her. "Couldn't live without her" should be rose-garlanded and cupid-borne, a conceit as unreal as the cow jumping over the moon . . . frail magic against reality.

What was he doing now? she wondered, since apparently

he was living without her very well. Was he filling the rooms of his newest lover, or perhaps his wife, with her favorite flowers, or buying her beautiful clothes? What kind of fur would he choose for his newest infatuation?

And while Empress's melancholic reverie took command of her mind . . .

Trey, in contrast to her speculation, was alone, lying in the golden autumn grasses of a clearing with only Rally for company. And while his paint cropped on grass, looking up occasionally as though she were listening, Trey talked to her about Empress. Leaning on one elbow, his torso bare, his moccasins kicked off, he lounged lean and bronzed under the unseasonably warm sun. "She would have liked it here," he said, gazing over the small meadow bordering a bubbling stream. "It's like the homestead on Winter Mountain." But then he remembered that Guy was a count now and the rough cabin on Winter Mountain was something to forget . . . along with everything else in Montana. "And then again, Rally," he said very softly, "I don't think Empress Jordan would appreciate the simplicity. She's after greener pastures and bigger game in the peerage, and all the glistening baubles."

Empress's preoccupation with her memories was punctuated suddenly by Eduard's piercing cry, and abruptly she looked up in alarm, but her face was wreathed in smiles as he ran toward her. She smiled back at her young brother, struggling up the terraced incline on chubby toddler legs, happy that he was happy. She hadn't been the only one missing Trey: Eduard still slept with the snowshoes he'd insisted on bringing from Montana.

A sudden excessive longing washed over her, and she sighed into the sunny sky, "Why didn't you come for us, Trey?" She desperately missed him today, missed his embrace, his warmth, the beauty of his smile, his hot-blooded wanting of her.

"Tiger Tom Cat's got kittens!" Eduard squealed, his short legs laboring as he negotiated the last several yards. "Me want one! Me, me *want* one!"

Apparently Tiger Tom Cat was misnamed, Empress thought whimsically as Eduard reached her and his dimpled hand tugged on hers.

"Come see!" he shouted, excitement dancing in his eyes.

And Trey's shining memory was displaced by sticky hands and high-pitched demands.

A month later, long after midnight, the prestigious doctor who attended all the royal accouchements shook his head sadly and said to Adelaide, "There's nothing more I can do." The large room was oppressive with heat and the odor of birthing, and in the predawn hours a gloom had settled over the interior as if the shadows had crept in from the dark corners and shrouded all in depression.

Empress had been in labor for a day and a half, thirty-six hours of dizzying white pain and mounting pressure, of screaming agony. The baby was in a breech position, and the doctor had done nothing but say, "Nature will take its course," until moments ago Empress's pulse had dropped dangerously low, and her screaming, which had subsided in the last few hours into whimpers, stopped.

"Incompetent!" Adelaide hissed angrily. "Imbecile! I'll see you ruined, you bungler," she swore at his retreating back and chastised herself for waiting so long to dismiss him. Although he'd been in attendance at both her deliveries, since hers had been uneventful, the extent of his inadequacies were only now apparent. Terrified, she sent for Beatrix, screaming at the servants she sent dashing off to collect her old nurse. Beatrix had been more of a mother to her than her own mother, and in times of peril or desolation she always called on her.

A scant twenty minutes later, her old nurse was shown upstairs and Adelaide burst into tears. "I should have called you sooner," she sobbed as she fell into the open arms of the old woman who had raised her.

Beatrix patted her back in brief consolation, and then, in the quiet voice that had calmed all her childhood fears, said, "Hush, hush, *mon bébé*, I'm here now and you must be strong." Releasing her grown-up baby, she murmured, "Come now," touching the tip of Adelaide's nose like she always had to cajole compliance, "wash your hands and help me." Without waiting for an answer, Beatrix went to the porcelain sink in the corner of the room and began scrubbing her hands. "We don't need a fancy doctor to bring this baby into the world. My Mama and Grandmère were birthing babies long before the fancy doctors were born."

"Thank God," Adelaide said with a heartfelt sigh, her burden of guilt lifting, feeling more confident by the moment.

"Don't thank God," her old peasant nurse said with iconoclastic pragmatism, wiping her hands briskly. "I'll be more help, but if you want to pray, pray that this young lady's uterus doesn't tear. We're going to turn this baby around."

It was a grim, taut, wrenchingly slow process as Beatrix massaged the baby slowly clockwise and Adelaide nervously followed orders to hold or press or push when the old woman murmured her instructions. "No! No!" she shouted once when Adelaide's pressure eased slightly and the baby slipped back. Adelaide broke into tears as their slow progress instantly reversed, and her shoulders sagged in defeat.

"Wipe your eyes, child, and we'll begin again," Beatrix said calmly, although she'd begun to fear for Empress's stamina. Her pulse was erratic, faint, the contractions slowing; even if they were able to turn the baby, she might not have the strength needed to complete the delivery. "Now this time," Beatrix cautioned, "hold *firmly*."

They were both drenched in sweat an hour later when, millimeter by reluctant millimeter, the small infant was persuaded to attempt the birth canal in more acceptable fashion. Thankfully Empress had remained unconscious through the laborious maneuver, but as the contractions forced the baby downward, her eyes opened in a restless flutter, as though she knew there weren't much time left. Though only half conscious, existing in a curious state between lethargy and agony, a dreadful alarm forced its way through the exhaustion and pain, and a harsh, angry face, beautiful even in its wrath, materialized like a vision of a vengeful god. "Trey!" she cried, half rising as though she'd seen a ghost. "Don't tell Trey," she whispered, sinking back and shutting her eyes against the frightening specter.

She wasn't lucid, Adelaide decided as she comforted her, stroking her shoulder gently. "Trey was her husband's pet name," Adelaide murmured as Beatrix looked up quickly from the imminent birth. "He died in America six months ago."

"Poor child," Beatrix muttered softly, supporting a small, dark head as Empress's child entered the world. "We'll have to make certain your Mama lives," she crooned quietly, easing the small body outward with exquisite care, "so you won't be an orphan."

The baby boy was swarthy-skinned, strong and healthy, with fluffy dark hair when it was rubbed dry, and enormous eyes, jewellike and shimmering, which laid claim to a heritage on the northern plains.

"His father was an American," Beatrix said, gazing down at the child she held in her arms. "Of the early variety, I'd say."

Adelaide looked at the sturdy infant and saw no resemblance at all to his blond, diminutive mother. "She said he was handsome and had jet-black hair."

"Did she say he was a red Indian?"

"No," Adelaide replied softly.

"Well, he was," Beatrix said plainly, without censure, "and he would have enjoyed his strong, healthy son." Turning back to Empress, as pale and motionless as death, Beatrix handed the baby over to Adelaide and withdrew a small bottle from her willow basket, which had been carried in from the carriage. With enormous patience she forced a black liquid down Empress's throat a spoonful at a time until she was content enough had been swallowed to serve the purpose. "Now she won't hemorrhage," Beatrix said with satisfaction, "and baby won't look out on the world as an orphan."

When Empress woke several minutes later, Beatrix had already bathed the baby and wrapped him in a snow-white blanket. "I want to hold him," Empress said, even before she was fully awake.

"How do you know it's a him?" Adelaide teased, her smile wide with accomplishment. She had actually helped deliver a baby and was exhilarated at her achievement.

What a silly question, Empress thought with an indistinct obscurity that resisted complete and rational thought. "I want to hold him," she repeated insistently, although her voice was no more than a hushed whisper.

Bringing her new son over, Beatrix laid him beside her.

Empress struggled up on one elbow to look at him, and tears spilled down her cheeks. Her tiny child was looking at her with Trey's eyes. How could they, she thought with wonder, be so perfectly duplicated? She lightly touched the soft, dark velvet of one downy eyebrow. "I love you," she whispered, and gathered him into her arms.

*   *   *

Amid heavily contested campaigns for a new constitution and slate of state officers, Montana had entered the Union in November. The usual accusations of graft and corruption ensued, and on the basis of disputed returns, both parties claimed seats, met in separate halls, and selected their favorites for U.S. Senate. The issue was ultimately decided by the Senate Committee on Privileges and Elections in December, which recommended the seating of Republicans Sanders and Power, rather than the Democratic claimants, Clark and Maginnis. From the purchase and manipulation of votes at a state level, the contested election had proceeded to the national arena of manipulative power, and with the current administration being Republican, there was harmonious agreement on seating the Republican candidates. And so went the will of the people in a state that was predominantly Democratic.

One cold morning in December, Trey walked into the breakfast room carrying Belle.

"Where do you think you're going?" Blaze said with that maternal emphasis that suggested he reconsider his plans.

Cheerfully oblivious to suggestions maternal or otherwise, Trey replied amiably, "What does it look like, Mama . . . for our usual morning ride?" He was dressed in buckskin with a Hudson Bay capote and fur-lined moccasins against the winter weather. Belle was wrapped in a fur bunting.

"Do you realize how cold it is?" Blaze looked to Hazard for support, but he only smiled and said, "Wind's from the northwest."

"Lot of help you are," Blaze murmured.

"Mother, Belle loves the rides, and nothing shows, anyway, but her eyes. See?" And he dutifully displayed her, plumply content in her bunting. "Now pour me some hot chocolate and I'll drink it on the way out to the stables."

"You're insensitive," Blaze grumbled, pouring his chocolate. "What if she freezes?"

"She's wrapped in more fur than a polar bear, and I'm not insensitive, she told me she wanted to go for a ride," he finished with a grin, and picking up the cup, he started for the door.

"Have you decided if you're coming to Washington with us?" Hazard asked, setting his coffee cup down. "Lowell asked me the other day, and I said I didn't know." With Montana a state now, its delegates could vote, and everyone with any interests to pursue would be in Washington for the congressional session.

Trey turned back. "I might. When are you going?"

"After Christmas. It looks as though the suits against the Montana Improvement Association are going to be dropped, so there's no rush to get there in time for the litigation that was expected. Sanders apparently convinced the Secretary of the Interior to intervene."

"Business as usual. That must have cost a pretty penny." Trey exhaled softly, the dark shadows of discontent having plagued him since Empress left, reinforced by yet another blatant pillage of Montana resources. The Montana Improvement Association was stripping much of the public domain of its lumber—illegally. "I don't know if I'm up to the machinations of Washington," he said with a faint grimace. "And if I don't go?"

"You'll miss Belle," Blaze said with a smile.

"In that case, I'll be joining you in Washington," Trey replied, his grin crinkling his eyes.

"You always were a reasonable boy," his mother said sweetly.

"Belle's good for him," Hazard said after Trey had left. "She takes his mind off Empress."

"I know, but I wish he'd play with her in the nursery today. It's so cold, and Belle's only three months old."

"When Trey was three months old," Hazard reminded her softly, "we were camping out at the mine." He smiled. "And Trey survived."

Blaze ruefully smiled back. "You're right, of course. . . . I worry too much."

"Your problem is you dote on that boy, and on Belle too." There was fondness in his voice, not faultfinding, and an indulgent tolerance in the dark beauty of his eyes.

"Well, you do, too, Jon," she returned promptly. "The only difference is that you don't talk about it as much." Blaze knew Hazard would go through hell for his son, had seen that Trey lacked for nothing, and adored him with a generosity of spirit untainted by censure.

"He turned out well," Hazard said, pride in his voice, "thanks to your mothering."

"And thanks to you, all the men at the mines and the ranch like him. Not to mention the admiration of the clan."

"He knows as much about the mines and the ranch as I do. The men respect that." Hazard grinned. "And as far as his *kon-ning* as a chief and a chief's son, as long as he wins all the races and brings in horses on the raids, his reputation as 'a man that knows and can,' his consequence is assured with the clan."

"Jon," Blaze chided softly, "you promised me the raids were over. You know how the authorities feel."

"They're just little raids, sweetheart," he soothed, but his voice was laced with playfulness, for the raids were the last unmitigated wild freedom left, like amusing games to a child. "You can't expect us to change overnight. Raiding's in the blood. Do you remember," he said, the timbre of his voice gentling, "that first palomino I brought back for you?"

As if it were yesterday, she saw Hazard standing in the dawn mist and golden sunrise. "I remember the flowers around your neck," she replied softly.

"You filled my heart that morning, *bia cara*, and I wanted to steal every horse on the plains for you." Their eyes met, and the special magic that existed for them alone shone, vital and enduring.

"It seems like yesterday, Jon."

"It does, doesn't it . . . as though the children and the years somehow flashed by and we didn't notice."

"They've been good years, haven't they," Blaze murmured, "in spite of—" She swallowed to press back the tears as memories of the children's deaths engulfed her.

Hazard was out of his chair before her first tear spilled, sweeping her up into his arms. "Don't cry, *bia cara*," he whispered into her hair, cradling her against his chest, his own eyes shiny with emotion. "We had them with us for a long time. Think of the happiness we shared . . . and all the good memories." Walking to the window, he stood holding her in his arms, gazing out on their land, stretching for miles beyond the mountains. The radiant winter sun set fire to the flame of Blaze's hair, illuminated the splendid planes of Hazard's face, glistened off the tears caught in Blaze's lashes, and brightened the glittering gold thread of her brocade wrap.

"Despite the sorrows, they've been wonderful years," Hazard murmured, his dark eyes turning back to his wife. "You're my best friend, you know," he said very low, "my very best friend. And also," he whispered, lightly brushing her cheek with his lips, "my passion." The cadence of his voice changed, less grave and vivid with amusement. "You're my favorite chess partner," he added with a smile, "and my most diplomatic critic. When you walk down the stairs in a ball gown and diamonds, my stomach still tumbles over at the sight of your beauty. But," he said, love in his voice and eyes, "I love you best as you look right now in morning sunlight. You've always been my sun, my moon and stars . . ."

Lifting her head from his shoulder, Blaze kissed Hazard in the gentle curve where his strong jaw met his ear. "In all the wide world, I found you." Adoration shone in the shimmering wetness of her eyes. "We were *so* lucky," she breathed softly, her small, pale hand lying against his bronzed throat.

He kissed her gently and then smiled that quick, dazzling smile she never tired of. "We *are* lucky," he said.

Kit returned to his mother for Christmas; the Braddock-Blacks spent Christmas at the ranch and, shortly after the New Year, set out for Washington. They had been in residence three weeks when a second letter from Guy arrived, forwarded from the ranch. The news was commonplace enough, although slightly out-of-date: Guy mentioned the rain, how Eduard had grown, the state of his dressage lessons, what the girls had been doing, how they all missed Trey. At the end of this mundane recital of events, Trey's breathing suddenly stopped. Guy's last sentence read: "Pressy's feeling fine now. She almost died last month."

When he remembered to breathe again, an intense, flaring anxiety, as boundless and voracious as desire, revolutionized his previous determined unconcern. She shouldn't have been ill or near death without his knowledge. It mattered to him that he knew she was *alive* somewhere in the world; it mattered fiercely, he decided in the next split second. If she had died, he would have had to face the awful finality: He could never see her again, ever. She wouldn't ever be coming back; she wouldn't be laughing somewhere else in the world, or just around the next corner, or walking in the rain although the rain was thousands of miles away. For the first time in months he cast aside prudence, intemperately refused to weigh the rational motives and explanations. *She had almost died,* ran like a pealing frenzy through his mind. Impetuously he rose, in a sudden, forceful movement that sent his chair crashing backward. He was going to France! The fearful bells stopped pealing, and a potent elation raced through his senses.

Whether Empress cared to see him or not, he wanted to see her. He wanted to see whether she looked different in cosmopolitan Paris, if her green eyes were still frank and sparkling with golden light when she smiled. He wanted to try to understand, possibly read the truth in her eyes. Perhaps it wasn't wise to go, but there was pleasure in his repudiation of prudent sagacity. And if nothing else, a trip would allay the boredom.

His explanation to his parents was brief, hasty, and irrepressibly buoyant. "I told Belle first," he said, striding into the study where Blaze and Hazard sat opposite each other at a partner's desk. "I won't be gone long, I explained, although I don't suppose she understands at all. I wonder if I should take her with me," he went on, dropping into an armchair near his mother. "With your notions of territorial rights, Mama, taking her would involve a bloody battle," he said with a grin, "so since I'm a dutiful son"—at which point both parents looked at him in mild disbelief—"I'll defer to your wishes."

Blaze and Hazard glanced at each other, and Hazard shrugged his incomprehension.

"Sweetheart," Blaze said, "this is all slightly ambiguous. Where are you going?"

"Empress almost died," Trey replied with what his parents considered undue cheer and even less insight.

"How did you discover that?" Hazard inquired, aware of the striking animation in his son.

"Guy wrote and mentioned it along with all the other news. I don't know the particulars, but I decided to go to Paris. I could see Erik again, and the Duchesse de Soissons has sent at least a dozen invitations in the last six months."

"How is Estée?" Blaze inquired, acquainted with the *duchesse*'s partiality for her son.

Trey shrugged negligently. "Fine, I suppose. You know Estée . . . elegant, keeping open house, impassioned as usual. Her newest infatuation is Expressionism. Impressionism, I'm told in endless detail in her letters, is passé. Maybe I'll have her take me around to the studios and I'll buy some of the new works."

"When are you leaving?" Hazard asked with the mildness he'd learned to cultivate with Trey's enthusiasm.

"In an hour," Trey said, rising swiftly. "I'll send you a cable from Paris. Remind Belle I won't desert her for long. Ciao."

He was halfway to the door before Blaze could inquire, "Do you need anything, dear?"

"Need anything?" Trey repeated abstractly as he whirled around. The prospect of seeing Empress again superseded mundane requirements. "No, no thank you, Mama, I've everything." His smile was brilliant.

When the door closed behind him a moment later, Hazard gruffly said, "It's about time."

"Meaning?" Blaze inquired with a smile.

"It's about time the stubborn fool went after her. I damn near went and fetched her myself to stop his infernal moping."

"He's as mulish as you, dear."

"He's more mulish than I," Hazard replied with a teasing grin. "He's as obstinate as you."

Blaze didn't argue, well aware of her headstrong temperament. "But a darling nonetheless," she noted with unconditional maternal affection.

Hazard laughed. "Of course, *bia cara,* he's perfect like his mother."

The trip took him six days of surging impatience, six days of logical thinking and unreasoning emotion. Trey warned himself to expect nothing and to avoid disappointment, cautioned himself about arriving uninvited at Empress's home. Since she hadn't written, he reminded himself numerous times that her feelings obviously had altered. He simply wanted to see that she was well, an altruistic, benevolent impulse, he reflected rationally.

And he doggedly repressed the swelling, sublime anticipation.

Twenty

OVER TWO MONTHS had passed since Max had been born, months in which Empress had devoted herself to her new son. She'd started writing to Trey a dozen times in the course of those months to tell him he had a son, Maximilian Laurent Saint-Just de Jordan, and the resemblance was so pure, even Trey wouldn't be able to deny him. Max had Trey's pale eyes and silky black hair, and when he smiled for the first time, poignant memories came flooding back with the force of a tidal wave. He had his father's way of smiling slowly, and then suddenly the full warmth would appear, like the sun in the morning.

But she always tore up the intended letters, for the words never seemed appropriate. She attempted amiable words—cool, objective words—and even tried writing in the third person. She considered a simple announcement. She wanted to tell him about his son and the joy she felt at having their child. Somehow, in each attempt, the phrasing always appeared awkward, like a petition, and she would recall all too vividly his resentment at Valerie's pregnancy and the number of females with gun-toting papas he'd evaded.

Could he have been wronged in that many instances, or was it just easier for a man to walk away from his indiscretions? It seemed too easy for him to say, "They weren't mine," as if saying the words set his conscience free and his life went on undisturbed. So she never sent the letters because she refused to ask him to love his son only as an obligation.

Recently Empress had begun to receive visitors again, a pragmatic decision based less on desire than on Adelaide's persistent persuasion. In the early months after her return to Paris, Adelaide had seen that Empress was deluged with invitations, and although a widow in mourning, her devoted admirers were numerous and solicitous.

The men, quite frankly, were dazzled by the beautiful woman they'd last remembered as a thin, lanky adolescent. Empress was voluptuous now, rather than coltish, and endowed with a rare, precious fairness that recalled Botticelli's finest work. Her sun-streaked hair was defiantly riotous even when she attempted to restrain her curls in a severe style commensurate with widowhood. And had she known how tantalizing she looked in black, all golden skin tones and pale tawny hair, she would have better understood the reasons for the besieging array of suitors.

Her green eyes, shaded by luxurious dark lashes, were languorous when they lifted to gaze at one, and she was immediately, although discreetly, dubbed the Green Temptress by the gallants surrounding her.

More than anything, her casual indifference was viewed as provocation, and her startled wonder, which so many of their fulsome compliments engendered, was translated into piqued fascination. Whatever the individual interpretation accorded her sentiments, there was no argument about the Green Temptress's physical beauty. She was an opulent woman, a lush, golden-toned sultana, all the more desired for her enigmatic wish for seclusion. Everyone understood her recent widowhood, but each young Turk hoped he would be the one she ultimately chose to end that seclusion.

And the offers of exactly *how* to end that seclusion ran the gamut from indiscreet to honorable. As the former Comtesse de Jordan, regardless of her marriage to an American, Empress was the recipient of many sincere and respectable offers of marriage. She was also, in the wealthy, aristocratic circle in which she moved, the recipient of several interesting, less permanent offers.

To all she extended the same polite response: after a year of mourning she would consider their offers seriously. Bets

were taken on the front runners in the contest for the Green
Temptress's favors, and the Duc de Vec and Prince Hippolyte
de Morne took those honors.

The Duc de Vec's offer, everyone understood, was limited
by his marital state, but to date this had not unduly hampered
his reputation as the foremost womanizer in Paris. Wealth,
looks, and a frankly sensual charm had all combined to
endow the Duc de Vec with advantage in his female relationships.

Prince Hippolyte, much younger and perhaps more vulnerable to romance, fell under Empress's spell to the extent that
he began composing sonnets and considered heeding for the
first time his mother's incessant demands that he take a wife.

So the wooing had gone on until Empress had retired to
await the birth of her child, and now that she was returned to
society—more beautiful, if possible—her drawing room was
thick with dashing men, each intent on pressing his suit.
Although the months had advanced, a year was by no means
past, but hope, as they say, sprang eternal, and each man
entertained the fond ambition that Empress would succumb to
his wooing and overlook her remaining interval of mourning.

Into this highly charged atmosphere of competition, albeit
gentlemanly in demeanor, Trey was to appear precisely two
hours after arriving in Paris.

During the six-day journey, Trey's mood had fluctuated
violently from happiness to moody resentment. When he'd
reread Guy's letter, which he did so often that he knew the
words by heart, he'd only think of his joy in seeing Empress
alive. Conversely—and these feelings surfaced generally
after several brandies—his bitterness would jostle aside the
clear-cut happiness. Empress said she'd write to him, dammit, he'd acerbically reflect, but she hadn't. Was she only
mercenary at heart, personally ambitious, easily convinced by
Valerie that he was unavailable as a husband? Was that why
she left? In retrospect, the brandy coloring his speculation,
Empress's indomitable spirit took on an enterprising character: her decision to come into Helena to sell herself was
certainly a practical undertaking; her offer to save his life may
have been prompted by the fear that his bank draft wouldn't
have been honored had he died; even her encounter with
Valerie had left Empress unscathed by Valerie's claws. She
had been angry rather than tearful.

And in Trey's gloomiest contemplation, Empress seemed

far and away the most pragmatic woman he'd ever known. Even in the expedient society of the frontier, white women did *not* put themselves on the auction block in a brothel. Her explanation that night at the ranch, when he recalled it, where she spoke of waiting for him in France, seemed cool and restrained in hindsight, without the emotional tears one would expect in discussing such a separation.

It was late afternoon, and he only took time to check into the hotel, bathe, and discard three coats before deciding on the conservative black. Gloves? No gloves. Money? He stuffed some large notes into his pocket, double-checked with the manager for Guy's address, and quickly dashed through the lobby to his waiting carriage.

He was not prepared for the splendor of the Hotel Jordan. As he crossed the threshold and stepped into the gilded and marble foyer, he was not prepared to have a haughty butler announce Empress Jordan as Mrs. Terrance Miles. His immediate reaction to news of her marriage was hostile, although, he bitterly concluded, he should have known better. Hadn't Guy announced in his first letter that Pressy had taken care of everything? he thought aggrievedly.

When the drawing-room doors swung open and the major-domo announced his name, he was *most definitely* not prepared for the veritable *crowd* of men surrounding Empress, seated in their midst like a queen holding court. And his response to the scent of white lilac was instant, intuitive desire. Blindfolded, he would have known she was in the room.

Visibly surprised, Empress gasped and stared, the blood draining from her face. *He has come,* was her first flashing thought.

A curious silence fell while every set of eyes noted Empress's pallor and then quickly veered to the open doorway and the handsome man standing there with a natural grace, looking every inch an exotic half-blood despite his impeccable tailoring. Tall, well built, with lustrous, long hair as black as raven wings, shading to iridescent blue-black where the light caught it, and skin so bronzed that the uncivilized, savage splendor of the West was immediately conjured in every mind. The black cutaway coat he wore over a citrine-and-azure waistcoat accented rather than mitigated the acute sense of physical virility. And when he smiled suddenly at the abrupt hush, the lift of his mouth was wolfish, his pale eyes narrowing in a predatory gleam, his intrinsic arrogance responding to the fascinated silence.

It was as though motion hung suspended, each of the men surrounding Empress stunned, caught off-guard; her obvious shock so unusual in a woman noted for her poise.

The striking dark man in the doorway emanated a confident power that rushed through the room like a gale. He didn't know what he expected the first time he saw Empress again, but he hadn't expected this—how did you put it, exactly? —this horde of hopeful men, and an ungovernable jealousy assailed him. It was clear now why she hadn't bothered writing, Trey thought, his luminous eyes scanning the score of men, some of whom he recognized from Estée's crowd of friends. Tall, short, muscular, lean, old, young, some in hacking jackets as if they'd come after riding in the *Bois*, others attired in prescribed afternoon dress.

But all rich.

He understood immediately.

But while he understood, powerful emotion overrode insight, and his sole consideration was that there was an excessive number of men around the woman he instinctively thought of as his. Regardless, he told himself, of her new name and new husband. With effort, he resisted the impulse to curl his fingers into fists and strike out at them. This was, after all, a Parisian drawing room.

So his voice when he spoke wasn't angry but self-possessed and scrupulously polite, only his soft Western drawl coloring the perfect fluency of his French. Like many wealthy young men, he'd been reared on yearly visits abroad. "Good afternoon, Mademoiselle Jordan," he said, deliberately overlooking her married name and the possibility that one of these men was her husband. "You're looking . . ." He paused while his glance raked her boldly. If she had almost died last month, there was no vestige now of illness. She was in full glory. ". . . splendidly healthy." The last two words were lazily uttered in a slow, sensual drawl, and his gaze leisurely drifted across her décolletage, noting with a connoisseur's eye that her breasts were measurably larger. If her husband was indeed in attendance, he decided with a dismissive assessment, he was obliging with his wife's . . . company.

Trey's insolent words and appraisal brought a rosy blush to Empress's pale face, while the shock of his appearance generated warring, irresolute emotions. Her first instinctive rush of pleasure had been instantly altered with alarm over Max, and reflecting on Trey's impertinent drawl and his refusal to acknowledge her new name, a swiftly rising resentment ruffled Empress's temper.

It was just like Trey, she thought, with growing vehemence, to walk back into her life with that unfailing assuredness, those polished manners, insinuating in that lazy drawl that he somehow had some proprietary claim to her. Was he still married? she wondered in the next flashing moment. Was his wife in Montana or traveling with him and left behind in some hotel suite? Was it possible he was divorced? Why was he here suddenly, after so many months? All unanswered questions she wasn't in the mood to deal with now after having slowly compromised and negotiated her feelings back into reasonable perspective. She had struggled too long to reconcile her ardent yearning, to reduce the potent, tantalizing memories of Trey to manageable levels. She wouldn't allow him, she decided heatedly, to casually walk in and overset her hard-won tranquillity.

Like Empress, the Duc de Vec immediately and justifiably took exception to Trey's proprietary tone. Only recently Empress had begun responding to his urbane courtship with a teasing amusement he'd found charming and encouraging. In his experience, young widows were by far the best possible lovers, and since the birth of her child, the countess was provocatively voluptuous. Rumor had it she'd insisted on nursing the child herself. Unheard of in the environs of the Faubourg St. Germain but typical of the startling independence he found so fascinating. He expected she would be unconventional in other aspects of her life as well, and he'd already selected a necklace of fire rubies as a remembrance of their first night together. This dark-skinned man with overlong hair and challenging presumption annoyed him, and turning to Empress, sitting beside him on the embroidered settee, he said in a low voice both casual and intent, "Should I throw the scoundrel out?"

The Duc's voice broke into Empress's critical intentions, and with relief she looked away from Trey's powerful masculinity. Deliberate and maturely considered as her intentions were, disobedient feeling was enticed by the sight of him. "That won't be necessary, Etienne." Encouragingly she found she could speak in a normal voice even while her heart palpitated uncontrollably. "Mr. Braddock-Black and I are old friends, and I'm quite used to his familiarity."

"You couldn't, anyway," Trey replied mildly, and vivid with challenge, he strolled closer to the group of men seated around Empress.

The Duc, conspicuous for his temper, immediately came to his feet, his anger graphic on his face, his skill with pistols or rapier distinguished and deadly. Before he could issue his own challenge, Empress touched his hand and murmured softly, "No, Etienne."

Trey's eyes shifted to Empress's small hand on the Duc's, then up to the Duc's proud face, its slightly heightened color visible beneath his tan. "Do you do her bidding, Etienne?" Trey inquired insolently, angered by the championship of the man seated so intimately near Empress. It didn't matter who he was or why he held the place of honor next to Empress on the small settee. The large whip-lean man in splendidly cut Harris tweed was a rival encroaching on personal property, and impulse rather than reason guided Trey's actions.

"Behave, Trey, you're not at Lily's," Empress admonished hotly, her green eyes fiery with temper.

"It sure looks as though I'm at Lily's," Trey drawled, his derisive smile tight-lipped.

Glowing with a furious incredulity at his rudeness, Empress drew a calming breath before she said very softly, "With your taste for self-indulgence, I'm sure you could scarcely distinguish the difference."

"You're right, of course, I never did learn how," he replied equally softly, his pale glance deliberately trained on her. "You know the old saying, 'In the dark'—"

Talk of Lily's meant nothing to the Duc, but the impending conclusion to Trey's remark brought De Vec's free hand up in anger, and he took a step forward.

Swiftly tightening her grip on his hand, Empress admonished in a hushed, intense murmur, "*Please,* Etienne." She refused to have a brawl, because Trey was impertinent and Etienne was territorial. "Please, for me . . ." she repeated in a soft, throaty tone.

Deferring to the intimate resonance of promise in Empress's voice, the Duc slowly lowered his hand and, stepping back, gracefully settled back down beside her. He'd deal with the upstart pup later, he thought, deliberately stretching his arm along the top of the settee so that it rested possessively near Empress's bare shoulders. "Perhaps we can discuss our friendship with the Countess at a more convenient time," he said, his smile pleasant, his eyes chill. "Privately. Will you be in Paris long?"

"As long as it takes," Trey replied, his smile urbane, his voice too soft, deadly provocation in his glance.

"For heaven's sake," Empress exclaimed, suddenly impatient with the quarrelsome men treating her as though she were a trophy to acquire, "would you two stop acting like rutting bulls? If and when I'm available," she said in that startling, frank way everyone agreed she'd developed in America, "the decision will be mine"—the furious look she leveled at Trey was resolute—"not either of yours."

"Hear, hear," the Prince de Morne cheerfully responded, always entertained by Empress's candid style of speech. She was an enchanting change from the other aristocratic ladies who always agreed with absolutely everything he said. "And please include me, dear madame, in your final decision."

Casting Hippolyte a grateful glance for his flippant lightening of the oppressive mood, Empress said, appreciation in her voice and gaze, "Dear Hippolyte, you are by far the most amusing of my friends, and I thank you, for I despise boredom."

"I would deem it an honor," the young prince replied with a practiced bow to Empress, ensconced on the rococo settee, "to devote my life to relieving your boredom."

The Duc looked afflicted. "Don't encourage him, Empress, in his lothario tendencies, or we shall *all* be excruciatingly bored," he said dryly, his heavy-lidded glance weighted with reproach.

"*I* need a drink," Trey said deprecatingly, apropos Hippolyte's fulsome compliments, his gaze sweeping the room in search of the liquor table. Perceiving it, he strolled away, thinking querulously, Lord, they're all panting after her like a pack of wolves. And in typical fashion, he decided, filling a glass with brandy, Empress was holding her own without difficulty. It was what most fascinated him—her ability to equalize the pleasant game of love. *Used* to fascinate him, he contradicted himself cynically. In this current hothouse atmosphere of numerous males after a bitch in heat, his feelings had altered to moody outrage as he contemplated the only possible assessment of this miscellanea, consisting of one woman, many men, an absent or complaisant husband, and flirtation. As in Montana, apparently, Empress was available to the highest bidder. Fortunately, he decided, ill-humored with jealousy, he had sufficient money to buy another install-ment of her time.

Lounging in a dainty chair sizes too small for him, his long legs casually crossed at the ankle, his heeled boots an incon-gruous note in the Boucher and Fragonard interior of shepherdesses and pastel hues, Trey stayed through the ritual of teatime because, much as she'd like to, Empress wouldn't allow Etienne to throw him out. Trey was much too unpre-dictable; she had visions of a Western-style shoot-out in her drawing room, but more importantly, she refused to be intim-idated by his challenging masculinity.

Drinking his brandy, he occasionally added a lightly abra-sive comment to the conversation, primarily concerned with the schedule of social events past, present, and future. With an uncustomary streak of puritanical virtue, the talk of idle, aristocratic leisure activities annoyed him today. Yet Empress clearly fit in perfectly, as if she'd never stood in range garb at Lily's looking like a misplaced gamin in worn flannel and tangled hair. Unlike the silky disarray he remembered, her hair was arranged now in an upswept mass of coquettish curls held in place with pearl-and-diamond clips. Her gown, of midnight-black velvet opening over faille with a fall of cream lace down the bodice, was costly. Having paid for a dress or so in the past, Trey was aware in a general way of prices for couturier gowns. Apparently Empress had overcome any fi-nancial difficulties, he sullenly mused, for she wasn't living in this style on his $37,500.

He watched her in the midst of the flattering males, cherry bright, smiling and gay, her lush lashes dipping in a sugges-tive, equivocal way when she spoke, her trilling laughter made to seem special somehow—personal. Even the way she sat—no, elegantly lounged—was intentional, her weight neg-ligently resting on one settee arm so her breasts swelled provocatively above the neckline of her dress, so every man in the room wanted her lounging in his bedroom.

Empress Jordan doing what she did best.

Something to behold.

If the anger didn't get in the way.

Once, midway between varying opinions on the hunting available near Paris, the Duc de Vec mildly ventured, "Do you find this tedious? Are we boring you, Mr. Braddock-Black?"

Trey briefly adjusted his emerald cuff link, thinking as he always did that it was unsporting for thirty men on horses and two dozen dogs to pursue a single small fox, and then his silver eyes came up. "I have never been so totally engrossed in my life," he replied amiably, his smile brilliant. "Mademoiselle Jordan's company," he went on pointedly, his manner irritatingly charming, "is, as always, paradise. Hunting, however, is not my forte, so forgive me if my attention wanders." This outrageous statement, from a man who spent weeks each year hunting game for his clan. Reaching for the brandy bottle he'd conveniently carried over with him, he filled his glass, saluted mockingly with the full glass, and proceeded to drink it down.

As the afternoon progressed, Trey's brandy bottle emptied, but his urbane sophistication remained intact if one discounted the occasional caustic comments bordering on misogyny.

Which generally Empress choose not to do.

And she would tartly respond.

To which Trey would mockingly defer, his eyes first on Empress, then on the Duc.

De Vec was the model of restraint but unnaturally quiet in his relaxed pose near Empress. He was drinking the aqua vitae he affected from the area near his hunting box in Logiealmond, Scotland.

Whose sangfroid would break first? many wondered, and the undercurrent of expectancy heightened.

Since no one intended to miss any possible excitement, Empress's guests gave every impression of staying indefinitely. She, however, was nursing, and her body chemistry had no way of relating to the intentions of the assembled males, only to regular time intervals. As the afternoon wore on, Empress became increasingly uncomfortable knowing that Max would soon begin fussing. With her eye on the Sèvres porcelain mantel clock, she finally pleaded an early-evening engagement, at which point the more courteous of her guests excused themselves. Trey, with his mildly ruffled air of displeasure, gave no indication of leaving, and when the Duc appeared intent on outlasting Trey, she gently promised to see him at the opera that evening.

"Are you sure you'll be all right?" he asked, loath to leave her with the rude savage from America who had consumed most of the bottle of brandy.

"I'm sure, Etienne, thank you. And thank you again for Tunis."

His attention to detail and fond consideration were only a portion of his engaging charm, and when the Duc had heard Empress needed a better mount for riding, one from his stables had been delivered the same day. "The pleasure was mine, mon chère." He bowed in casual gallantry, his extravagant gift dismissed. "Until tonight, then. You're sure now?" he asked cryptically, with a short, studied look at Trey.

Empress nodded and smiled.

He flashed a swift, answering smile and left.

"What," Trey said brusquely when the door closed on the Duc, "is Tunis?"

His question annoyed her. It was none of his business. The fact that he had intentionally outstayed his welcome *annoyed* her. The other men had had enough courtesy to leave. And she said as much.

"Tunis is none of your business, and you've long outstayed your welcome. Don't you have any manners?"

"Just curious about the odd name," he replied casually, immune to her censure, "and I don't have any manners. I thought you knew. Did your cicisbeo give you a black slave? You don't seem the type." Every word was provocation, every drawling inquiry thinly veiled mockery.

"Oh, good God," she exclaimed, "if you must know, Tunis is not a slave, Tunis is a small mare Etienne gave me. She was trained in North Africa, hence the name. And to fully assuage your curiosity, she was also trained at the Spanish Riding School. Her gait is remarkably smooth, she's a champion in dressage, and can count to twenty." Empress finished in a huff because he hadn't moved a muscle in his lounging pose, except the cynical adjustment of one eyebrow upward.

"That's an improvement over the mountain mustang Clover, I'd say. You've done well for yourself," Trey murmured dryly, his gaze drifting around the luxurious room, alcohol tempering his words, "but then you've always been resourceful. Are the prices higher over here?"

Empress flinched, and the anger that had been building in her all afternoon, while Trey nonchalantly drank in her drawing room as though he not only belonged but somehow outranked his rivals, finally exploded. "I don't *need* money now," she retorted acidly. "Would you please leave?"

"If," Trey said pleasantly, disregarding her plainspoken ejection, his eyes straying to the baroque pearls around her neck, "you continue living in this splendor, you soon may."

"I don't know why I feel compelled to explain to you, but this is all Guy's. His inheritance was restored along with his title. There *is money*." Her words were chill and plain and dismissive.

"And for you as well?" Trey inquired gently. His smile, which was not natural, owed its tightness to a restrained fury. After the long afternoon watching Empress being charming to other men, he wasn't in the mood to be dismissed.

"A sufficient amount," she said with brevity.

"I hope it's a large enough fortune to counter the reputation you're no doubt acquiring with this male harem you're entertaining." Although Trey lived his life ignoring society's strictures, he was fully aware that a woman was not allowed such freedom without censure.

"It's sufficient," Empress repeated, her voice brittle with control, determined to let Trey think what he wished. She had no intention of enlightening him on her celibate life. It would only increase his arrogance.

An arrogance, she had to admit, was justifiable, seeing him lounging in her pastel rococo chair. His looks were the kind women followed with their eyes; even men did with surreptitious dismay, so purely was his face wrought in line and plane and form. And when his pale silvery gaze held hers, as was now the case, it was impossible to disregard the potent energy. Trey was not like other men; he had a hard resilience lightly restrained in his powerful body that lured and dazzled. The catalog of faultless attributes lavishly bestowed on him was unfair.

But while Trey was delight and beauty and excitement, his air was too rarefied for her breathing. He'd only offered what he did to all women, and she'd been artless enough to expect more. Like the others, she should have been less addled by his charms. He gave pleasure and wished nothing more in return. So while he might be the ultimate enchantment, as a lover she'd become sensible away from him, she reminded herself, sensible and capable of dealing with his facile charm.

"I want you," he said casually, startling her with both his words and his insolence. It was a rich man's son speaking, brazenly overlooking all that had transpired in the intervening months. It was Trey Braddock-Black, with a millionaire fa-

ther and mother, mines and horse-breeding ranches, and extraordinary beauty of face speaking. She shouldn't have been
so startled; she should have remembered.

"I'm sorry," Empress replied crisply, fighting the acute
emotional response his words provoked. "It's out of the question." But his heated glance and lazy words touched her as
only he could, and a small flutter of longing trembled through
her senses. Her milk-full breasts reacted to the quivering
pleasure, and she rose abruptly, resolved to resist Trey's
sensual lure. She didn't flatter herself that he wanted more.
His words were quite plain. Drawing a quick breath to steady
the trembling sensations that persisted despite her better judgment, she said in as neutral a voice as possible, "If you'll
leave now, I must dress. It's opera night. *Thaïs*."

There was a silence.

"*Thaïs*, my favorite, and I'm not invited?" Trey's smile
was enchanting.

"No," she said resolutely, trying to control her breathing,
difficult with Trey in her drawing room, close enough to
touch. Her fingers crushed the velvet of her skirt.

"A pity."

"I'm sure you'll manage to entertain yourself somehow.
Have you," she asked in what she hoped was an impersonal
tone, "brought your wife along?"

"Fortunately," he replied pleasantly, "I don't have a wife."

A flare of anger reacted to his insouciance. "Are congratulations in order?"

"Very definitely." His smile was a lush invitation.

"Consider them given, then," she said curtly, moving to
the door and opening it. How typical of Trey to neatly
dispose of an unwanted woman. His tone was bland, his
smile tranquil, as though dealing with an unwanted wife were
a transitory inconvenience.

"Where is Mr. Miles?" he asked nonchalantly, taking her
hint and rising. His question was casual, his unconcern that a
Mr. Miles existed blatantly apparent.

"Fortunately there is no Mr. Miles," Empress replied in
parody of his flippant disposal of his wife.

His dark brows winged in mild inquiry. "Why the pretense?" he said. As a man of the world, the reason was
obvious, but he was ill-tempered enough after her flirtatious
availability that afternoon to insist ungraciously on being told.

Empress hesitated, not from embarrassment over her position but intent rather on keeping Max a secret from Trey. "I prefer being viewed as a widow, you see—"

"Ah, yes, the merry widow," he interrupted deprecatingly, graphically recalling her avid sexuality. "I see how it would appeal to your—er—friendly nature." His tone was amused; his eyes were not.

"Why do you insist on sexual connotations to every utterance I make?" she retorted, closing the door again so the servants weren't party to their conversation.

"I should entertain other connotations," he retorted mildly, "after seeing such patent, unmistakable lust at teatime this afternoon." His fringed lashes half lowered fastidiously. "I admire your capacity for cordiality," he went on dryly. "No one left with dashed hopes." Her manner, damn her, was perfect. Gracious, hospitable, with glimpses of spirit both vivacious and, when she looked up through her heavy lashes, encouraging.

"Don't take that deprecatory tone with me," Empress snapped, almost stamping her foot in indignation at his sanctimoniousness. "Not after reigning as the uncontested stud west of the Mississippi!"

"It's different for a man."

No polite denial, only that impossibly bland rejoiner. How typical. "In what way," Empress replied icily, "is it different?" Trey's cliché phrase, in addition to his damnable arrogant hypocrisy, was guaranteed to bring her temper to the boiling point. Whether she was virginal or sexually active didn't matter; it didn't matter that she had, in fact, been celibate since Montana. What mattered, she defiantly thought in answer to his damn masculine bias, was that the decision was hers. *Not* society's, *not* his, *not* some stranger's on the street.

"We have more freedom." His tone was lazy, only the words were overbearing.

"How nice for you. I've discovered, however," she said, her voice dry and astringent, lifting her chin slightly in response to his bold eyes, "that my freedom is quite adequate."

He had been standing some distance from her near the chair he'd risen from, and he moved toward her now with that soft, gliding walk she'd often thought would be silent in dry, fallen leaves. He stopped too close for politeness and, towering over her, his temper curbed with effort when he thought of Empress making love to any of those men, said with quelling gentleness, "To be brutally mundane, darling, as a woman there are sometimes physical consequences to that freedom."

Empress's stomach lurched. Did he know about Max? Was all this mocking repartee an exaggerated cat-and-mouse game? Why did he seem so much larger than she remembered? "When did you arrive in Paris?" she asked too quickly, too bluntly, overwrought suddenly at the prospect of challenging Trey over their son.

He inclined his body briefly in an understated bow, and the sapphire buttons on his waistcoat winked and glistened as if reminding her of the wealth at his command. "This afternoon," he said. "May I call later tonight after the opera and sample some of your *freedom*?" His tone was exactly correct, as though a chaperone were seated near, the deferential dip of his head unerringly proper; only the soft emphasis of his words and his mocking eyes were disrespectful.

He didn't know about Max, she decided, looking into those derisive, languorous eyes. They were too dissolutely sensual under the idle mockery. He was simply interested in gratifying his carnal urges. "I'm afraid tonight is busy." The implication in her voice and expression insinuated that she would be busy—permanently.

"Tomorrow, then?" he suggested smoothly, unimpeded by either the substance or spirit of her refusal.

"No," she said flatly, rankled by his careless presumption that she would succumb to his blunt declaration that he wanted her, singularly irritated that she was inexplicably drawn to the heated, impatient invitation in his pale eyes—as though she stood suddenly restless and fevered, waiting for him to put out his hand and say, "Come."

"Are you too heavily scheduled?" he asked with that charming effrontery she'd watched all afternoon. "I'm prepared to buy a substantial time slot. What are the rates here in Paris," he drawled languidly, "now that you are not barefoot in the market?" And he stood there, the familiar blandness returning to his face as he watched her.

Her skin flushed to the roots of her hair, and she drew a breath of unprecedented, murderous rage. "Naturally I find your invitation irresistible," she replied with smooth venom. "Unfortunately," she said tartly, "you can't afford them."

He looked surprised and then smiled "I can buy every whore on the Continent, sweetheart," he said, his voice cordial, "and you know it."

"A pleasant holiday, then, Mr. Braddock-Black," she said. If she had been a man, she would have killed him. Twirling, she wrenched open the door and escaped from the smiling rudeness and the overpowering urge to rake her fingers across his face until the insulting smile was marred with blood. Fleeing into the first room, she reached and, slamming the door behind her, leaned back against the polished fruitwood, trembling in fury. If she had a weapon, she would have used it on him and eradicated his calculated rudeness and bigotry. How dare he inflict the double standard on her conduct! How dare he call her whore for the same activities he saw as male prerogatives! "Fuck you, Trey," she swore under her breath, "fuck you to hell and beyond!"

The tall case clock in the corner chimed, reminding her that Max would be frantic soon, his feeding long overdue. Consciously she forced her thoughts away from Trey to still her fury and agitation. Placing her palms on her cheeks, she drew in slow, calming breaths, exorcising her flush of anger, exorcising the provocative image, smiling, as dark as the devil, single-minded, and dammit, seductive and as fascinating as a lodestar. With a peremptory toss of her head she dispelled the image and pushed away from the door. At least, she thought with satisfaction, her refusal was overwhelmingly clear.

She had seen the last of the magnetic Mr. Braddock-Black.

Twenty-one

HE WAS THERE the next morning.

He was *rolling* on the floor of the breakfast room with Eduard while Guy, Genevieve, and Emilie tugged and shouted at him, wanting their turns at his attention. Colorful paper and ribbons, torn and crumpled, were strewn on the golden Tabriz carpet, along with lavish gifts, jewelry and dresses, stuffed toys and dolls, paintboxes and books, a saddle from Hermès that must be for Guy, Trey's usual largesse with the children. Emilie's blond curls were peaking out from under an expensive new bonnet, and Genevieve's slender neck was circled with three splendid ropes of pale pink pearls, the tiniest, most perfectly matched pearls she'd ever seen. Guy had a good hold on Trey's sleeve and was demanding he come to the stables with him. "You must, Trey. Leave *off* now, Eduard, it's *my* turn!"

"He can see your old horse later," Emilie declared grudgingly, the violets on her lavender silk bonnet quivering with her denial. "He has to see my new ball gown first. It's my very *first*, Trey," she said, pulling on his hand, "with sparkling gauze over white silk, and it makes me look . . ."

"Like a fairy princess," Trey responded smilingly, sitting

upright suddenly in the melee, Eduard snuggled happily in his lap.

"It does! It really does," she agreed happily, her answering smile reminding him wrenchingly of Empress. So she must have looked at twelve, fair-haired and rosy-cheeked with dancing lights in her eyes. "And Pressy says I can wear my hair up because it's a family party and—"

The door shut with a quiet vehemence, and everyone turned to see Empress standing stiffly at the entrance to the room.

Her morning dress was a severely cut jonquil silk, and Trey thought again how noticeably fuller her breasts were. Perhaps a tailoring device, he speculated, to add allure to a courtesan's image. And effective, he decided with a touch of asperity as desire flared through his senses.

"See who's here, Pressy!" Guy exclaimed.

"Isn't it *grand*! Trey's on holiday and came to *see* us!" Genevieve was wide-eyed with pleasure.

"Look, look at my new bonnet. Trey says it's *very chic*!" Emilie said with a grown-up modulation that ended in a fit of fourteen-year-old giggles.

Exultant smiles wreathed every young face, and each voice was filled with jubilation as they stood surrounding Trey, but what moved Empress most was Eduard's small arms hugging Trey tightly. All the children had missed Trey, talking of him incessantly, until several months ago, when Empress, in a fit of temper, had hotly forbade them to discuss him. "I do not want that man mentioned in my hearing. Is that clear?" she had said, her voice grating, and the children's eyes had dropped before her cold gaze. But Eduard, too young to comprehend the order or the complex confusion that prompted it, had persisted in asking for Trey. He was clinging to him now with fierce determination, his large baby eyes viewing Empress warily. She felt tears starting.

"Good morning. You sleep late in Paris," Trey said blandly, his long-fingered hands resting lightly on Eduard's waist.

"Oh, Pressy never gets up early, do you, Pressy?" Guy interjected, trying his best to soothe away the severity from his sister's expression, his voice earnestly helpful.

"I expect it's your busy nights," Trey remarked softly, curtailing the tears.

Empress refused to account for her schedule to a man who lived consistently outside convention. She slept late many mornings because she was often up during the night nursing

Max and had in fact just tucked him back into his crib. "You're up early yourself," she replied, thin-skinned and waspish. "Did Paris offer no entertainment last night?"

"Actually," he said, his voice peaceful, "I haven't been to bed yet—that is, to sleep yet," he corrected with a faint smile.

Hot resentment flooded through Empress as she noted the slight, marring traces of a sleepless night on his fine-boned face, and of course his evening clothes, she observed tardily. Damn his libertine soul, she thought indignantly, and schooling her voice to a calmness she didn't feel, said, "I hope you were suitably entertained."

"Very well, thank you." He exuded an air of insolent decadence. "And you?"

"I find my nights quite eventful," she replied, maliciously tinging the last word with sly suggestion.

The silver depths of his eyes glowed with ungovernable fury as territorial prerogatives overwhelmed him. "And maybe more so in the future." His chin was resting on Eduard's dark ruffled head, his pose tame and tranquil, but his words were murmured with a deep, husky resonance, and the smoldering menace in his eyes sent a shiver down Empress's spine, a shiver that capriciously altered into a strange quivering warmth, and she pressed her open palms against the solid door at her back as if the smooth, cool mahogany could steady her body's response to his implied threat.

"Trey *must* see my party dress," Emilie broke in, unconscious of the silent, heated exchange, and both adults forcibly turned their attention to the young girl.

With an aplomb that arose to the occasion with practiced ease, Trey answered before Empress found her voice. "Very well, Princess, bring it down and show it to me, and if you tell me what your favorite jewels are, I'll buy you a necklace for your grand party. Every young lady needs jewelry for her first grown-up soiree." When he smiled, Empress saw his potent charm in full effect, and for a quicksilver moment she recalled a stormy winter night when he'd asked her what her favorite flowers were.

"Oh, Trey! Will you? Will you buy me diamonds?" Emilie inquired ecstatically, and leaning forward so that her eyes were level with Trey's, she breathed with delirious relish, "Will you *really*?"

"Emilie, mind your manners!" Empress snapped, seeing

Trey nod his smiling approval. "Of course he won't buy you diamonds!" she repudiated irritably, on the edge of a ferocious mood with Trey's impulsive generosity so obvious, with the children's adoration so plain. Damn him. Everyone loved him.

"Trey says he will," Emilie said defiantly of her champion, "and I want diamonds."

"Run along, Princess, and fetch your dress," Trey proposed quietly, his tone conciliatory. "Your sister and I will discuss the necklace." But he shot a glance full of conspiratorial delight at Emilie.

"We certainly will *not*," Empress declared defensively, as Emilie, after a glowing smile at Trey and in a flurry of twirling skirts, raced for the door. For a moment Empress considered standing her ground and concluding this argument once and for all.

"Not in front of the children," Trey said smoothly, his smile easy, his eyes sliding obliquely toward Guy and Genevieve, his fingers moving up to stroke Eduard's silky hair. It was as if he'd read her thoughts and warned her off. "Now, if you two want to get Eduard ready for a ride," he suggested to Guy and Genevieve, "my carriage is outside and ready to take us to the zoo."

Before Empress could protest, Eduard had scrambled up from Trey's lap, yelping, "Elephants, elephants, elephants!" in a voice that ricocheted around the room.

"You know who loves carriage rides, Pressy," Guy said excitedly, joy vivid in his voice. "Should we get—"

"Run along now if you're going to go," Empress said, swiftly interrupting before Guy could mention Max and the fact that carriage rides were his favorite diversion. Flustered, she quickly turned to Trey and said, "I'll help them get ready . . . you know, coats and things," she added hastily, and shooed them out of the room.

A vague suspicion stirred at Empress's sudden acquiescence and restless agitation, but Trey shrugged away his mild unease, content that the children were coming.

Ten steps down the hallway, Empress caught Guy by the arm and, pulling him to a stop, hissed, "You are *not* to mention Max!" She swung her glance to Genevieve, who had stopped at Guy's muffled yelp of pain as Empress's fingers bit into his arm. "Don't argue, just do it. And tell Emilie. I'll explain later."

They stared at her, startled at the vehemence in her voice, stupefied at the curious command, but her voice shook as it had when she'd demanded they not mention Trey months ago, and both children knew better than to argue. "Eduard might—" Guy began, but Empress shook her head.

"Whatever he says won't be clear, but for heaven's sake, ignore it if he says something about Max."

"Don't worry, Pressy, if you don't want us to, we won't," Guy replied quickly, intent on protecting her and Max if she felt it was necessary. But while his loyalties were with his sister, he longed with a young boy's hero worship for Trey to stay. He idolized the lounging man in rumpled evening clothes lying on his breakfast-room floor, and he hoped that whatever had gone awry between the two adults wouldn't compromise *his* friendship with Trey. "I'll tell Emilie," he said, trying to pacify. "Don't worry, Pressy, no one will mention Max."

"You understand now, Genevieve?" Empress asked tersely.

Her deep blue eyes as large as saucers, not understanding in the least about Max or why Empress always snapped at Trey's name and presence, she silently nodded her assent.

"Hurry, then, and put on your coats."

She leaned against the wall as they raced away and shut her eyes. This wasn't going to work, she thought fearfully. Somehow Max's name would inadvertently slip out. . . . How could you expect young children to hold their tongues? Lord, what was she going to do? Yesterday she thought Trey was gone out of her life, that she had sufficiently discouraged him. She should have remembered how assertive he was, how he did as he pleased, how Trey Braddock-Black set his own rules.

Nervously smoothing her hair, she checked to see that her gown was all rebuttoned after nursing Max and, squaring her shoulders, went to face the man who could ruin her life, who almost had. She stepped back into the sunny room to find Trey still comfortably sprawled on the floor. How like him, she thought heatedly—not a care in the world. Not concerned that he had a son upstairs, not concerned that he was disrupting her life, making chaos out of the new existence she'd carefully rebuilt, totally unconcerned that most people considered it rude to call at this ungodly hour of the morning.

"I won't have you buying diamonds for Emilie," Empress said curtly, in lieu of telling him what she really felt—that he irritated her and, more disquieting, left her strangely restless.

"And"—her arms swept in the direction of the presents scattered on the floor—"all this."

Trey's dark-lashed eyelids lifted negligently, the only movement in his lounging form. He knew that tone in a woman. "Why not? I'm fond of them." His own voice was placid. It was too early to fight, or maybe he was too tired, or maybe on the issue of the children he didn't care what she thought. Shrugging away her critical tone, he felt suddenly that he should have come to Paris earlier, for the children at least.

Momentarily nonplussed at his simple reply, she only knew it angered her—his casualness, in effect his saying, "But I want to," leaving her in the awkward position of saying, "You can't."

To which, knowing him, he'd reply, "I can and I will."

Damn his nonchalant entry into her household, she fumed heatedly, and damn the enormous influence he had on the children, she fretted, refusing to acknowledge what piqued her most was not his casual fondness for the children, nor the gifts or the early hour, but the dark circles under his eyes and the disheveled aspect of his evening clothes . . . as though he'd carelessly redressed. His jacket collar was turned under, his white tie hung loose, his starched shirt was partially unbuttoned, several of the jeweled studs were missing, and he smelled headily of musk-scented ambergris,[12] all the rage in Paris now. Inhaled, it was thought to be both an aphrodisiac and an exhilarant, sensations Trey was sure to appreciate. As her eyes slid down his lean body she noticed for the first time the bits of glitter on the toes of his Western boots, mute evidence of his proximity to a diamont ornamented gown. Of course, his activities had been predictable from his first insolent comment about no sleep; he'd been up all night gratifying his senses . . . with a woman. How dare he come directly here from his . . . orgies. "Must you wear cowboy boots in Paris?" she said acerbically, causing a swift, upward look from Trey.

"I always wear boots or moccasins," he replied softly, ignoring her abrupt change of subject and nettled tone, "Paris or not." He restrained himself from adding that the state of his footwear was no concern of hers. She was bent on a fight, and he was not.

"Was she entertaining?" Empress blurted out, unable to suppress her impetuous compulsion to know, having to admit even with shadowy smudges beneath his eyes and untidy evening rig that he looked magnificent. Moving several steps closer, she archly indicated the toes of his boots.

For the first time Trey noted the silver glitter clinging to the black leather and recalled the circumstances under which he'd been bespangled with diamont.

The Duchesse de Soissons had somehow heard that Trey was in Paris—from one of the men in Empress's salon, perhaps—and when she'd called to invite him to her soiree, he'd first politely declined, annoyed with Empress's peremptory dismissal; more than annoyed, angered at her popularity, incensed at her array of panting suitors. He hadn't been in the right frame of mind for Estée's frantic press of friends.

"But *chéri,* we need your wildness," she'd insisted in her special husky voice.

"It's not turned on tonight," he'd growled, brooding and moody.

"And your sweet charm," she'd placated, sensitive to his low growl. "You can play my new Bösendorfer. I'll have it moved into the library so you can brood alone if you please and play Liszt on Empress Eugenie's grand piano. If so much as one person dares bother you, I'll have their head."

Trey laughed. "You always were the perfect hostess, Estée. I warn you, though, I'm not good company tonight."

Having known Trey intimately, the Duchesse rather doubted anything could make him poor company, but she knew better than to argue. Estée had a wealth of friends because of her flawless tact.

He came late and attempted to wend his way quickly through the crowded rooms to the library.

The Duchesse, politely intent on the Marquis Bellemont's recitation on the current outrages of the socialist rabble, caught sight of him and, waving discreetly, pointed toward the library.

The exquisite piano with gilded, carved legs and fourteen different wood inlays drew the eye in the muted shadows of the gaslights, like a special creature of beauty, an extravagant ornament in the dark-paneled, book-lined room. And with Estée's usual thoughtfulness, his favorite brandy was conveniently at hand.

Standing, he ran his fingers over the keys, poured himself a drink, and then sat down to play. He knew Estée would find him later; he also knew she'd bring in a friend or so. But she'd allow him the promised time to himself. In moments he'd forgotten everything but the desperate sadness in Liszt's minor-key poetry put to music. His long-fingered hands moved gracefully, effortlessly, playing Liszt with a constrained power, feeling the intensity of the music in the tips of his fingers, in every nerve ending, and in his very soul.

Much later he looked up, startled to see that the room had filled, and prominent near him were women, smiling, their eyes all lush invitation. Famous for his looks and wildness, all the flirtatious women hoped he'd not outgrown the wildness, and in the past he would have taken pleasure in the variety and the invitations. Since Empress, though, the keen, piquant desire was gone, only the words and nuance, the facile charm was automatic—effortless. Like a familiar exercise, mindless with practice. So tonight he smiled and flirted and entertained with his usual seductive effrontery, but he gracefully refused them all.

Sharing a last drink with Estée and her husband before he left, the young Comtesse Trevise, slender and Mediterranean with sultry eyes and olive skin, had come into the room and, gliding across the room like some nymph of night in black tulle and diamont sparkles, sat down next to Trey and smiled up at him. Smiling back politely, he'd resumed his conversation with the Duc de Soissons. A moment later she touched his arm and whispered softly into his ear.

And he'd shaken his head. But she'd leaned closer and murmured something outrageous. She was newly married, and it had excited him briefly, so he reconsidered, finished his drink, and offered her a ride home, but later, when he'd been kissing her in her boudoir and she'd been frantically ripping his shirt open, it struck him suddenly that she was too tall, that her hair was the wrong color, that he didn't derive pleasure from the warm softness of her lips.

More than his normal diplomacy was required to disengage himself because her husband was very old and dull—and she was not. Since his carriage had been sent away because of his usual consideration for his driver's sleep, when he capriciously changed his mind, he was without transportation. He didn't think that the comtesse—roused, nude and angry—was in the mood to lend him her carriage, and though he soothed her as best he could, with a skill refined by practice, she was pouting when he left.

It had been extraordinarily rude of him. He'd have to send

her something expensive from Chaumet. And an apology, he thought, standing on her doorstep in the cool, gray predawn.

On impulse he decided to walk over to Empress's from the Hôtel Trevise, a short distance, since all the old titles lived in Germain. And he'd enjoyed the light of dawn in Paris, the same delicate coral as the sunrise over the Bear Mountains, and found peace in the solitude of the sleeping city. When it occurred to him as he strolled that calling at the Hôtel Jordan this early was perhaps slightly irregular, he detoured to buy gifts for the children. Dozing in a cab, he waited for the shops to open and then filled the carriage to overflowing after walking through several shops and pointing. Laden with presents, lighthearted and cheerful, he told himself he was going to see the children . . . it was only courteous. Empress was of no interest to him.

Since their conversation that morning hadn't been frankly open, but rather one qualified by omission, Trey lazily replied to Empress's blurted inquiry, "The lady was entertaining enough to keep me up all night. How do you explain the men to the children?" he asked in the next breath, each parrying for answers, each jealous and resentful, each wishing vengeful compensation for the months of misery.

"I came back from the opera at midnight."

"Ah—and the children were sleeping?"

"Very astute," she said, walking to the window and looking out as though his presence were of no consequence.

So the merry widow was entertaining men late the previous night, he thought, gazing at her trim form, silhouetted against the light. Why was that such a surprise? If anyone understood her whorish ways, it was he. How could she look so fresh and innocent, like a new spring flower this morning in jonquil silk, her pale hair like a young child's, so newly minted in its tawny gold, and yet play the courtesan with such ease each night? He felt an urgent need to place his hands around her trim, small waist, draw her back so he felt her warm against his body, and bury his face in her lilac-scented hair. He no longer deceived himself that the children were the only reason he was here, and tainted with jealousy of all the men in her life, he said in a decretory voice he'd never used with a woman before, "I won't wait much longer."

Twirling back, she didn't pretend to misunderstand what he meant, and she glared at him for his arrogance, damn him and his insufferable confidence! "You can't force me."

He smiled. "I won't have to."

His assurance, his disheveled appearance, and his insouciant sensuality all galled her. But she knew that if she was honest with herself, he was right. And that galled most of all. How could he—with a lazy, smoldering look from those silvery eyes—make her weak with wanting him, make her feel exquisite quivers deep inside, when all the men courting her with such fervor didn't cause a ripple of interest? He offered nothing but transient pleasure, then heartbreak, and she hated him. "I would appreciate it if you wouldn't come here," Empress said, incensed with his self-confidence, angry with her own reaction.

"We'll have to vote on it," he said with wonderful perceptiveness. "I think I hear the children."

Empress's color had risen. "Damn you, Trey," she said, wanting to scream, wanting to slap the smugness off his face, "you can't just walk back into their lives!"

He bestowed on her a warm, indulgent smile. "Watch me," he said without rancor, and uncurled from the floor to a standing position in a single fluid motion.

Twenty-two

WHILE TREY AND the children were gone, Empress spent the greater part of those hours nervously wondering if any moment Trey might discover with some careless remark by the children that Max had been born. Not that it would matter a scrap to him, she thought in the next fluttering heartbeat, but her unease remained inchoate and distracting, hovering prominently in her thoughts. What would he do if he knew? Would he come barging in demanding something of her? Would he threaten to expose Max as illegitimate? Of course he wouldn't do anything of the kind, she decided in the next anxious moment. She must stop worrying; if Arabella McGinnis could be believed Trey Braddock-Black would be unconcerned about his child.

Each time the drawing-room door opened to a new visitor that afternoon, she was noticeably apprehensive despite her logical assessments, fearful that Trey would intrude into the midst of her friends again and with an ill-placed word lay her whole life open to scandal. If he were to say he'd bought her in a brothel, or even insinuate with his drawling sarcasm that she had been for sale, she'd never live down the shame. The possibility of that terrifying scenario caused her profound trepidation throughout her usual lighthearted bantering teatime, and she sent everyone away early with the flimsiest pretext of a headache.

When Trey entered the drawing room in the children's wake just as the sun was setting, he immediately said, his glance sweeping the quiet interior, "No harem today?"

Seated near the fire, Empress was sorting through the invitations that had arrived that day, but her hands trembled at the sound of his deep voice, and she prudently set the cards aside. "Tea was over at six," she said, ignoring his jibe.

"Is that what you call it?" he replied derisively, well aware of the tea hour, intentionally absenting himself today. Then Eduard began tugging on Trey's hand with some urgent child's business, and as he bent low to hear the whispered words, Guy, Emilie, and Genevieve converged on Empress with animated, breathless accounts of their day's activities. Each animal at the zoo was described in great detail, and their newest gifts were displayed. They explained in high-pitched excitement how they were allowed to set up an easel in the Louvre, and to please Guy's passion for horses, everyone painted from Delacroix's Arab battle scene. "You should see how Trey paints horses," Guy declared, and the litany of Trey's perfections was eagerly enumerated by first one child and then another. Listening politely until there was a moment of silence while they all caught their breath, Empress took the opportunity to arrest the various descriptions of Trey's glowing attributes and reminded them that dinner would soon be served. "Thank Trey," she instructed, "then run upstairs and tidy up before dinner."

Amid discussion and recommendations for tomorrow's itinerary, the children offered uproarious, effusive thanks before they ran off crying, "See you tomorrow at ten. Don't forget!"

When the noise of their departure subsided, conscious of her manners, aware of the pleasure the children found in Trey but annoyed nevertheless that he chose to exert his charm on them, Empress stiffly declared, "Thank you for your kindness to the children."

"My pleasure," he said simply.

"You can find your way out, I'm sure," she said crisply, having to see to Max before the children's dinner. She wondered how intricate a tangle of adjusting feeding schedules and visitors against Trey's presence would evolve if he stayed in Paris long.

"No invitation for dinner?" Trey drawled lazily, thinking

that he liked her better with her hair down, and the brooch under her chin cast away, and next the prim navy silk dress she was wearing today, the one she'd selected as superficial defense against Trey.

"No invitation," Empress replied discourteously. Trey could force her hand when it came to the children's happiness; she couldn't deny them his company when they adored him so, but the familiarity didn't extend to herself. Trey Braddock-Black was an unprincipled, self-indulgent, too wealthy young man, and her hard-won struggle to overcome her feelings for him was too recent to allow any unnecessary exposure to his undiluted charm.

"It seems I'll have to dine alone." The message in his eyes had nothing to do with food.

Empress looked down at her hands briefly to still her intoxicating response, then swung her gaze back. "If I were more charitable," she said briskly, "I'd extend my sympathy. However, I'm not. Perhaps your companion of last evening is available." No longer even mildly courteous as she recalled his state of dress that morning, she rose from her chair, lifted her chin so her eyes met his, and said, "Good evening, Trey."

"How long do you intend to keep pushing me out of your house?" She might not have spoken, for all the reaction he showed to her comments.

Now that she was standing, he was too close, too unbridled, his pale eyes intemperate with inquiry, and she inhaled softly before she answered, "As long as possible."

He smiled that celebrated smile, devastating and suggestive. "At least you're sensible enough to realize that it won't be forever." His voice was low and husky and doing disastrous things to her resolve. "And remember, you can't keep the children around every moment—"

"Get the hell out," she ordered quietly, controlling her impulse to point a commanding finger at the door like an actor in a bad play. "You have to leave my house," she said explicitly and discourteously, but her voice shook slightly on the last words, and the flush on her cheeks wasn't from anger. Even quietly standing as he was now, dressed in subdued tweed like other men, Trey exuded beneath the calm conformity his notorious intensity, as infectious and riveting as silver flame. How could his ardent promise of pleasure rouse without words or movement?

Pleasantly conscious of her agitation, he bowed sardonically and murmured, "*Au revoir,* darling." His dark, silky hair was close enough to touch when his head lowered briefly and it took all her will to resist stroking its sleek beauty. "I'll be back."

And when the door quietly closed on his tall form, Empress sank back onto the chair and sat unmoving for several minutes, allowing her tremulous reaction to subside or at least diminish, she nervously reflected as her pulses still throbbed long moments later. Damn his galvanic attraction and redolent charm! She'd probably been celibate too long, she reminded herself in her next hurried heartbeat—that was all—and her body's response was simple circumstance, not Trey. All she needed was another few moments of calm repose and her objectivity would be restored.

But calmness refused to surface, and objectivity seemed stubbornly elusive. Perverse and self-willed, Trey stayed in her throbbing senses and would not disappear until she was roused from her absorption by servants busy in the dining room. Their activity reminded her suddenly that Max was waiting, and hurrying upstairs, she walked rapidly down the corridor, expecting to hear unhappy cries. But the paneled hallway was silent. Hopefully Nanny had pacified Max with sugar water as she did occasionally when Empress was delayed. "I'm sorry," Empress said, her apology already begun as she entered the colorful nursery, "there were people I—"

The words died in her throat.

Trey stood against a backdrop of animal murals and stuffed toys, holding Max.

"What are you doing here?" Empress demanded when she'd regained her voice. He looked up from the baby he held in his arms, and she saw with a start that he'd been crying.

"I'm telling my son about Montana," he said, his voice soft with emotion, and he thought with gentle gratefulness that he could forgive her anything for this—his son.

"He's *not* your son." The sentence was graceless, cold, and spoken with such intensity, it seemed to glitter briefly in the air before it perished.

Gazing down at Max gurgling happily in his arms, Trey reviewed the undiluted imprint of his features on the small face, breathtakingly vivid, glanced back at Empress, and quietly said, "Like hell he isn't."

"Prove it."

There was a catastrophic silence.

He took a deep breath, his eyes brilliant with anger, tender forgiveness demolished by a few malevolent words. "You coldhearted bitch." His voice was low so not to disturb his son, but harsh and contentious and underscored with an implacable menace. "You would have kept my son from me."

"I thought you'd be too busy with all your lady friends—and your other child." She said it plainly, like a mountain blotting out the sun, as if the few simple words explained all the perceived neglect and omissions.

"I don't answer to you for my social life, and as far as Valerie's child is concerned, it wasn't mine." Her mountain was leveled casually, his tone impassive—no mountain to him, only brief phrases negligently delivered to remind her of his independence, and the same denial of Valerie's child she'd heard from the beginning.

"What about the others, then?" she replied hotly, refusing to accept his cool disclaimer.

His pale eyes widened appreciably. "What do you mean, what about the others?"

"Your *other* children." She advanced with authority across the flowered carpet, her dark blue gown trailing over Aubusson moss roses and sculptured garlands. He couldn't deny them all, she thought belligerently.

The momentary surprise had vanished from his eyes, and her authority was less than alarming since she only reached his shoulder. In any case, he knew with considerably more certainty than she that she was wrong. "I don't have any," he said unequivocally.

"*Arabella* says you have several," Empress informed him with an instructive enunciation that further irritated him.

"At the risk of disabusing this expert opinion, Arabella's not privy to my personal relationships and is distinctly *not* in a position to know anything about *my* supposed children." His voice was suddenly chilly and distant.

"I knew you'd deny it," Empress maintained, her own conception of Trey and responsibility unaffected. "Just like you deny Valerie's."

"But not yours," he reminded her succinctly. "Look," he said with a weary sigh, his hand half rising to his face, "this is why this baby is mine and anyone with eyes knows none of the others are. You can't hide this skin or hair, and you know it."

"I don't know anything of the kind," Empress replied unreasonably, even as her son was graphic evidence of his allegation. At the moment she was out to refute his complacent, profligate freedom and to wound him as he'd hurt her. "Actually, I hardly know you at all," she snapped, "except for your amorous skills."

He surveyed her from slippered feet to tawny crown with chill, pale eyes. "And I find I know you even less, mademoiselle," he replied coolly, "after sitting through one of your afternoon teas. Do your suitors draw straws, or do *you* pick the lucky winner each night?" His mouth quirked in a parody of a smile. "It must be exhausting accommodating so many panting men."

"They're all merely friends to me, although I'm sure you have no concept of the notion," she replied indignantly. "You can like men for a great *number* of reasons."

Fascinating choice of words, Trey thought bitterly. Very professional, although the dramatic indignation was slightly overdone. "Oh, I understand friendship, darling, I was once your friend." His voice dropped to a hushed, dangerous murmur. "And I remember exactly how you like your friendship—*all* the ways you like it."

"You're wrong!" Resentfully she repudiated his assumptions concerning her suitors.

Their conversation at cross purposes, he observed sardonically, "You're a marvelous actress, then, darling, because you always *appeared* to be enjoying yourself."

"Arrogant bastard!"

"*Au contraire,* mademoiselle. Just another humble petitioner for your favors." The lazy insouciance was prominent again. "And incidentally, the father of your child—does that count at all in the drawing of lots?" His face was bare of courtesy. "If so . . . I'd like my time—is this too short notice?—*right now.*"

Empress gazed at him with astonished fury, and it took a short space of time to catch her breath. "Get out!" she ordered.

Trey looked affectionately at his son. "No." A simple response touched incongruously with delight.

"I'll call the servants!" Empress threatened hotly.

His brows rose and fell in swift assessment. "Call away," he said. Trey had never in his life been intimidated by a servant.

"I'll call the gendarmes!"

"Suit yourself," he replied blandly. "I believe paternity rights are adequate in France."

"*Damn you!*" she screamed finally, servants or not, Max or not, so provoked that she yielded to her fury.

Trey's expression was unreadable. "The feeling, Empress, darling," he said, very, very softly, "is reciprocated."

Max's tiny face had twisted up at the sound of his mother's scream, and after three small whimpers in response he had swiftly launched himself into a full, piercing, red-faced wail.

"He wants to eat," Empress said nervously, moving a step nearer, faintly fearful that Trey might not relinquish Max after his remark concerning paternity rights. Putting her arms out for her son, she waited anxiously. For a brief moment Trey hesitated, then, brushing a kiss on his son's forehead, he handed him over to Empress.

"Now, if you'll excuse me . . ." Empress said pointedly, secure now that she was holding Max.

Trey sat down on a convenient chair, ignoring her blunt dismissal. "I don't care to be excused," he replied lazily. "This is my first child, whether you believe it or not. What's his name?"

Empress debated refusing or arguing again, and then decided it couldn't hurt to divulge that information. "His name is Max," she said, foregoing the numerous other family names.

"How did you think of that?" His voice was mild over the screams of his hungry son, and making himself comfortable, he settled back and crossed his legs. He'd changed from his rumpled evening clothes to a gray tweed jacket and suede riding pants, since Guy had insisted he try out his black gelding, and he looked very English in his understated clothes, except, of course, for his spectacular long hair.

"It's a family name," Empress returned briefly, sitting in a rocker opposite him. She would have preferred not nursing Max in front of Trey, but one glance at his lounging posture convinced her he could outlast a glacier. Short of shooting Trey where he sat, there was no way out of the situation, so she nervously began unbuttoning her dress. "What did you do with Nanny?" she inquired, inclined to feel that Nanny would lend an air of professional authority to this nursery scene in addition to diverting her from the intensity of Trey's indolent gaze. Arranging Max at her breast, she forced herself to a reasonable equanimity, as though she nursed her son before Trey every day of his life.

Although Trey didn't answer immediately, Empress kept her glance lowered, knowing his eyes were on her, knowing the riveting focus of his gaze was fixed on her bared breast.

His voice sounded preoccupied when he answered. "In the five minutes I had before you arrived, I cut her into little pieces and chucked her out the window. What a stupid question." His voice was soft. "I sent her away." He had a son, he was thinking. *My son.* He experimented with the pure, sublime sound of those two words.

Empress looked up, startled at his gentle answer. "And she went?" Nanny was a Scotswoman who could meet even Trey eye-to-eye.

He only raised his dark brows fractionally at her naïveté and slid a little lower in the soft-cushioned chair, his pale eyes intent on the scene of mother and child. Both his. It was feeling, not reason, and it was so powerful, he held on to the chair arms to keep from jumping up and pulling them both into his arms.

The room was suddenly quiet except for the faint suckling sound, and Empress quickly looked back down at her son to escape Trey's disconcerting gaze. How could he reenter her life with such abruptness and yet, in his quiet, comfortable sprawl, seem as though he sat here every day? What was worse, his potent presence was like a powerful door knocking in the dead of night: insistent; compelling; impossible to ignore—the only man she knew who activated and quickened her amorous instincts simply by looking at her. And she fought those feelings, that white flame of excitement, by reminding herself that she was only one of a long line of women equally affected. That mercurial sensuality was Trey's trademark, second nature to him, as effortless as breathing. But too difficult for her to deal with, too fickle. There would be no more weak, helpless succumbing to Trey's passion. She wouldn't.

"I don't want you with other men," Trey said abruptly and very low into the quietness, so it seemed to vibrate through the still air like a living current of sound.

After the first repressed shock at his statement, Empress closed her eyes briefly to resist the defenseless feelings flooding through her at the hushed words, words inflected with infinite shades of meaning and interpretation. Words tinged with wanting, rendered with authority, pronounced in that rich, caressing resonance that recalled warm bodies and soft beds. "I didn't want you with other women, either," she replied, lifting her dark lashes, her voice trembling with the inner struggle she was waging to resist him. Her tone grew suddenly steadier when she thought of her last interview with Valerie, "But it didn't matter," she added, "did it?"

"I haven't been," he said gently. He didn't say he'd spent tortured days in an opium world because of her, killed a man because of her, avoided female company, left the comtesse this morning because—of her.

"I don't believe you." With effort she matched his moderate tone, but a simple denial was unsatisfactory now . . . and too late. Too many tearful nights with visions of Trey and other women repudiated acceptance of his word. "When was the baby born?" she asked to deliberately remind him of his faithlessness.

"September fourteenth. A girl," he added before she asked. "Valerie relinquished custody to me. She didn't want her. Her skin was too dark." He spoke with no implied censure, but the plain statements were shocking nonetheless.

"Where is she?" The baby must be his, Empress thought with a sinking heart, if he was caring for her. Trey wouldn't do that for another man's child.

"My parents have her in Washington, and Belle is going to be the first woman president if Mama has her way." His smile now was very different from those of the last days. The cynicism was gone, the warmth genuine, and when he said, "Belle and Max can be great friends," in a soft tone saturated with pleasure, it took every concentrated bit of willpower Empress possessed to withstand the splendor of his smile.

"It won't work!" she retorted so violently, Max's arms and legs flew out in a startled reflex, and he whimpered softly before resuming nursing.

Although Empress's sharp rebuttal was completely out of context, Trey replied promptly, "It *will*." Nothing had ever pleased him so as the sight of his son and Empress.

"No!" She didn't want to argue or debate how much her wanting him counted against his notorious reputation for dalliance. She didn't want to weigh passion against security, or gauge degrees of passion and love. Even the strongest love died without honesty and faithfulness, and Trey wasn't capable of faithfulness. Never had been . . . never wanted to be, she sadly thought. "Go away!" she ordered angrily. "I want you to leave and never come back," she added emphatically, as though saying the words would serve as protection against her tumultuous feelings.

The stark rejection reminded him that Empress Jordan was settled in her new life, and while they shared a son, apparently they shared different memories of their weeks together. "I *want* my son," Trey countered bluntly. She could turn him away in favor of other men, but he would not be refused his son.

"I'll fight you with my last franc. He's *mine*."

"He's *ours*," he said, hard-featured and grim. He had a prize horse stolen from him once when he was fifteen in one of the continuing internecine raids between the Blackfeet and the Absarokee. After the rest of his party gave up in the January cold, he'd tracked it alone, tracked it for four hundred miles far beyond the border into Canada. And recovered it. If Empress had known, she may have reconsidered her answer.

"Never," she said.

"Never?" Trey laughed unpleasantly. "Don't you think it's a little late, darling?" If Empress wanted preemption, he was more than willing to oblige; in fact, he never doubted his power to take what he wanted. But with Mademoiselle Jordan's penchant for business, surely they could come to some more amiable agreement. "Now then, dear," he began mildly, "you were always good at bargaining and after seeing the full array of . . . what's the polite term for those lusting men you surround yourself with?"

"You should know," Empress replied, maliciously sweet. "When it comes to lust, you've investigated the sensation a thousand ways, I'm sure."

"Let's not get into name-calling, sweetheart." The anger in his voice was controlled, a skill he'd acquired in his legislative battles. "Shall we simply say 'your friends' are all being juggled with that complacent frankness I've always admired in you? All I'm asking is you include me in the juggling act and add a codicil for time with my son. I'll happily pay for the privilege. Surely your mercenary soul will consider the practical aspects of such an arrangement. It must cost dear to keep up this house."

"And if I say yes?" she remarked acidly.

"Well, then, since all the world knows you for a 'friendly' widow, I'd say why not extend that cordiality to an old friend? Put little Max to bed since he's apparently fallen asleep, lock the door, and we can test out Nanny's narrow cot over there. It only remains to ask," he said with charming mockery, "whether you would prefer francs or dollars."

His rudeness was beyond belief. "I'd prefer you take your silky lust," Empress said, quivering with rage, her voice barely controlled, "and entertain some other woman."

He gave her a glittering smile. "But I want to entertain you."

"Get in line, Trey, darling." Her malice was as sparkling and tinsel-bright as his glittering smile. "I seem to be much in demand."

"And with good reason," he replied, his glance slowly drifting down her body and then up again to rest indolently on her full, exposed breasts.

"You haven't changed," she snapped.

"Well . . . neither have you, except," he murmured very softly, "for those extremely lavish breasts. The Earth Mother becomes you, love."

"You can look all you want," she said, ill tempered, deliberately lowering the sleeping baby into her lap so Trey's view was unobstructed, "but that's as close as you'll get." If he thought she was for sale, she wanted to make it plain she was *not* for sale to him.

"Don't challenge me, Empress." He measured the distance between them with his eyes. "I never lose. You'd be wise to remember that."

"There's a first time for everything," she replied sweetly, complacent in her position of strength with her small son as bulwark, irritated at Trey's assurance and presumption.

"I remember *your* first time," Trey breathed softly, and was rewarded with a spontaneous blush that pinked even the pale fullness of her heavy breasts.

She covered herself up then, as though a thin silk barrier was enough to nullify the spiraling heat his words provoked in the pit of her stomach. Forever etched in her memory was the stark, handsome sight of him, his luminous eyes hot with wanting her that first moment when she stepped out of the tub at Lily's. She had never seen a maid dismissed with less movement and more authority.

He knew what she was doing when she bared herself to

him, and he kept his feelings tightly leashed. No callow youth, he refused to respond to the deliberate provocation. But he'd seen her hasty, fluttering gesture before she'd pulled the bodice of her dress shut, and experience suggested that the lady was feeling the same prominent desire as he. Did she really think she could keep him out?

The men in her life angered him more than he cared to admit; he wanted her more than he wished; Empress Jordan was more of a callous businesswoman than he cared to consider. All seething, frustrated emotions combined to temper his compassion and force a merciless bluntness to his statements. So when she said, dismissively, "That was a long time ago," he rose in one swift movement, intent on making his position clear.

As he advanced toward her, she shivered, his towering size menacing, his expression ominous. But his voice was gentle when he spoke. "It *has* been too long, hasn't it?" And standing beside her now, he reached down and touched her shoulder, his hand slowly sliding downward until his fingers covered the swell of her breast, the weight of his hand heavy for a moment like an explicit demonstration of ownership. She should fight such conspicuous power, Empress thought, but her traitorous body sighed into the authoritative pressure, and her eyes closed to absorb the sensations. "And regardless of the line of men in front of me," Trey whispered, stroking the fine silk, feeling the warm resiliency of her breast beneath, watching with satisfaction her closed eyes and the blush stealing up her throat, "I'm not waiting my turn. I'll be coming into your house." His thumb circled her nipple, rising through the dark silk. "Your room." A drop of milk oozed through the fabric, and Empress groaned, a small stifled sound, her eyes opening languidly to follow his velvety voice, as exquisite, pulsing heat descended downward. "Your body . . ." He lightly touched the telltale stain, and a muted whimper escaped Empress's lips as an intense pleasure spread from the feather-light pressure of his fingers. "So be warned." His hand moved upward until his palm rested on the pulsing vein under her ear, then his fingers splayed out, twining in the softness of her hair, holding her head gently. "And my apologies for not using prettier language," he murmured, his grip tightening so her face was lifted to his, "but I mean to fuck you."

He smiled, just the faintest curving of his mouth, and

released her hair. The pad of one finger touched the fullness of her lower lip. "Lock your doors if you wish, Empress, darling, but I'm coming in."

She was still sitting in quivering shock when he turned and walked from the room.

Twenty-three

AND IN THE following days he was underfoot, at lunch, or taking the children out on excursions, in the nursery every time she turned around, it seemed, insinuating himself—damn him, she thought—into the very fabric of their life. But she would have been a brute to refuse the children the enormous pleasure he brought to them. She hadn't seen them so happy in years.

Guy was learning Absarokee horsemanship in addition to his dressage, and the day she went out to the riding ring to view his accomplishments, her heart almost stopped. Guy was balancing atop a galloping horse, standing with his arms out and swaying precariously, it appeared from Empress's vantage point, as the horse thundered down the length of the ring. Forcing her scream back, she watched, terrified, expecting any minute that he would tumble from his unsteady perch. Seeing her, Guy waved gaily, and rigid with fear, she waved back, her heart only resuming its regular rhythm when he slipped back into a seated position. Trotting up to Trey, who was supervising his lesson, Empress watched her brother speak to him in an agitated, gesturing conversation that appeared to be a coaxing monologue. Trey, mounted on a sleek bay, listened without responding for several moments and then nodded his head once. Apparently Trey had agreed to Guy's persuasion, for a moment later Guy wheeled his mount and shouted, "Watch us now, Pressy, watch us!"

Empress anxiously grasped the fence rail as Guy and Trey cantered off to opposite ends of the riding ring and, turning slowly, set their mounts in a collision course. They trotted first, then moved into a canter and, urging their horses to more speed as they began nearing the center, eventually rode headlong toward each other. Galloping flat out, each rose to a standing position on his horse's back, balanced, carefully judging distance and stride and, jumping, exchanged positions as the bay and black gelding streaked past each other.

Guy performed with a young boy's determination and slightly awkward verve, while Trey executed the astounding maneuver like he'd been born to the saddle, his movements economical, graceful, effortless. And Empress was reminded that under the image of idle young man of leisure was a warrior chief's son trained in his father's ways.

Trotting up and stopping his mount just short of the fence, Guy exclaimed exuberantly, "Have you ever seen anything so amazing? And it only took me two days to learn! Trey said he'd show me how to jump on and off, too—at a gallop!" Guy was beaming from ear to ear, dirt smudges on his face and riding pants. Trey, dressed in plain-cut chamois and elaborately beaded moccasins, sat his mount quietly behind Guy, his bearing relaxed, his bronzed hands resting lightly on the short knotted reins, his face expressionless but for the amusement in his eyes. "Isn't Trey the best teacher in the whole world? I never could have learned this from Laclerc, not in a million years!" Guy went on effervescently. And when Empress didn't answer immediately, he urged, "Isn't he just, Pressy? You know he is. The absolute *best* teacher!"

Empress was forced to agree. "Yes," she said, speaking automatically.

And the lounging horseman smiled at the beautiful woman cloaked and hooded in lynx fur.

But both adults' thoughts were on another form of teaching.

By week's end, Max recognized Trey whenever he walked into the nursery, and his eyes, so like his father's, would shine in welcome. Then his plump arms and legs began pumping wildly, like tiny churning pistons until Trey picked him up and said, "Give Papa a smile," which he always did

on cue, a wet gurgling that ended in cooing bubbles. His
Papa's smile in return was proud and doting. Even Nanny had
succumbed to Trey's charm after she discovered that he spent
a week each year salmon fishing near her home village in
Scotland.

Empress found it detestable when he and Nanny lapsed into
Robert Burns's poetry, and when she vexatiously asked one
time how Trey had become so familiar with the Scot's brogue,
he had mildly replied, looking entertained, "You wouldn't
care to hear. It has to do with a country school hidden away
in a mountain valley and the schoolmistress who—"

"I'm sure I'm *not* interested!" Empress interrupted hotly,
wondering if there was a woman in the world who hadn't
yielded to the warm, shining light in his eyes.

Max was always included in the children's activities now,
and whatever their schedule of events, Max would be cradled
in one of Trey's arms, and Eduard in the other, and they'd all
leave in a raucous clatter of running feet and screaming
voices.

But on Saturday—Nanny had her afternoon off—somehow
the children were all in their rooms and Trey rested quietly in
the nursery while Empress nursed Max. He had taken to
settling into the same armchair whenever he visited the nursery; and he was comfortably sprawled in shirt sleeves, his
collar undone. Their glances would meet occasionally, and
Empress would always look away first, from the frank need
in Trey's eyes. But he didn't make a move to touch her,
fighting his own inner battle.

"What am I to do with you?" he said into the quiet
twilight-shaded room, the words involuntary, musing thoughts
unconsciously spoken. He smiled a quick, rueful smile and
shrugged away the inadvertent words.

"Anything you want," Empress was inclined to say but
didn't, her own desire sensitive to his powerful presence.
Trey's lean form was cast in lavender evening shadow as he
sat near the nursery fire, his head resting against the chair
back, his hands lying gracefully on the unicorn-print upholstery. It would be heaven, she thought, to have those elegant
hands caress her, but Trey's casual words were based on his
physical need, and if she was fool enough to read anything
more into it, she'd only cry tears of remorse later. So she
replied in as placid tone as she could muster, "If you care to,

you could take me down to dinner in a few minutes. I think
Max fell asleep.''

The invitation was the first Empress had extended to him
since his arrival, and warning himself not to construe too
much from the simple offer, he accepted.

Dinner that night was *en famille,* noisy, boisterous, and
dangerous with undercurrents of passion. Under the soft glow
of gaslight the small dining room, decorated in crimson and
polished mahogany by a Jordan weary of rococo pastels, took
on a cloistered seclusion, as though Trey and the Jordans
were cut off from the world. The shadows in the crimson-
walled room were denser, the carpet scarlet duskiness, the
dark mahogany furniture somber shapes melting into masking
darkness; only the animated children under the chandelier
light and two quiet adults were illuminated. It was like a play
being enacted on a very small stage.

While the children laughed and teased in their normal
fashion, Trey was subdued, pleasant and agreeable but distracted when they tried to draw him into their silliness. He ate
in a desultory way, refusing the first course and leaving the
second uneaten. He tasted a portion of the veal but motioned
to have it taken away after a few bites. Empress found she
had lost her appetite completely, her heart thudding so loudly
in her chest, she was sure the sound could be heard above the
children's laughter. They were much too close across the
polished table. When she looked up, he was *there,* correct
again, his suit coat and cravat restored, scowling a little when
he wasn't responding to the children, resting against his chair
back, trying to keep his eyes off Empress. Dinner with the
children joltingly reminded them both of the snowed-in days
at Winter Mountain.

Guy had to ask Trey twice whether he had tickets for the
circus, and when Trey finally heard the question, he only
nodded in affirmation, his mind immediately distracted by the
rosy blush on Empress's cheeks. The twin spots of color high
on her cheekbones, so perfectly pink and balanced, looked as
though they'd been brushed on from a paint box. She always
flushed that way when they made love, he remembered, and
he shifted slightly in his chair as his erection rose.

"Dessert, sir?"

Trey looked up and automatically shook his head.

"Trey, you have to have some," Emilie said.

"I ate before I came here."

"No you didn't. You were with us."

Then he remembered he *hadn't* eaten. He'd drunk too much last night with Satie at the Chat Noir where the Duchesse's party had ended the evening, and he hadn't been in the mood for food today.

"It's chocolate mousse, Trey!" Emilie insisted, the pearl earrings he'd bought for her that day bobbing in her ears.

So he nodded; the serving man carefully placed a portion on his plate; Trey took a spoonful, said, "Wonderful," a moment later to Emilie's expectant, shining face, and wondered what he'd just eaten. It could have been boiled bark and he wouldn't have noticed.

Less cautious of the possible hurt feelings her siblings might suffer, Empress didn't even make a pretense of eating. She simply said, "I'm not hungry," and tried to keep her eyes from straying to Trey.

It was the longest dinner of his life.

Empress seriously considered snapping, "Go to bed this instant," to the children, but dizzy with bewilderment, she didn't know what she'd do if they did and she was left alone with Trey. *Get a grip on yourself,* she thought, and smiled at Genevieve, who had just finished telling a story and had a smug grin on her face. "Genevieve has such a marvelous sense of humor," Empress said to the table at large and met the children's confounded faces.

"I was telling Trey about my canary. The one Guy *stepped on!*" Genevieve said, retribution prominent in her arch expression. "He has to confess at Confession now, and do penance and—"

"How many times have I told you, it was an accident! It wasn't my fault!" Guy protested.

"Was too!"

"Was not!"

"Was too!"

"Oh, dear," Empress murmured.

Trey looked at the clock and gave a nod to have his wineglass refilled.

Eduard was tucked in first after dinner, and slowly over the next two hours the other children went to bed, each insisting on Trey's good night.

With the last child settled in for the night, Empress and Trey stood outside Guy's bedroom door, an awkward silence lengthening now that they were alone without childish banter and questions and the distractions that had diverted them from their own unguarded desires. Glancing up, Empress met Trey's eyes for only a flashing moment, her gaze dropping instantly at what she saw in their heated depths. "I'd better . . . I'll check . . . on Max . . . one more time," she said, stammering, imperiled with Trey so close, with the intimate, dusky silence of the hallway enveloping them . . . with her own dangerous feelings demanding release.

Swiftly walking away, she fled down the long corridor to the nursery, praying Trey would politely leave and save her from her own susceptibility. But after she'd verified that both Max and Nanny slept peacefully, she shut the door behind her to find Trey lounging against the paneling in the hall.

"Is he sleeping?" he asked, pushing away from the hand-rubbed tulipwood.

She nodded, unable to find sufficient breath to answer.

"And Nanny?"

"Sleeping," she whispered in the merest exhalation of sound.

"Everyone's sleeping." His pale eyes shone out of the darkness of his face, his wide shoulders wider suddenly in the half shadows of the dimly lit corridor, his stature sharpened by her own vivid trepidation. He seemed very large. "You're not going out tonight?" he asked so softly, the words were almost a whisper.

Empress swallowed once before she answered in the negative, nervously looking away from his lambent eyes and mesmerizing strength. Anticipation was poised, taut, screaming through her senses, and she began counting the medallions in the carpet in a frenzied attempt to resist throwing herself at him.

"Where's your room?" he said, low and hushed.

"No!" she cried, turning back to him, demonstrable alarm unmistakable in her huge eyes and suddenly clenched fists.

But Trey noted her quivering tremor, perceptible beneath the overt alarm, and he knew how little the no meant. "You have an evening free . . ." he murmured, the unfinished sentence ripe with meaning.

"No, please," Empress breathed, but the no was several decibels softer than her first emphatic reply, while her "Please" was more a plea than a refusal.

Experienced with the physical manifestations of women

who said no when they capriciously meant yes, he reached for her slowly, his rings flashing in the subdued light, and she didn't move, only watched his arms come out to touch her, knowing she couldn't stop herself from shaking. His slender hands gently closed on her shoulders, and she shuddered in a silence so solid that their breathing seemed to part the air in waves. With deliberation he drew her near, the scent of white lilac mingling with the fragrance of mountain pine permeating Trey's clothes as the distance closed between them, her body unresisting beneath his hands, her face unconsciously lifting for his kiss.

Both struggled unsuccessfully against the resplendent passion overwhelming their senses, and in the hovering moment before their lips met, Empress whispered, "Please go."

"Yes," he said, the curve of his lowered lashes like ebony silk, and touched her lips with his.

It was a tender, butterfly-light kiss for only one scant moment, and then Empress threw her arms around his neck, his slid down to her hips, and he pulled her fiercely close, with such violence that she cried out. Selfishly he ignored her cry, intent on tasting the hot sweetness of her mouth, ravishing the welcome submission of her parted lips, crushing her body into his until every soft, silken curve melted into his hard-muscled frame. Only short moments later, with restless turbulence his mouth lifted from hers abruptly, as though his patience had a brief, measurable limit that suddenly had expired. "Which room?" he said, the words curt and urgent, his mouth drifting across the smoothness of her cheek, his hand brusquely forcing hers down to the rampant rigidity of his manhood.

She trembled at the enormous pulsing size of him beneath her hand, and as volatilely as his abrupt question, she felt her body open in a melting rush. Restlessly he forced her the few steps backward until she was trapped between himself and the paneled wall. Not waiting for an answer, quicksilver with intemperate need, he pushed her hand aside, grasped a handful of silk skirt, and shoved it out of his way. Overwrought and compelled by months of abstinence, he'd find the bedroom . . . later.

"You shouldn't be here," Empress moaned, shaken by her swelling desire, feeling the coolness of the air on her legs, hopelessly aware of Trey's strong hands sweeping up her thighs.

"I know," he replied with soft gruffness, crushing the emerald silk of her gown, pushing the fabric and petticoats upward with rough swiftness, his fingers closing on the ties to her drawers. "This won't take long."

"Damn you," she whispered at his blunt crudity, shocked back to reality from her tantalizing pleasure-drenched rapture.

"Damn you to hell, Empress Jordan, for doing this to me," he growled, jerking on the tie with an abrupt tug.

"No, Trey, please," she cried, alarmed at his intent, pushing at his intractable strength. "Not here. What if the servants . . . the children—"

And he stopped suddenly as if she'd struck him, the word *children* effective against his raging fever . . . but only for a brief moment. He was beyond reasoning, guided by an aching need that precluded logic. "Where?" he said in a harsh, deep tone that vibrated with urgency, his hand burning like a brand through the sheer batiste of her lingerie.

"There," Empress answered, understanding the incautious hunger, hardly able to control her own ardent desires, although the requisite words of denial had been spoken. On the verge of her own compulsion, which overlooked probity and principles, she pointed toward her room so she could feel him inside her again, so she could still her ravenous craving for a faithless, beautiful, and thoroughly selfish man who made her feel like she was on fire.

Picking her up in a swift, sweeping scoop of his arms, Trey strode toward her room, pushing the door open with a crash, and heedless to the sound, kicked it shut with equal force. His glance rapidly surveyed the room looking for the bed, although in his current near orgasmic state it wasn't a requirement. Dropping Empress roughly on the white satin coverlet of the gilt-and-amber shell-shaped bed, he pulled off her slippers, tossing them aside without looking, pushed her skirt and petticoats out of the way with tense impatience, stripped her drawers down with deadly quiet speed, unbuttoned his trousers in a seeming blur of motion as the pulsing urgency in his body drummed in his ears, and climbing on top of Empress without preliminaries or care, plunged into her.

Expeditious and selfish, he was finished in seconds, as though she was no more than a convenient receptacle for his lust, and withdrawing as abruptly as he had mounted her, Trey rolled away, still angry, still frustrated, orgasmic but not satiated. His arms flung over his head, he lay beside her, tense and agitated. He blamed Empress for the chaos in his mind, blamed her for the crying need inside him, for this hot, fierce wanting that ate at his reason, lawless and violent. He was never like this with women. Never. And he swore at the cupid-painted ceiling as though the smiling and oblivious garland-draped putti were the instruments of his discontent.

Lying curled on her side, her back to Trey, Empress cried silent tears of misery and self-pity. Even with his cynicism and sarcasm of the past fortnight and all the vicious insinuations, she had never expected this: a cold, impersonal coupling without a scrap of feeling, detached as though they were strangers—worse, enemies. She no longer knew this man and couldn't continue deluding herself with rainbow-colored dreams or cling to the memories of her weeks with Trey. The man lying beside her was different, harsh, and pitiless—a stranger—and she had no wish to prolong this particular wretched style of warfare. Sitting up, she slid off the bed to escape the disaster that had transpired, but Trey's hand stopped her before she could move away, closing around her wrist like a shackle, hauling her back.

"I'm not finished." His half-reclining sprawl was languorous; his expression, in belligerent contrast, mirrored his turbulent emotions—emotions, he realized with the saner sensibilities still functioning beneath his insanity for this woman, that were the grossest impudent folly.

"Please, Trey, not this way," Empress pleaded, regret in her voice and eyes.

She saw him try to master his response and fail. "Why not?" he said softly, unsettled and high-strung. "You've an evening free." His fingers were hurting her, his face hard. "Consider me your Saturday night. Offer me some of your popular, generous . . . hospitality. I'm no different from the other men."

"There aren't other men," Empress replied quietly, no longer interested in the deception, trying to reach this chill, cold man who was gripping her wrist painfully tight.

"You're lying," he retorted harshly.

"Ask them," Empress entreated, only wanting surcease from this battleground of misunderstanding.

"How droll. Should I do it individually or save time and ask them en masse whether they've slept with you? My compliments, sweetheart, on your bold offense . . . you certainly know the subtleties of when a bluff is a bluff is a bluff.'' He winked at her gratuitously and smiled his most dazzling, mocking smile.

"The simple truth," Empress said levelly, looking at the darkly handsome man who had slept with so many women that he should be the last person on earth to take a proprietary virtuous stance, "is . . . you're the only man I've ever slept with."

"Charming lie, I'm sure," Trey said with elaborate courtesy, untouched by the sincerity of her words, his own internal images of the merry widow of Paris quite different. One was not awarded the sobriquet the Green Temptress for the table one set. "Is that innocent denial normally effective?" he added as a facetious afterthought.

"What do you want from me?" Empress asked wearily, her emotions crushed and bludgeoned, her expectations and dreams in shattered fragments, all because of a beautiful man who'd shown her kindness once.

"I'd like to fuck you steadily for a week or so to begin with . . . and then I'll reassess my priorities. How does that sound?"

"It sounds like Trey Braddock-Black, world-class stud," Empress replied sharply, reminded instantly of how little her dreams meant next to the reality of his libertine life, "and I don't care to accommodate you!" she added heatedly, attempting to pull loose from his punishing grip.

He didn't move, her struggles ineffective against his effortless power. "I'm not sure your acquiescence is entirely necessary, darling," he drawled, his pale eyes raking her intransigent figure, his tone as heated as hers. "Maybe it'll be just as interesting to tie you to my bed for a fortnight and see if I can remember everything you like."

"So sorry to disappoint you," she retorted maliciously, standing defiantly before him in tumbled hair, stocking feet, and crumpled gown, "but with Max, my schedule is limited."

"You don't have to be untied to nurse Max."

"You beast! This isn't the hinterlands of Montana where your word is law!" Her voice trembled with rage. "The Jordans have been noblemen since Charlemagne, long before your people had even *seen* a horse, when the Absarokee were still hunting on foot!"

His entire person went still, not a muscle moved, his face like a mask. "I don't care," he said, each word as unyielding as his posture, "if the Jordans were here before the Flood."

A muscle high over his cheekbone clenched, marring the perfect stillness, and his voice lowered to a grating rasp. "I don't care if they rode horses for a thousand years before we did. If I want to take you away tonight, I will. Do you understand? And a nursemaid for Max is hardly a problem. Don't be naïve about my capabilities and resources." He was crushing the bones in her wrist.

Her face went pale, reminded of Trey's autocratic impulses, conscious, too, of the full extent of his compulsion. He was not a gentleman pressing his suit. And all the accoutrements of Braddock-Black power rushed back: the personal guards; the small army of clansmen; the private train and railroad track; the influence on politics; the limitless wealth. She remembered, too, a time at the ranch when she'd asked Trey what he intended doing with his life, and he'd said, "Rule my half of Montana."

"Would you?" Her eyes were deep green and large in the whiteness of her face. "Would you imprison me?"

"Maybe," he said flatly. "Come here and we'll discuss it."

"I despise you." Each word was separate, frigid, and inescapably poisonous.

"This whole situation is lunacy," he said, coolly indifferent, "so it doesn't matter as long as you flatter me with your enchanting company."

"I never will by choice," she spat, her bitterness keen-edged and surly.

"Let's see if we can remedy that." His smile was so unpleasant, she shivered at the unctuous animosity, and when he jerked on her wrist, she moved forward with trepidation. This hard, implacable man frightened her. "Undress," he said, the single word imperious. "I haven't seen you in months."

She hesitated briefly, but the expression on his face was wintry, precluding dissent, and when his fingers uncurled slowly as if testing her obedience, she obeyed.

Standing before him, faltering and uncertain, she looked at him from under the lush fall of her lashes, the green of her eyes like a magnet with that damnable capricious flicker of innocence. The lure of innocence, that was the temptation, he thought . . . wanting that trembling innocence. And he understood perfectly why they called her the Green Temptress over drinks at the clubs.

"I'm waiting." Relaxed against the ornate headboard, he ran both hands through his long hair, insult in his gesture.

Empress reached for the small enameled buttons on her dress.

"Take your hair down first," he ordered, wanting her to look as he remembered, without the fashionable Parisian hairdo of upswept curls. "I want to feel your hair."

Reaching up to slide a tortoiseshell comb from her hair, her expression mutinous after his imperious command, her transient fear nullified by her ready temper, she muttered disdainfully, "Yes, sire, will there by anything more, Your Highness?"

"There'll be substantially more, darling, before you're through," he murmured lazily, his silver eyes wolfish. "We'll be testing your docility and my imagination . . . all in due time."

"I refuse," she hissed, her eyes sparking flashes of green flame at his high-handed coercion, "to be treated like some . . . some . . ."

"Trollop?" he supplied mockingly.

"Exactly! And I *won't*!" She stood holding the jeweled comb like a weapon.

"I should think the role quite comfortable for you, Mrs. Miles. Certainly I'm not the first of your harem to make a request for some particular fancy. I *like* the feel of your hair," he noted incidentally, as though they were discussing the merits of his request and her bitterness were irrelevant. "In any event"—and his voice lost its pretense at lightness—"I'm not concerned with your opinions or sensitivities, only the availability of your body. And I'm waiting . . . the south of France is waiting . . . or if you prefer more exotic locales, North Africa."

She threw the comb at him, but he only caught the flung missile and smiled. "It's entirely up to you," he said with gentle mockery, "my *dear* Mrs. Miles."

He watched her grudgingly take down her hair and with a faint smile caught each comb she hurled at him, neatly placing them on the bedside table. She struggled a moment to work the small buttons at her wrists free, then shrugged out of her dress, dropping the glistening gown with a studied, deliberate affectation. Trey's gaze idly followed the fall of spring-green silk as it rippled to the floor at her feet. "Do you really intend on going through with this despotic charade?" she asked resentfully, standing before him in her chemise and petticoats.

"I prefer more tranquillity—or at least a restful neutrality, to be perfectly honest." He shrugged. "But Paris has made you less cooperative." Because all the other men have profoundly expanded her options, he thought censoriously.

"And Paris has brought out the bloody autocrat in you," she replied tartly.

"Ah, dear." He sighed mockingly. "Both of us with blighted hopes in paradise. But let's see what satisfaction we can salvage from the discontent. Personally," he went on with a sardonic smile, "I've always found a good fuck breaks my concentration on the disillusions of life."

"Someday," she vowed quietly, "I'm going to exact retribution for this damned servitude."

You already have, he wanted to say; *you've made ten months of my life hell.* "If you've finished playing God's avenging angel, could you move on to your next role?" he said instead, his voice deliberately mild. "Finish undressing."

Her petticoats were stripped off in quick succession as Trey watched. But his arousal was a less dispassionate gauge of his emotions, his erection prominent, rising markedly as each petticoat was discarded until she stood finally in only stockings and chemise, the focus of all sexual attention framed by her two remaining articles of clothing. He only motioned this time to have her finish, and in moments she was nude.

"Are you satisfied now?" Empress snapped, tossing aside her last stocking, her tawny hair tumbling around her shoulders, her eyes blazing.

"Hardly." His drawl was punctuated with a quick lift of his eyebrows. "Surely you understand the sequence of events in these fascinating, amorous games, sweetheart. Satisfaction comes . . . much later. But I see," he went on in the same insolent tone, "you're becoming interested. Cooperative at last—"

"I *am not,*" she repudiated hotly, his derisive murmur impelling her heated rebuff.

"Then what's that?" He raised a slender bronzed hand and languidly gestured.

Shamed, Empress felt milk oozing from her breasts, dripping on the rumpled clothes at her feet, her senses immune to her hot-tempered offense at Trey's barbaric conduct. "I'm *not* interested," she maintained stubbornly.

"Good," he said calmly, "we'll keep this businesslike."

"Fine," she replied with a toss of her head, her tone outrivaling his in indifference.

He stretched out his hand, and after one considered moment and Trey's curt, "Now," she walked forward and put her hand in his. Sitting up fully, he swung his legs over the side of the bed and pulled her close. "We can't have you ruining my suit . . . with this," he murmured as his elegant finger caught two drops of milk trickling from her nipple, and mortified at her body's brazen response, she felt the flush of embarrassment creep up her cheeks.

Trey saw the rosy blush, too, and smoothly remarked, "What a marvelous actress . . . virtuous modesty after all we've been through . . ." But it roused him, that feigned naïveté and angered him, too, when he considered how many other men had enjoyed its captivating enchantment.

"How much more," she said in a small, tight voice, "do you want?"

"I haven't," he replied very softly, gazing at her splendid glowering rage, "even started."

And if she'd dared, she would have shoved him away a short moment later as he bent his head and lowered his mouth to her breast. His lips closed gently over her peaked nipple, his tongue licking the tip, sliding over and around the hardened, tingling crest, teasing for one heartbeat, two, while she tautly waited for the full pressure of his mouth. And then it came—hard, firm, sucking—and her milk came rushing down, her knees went weak, every pleasure receptor in her body opened wide. His hands came up swiftly to steady her, clamped hard on her hips, and supported her while he teased and sucked and nibbled and made her think: It's been too long . . . too long . . . *too* long. She shouldn't respond so acutely, *she mustn't,* Empress thought in the next instant, desperately fighting the dizzying sensations. He was everything she hated in a man—arrogant, insolent, selfish. But a thundering pleasure pealed through her body, drummed, roared, swelled through every quivering nerve, obliterating judgment, scorning cognitive thought, only wanting lavish, unrestrained fulfillment. And she felt a wayward wetness not only at her breasts but also sliding down from the pit of her stomach, a hot, tropical, steaming heat that wantonly disregarded "shouldn't" and "mustn't," overlooked the flagrant flaws in Trey's character, and waited, poised breathlessly, for the surging rapture to intensify.

With gentleness and skill, with luscious calculated languor, Trey sucked on each of her breasts while the heat centered in the spiraling core of her stomach radiated outward until a rosy flush adorned her body and desire burned like a wild and violent flame inside her.

"I think," Trey murmured, lifting his mouth away at last, his husky voice fragrant with exaggerated courtesy, "we've remedied the indifference . . . don't you agree?"

Her eyes half shut, her breathing small, incoherent sighs, Empress fought the lazy, rankling confidence in his tone. "No," she obstinately whispered.

He shrugged, touching each nipple with a light brushing finger and murmured negligently, "I suppose we could quibble over our interpretations of indifference, but I won't be ungallant when you're being so amenable." He circled a nipple delicately. "On one thing perhaps we can agree. At least now"—he lightly squeezed each nipple—"you won't drench my suit." And like an appraiser might estimate or consider what next to do, he placed his palms over her breasts as she stood, beset by her tumultuous feelings, trying to control her breathing, trying to deny the pulsing need, splayed his long fingers over their ripe fullness and rested his hands on the pale, high-swelling curves like they were his property. Her breasts had always been voluptuous, but they were ostentatious now, jutting out, her fair skin showing a trace of veining on the full outer curvature, as though the pressure of their swollen weight was making the pale flesh translucent.

Like a small, flaunting goddess of fertility, he thought, Empress lured and beckoned. *Touch me and I'll give you pleasure,* she enticed, *suckle me and I'll give you sustenance.* His warm palms drifted over the flamboyant curve of her breasts, trailed down her ribs and narrow waist, traced the smooth roundness of her hips, gliding slowly to the splendid juncture of her thighs. Stroking the smooth, heated flesh and her pale silky hair, he felt her rise into the pressure of his hand, and his calm assessment abruptly ceased, his own intemperate passion flaring in response. The goddess offered more than pleasure and sustenance; she offered glory in the heated, sweet center of her body, a glory he wanted so badly, he could feel a pulsing ache creep up his spine. Sliding his long fingers into her dampness, into the luxurious haven that tantalized, he delicately stroked the velvety softness and watched her face, slipped upward slowly until he touched the precious, throbbing focus of her rapture, and heard her blissful sigh of pleasure. Completely detached from every reality but Trey's exquisite stroking fingers, Empress swayed slightly into each luscious ascent of his hand, purred low in the back of her throat, and damned him for being so good. She should be standing here coldly and indifferently, not craving the delicate pressure of his fingers, not wanting Trey to make love to her, not feeling as though she were going to die from the pleasure. "Please, Trey . . . I can't wait . . ." she breathed, "please . . . please . . ."

She was absolutely ready to dissolve, he noted with an expertise honed to perfection through endless observation. He had found his delightful heaven on earth and, after months of exile, was about to enter Empress's luscious gates to paradise.

The long, frustrating wait was over.

Withdrawing his fingers, he moved away from Empress to lean against the carved headboard. Despite Empress's earlier denials, she was aroused, past aroused, and his own passions had been urgent since he first set eyes on her two hours after arriving in Paris. The time for unnatural constraint was over; he intended to consummate his intense craving for the beautiful woman who had left him, who had the attention of every hot-blooded aristocratic male in Paris, who had refused to acknowledge that she wanted him but would please him tonight despite her denial and rancor because she was flame-hot right now, exactly as he remembered. "Come here," he said in a brusque, raspy tone. "Come and sit on me."

Passion was clamoring for release in Empress's mind—in her body; her hot, flushed skin and nerves and stretched-taut pleasure centers—but pride stopped her, and unmoving, she gazed at him with wild, tempestuous eyes.

"If you don't care to obey *here*," Trey said very low, "you will in the charming prison I can arrange for you. Good manners are not my strong suit." And he surveyed with appreciation the magnificent woman before him, proud and defiant, her fragile beauty paradoxically juxtaposed to a riveting, untamed sexuality.

Her eyes, frankly hostile now, met his.

"You decide," he said softly.

She went then to where he reclined, braced against the gilded wood, his splendid erection blatant. Fully clad with only his trousers unbuttoned, his clothing, opposed to her nudity, was a calculated conceit to underscore her servility.

Like the afternoon round of the brothels by the Jockey Club members before they went off to the races, where there was no need to disrobe for their brief encounters with the courtesan, or at least only a minimum of uncovering was required. It wasn't even necessary to get into bed if one's trouser crease took priority. "I'm sure you're familiar with this . . . I *know* you are," he amended, his pale eyes slowly traveling over her voluptuous body as she kneeled beside him, hesitant. "The feigned reluctance is unnecessary." And he lounged mere inches away, offering no assistance, only loosening the foulard cravat at his neck, exposing a glimmer of gold chain.

"You sanctimonious hypocrite," Empress hissed furiously, and her hand lashed out to strike him.

His reflexes were superb. He even allowed her the tenuous satisfaction of almost succeeding, his fingers closing cruelly around her wrist just as her fingertips grazed his cheek. "Let's not make this difficult," he said softly, his grip harsh. "I'm not asking you to enjoy it, only do it . . . or I'll take you away and you'll service me in the quiet of the country." He held her hand upright between them, his grasp relentless, her entire body rigidly aggressive. "You're not strong enough," he whispered, her stormy expression pugnacious, as though she'd spring at him in attack if he released his hold. "I hope we understand each other. I wouldn't," he said with exquisite delicacy, "want to hurt you."

"The man who'd force himself on a woman has scruples," Empress said with a sneer.

"Sweetheart," Trey murmured smoothly, "the only thing I'd be forcing, from the looks of your primed body, is forcing you to . . . wait."

Her free hand hotly came up, and no longer as indulgent, his own anger rising, Trey caught it before it neared his face. "I'm getting tired of this damn melodramatic resistance," he growled, "so make up your mind . . . the south of France, North Africa, or this very convenient bed."

Their eyes were level as she knelt beside him, both her hands held prisoner by Trey, and for a long moment she resisted compliance.

Then her eyes dutifully lowered.

And he slowly released his grip on her wrists.

But for all his flaunted indifference, his hands closed on her hips as she began to lower herself onto him, and when she'd fully absorbed his hard length and he could feel her hot around him, his eyes shut briefly and he groaned deep in his throat, a sound as familiar to Empress as her own shuddering sigh.

Without effort he lifted her, then lowered her with deliberate slowness, raising her again until she maintained his rhythm herself, rising and descending with measured smoothness, her thighs rubbing against the wool of his trousers, her full breasts grazing the texture of his jacket as she complied to his demands. His loosened cravat felt cool when it slipped between her breasts, in contrast to the warm friction on her thighs and breasts where the wool fabric touched her skin.

Empress had no intention of responding to Trey's calculated act of tyranny, but her traitorous body, so long in hermitage, discounted grudging intent and shamelessly, within only a few fugitive moments, undutifully dissolved into throbbing, impassioned need.

Trey intended to sit collected and let Empress do what she did as the merry widow of Paris, but she was peaking so fast, his own passions spurred and heightened at her tempestuous, hot-blooded hunger. Holding her with his hands firmly on her hips, he impatiently rose to meet her restless ardor, thrust upward at the same time he pressed her hips fiercely down, and she screamed as intoxicating sensation flooded her body. At her wild cry Trey felt himself swell inside her so it hurt for a moment, the violent intensity clamping his teeth shut until a second later savage, unrestrained pleasure washed over him. Feverishly he drove violently into her again, and in the next flame-hot moment she was plunging over the edge. With an uncurbed, hammering wildness he joined her, his hands rising against his will at the end to twine in the pale silk of her tumbled hair, and he crushed her so tightly, he could feel her melting into him as they climaxed. A convulsive shudder shook him when it was over, and Empress collapsed on his shoulder with a great, gulping sigh.

Burying his face in her cloud-soft hair, he held her close as the delicious sweetness pulsed with diminishing intensity. Making love to her, holding her, felt like a homecoming, he thought with blissful contentment. Empress could hear Trey's heart beating in a frenzied echo of her own as she lay on his shoulder, and reaching up, she tenderly kissed the curve of his throat in gratitude. She had forgotten the profound, unmitigated intensity that took one away like a tidal wave, and also the winsome, snuggling warmth when he held her like he was doing now. His hands were gently stroking her back, and she suddenly wanted to feel his skin next to hers.

He felt her fingers on the hot, damp skin of his neck, and in the next moment his cravat slid free with a single swift tug. When her hands moved to the buttons of his suit coat, they were excitable and urgent, no languid female gentleness or timid awkwardness, and every sensitized cell in his body responded to her restless, demanding haste, his passions re-kindling as though he had never climaxed. "I want you," she whispered, and touched his lips with the tip of her tongue.

"You have me," he breathed, moving in slow suggestion inside her so she felt a sumptuous, undulating surge of excitement.

She had his shirt undone, and her hands slid inside to caress his muscled chest. "Take your clothes off." Her voice was liquid enticement, and the slow, gliding rotation of her hips so provocative and rich with invitation that all the previ-ous women in his life were relegated to novices.

And when he said no to her command on principle, his dislike of women giving orders in bed intrinsic, Empress whispered, "Yes," and bending low, ran her tongue over the velvety lobe of his ear, murmuring an impelling reason for changing his mind. He helped her tug his clothes off in a feverish rush, and there was no courting, both deprived too long, both resentful beneath the tumultuous passion that over-whelmed all impulses like a wall of flame roaring across parched grasslands. The third time was as selfish as before. He couldn't get enough of her, nor she of him, and when it began the fourth time, it was as though a desperate force overcame them both. He rolled her beneath him in one fren-zied movement, and she clung to him as though she thought he might leave her. He realized she wouldn't have let him go—he couldn't have released her this side of death, in any case, and with a mad, dizzying urgency he took them both with an insistent, only partially contained, violence to a high pinnacle, keeping them there with practiced timing for long, extended moments of agonizing pleasure. He bit her at the very peak of conspicuous, glittering sensation, a small nip-ping bite on the scented skin of her shoulder, lush and tingling.

And she reached up in scorching response, sinking her teeth into the dark bronzed skin just below his ear, brushing his hair aside with an abrupt sweep of her hand when it slid through her teeth. She bit urgently, sharply, her teeth closing with a savage ferocity. And he felt his next orgasm begin. The resulting explosion left them both gasping for breath, and they lay in stunned oblivion, feeling as though their bodies had melted.

When Empress looked up finally, Trey's eyes were shut, his breathing still labored as he lay above her, propped lightly on his elbows, protecting her from his full weight. Holding him gently, her small hands resting on his powerful shoulders, she felt a contentment so rich, it vibrated in palpable ripples over her skin and deep into her soul. How had she ever thought she could live without him?

How, he was thinking, can she sustain this pace with so many men? Then a slurred male voice demanded from the vicinity of the stairway, "I tell you, dammit, I want to see her!"

The butler's voice could be heard in rebuff, although his lowered tones didn't carry with the clarity of the inebriated caller.

Trey went rigid, his breathing in abeyance as the sounds of a scuffle punctuated the quiet of the evening. With diminishing volume the insistent man was shown back downstairs and the voices died away. Wordlessly Trey detached Empress's clinging arms and rolled away. As he silently withdrew, Empress whispered, "Don't go," in a small, artless voice that reminded him of the first night at Lily's when she'd coaxed him to stay. The words sounded wanton in his suddenly grim, black mood, and her eyes when he glanced at her lying only inches away, warm and softly available, were . . . accommodating.

Her courtesanlike ways disgusted him, his own jealousy an unrecognized emotion. No wonder, he thought, she was so in demand. Few women were so explosively receptive, so spontaneously, *immediately* receptive—as orgasmic as a nymphomaniac. "You may have a caller waiting downstairs," he said, his voice remote, "and I have another engagement." Leaving the bed, he walked to the small sink in the corner, wet a towel, and wiped the sweat and residue of lovemaking from his body.

"I don't know who that was," Empress said quietly, Trey's resentment visible in his eyes, the severe set of his mouth, in the very stiffness of his posture, "but he's gone now. Please stay." She was without pride, she sadly thought as she uttered the words, without pride or shame in her passion for this man.

Trey was retrieving his clothes from the floor, and he glanced up sharply at Empress's words. With the taste of her still in his mouth, his wanting her as pungent as the sweet flavor lingering like savory memory, it took significant self-denial to say finally, "I can't."

"I wish you would," she said softly, torn between fighting for his interest and the humiliation of pleading.

Shutting his eyes briefly against his own powerful feelings, he inhaled softly before his luminous eyes opened and he resumed buttoning his shirt. "I promised the Duchesse de Soissons," he said levelly "to make an appearance at her ball." Although until Empress's drunken caller had interrupted the evening, he had forgotten the commitment.

"Could we talk about this?" Empress asked, sitting up in the shambles of the bedclothes and directing the full intensity of her perplexed, inquiring glance at the silent man swiftly dressing in the center of the room.

"There's no point in discussing anything," he replied tersely, tucking his shirt into his trousers, "although I sincerely thank you, Mademoiselle Jordan, for your time." He could have been talking to a shopkeeper, for all the warmth in his tone. Raking his fingers through his long hair with brisk economy, he reached for his suit coat and, taking out the thin leather wallet large enough for French bills, extracted several and tossed them on the dresser. "Bill me if that's not sufficient. I'm unfamiliar with the price of mother's milk, but knowing you, I'm sure it's costly." A flicker of tenderness softened his harsh features before he added, "My lawyers will contact you concerning my son, mademoiselle, and I'd suggest you cooperate." His light eyes went flinty, and his voice took on an astringent quality as he appended softly, "Just a friendly warning—if you try to keep my son from me, I'll destroy you. . . ."

Empress went deathly pale at the primitive menace beneath the softly uttered words, instinctively drawing back, as though Trey's dangerous voice alone could harm her.

Devastated by her flaming passion and its impact on him, Trey wouldn't look at Empress again as she sat on the bed in beautiful disarray. He wouldn't because he wanted her still, could never have enough of her, and his pride—bred through generations of Absarokee chiefs—wouldn't allow him to want the most popular widow in Paris. But the vice of pride served another purpose as well: It kept his voice steady when he bade her good night.

Neither, however, passed a pleasant night. Tormented, Trey decided to return to America and, after packing, spent the remainder of the night pacing the floor. Empress found sleep impossible, her heart shattered and bleeding. The anger in his voice had been killing . . . and fraught with coldness.

By morning, numbed and listless, she couldn't cry anymore, drained of emotion, along with her tears.

Trey inaugurated the sunrise with a brandy.

Twenty-four

———————————•———————————

AS SOON AS it was decently possible, Trey had the concierge come up and arrange steamship tickets for New York. Once he had decided to leave, he had hoped to make connections that morning, but the earliest departure was a day away, so he pleasantly thanked the man, swore roundly the moment the door closed on his uniformed back, and poured himself another brandy to lighten his dismal mood. His trip to Paris had been an unfortunate mistake, except for the glorious fact that he now knew of his son. And weighed against the bitter distaste when he thought of Empress, Max more than balanced the equation. The other children, too, were important to him, and he would have to see if arrangements could be made for visits, although after last night more than a polite request would probably be required. Fortunately with Empress, the leverage of large sums of money was sure to produce results . . . and fortunately he had large sums of money. She was at least predictable, he thought caustically . . . so *very* convenient.

After finishing his brandy he went out to wire his parents, informing them of his return, and after the usual delays with bureaucratic red tape, it was mid-morning when he walked back through the grilled doors of the Hotel Athenée. The

SUSAN JOHNSON

lobby was mildly adrift with those who included a morning constitutional in their regimen and were coming or going in pursuit of this healthy endeavor. Sam Chester stood out flagrantly in his evening clothes, but then so did Trey, as the only red Indian in the conventional assortment of businessmen and leisured gentlefolk. Sam shouted a greeting across the quiet lobby, obviously not entirely sober, and Trey smiled politely at all the curious darting glances, decided Sam was exactly what he needed today to take his mind off Empress, and from all appearances he had some catching up to do in the consumption of alcohol.

After the surprised questions were sufficiently answered in the usual laconic male fashion that disregarded past, future, and all but the immediate, nonemotional present, Trey and Sam retired to the Jockey Club to idle away the day. They talked horses, then inevitably women, in a quiet corner of the club and compared the merits of various cognacs as the day progressed. With the sun shining warmly through the tall windows, the cognac, drunk Trey's favorite way, with a slice of sugared lemon as prelude, felt even warmer going down . . . and soothing, tempering the raw, brutal edges of his discontent and disillusionment. Talking with Sam, Trey was reminded of their carefree days at college when pleasure and play were prominent, problems were nonexistent, and nothing more serious than a tutor's displeasure sullied the genial drift of days. Was it only a few years ago? He felt tired today, like an old man.

"Did you hear about the duel over the Duchesse du Montre?" Sam's sandy brown hair stood on end with an electric energy commensurate with his vitality. At school he and Trey had always led all the youthful pranks, more reckless than most, their impulsive personalities recognizing a kindred spirit in each other, and Sam's eyes were alight now with the delicious scandal of a young army officer fighting over a married woman fifteen years his senior.

Smiling benignly at Sam's irrepressible interest in excitement of any kind, Trey said blandly, "Who hasn't?"

"I can't imagine dueling over her. She's old." Sam viewed any woman over thirty as ancient.

Looking at him over the rim of his glass, Trey pleasantly dissented. "I saw her at Dunette's, and I think most would disagree with you. And *you* wouldn't fight over a woman if you found your wife in flagrante delicto."

Sam grinned. "True . . . with all the women in the world, it doesn't pay to get overly excited about any particular one."

Before Empress, Trey would have wholeheartedly agreed with his friend's *dégagé* opinion, but circumstance had forever altered his former nonchalance. He wasn't currently in the mood, however, to divulge his passion for one of Paris's newest *horizontales*. "There do seem to be a great number of available women," Trey said noncommittally.

"Aren't there always," Sam agreed with a dismissive shrug. Endowed with healthy good looks, a fine athlete's body, and his father's millions, Sam understood female surfeit. "Guiley had to flee to Belgium," he declared, back to his amusing gossip.

"It won't be for long," Trey remarked, pouring himself another drink. "Form's sake."

"Her husband bought drinks here afterward, and bored everyone with tales of his young mistress," Sam said. "You know the young dancer from the Comédie Française?"

Trey nodded. Who didn't know of the newest star in the chorus?

"Montre doesn't care about his wife, but who does, I suppose? You're not married, are you?" he asked in hasty afterthought, since he and Trey hadn't seen each other in two years.

"No." Trey's voice was crisp and clipped.

"Didn't think so . . . not exactly the marrying kind, are you," Sam said with a grin. "But if you ever *did* marry, would you consider fighting a *duel* over your wife?" The European custom seemed an anachronistic curiosity to Sam, particularly with his abstract disregard for female company other than in bed.

Trey thought of the rage he felt when he contemplated Empress's admirers, and how he wanted to kill every man who touched her. He opened his lips before he spoke and then said very slowly, "I don't know."

It was the chill voice that prompted recall of the rumors about Trey through Sam's increasing cognac fog. "Jesus, I forgot," he blurted out. There had been a duel once after a long night of drinking in Montmartre when hardly anyone had been sober enough to count off the paces. Except Trey, of course. His hand had been firm and unwavering; only his glittering eyes were uncommonly brilliant. The man had died.

And it hadn't been over a woman, now that he recalled, although a woman was involved.

"I was trying to miss him," Trey said, his voice moderate, his dark brows drawn together in a faint scowl. "Damn fool didn't stand still."

As the day progressed, Sam began insisting that Trey accompany him to LeNotre's party that evening. "Can't miss it, Trey. Best damn wine cellar in France."

In his current frame of mind that suddenly sounded like a sensible reason for attending a party. "Might as well, Sam, it's my last night in Paris."

"Have to go, then," Sam replied succinctly. "Need a drink and a woman on your last night in Paris."

"Why not," Trey said softly. It was over with Empress . . . finally. He could never share her, and she wasn't the kind of woman to settle for one man. Ironic justice, he thought with bitter wistfulness. How often had he politely discarded a woman, lived his own life without limits. Now he'd met a woman doing the same . . . no limits for her. He felt suddenly, despite his years, weary, burned to ashes.

Although Empress had been committed to go to the LeNotre party for several weeks, she called Etienne, who had been planning to escort her, and left a message of regret, pleading illness.

Her heartache that morning was as unendurable as ever, fresh, as though Trey had left only minutes before, and she hurt so, she didn't know whether she was capable of forcing a smile and exchanging pleasantries. Food made her sick, her throat closed up every time she thought of Trey's cold eyes, and only Adelaide's perceptive invitation to take the children for the day saved her from the dread prospect of explaining Trey's departure to them.

After a morning spent wallowing in self-pity, alternating with rage at Trey's insulting contempt, Empress decided there was little future in either course and she had already shed enough tears over Trey Braddock-Black in the last months to float the French fleet. It was time to go on with her life. So when Etienne refused to acknowledge the butler's polite, "Madame is not home today," he said, "Thank you, Bartlett, you've done your duty," handed him his hat and gloves, walked through the door of Empress's sitting room a moment later with a boyish grin, and declared, "You can't be ill, I'm taking you out tonight.'' Empress greeted him with genuine affection.

In the course of his visit, he cheered her with his wry humor, distracted her with amusing anecdotes, made her feel cherished as a woman and valued as a friend. And after last night she was vulnerable to his captivating charm; she agreed to have him come fetch her at nine. He had ten dozen of the new Madame Isaac Pereire roses sent over to help buoy her out of her doldrums. Massed in all their lush magenta beauty in the foyer, the world's most fragrant rose lifted her spirits. As did Etienne's endearing gallantry.

The teasing tone of his enclosed note blended with a beguiling charm that amused and made no overt claims. In a bold scrawl that moved across the armorial embossed paper with an unconstrained rhythm matching his character, he wrote, in place of sonnets he was hoping to make her dizzy with the attar of roses at which point she might become giddy enough to say yes to him. Even his seduction was genial, nonthreatening, an offer to pleasant pleasure for them both, and upon reading his note, Empress abruptly decided that Etienne would be the most sensible, agreeable, and satisfying way to forget Trey. She had preserved her passion for him long past prudent judgment, and last night had coldly demonstrated the extent of Trey's feelings for her.

She'd burned the money last night after furiously trying to tear it into shreds without success. In a tearful frenzy of strewn perfume bottles and frantic, hiccuping sobs, she'd found her manicure scissors on her dressing table, taken the bills she'd twisted out of shape, and sitting on the floor, cut the large-denomination francs into thousands of tiny pieces, as if each slash of the minute blades were another jagged cut into Trey's cold, black heart. Gathering the scattered scraps and fragments, her hysteria unabated by their mutilation, she'd flung them into the fireplace and kept the fire roaring till morning.

That night, she decided, Etienne's crested letter in her hand and the rose perfume permeating the house, she was going to end her long celibacy, her misguided fidelity to a man who had no conception of the word. Etienne would be safe, no melancholy or broken hearts . . . and amusing. He'd also stave off the more serious suitors who wanted their love returned. She wasn't ready for serious love and commitment and all the earnest tenderness and gravity that a consideration

of marriage would imply. Her suitors who importuned for a
wife would have to wait until her bleeding heart healed. For
the moment all she wanted was to blot out Trey's memory,
and Etienne, if rumor was true, was skilled and seductive
enough to eradicate Trey from her mind.

And all seemed pleasantly on track with Empress's newly
planned future: Etienne arrived looking magnificent in his
evening clothes, living up to his reputation as the handsomest
man in Paris. He was attentive to the children before they
left, amiable as they rode to the ball in his specially designed
carriage that allowed room for his long legs, devoted at
LeNotre's as an escort, conversationalist, and dance partner.
And brightly amusing. Empress found herself genuinely laughing, something she'd thought forever impossible after the
previous night.

In recognition of her new intent, Empress had discarded
her pretense of mourning and worn vivid magenta silk,
embellished with black lace and yards of silver ribbon, an
elaborate, extravagant evening gown that matched her glittering, frothy mood and Etienne's roses. Several of the fragrant
blooms were adorning her hair, others were tucked seduc-
tively into her low décolletage, and when she walked into the
ballroom on Etienne's arm, a sudden hush indicated that all
present were aware the Duc de Vec had taken the prize as
winner in the club betting. Out of mourning, the former
Comtesse de Jordan was breathtaking, her fair hair and skin
set off to perfection by the intense shade of pink, the decorative lace lending a tantalizing wickedness to her image, her
intoxicating gaiety heightening the sinfully romantic contrast
with the Duc's dark, suave sensuality.

"Well, the girl has recouped the family fortune—and in
spades, if she has de Vec's attention. He's a very generous
man." The speaker was viewing Empress through a finely
enameled lorgnette.

"She's bold like her father in that magnificent gown, and
on de Vec's arm, as conspicuous as you please . . . but blood
holds true," her companion remarked, her own glass lifted to
her eyes. "Who but Maximilian Jordan would have carried
off the English ambassador's son's betrothed. Even though every
man was flirting with the English earl's daughter and playing
the amorous games—she was, after all, the most beautiful girl
in Paris that season," she went on, scrutinizing Empress with
the critical eye of a dowager who had watched decades of

beautiful young girls pass by, "everyone else had sense enough to know the limits of flirtation. Leave it to Max to want what he shouldn't," she finished in the fashion of the elderly discussing the past as though it were the present.

"Heloise spoiled him."

"He was her only child." Since both elderly ladies had known Empress's grandmother, the brief sentence was explanation enough, and they nodded solemnly in agreement.

"Even the Rochefort duel was rash. No one in their right mind would have taken on Rochefort. He was ruthless. No one but Max . . . and all for his darling wife."

Both lorgnettes came up simultaneously, assessing Maximilian Jordan's gorgeous daughter in the arms of the Duc de Vec, waltzing past them so close, the fragrance of the roses drifted into their noses.

"She's more beautiful than her mother." Was it waspishness or a compliment? The tone was abrupt, the sentence ending with a sniff. Or was it nostalgia for the past that tainted the ambiguous tone?

"She has Max's eyes . . . spectacular with her coloring."

"Max put those enticing eyes to good use for years." And for a moment both recalled the splendor of the Third Empire when they were still young enough to partake in the gaiety.

"Until he fell head over heels for La Belle Anglaise," came the curt reminder of reality.

"How serious is de Vec?" Their attention was focused once more on the present and the eye-catching couple waltzing across the floor.

"He's more interested than usual. Isabelle was short with me earlier when I mentioned that her husband seemed to prefer dancing this evening in contrast to his usual interest in the gaming tables."

"You're right. He never dances."

"I love dancing, Etienne." Empress smiled up at her partner. "You're a wonderful dancer."

His own smile was indulgent, his heavy-lidded eyes amused at her obvious pleasure. "And I love dancing with you." She was champagne bright and so beautiful, he was tempted to kiss her. The roses had been a good choice; the coloring was superb with her hair and skin.

"Will your wife mind?" Empress asked delicately, because this was their tenth consecutive dance and she only just realized that Isabelle was at LeNotre's as well. When Etienne had offered to escort her, she'd assumed Isabelle was in the country or engaged elsewhere, and while she understood that Etienne's marriage was a dynastic one, she wasn't certain what decorum required when he and his wife were both in attendance at the same party.

"Mind what?" the Duc replied absently, his attention concentrated on a tall, dark-haired half-blood walking in from the card room.

"Mind me dancing with you."

He looked down at her. She wasn't that naïve, surely, not with her frank personality, which he found so attractive. "Isabelle and I understand the social courtesies. I'm sure she won't mind." His answer was neutral in the event that Empress was sincere in her query. He and Isabelle understood the social courtesies to perfection: he paid all her bills; she raised the children; and if she wished to speak with him in person, she sent a note by a servant setting up an appointment. It was all very civilized. The Braddock-Black cub was glaring at them, he noticed over Empress's blond curls. No . . . he was distracted now by a woman tapping him on the shoulder with her fan. Ah, Clothilde Chimay. She was without doubt a distraction. Perhaps the American would be diverted.

As the evening pleasantly advanced, Empress was convinced she'd made the right decision. She'd enjoyed the ball enormously. Etienne was not only a superb dancer but also so entertaining, she'd not thought of Trey once. How easy this all was going to be, she decided complacently, and chided herself briefly for not seeing the advantage of a fascinating man like Etienne sooner.

Her complacence was seriously shaken a short time later, however, when she caught sight of Trey's dark head bent attentively toward a glorious woman with pale hair like dandelion down and daringly bare shoulders which he was holding lightly as he smiled down at her. Momentarily sickened at the intimacy of his smile and the suggestive position of his hands, Empress misstepped, clumsily breaking rhythm and treading on Etienne's toes. Smiling her apology, she forced her eyes away from the devastating sight—it was Clothilde Chimay he was holding, she saw as they danced closer, the most sought-after young heiress in Europe. And her appeal wasn't exclusively monetary, although rumor had it her family had financed the Franco-Prussian War. She was always described as that Baltic princess's daughter, as though it not only accounted for her pale white hair but her wildness as well.

A fluttering tremor shuddered through her as she visualized Trey and Clothilde in bed together, and as soon as the dance ended, she asked for champagne. "Two glasses, please," she said with a tight smile. And when Etienne returned with them, she gulped them down in an unfashionable rush.

"I hope that's not Dutch courage to face the coming hours with me," he said facetiously, with a smile calculated to disarm.

Empress flushed at his assumption and lied, unable to reveal that she was hopelessly jealous of Clothilde Chimay over a man who had no feelings for her beyond carnal lust. "No, of course not. Dancing makes me thirsty, that's all."

"Another, then?" he asked courteously, intent on making her comfortable, intent on altering, before the night was over, her brittle elan.

"Yes, please." And that portion went down as quickly.

Very late, just as they were preparing to leave, Trey came up to Empress and the Duc. He had been aware of Empress all evening, as she had been conscious of him since first seeing his dark head bent low to Clothilde's flirtatious banter, and despite his best intentions to ignore her, he found himself unable to leave for America without saying good-bye to her one last time. He had not expected it to matter so much, but it did . . . the thought of never seeing her again.

"Good evening," Trey said to them both, his eyes on Empress.

The bite showed under his ear, a perfect oval of teeth marks, reddened and darker than his bronzed skin. The Duc saw it and negligently wondered what else the lady had bitten. Empress colored furiously at the sight of her passionate brand.

"I didn't know you were a friend of LeNotre," the Duc said.

"I'm not." Trey didn't take his eyes from Empress.

"I hear you were at the Jockey Club today," Etienne said. "LeNotre's the steward. Perhaps you met him."

"No," Trey said.

Empress crushed her ostrich-feather fan to keep her hands from trembling.

The Duc thoughtfully took in both Empress's and Trey's stiff, frozen postures and the yearning in their eyes. It was a mistake to show that longing so clearly. Unguarded youth. One learned.

"I'm leaving in the morning," Trey said, a muscle clenching along his jaw, "so I thought I'd say good-bye. Tell the children I'll write." His voice was low and perfectly level.

Empress felt her heart stop at the finality of his statement, but there was no alternative other than to respond politely, as calmly as he'd spoken. "*Bon voyage,* then. The children will be pleased to hear from you." With sheer willpower she kept her voice from breaking.

So it was the Duc tonight, Trey thought bitterly, feeling the bile of jealousy rise into his mouth. He swallowed and, with a small bow in the Duc's direction, smiled that effortless smile that charmed so many people. "*Au revoir,*" he said.

Empress could not smile back, less experienced in the politesse that passed for feeling. "*Au revoir,*" she whispered, and watched him walk away. Pale-haired, beautiful Clothilde was waiting for him, Empress noted as Etienne slid her velvet wrap around her shoulders. God, it hurt to love him.

"I think I need a drink," she said.

With new resolution Empress climbed into Etienne's carriage, and when he put his arm around her shoulders and drew her near, she leaned into his solid strength. She needed him tonight, desperately needed to erase all the sensual images of Trey demolishing her reason and to free herself from the tenacious hold he had on her sensations. Etienne's mouth was warm and gentle as it touched hers lightly, but as his embrace tightened and his kiss deepened, a sudden panic assailed her. Shuddering slightly, she unconsciously pulled away.

The Duc instantly recognized her uncertainty. "You're too beautiful," he said in a gentle murmur. "Forgive me, *ma petite,* for rushing you."

Empress apologized, stammering, abashed at her virginal reaction. "No, Etienne . . . it's . . . my fault."

"Is this the first time since your husband's death?" His hand was warm on her shoulder, his voice soothing.

Empress nodded mutely. Although Trey was not her husband, it would be her first time with another man.

"Come, sweet, we've all night. There's no urgency."

Unlike Trey, she thought, whose urgency matched her own. He pulled her against his chest and, leaning his head back, said pleasantly, "Tell me now, did you enjoy LeNotre's ball? If nothing else, his chef is superb." The Duc wondered if her husband had been boorish in bed, occasioning this tentativeness for lovemaking. Or maybe she was simply shy. Either was easily remedied with patience and skill, both of which the Duc possessed.

Smiling up at him, Empress whispered, "Thank you, Etienne, for being so understanding . . . and yes, I enjoyed myself immensely." She may never experience the rash, ungovernable passion she had with Trey, but Etienne offered a tenderness with which she was willing to be content, and looking up into his lazy, heavy-lidded eyes, glinting with a restrained sensuality, she understood that he offered more than tenderness. Which accounted, no doubt, for his vast reputation as a lover and explained why so many women had been undone by his charm.

As Empress and the Duc walked into the foyer past the massed roses and ascended the marble staircase, they whispered quietly to avoid waking the servants. Entering her boudoir, Empress was laughing softly at Etienne's droll rendition of a stuffy princess who had asked him about his mother's health, all the time casting Empress a flintly-eyed look.

"You were very gallant," she said, reaching up to kiss him lightly on the cheek, "when you said your Mama and I were dear friends."

"She would adore you. Mama is more pleasure-loving than I and didn't spend her entire life minding her flower gardens," Etienne replied with a swift, vivid smile.

"Then I shall have to meet her someday," Empress declared happily, her mood altered again from her timidity in the carriage. Lighthearted and at ease, she was enjoying Etienne's casual courtship, confident once more that he was the perfect companion to amuse and divert her. For the first time in her life she felt a wicked sense of sophistication, a new worldliness that she owed in part to Adelaide's counsel. Her cousin had been urging her for weeks now, since Max's birth, to take a lover. And thanks to Adelaide, she needn't fear another pregnancy, for she now had Greek sponges her cousin had assured her were efficient. "Really, darling," Adelaide had said, "look around you. Do you see anyone with more than two children? Valentin has his heir; I've my sweet

Stephanie to dress in ruffles, and my duty is done. And Valentin approves. He prefers me slim and attractive, and I quite agree. Also, how would it look if every time a lady took a lover she presented her husband with a bastard? There are women who do, of course, but they're the ones foolishly enamored of their lovers." So tonight Empress intended to step into the fashionable world of dalliance and *amour* with her eyes wide open and her heart conveniently on holiday.

Twirling away from the Duc in high good spirits, she untied her evening wrap, tossed it on the bed, and turned back to him with a welcoming smile on her lips. But a moment later, as he gently embraced her and leisurely began kissing her, a ghastly panic engulfed her. She felt nothing. Guy could have been kissing her good night for all the sensation Etienne's warm lips were provoking. Dear Lord, she thought desperately, could she really go through with this without desire? Would the heated feeling and turbulent passion she felt stir when Trey touched her or simply looked at her, would those overpowering sensations develop later as Etienne began making love to her?

Her hands trembled as they rested on Etienne's chest, indecision and unease washing over her with perturbing, distracting intensity. It was utter infantile madness to expect drumrolls and a heavenly chorus, she reasoned, and it was time she grew up. Certainly she should have learned with brutal frankness last night that only a single emotion was enough to initiate lovemaking. The perfect alignment of love, passion, tenderness, sentiment, and caring was a fairy-tale concept. The previous night, lust had been enough. Tonight she'd learn of tenderness, perhaps . . . and only innocents indulged in fantasy dreams unrestrained by undeniable reality. The man holding her in his arms was the essence of all that was charming and gallant. Who better to obliterate memories of Trey and show her new delights?

But in the next instant Etienne's dark head dipped, his mouth traced a path down her throat, and all she felt was overwhelming terror. *I'm not ready,* she thought agitatedly, *I can't . . . I can't,* and breathlessly she began pushing at his chest.

"Don't be afraid, *ma petite,*" he murmured, drawing her back, his hands soothing her as they would a frightened child. Confident in his expertise, the Duc knew he could rouse her, intrigued after so many practiced women to find such artless virtue. How enticing her simple, unsophisticated reserve! For the first time in years he felt more than a moderate excitement. "I won't hurt you, darling," he said, holding her face in his hands. "Kiss me now," he murmured, "and I'll show you—"

"Monsieur Le Duc, could I have a moment of your time?" The familiar voice, deadly quiet, paralyzed Empress. The Duc's hands dropped from her face, and they turned, seeking its origin. Trey, lounging in a chair near the window, rose slowly and stepped out of the shadows into the faint glow of the firelight.

At ease, a half-smile on his face, his dinner jacket unbuttoned and his tie loosened, the costly diamond and lapis studs twinkling, he gave the appearance of casual tranquillity, but underneath the gently put words was an unmistakably hard edge to his voice and a primitive desire to devastate them both. They stared at each other for a moment, and then Trey smiled and bowed, a sardonic gesture. And all Empress could think in that instant was: How can he always look so handsome?

The Duc took in their expressions, the hushed expectancy, Trey's words and audacious, uninvited presence; he could almost feel the young male impatience kept tightly leashed. This suitor was determined, and his face had changed, the insouciance stripped away. Warfare over a woman. It reminded him of feelings he hadn't experienced in years, had forgotten until this explicit moment that he'd ever felt them at all. With a compassion he rarely showed and an inherent aplomb that was universally agreed De Vec had perfected to a fine art, the Duc rose graciously to the occasion. "Of course, Mr. Braddock-Black," he responded politely. "Would you prefer the library or my carriage?"

And when Trey brusquely said, "The library," without taking his eyes off Empress, Etienne turned to her and gallantly said, "Excuse me, my dear, for a brief interval."

"Trey!" Empress exclaimed sharply, finally coming to her senses, Etienne's words returning her to the present. "Damn you"—she exhaled softly—"who the hell do you think you are, breaking into my boudoir?"

"A friend," Trey replied sardonically. "A very *dear* friend," he added with pointed emphasis.

"Etienne!" Empress appealed. This couldn't be happening to her. If Trey thought he was going to start playing guardian to her virtue—or call Etienne out, or interfere in any way in her life—*damn him,* he had *no* right! "Damn you, you arrogant bastard," she hissed, turning on Trey with snapping eyes.

"Hush, darling," Trey said dryly. "Etienne will be frightened off by your ungovernable temper."

"Or your damnable presence!" she stormed.

"That remains to be seen. . . . Now, if you'll excuse us . . ." he drawled lazily.

It was Etienne who calmed her. "I'll be back, darling, as soon as Mr. Braddock-Black and I have settled things." He was serenely undisturbed, as though bedroom scenes were commonplace for him.

The two tall, dark men stood facing each other in the library, both exquisite in evening dress, the Duc still wearing his black cape, their eyes of a height and matching hardness.

"I could kill you," Trey said very low.

"You could try," the Duc replied, and untying the braided silk cord at his throat, dropped his cape on a chair.

Trey carefully assessed the lean man who had replied in a mild, expressionless voice and saw a member of an ancient, powerful family, perhaps fifteen years his senior but hard and trim, obviously conditioned by more than idle frivolity.

"I'm the father of her child," Trey said with distinct querulousness.

"I knew that the moment you stepped into Empress's drawing room, your first day in Paris. The resemblance to your son is"— there was the slightest pause—"exotically obvious." The Duc had heard of Trey's reputation with women. In previous visits, apparently, he'd slept with nearly every highborn woman in Paris. It surprised him—the adamant tone when speaking of Empress's son. Surely a man who'd enjoyed so many women would be blasé about children. "It's not enough to be the father," the Duc went on, disagreeing amiably. "Every child has a father. What I'm interested in is whether Empress wants you, and quite frankly, in the last fortnight it appears very much as if she doesn't. Perhaps," he continued with the beginning of a smile, "you haven't persuaded her properly."

The Duc was no tyro in interpreting the female sex. It was his greatest asset, his ability to see beyond the sparkling repartee. He'd also attentively watched the farewell scene that night between Empress and Trey at LeNotre's and had perceived a wrenching display of unrequited love. A surprise to him. It had almost made him give up his own pursuit of the fair Mrs. Miles, and if he'd been a less selfish man, he may have. But he'd wryly concluded when the young people's sad parting was complete that Empress would need a shoulder to cry on and eventually . . . other things. All of which he was more than willing to supply.

Trey thought of his brutal possession of Empress the previous night and winced inwardly. Damn, it probably *was* his fault. But instantly he reconsidered taking the entire blame, thinking Empress was at fault, too, driving him to distraction with her damn courtesanlike ways and endless admirers. "Oh, hell," he swore softly, his dilemma no nearer solution than before, the Duc's reasonable words disconcerting, the hours of drinking that day not conducive to clear and rational thought. He had come on heated impulse and now was indecisive beyond the knowledge that he wanted Empress for himself alone. And that feeling wasn't novel to this particular time and circumstance. He'd felt the same from the first night he'd met her. "I need a drink," he said quietly, with an exasperated sigh, and stalking to a side table stocked with liquor, uncorked a decanter, tipped it up, and took a healthy draft. Rinsing his mouth with the liquor to wash away the dozen hours of drinking, he swallowed the cognac and, turning back to the Duc, who had been watching with amusement, said wryly, "Maybe we don't have to kill each other tonight, after all. Care for a drink?"

They were seated a few moments later, gazing at each other over brandy snifters and an ornate marquetry library table.

"My apologies," Trey said first. "I feel like a damn fool. I don't know what there is about her." He smiled then, a faint, private smile, and added, "Actually the list is quite long, but I won't bore you. I'm sure you've discovered yourself; she's most unusual."

"She's the only woman I ever considered leaving Isabelle for," the Duc said in a musing tone. "There've been many women over the years." He shrugged in that particularly Gallic way. "Ours was a dynastic marriage entered into with practicality. Not unusual. But I'd never seriously considered another woman with any permanence . . . not until I met Empress. She's like fire in your blood."

"And in your soul," Trey said with chafing discontent.

"Ah," the Duc said, smiling over the rim of his glass. "It did rather look that way at the ball tonight."

"I almost shot you out of hand when you walked into Empress's boudoir."

"I understand. I once shot a man like that—not over love, over jealousy. I was very young."

"I'm jealous of every man who looks at her. And there's too many," Trey concluded bitterly, lifting his glass to his mouth and draining it.

"There always will be with a beautiful woman like Empress."

The Duc's words only reinforced Trey's own unpalatable conclusion. "*Merde*," he swore softly into his empty glass.

Whether it was a philosophical expletive concerning life's inequities or, more prosaically, notice of an empty liquor glass, the Duc was uncertain, but of one thing he *was* certain. Empress was not likely to seek comfort from him that night with this wild ex-lover lurking about, so he rose and, looking down at the despondent young man seated at the Boulle table, said, "Thank you for the drink, and please make my regrets to Empress." Etienne was a practical man and long past the rash eagerness of youth when it came to matters of *amour*. Empress would still be here tomorrow, and if not . . . no one died of love.

"Regrets," Trey replied caustically, looking up, his luminous eyes cynical. "Don't we all with her?"

The Duc, while gracious, was not excessively benevolent, and additionally, his own feelings apropos the beautiful Empress were less philanthropic than carnal. Not inclined at the moment to serve as father-confessor to this disillusioned swain, he only smiled in reply. They would have to deal with their problem without his assistance.

Trey hardly noticed when he left.

Empress paced the floor after the men had gone, wondering what outrageous idiocy Trey was disgracing her with now, fretting over his incredulous intrusion into her evening with Etienne, becoming increasingly out of temper at his damnable presumption. Sitting in a chair by the window, she drummed her fingers restlessly on the chair arms, looked out into the black night, and tried to visualize the conversation in the library. The possibilities were appalling; she could see her entire life permanently destroyed by scandal, and she nervously turned her thoughts to less disastrous reflections. She rose impatiently a few moments later, picked her cape up from the bed, and hung it in the armoire as if a fit of neatness would restore order to her life. Looking at herself in the armoire mirror, she smoothed her hair with agitated fingers, then made a face. Damn men, anyway. Surely Etienne would be back soon. It was disconcerting being left alone, utterly preposterous to have been bearded in her own boudoir in the first place. Leave it to Trey to be unconventional. Fitfully she returned to her seat on the gilded chair, and the drumming began again, this time on the windowpane.

How long would this "discussion" go *on*? she pondered exasperatedly, on her feet again a few seconds later. It had begun to rain, she noticed distractedly. When the small clock on the mantle chimed some time later, she looked away from the rain-wet window and was startled to see how late the hour was. Why, she thought indignantly, was she waiting here like some penitent child? This was *her* home, she was a *grown* woman, long since independent enough to make her own decisions. Additionally, she was not some damn chattel that Trey Braddock-Black, with his bloody imperiousness, could command at his whim!

And on that heated thought she stalked to the door, jerked it open, and, holding up her silk skirts, ran down the stairs to the library. This was not a medieval century! She was not going to wait submissively upstairs while two men discussed her like she was some *commodity*!

Livid with growing rage at the whole anachronistic drama—long, *long* outdated—she pushed open the library door and swept into the room, ready to do battle. "If you think you can order my life around, Trey," she began hotly, already several steps into the room before she noticed the absolute silence. Stopping, she searched the dimly lit interior, her gaze drawn to Trey's powerful form, seated at the library table. "Where's Etienne?" she snapped.

"Gone," he said quietly.

"Did you threaten him?" she inquired heatedly, incensed at his actions, his intrusion into her home, the very way he commanded the room with his presence.

"Naturally." His voice was flat, the answer simple.

"Why?" she almost said in anger, until she reinterpreted his curious intonation and uncharacteristic mood. "Why?" she asked then in a hushed, hesitant voice, all her anger draining away, her nerves suddenly on edge, like a general waiting for a scouting report that could prove disastrous.

Trey sighed softly. "I don't know." He'd been drinking all day. Rubbing his head with both hands, he tried to clear his thinking, then, abstractly raking his fingers through the black silk of his hair to smooth the disheveled roughness, he slowly looked up at her from under heavy brows. "Yes, I do know." And after another deep exhalation of breath, he said quietly, "Because I wanted to kill him when he touched you."

"You can't do this," Empress declared softly, "every time I bring someone home."

Leaning back in the heavily carved chair, he rested his head wearily against the intricate design. "I know that too," he murmured with a faint grimace. She was everything he needed, and the awful truth was . . . only she made life sweet. Abruptly rising from his chair, he pushed it aside with a harsh gesture and strode away from her to the window overlooking the rain-swept garden. The odor of brandy was pungent as he moved across the room, and underlying it was the faint essence of ambergris.

"You're drunk," she said quietly.

He shrugged, his powerful shoulders in his black evening clothes outlined against the glistening glass. "Maybe," he murmured. "Probably. It wouldn't matter," he replied softly, standing motionless before the window, looking out as though there was something to see in the desolate winter garden.

"What do you want? Here, tonight?" Empress rested her hands to steady them on the inlaid table, her heart beating very rapidly, like a young girl's, under the magenta silk and black lace and yards of silver ribbon of the magnificent, sophisticated gown that should have shielded her in worldly wisdom.

"What I shouldn't," he muttered gruffly into the black night, his pride wanting an accounting of all the men, a denial, an apology . . . her new life wiped away. Turning, he faced her, in shadow still, his expression shrouded. He took a step forward, and the glow of the fire underlit his face, the stamp of weariness stark against the fine bones. "It's unendurable," he whispered, "seeing you with other men. My feelings are—" There was a flat silence, and then he said softly, "It frightens me." And for the first time Empress saw him devoid of arrogance.

Her heart began a tremulous beating rhythm of hope, but

wary still of Trey's past, his child-of-fortune mentality capricious in its wanting but never for long. "I know the feeling," she said, "with Valerie, with Arabella, with Clothilde at LeNotre's tonight . . . with all of them," she finished in a subdued murmur.

His head came up like a wolf scenting the wind, and the power, the energy so characteristic and enviable, was plain to see. He was sure, at least, of his own feelings, and her words were like a freshening wind to an alert animal, sweet with promise, fragrant with hope, the answer he'd been searching for. She saw him take a deep, controlled breath. "Could you give up"—he paused, and she saw, as he stepped closer, the merest shadow of the teasing smile he used so effectively—"the harem?"

"If you were less cynical, you would have believed me before." Her small smile was the half-tempting, playful one he loved best. "There have not been other men."

"The Duc," he reminded her, his scowl reappearing.

"My answer to your good-bye last night . . . and pale-haired Clothilde at LeNotre's," she jealously reminded him.

"She wasn't you," he said very simply, "so I jumped out of her carriage halfway to her house and took a cab here."

He had come for her. Finally. When she had given up hope completely. Even if all her dreams didn't come true in this world, at least the most important one had—he was here. "Is this love?" She said the word first, less afraid than he to admit to her feelings, daring to hope, even though his scowl was not completely erased.

His scowl disappeared, and his eyes took on a tenderness she could imagine his mother had seen when he was very young. "If it isn't, I wouldn't wish this appalling misery on anyone," he said with a humility she had never heard from him.

"Do you want your son?" she asked. After all the unanswered questions concerning Trey and babies and paternity, she had to know if his wanting Max was based on contentious possession or genuine affection. She had seen his charm used too effortlessly to be certain when it was sincere, and her maternal feelings were as intense as those she felt for Trey.

"Almost as much as I want you," he answered, his heart in his eyes, then he amended, trying to properly convey his feelings, "the same as I want you—oh, hell . . . no, it's different, but the same," he finished softly, shaking his head slightly and reaching out his hand to brush her cheek gently. "I want you both . . . want you desperately." He took a deep breath, this favored young man who had never lacked for anything until he'd met Empress, and very quietly asked, "Will you have me?"

"Now?" The lighthearted teasing of victory shone in her fresh green eyes and wreathed her face in happiness.

His luminous glance took in the furniture arrangement, noted a suitable couch, and with an answering smile of jubilation he replied, "Now would be extremely convenient."

"I warn you, I am so in love, I may fall into pieces before the overwhelming torrent. . . ."

"In that case I should lock the door," he said, his smile lavish. "This could get excessive." But he was earnest beneath the teasing, wanting to hold her in his arms for a thousand and one years and beyond. She was a courtly lady tonight in her beribboned and lace-trimmed glistening silk with jewels in her ears and at her throat and the fragrance of de Vec's roses taking second place to her own sweet perfume. But he loved her as much in worn cowboy gear or in nothing at all, and he said it silently to himself in quiet wonder, *She loves me*.

"Will you give up your harem as well?" Empress asked softly, following him as he moved to the door and secured it. With her usual unreserved directness she wanted certification and only one answer. An experienced man, Trey knew what she wished to hear, but this time, unlike all the soothing phrases in his past, it was true. He turned back to her, his pale, silvery eyes the color of moonlight, his stark cheekbones crinkled across the top from the smile lifting his fine mouth.

He was as beautiful as sin, she thought. Still. Always.

He opened his arms and she rushed into his embrace, lacing her hands around his waist, clinging tightly. Looking up at him, she said tenaciously, "Now tell me," wanting to feel safe, wanting his undying love like a young girl.

"There is no harem," he said, his rich, deep voice gentle. "It's been gone a long time."

"You still smell of ambergris." There was a touch of distrust and suspicion in her green eyes. She knew what ambergris was used for . . . to heighten sensuality, to make sensations more vivid.

"It's a toy," he replied dismissively, his hands warm on

the magenta silk of her back. "The ladies love it. It makes them feel wicked—it's nothing." Ambergris was always available at the parties for the daring ladies and venturesome men. And opium, too, for those searching more serious escape. He always politely declined the opium.

"What do you *do* with the wicked ladies?" Empress persisted, jealous of every woman who looked his way.

He shrugged and wished he could make her understand how none of them mattered. "We laugh a little," he said mildly, "then—nothing. Someone says something silly, and everyone laughs again. Sweetheart, you know how banal this frivolous life is. But from now on," he said, taking her face in both his hands, "you're my ambergris." He buried his nose in her scented hair, inhaling deeply, and murmured, "You're my ambergris . . . my intoxicant . . . my aphrodisiac." Lifting his head slightly, he rubbed his face against hers, sliding his cheek over the smoothness of her skin, his fine, straight nose tracing the curve of her jaw. He inhaled again. "You're my opium dream come true." And he kissed her very hard.

Even while she felt the warmth of his lips, tasted the sweet flavor of the cognac, and felt the exquisite flutters begin when the delicacy of his kiss changed swiftly to a luscious intensity that was the familiar, impatient passion she adored, she wondered in a tiny corner of her brain whether he'd kissed Clothilde this way tonight. Why did it matter about the women now? Still, why did she have to know when everything she wanted in the world was in her arms? Wouldn't it be more sensible *not* to know? But she wasn't sensible and never had been, so she wanted more clarification than a casual disclaimer about the women in his life. So when she drifted back from the sighing wonder of his kiss and Trey was tracing the gentle curve of her eyebrow with his tongue, she said in a determined way, "Trey, I want to know about the . . . wicked ladies." Her voice was serious, and he knew what she was asking.

There was no teasing now in his voice, but a quiet graveness that reminded her of his tone when he spoke of the battles in the legislature. "I have been celibate," he said softly. "Word of honor, strange as it may seem. Which might," he added by way of apology, "account for my unfortunate behavior last night. I'm sorry," he said in low tones, "if I hurt you, although," he amended, "you're partly to blame, too, goading me with all those drooling males forever around you.''

"You're jealous," Empress said joyfully, a warm glow of contentment spreading through her senses.

"And possessive," he replied gruffly, tightening his hold on her.

"The next time you look at a woman like you looked at Clothilde at LeNotre's tonight, I'll show you what possessive is." Empress's chin jutted out with a belligerence that was only half mocking.

"You always were hard to handle."

"And you were impossible."

"A charming combination—the difficult with the impossible." His grin was roguish. "At least it won't be boring."

"Have you, really?" she said, completely out of context, wondering in the next breath if she was going to drive him away with her demanding questions when she'd only just found him again, because she was so outrageously jealous and his answers were always just short of absolute, definitive answers, which she wasn't sure was only vaguely male or by design.

"Really, what?" he teased, and that made her even more acutely suspicious, because he knew exactly what she was talking about.

"Been celibate," she said with a pouty look, because he was smiling down at her with dazzling sparkles of amusement in his eyes. And his dark hair was much too beautiful for a man—any woman would kill for it, she thought as she gazed upward. And if another woman *had* run her fingers through that long, silky hair yesterday or last week or anytime . . . she would kill her instantly. How did one ever come to grips with an irrational jealousy such as hers, she wondered, and stay out of prison?

"Have *you*?" he asked much too impudently; she would put him in his place.

"Is this a test?" she replied sweetly.

The amusement instantly vanished from his eyes, and his voice was definitely a growl. "Yes," he said, "it damn well is."

"Do you get points for partial answers?" she inquired with an arch smile, which she thought decidedly good enough for the stage.

"Only one answer is allowed," he rumbled deep in his throat, and his large hands tightened around her waist.

"Oh, dear," she said, and then when his dark brows had drawn together like great, dark wings, she answered very softly, "Yes, I have." And grinned.

He laughed out loud, then kissed her nose. "I adore you."

"Just so long as I'm the *only* one you adore."

"You are, you have been, you will be. Is that clear enough, or would you like sworn affidavits from my parents that I was underfoot for months?"

"Speaking of parents, and truly I don't mean to be difficult now when everything is absolutely heavenly"—she was giddy with happiness, and so was he or she never would have dared to be so outspoken—"but I might as well tell you, I won't live at the ranch. Just because we're married doesn't mean I'm going to become an automatic part of the Braddock-Black empire." The frantic pace at the ranch was all too overwhelming for her. Everyone was kindness itself, but lawyers were always underfoot, and accountants, and three telephone lines into the house constantly ringing from all the companies and mines and lobbyists who needed money or orders or help in a hurry. She was selfish. She wanted Trey to herself, at least part of the time.

"Who said anything about marriage?" Trey said blandly, and was gratified to see, for the first time, visual evidence of the phrase *struck dumb*.

"Should I call the Duc back?" Empress replied silkily when she'd regained her breath.

"How does marriage, say at ten tomorrow morning, sound?" Trey's smile was pure sunshine.

"I adore the sound of that." There was triumph and assurance in her voice.

"I thought you would."

"Arrogant man! Do you think every woman in the world wants to marry you?"

"Whatever," he said modestly. "As long as the merry widow of Paris does, I'm content."

"I love you," she whispered.

"You're my life, fierce kitten, for now and always," he replied softly, and kissed her very tenderly, as though the taste of her was new. "Come home," he whispered, his breath warm on her lips. "Come home with me." His slender hands stroked her hair.

"To the mountains?"

He nodded. "Blue wired the other day. The crocus are

coming through the snow in the sheltered areas on Winter Mountain. Clover misses you.'' His palms drifted down her back, his smile for her alone.

''Springtime,'' Empress breathed, remembering the lush and majestic peace, the promises Trey had made in the night silence of their hayloft bed.

''On Winter Mountain. Our first, like I promised you.'' His voice was low and tender, his own memories of their love in the mountain valley filled with an aching poignancy. How much they had had, how fragile it was . . . how near he had come to losing it forever.

''Will it be the same?''

He knew what she was asking. ''The same . . . and better.'' He smiled with the old assurance. ''I'll build you a house.''

''With balconies.'' Her voice was gentle.

He nodded, smiling.

''And turrets.''

He kissed her yes. ''With rooms for the children.'' Then quickly, in guilty afterthought to his own intense happiness, he asked, ''Will they mind going back?''

Empress laughed. ''I had to drag them away.''

''Good, then rooms for the children.''

''And a nursery for Max,'' she added softly.

''And for our little blond-haired girl,'' he said, his voice husky, his heart in his eyes. Then he slid his fingers into her hair and, bending to her, kissed her with love and grace and care. And pleasure played upon pleasure.

And the door stayed locked in the library until shortly before ten the next morning.

Epilogue

———————————

THEY WERE HOME for the trillium. And the turrets were all in place by the first snowfall. The following spring, the first baby born on Winter Mountain was christened Solange Braddock-Black. Sunny for short.

And her godmother, Daisy, went to Paris to see her god-daughter's status as the heir to Empress's portion of the Jordan inheritance.

Quite by accident, Daisy met the Duc de Vec. Their instant antipathy was mutual. She was in control of herself, aloof, immune to gratuitous charm—all personality traits similar to his own. It was natural that they would dislike each other.

But Daisy was also darkly exotic, beautiful. And intelligent. He'd never met a female attorney.

Of course, she was immune to his charm.

A challenge, he thought.

A challenge to bed.

It turned into more. It turned into a dark and forbidden passion.

Notes

1. Chinese women were brought to America, taken through customs with forged papers representing them as wives of Chinese men in the States, and then sold at auction. Chinese men, too, often sold themselves to American companies contracting for labor. The price for strong young men was between $400 and $1,000; they could, however, buy out their papers much like an indentured servant over many years. Women sold for higher sums ($2,000–$10,000), but their sales were permanent—into prostitution or slavery. The biography of a young girl named Lalu, sold at age 17 at an auction in San Francisco to a Chinese saloon owner in Idaho, is typical. Eventually her life had a happier ending than most of her peers. She was won in a high-stakes poker game by a gambler who cared for her and married her. She died at age 80 in 1933.

2. It was not uncommon for young girls to be sold by poor families in China in order for the rest of the family to survive. Women were trained to accept this (at least in theory); one of the four virtues of a woman was that she must reconcile herself to her fate. During a famine, Lalu, the woman cited in Note 1, was traded to a bandit chief for two small bags of

soybeans. He in turn sold her to a madame in Shanghai who operated a profitable business of supplying American buyers.

3. An excerpt from reporter Martin Hutchens's biography best explains the etiquette apropos of names. He had arrived in Helena, Montana, in November 1889, and, on his first day in town, found himself living quarters in a redbrick boarding-house and then dropped in at one of Helena's finest saloons, where the chandeliers shone on reasonably good copies of Renaissance masters. As he entered the saloon an intoxicated drinker was arguing violently with the bartender. The cus-tomer, angry at being invited to leave, pulled out a Colt six-gun, aimed it unsteadily at the bartender, and fired. He missed. The bartender wrenched the gun away from him, turned it on its owner, and shot him, considerately, in the shoulder. The young reporter glanced around the room. Not another person on his side of the bar, except the wounded man, was in sight. The people who had been lining the bar were on the floor or under the tables. A distinguished-looking man in a well-tailored suit dusted himself off and observed amiably to the young man, "You come from places where these things don't happen, or you would have taken cover like everyone else."

Martin Hutchens agreed this was true. They fell to talking, and presently Martin was asking what he deemed a perfectly acceptable question: "And what part of the country do you come from, sir?"

The distinguished-looking man's affability vanished behind a chilly stare. "No questions west of the Red River, young man. *No questions.*"

Martin Hutchens concluded, "I learned two extremely im-portant lessons about the West before the end of my first day."

Walter Cameron, in his recollections of his early years in Montana helping to build the Northern Pacific railroad, de-scribes this phenomenon in a little different way:

My first day in Miles City, I began looking for a job and a man told me there was a railroad outfit camped in a cottonwood grove at the head of Main Street that he thought wanted team-sters. I went down to this camp and inquired of the man in charge (whom none of us ever knew by any name other than "Tex"), I suppose he hailed from Texas. It was customary in those days to inquire of a man, "What shall I call you?" rather than to inquire, "What is your name?" Later on I got acquainted with many men, who for reasons best known to themselves, were sailing under aliases not wanting their true identity disclosed.

4. History suggests the almost universal bad faith of Indian agents toward the Indians. The practice of defrauding them out of the annuities and presents granted them by law was widespread. The agents, mostly political appointees from the East, were supposed to be responsible for the Indians, but Martin Maginnis, longtime congressional delegate from Montana, describes the majority of agents he was familiar with:

> They will take a barrel of sugar to an Indian tribe and get a receipt for ten barrels. For a sack of flour the Indians sign a receipt for fifty sacks. The agent will march three hundred head of cattle four times through a corral, get a receipt for twelve hundred head, give a part of them to the Indians, sell a part to the white man, and steal as many back as possible.

The Indians were well aware of the fact that they were being cheated, and their agent, a representative of the great government with which they had signed a treaty, was a thief. However, their options were limited.

In Montana's climate, winters were particularly hard, and every year many Indians froze and starved to death on the reservations. The buffalo were gone, the ranges overcrowded, and below-zero weather brought disaster. "The Starvation Winter of the Pikuni," depicted by J. K. Howard, is only one instance of many.

A day or two after Christmas, 1883, a luminous and glittering mist formed over the northern and eastern Rockies slope—where Glacier Part is today. Frantically the Pikuni-Blackfeet prayed to Aisoyimstan, the Cold Maker, not to persecute their people; pleadingly they sought of their Indian agent a few extra rations. But rations were low: the agent had reported (seeking to make a record for himself) that the Blackfeet were now nearly self-supporting.

The mercury dropped to 40, 50 below zero, and stayed there for sun upon sun. All travel ceased and the hungry Blackfeet huddled in their lodges. Every day was as the day that had gone before; the sun was a faint light in a colorless void, and it set far to the south. There would come slightly warmer days, and it would snow, hour after hour.

Now the hunters would go forth to seek game afoot, for their horses had long since died or been killed for food; and when there was no more game, they brought back the inner bark of the fir and pine trees, or tissue scraped from buffalo skulls, or the hooves of cattle, left by the wolves—or even rats hunted out of their homes in the rocks.

They were deserted by their agent, who was being replaced; his successor arrived in the midst of the worst suffering and did his best. Word of their plight reached Montana towns and rescue expeditions were organized. George Bird Grinnell, famous naturalist and friend of the Blackfeet, stirred the government to action. Cursing freighters fought their way over drifted trails to the reservation with wagon loads of food. They found some of the survivors mad with hunger and grief among the bodies of their kin; they found coyotes and wolves fighting in the lodges of the unburied dead; they found six hundred Indians—one quarter of the tribe—starved to death.

The next winter was nearly as severe, and the *Mineral Argus* remarked casually in January 1885: "Many of the Pikuni Indians are reported frozen to death." That was the extent of the story.

5. The Gilded Age was marked by corruption, crass materialism, and close links between business and politics. Montana was no different from other states and territories. For instance, a violent fight erupted over the placement of the capital, and in the struggle between Helena and Anaconda (owned body and soul by Daly's Copper Company), Helena won. Daly's rival, Clark, supported Helena. Later Clark admitted before the Committee on Privileges and Elections of the United States Senate that he had spent $100,000 in the capital fight. John R. Toole, Marcus Daly's political lieutenant, testified before the Helena grand jury, which pretended to investigate Clark's briberies, to an expenditure of $500,000. But former Governor Hauser, in his testimony before the senatorial committee in Washington, gave the Daly figure as over $1 million. Taking into consideration the vast sums of money Daly afterward gave away in the form of mining leases to his supporters, he must have spent, in round figures, over $2.5 million in the contest. Clark and his friends

must have spent over $400,000. The vote of the state did not exceed 50,000 people in the capital election. The cost of each vote was, therefore, approximately $38.

Another interesting case of the power of money in Montana politics concerns Clark's bid for a senate seat. Before the election, Clark's son, his political manager, was reported to have said, "We'll send the old man either to the Senate or the poorhouse." C. P. Connolly says that as a result of this resolve, there began in Helena a series of such astounding briberies that they almost managed, by the commonness of their occurrence and the openness with which they were offered, to change the public mores. If a legislator had a weakness in his nature or his circumstances, Clark's lieutenants found it. Forty-seven votes were bought in 18 days, for a total of $431,000, the individual price ranging from $5,000 to $25,000. Thirteen senators refused bribes that totaled $200,000. Clark, a Democrat, was able to buy all but 4 of the 15 Republican votes in the Senate. Tracing the course of bank accounts opened or increased, mortgages paid, debts suddenly resolved, new businesses and land purchased is a fascinating paper trail.

6. Until 1888, everything to the north of the Missouri River was Indian reservation, as was much of the area south of the Yellowstone, and opening of the Indian lands was a common, relentless theme in government. Charles Broadwater, Samuel Hauser, William Clark, and Marc Daly, the "Big Four" of Montana Democrats, were influential in territorial politics. Martin Maginnis, Territorial Delegate to Washington for twelve years, was widely regarded as a Broadwater–Hauser man, and neither of them was shy about making demands on him. Broadwater informed Maginnis in 1881 of reservation boundary changes he desired, going so far as to send Maginnis a map, redrawing to his own satisfaction the boundaries of Indian lands and indicating which should be thrown open for white settlement. "I must have it," he wrote, "or damned if I don't go back on you next election."

Governor Hauser in his message to the 15th legislature (1886) insisted that Montana's Indians were better off in Indian Territory (Oklahoma) in a climate more conducive to agriculture. "If the Indians are to subsist by agriculture and become civilized and self-sustaining, a country further south, and with more natural rainfall, would suit them better." His magnanimity is apparent.

The greatest single reduction occurred on May 1, 1888, when Congress passed an act that provided for diminishing the northern reservation, followed in December 1890, by reductions in the southern Crow reservation. Nearly 20 million acres were added to the public domain.

As late at 1909, Indian reserves continued to be encroached on if powerful interests would benefit. J. K. Howard relates an instance having to do with James J. Hill's son, Louis. In a special train, Louis was taking delegates to the Dry Farming Congress in Billings. En route the party stopped off in Culbertson and took a trip over some lands that had been set aside for an Indian tribe. They then telegraphed Secretary of the Interior Ballinger, urging that he open these lands to homestead entry. He obliged within three months. What the Indians thought of the deal is not on record.

7. Many of the cattlemen enclosed large areas between barbed-wire fences, even when all or part of the range belonged to the public domain. To combat this illegal practice, in April 1884, the Commissioner of the General Land Office issued a circular giving notice that "the fencing of large bodies of public land beyond that allowed by law is illegal." This rather weak measure was supplemented, in 1885, by an act of Congress that declared, "all inclosures of public lands" to which the incloser has no "claim or color of title" are illegal. By 1887, enclosures of over 200,000 acres of public grazing land in Montana had been reported. Some of the most prominent cattle companies in Montana were involved in these illegalities. There were constant battles over grazing land and water rights, and only a portion of the contests ever came to court.

An interesting account in *Montana* magazine details an incident occurring in 1894 that never reached court. It was handled privately. The story is written by B. D. Phillips's son, so may be influenced by consanguinity.

In 1894 B. D. Phillips found a large natural hay bottom between Malta and North Central Montana's Little Rocky Mountains. Although some settlers were already there, Father liked the idea of so much open range. He thought it would remain open indefinitely since it wasn't fit for farming. He had had to move twice before, mainly because of losing range to farmers and he didn't want it to happen again.

Settlers on the land gradually sold out to him.

One man, who had been roughing up other settlers in the area, finally tangled with B. D. Father was irrigating when this rancher rode up and demanded that B. D. open his diversion dam and let the water go down the creek for his use. Father told him, "I have the first water rights, but I'll turn the water down the creek just as soon as I've finished with it."

The rancher was back in a couple of days with, "I thought I told you to turn the water down the creek." My father answered, "If you bother me any more about the water, I'll turn it into Wild Horse Creek and you won't get any more water."

A few days later, we learned from a friend that the rancher and his sons planned on murdering our family at the first opportunity. Not being able to live under such a threat, the next day at daylight, Father took his rifle and rode over to the neighbor's place. He kicked the door open and found the family at breakfast. Covering them with his rifle, he said, "Finish your breakfast because this is your last meal."

He accused them of making the murder threat, and it was obvious from their reactions that they had made it. Then he said, "This bottom isn't big enough for both of us and I'm not leaving."

The rancher quickly agreed to sell out to B. D. and leave the area. Terms of the sale were agreed upon. As my father left, he told them, "All this depends on your being out of the bottom this afternoon by two o'clock."

By one o'clock the troublemaker and his family were "stringing out across the bottom with their wagons," according to Father.

Phillips continued adding to his holdings.

The beginning of the new paragraph causes the reader to think, "I'll bet he did." In accounts like this, often written for historical societies or in memoirs, one point of view is presented. Questions arise when reading this narrative: Why did settlers on the land gradually sell out to B. D.? Why was the last remaining settler on the bottomland roughing up settlers? Why did B. D. suddenly dam up the creek after he'd bought out all the settlers save one? Why would a man who had been threatened with murder by a neighbor and his sons beard them in their own home single-handedly? Some details, one suspects, may have been omitted.

These accounts, which appear with some frequency, verify two points. Power and protection of one's land often rested on violence and lawlessness. And a certain objectivity is required in interpreting "pioneer memories."

8. In February 1889, the legislature amended the statute prohibiting women from practicing law in Montana. During the Christmas season of 1889, Ella Knowles passed the bar exam without difficulty, becoming the first woman lawyer in Montana. One of her examiners noted in his diary that night, "Examined Miss Knowles for admission to the Bar and was surprised to find her so well read. She beats all that I have ever examined." By 1890, only 50 women nationwide had been licensed as lawyers. By 1910, there were only 558 women lawyers and judges in the country, making up 0.5% of the profession.

9. Trey's carrying Empress down-mountain is based on a true story. Thomas Faval and his wife with a partner named Charboneau had been sent out by a fur company to trap for the winter. Charboneau had a vicious reputation, but young Faval needed the job and wasn't in a position to refuse orders. Although given supplies, they were expected to live largely off wild game. Soon after their winter camp was readied, four feet of snow fell in a week, and all the animals moved out of the area. They kept waiting for the wild animals to drift back once the snow settled, but they never did. Shortly before Christmas, Charboneau set out for the fort. He was to return with supplies, for they were out of food. By dogsled, it was a ten-day round trip. When he didn't return, Faval and his wife began their trek out, but by that time they were much weakened by hunger. After the first day Marie could no longer walk, so Faval carried her. There was no evidence of game anywhere, although Faval hoped each day that they would find some. It was as though they had disappeared off the face of the earth. On the sixth day Marie fell into a stupor, but he knew it wasn't much farther to the fort, and if he traveled all night and all the next day, he was sure he could get there by dusk—if his strength held. Faval stumbled into the fort late the following afternoon and lay his wife on a bed; after opening her eyes and smiling at him, she died.

"How came it you starved out there?" the company factor asked him. "When Charboneau came in, he reported that you

were doing well." And Faval discovered that Charboneau
simply had said he wasn't needed at the winter camp. Faval
was so enraged, he could barely speak. "Where is he now—
this moment?" he said in a whisper. When he was told that
Charboneau was playing cards in an adjacent room, Faval
rushed into the room and killed him with his bare hands.

10. Newspaper comment on Indian matters was often laconic.
On November 27, 1884, the *Cottonwood Correspondent* reported: "The Crow Indians are raiding the Musselshell for
horses." Ten days later the *Mineral Argus* carried the correspondent's "follow story"—a succinct line: "There are seven
good Indians on Cottonwood Creek." The stockmen had
taken matters into their own hands and hung seven Indians
from the cottonwoods near the Musselshell.

11. In a letter to the editor of *Montana* magazine, information
is furnished about George Parrotti, a bandit portrayed in
several of Charles M. Russell's paintings. The rather unusual
facts are related in a bland, objective fashion:

George Parrotti, a train robber and murderer was lynched at
Rawlins, Wyoming at 7:30 P.M., March 22, 1881. His skin
was tanned and made into a medical instrument bag, razor strops,
a pair of lady's shoes and a tobacco pouch. The shoes are
on display in the Rawlins Museum. Part of his skull is in the
Union Pacific Museum in Omaha, Nebraska. Two future gover-
nors of Wyoming, Osborne and Chatterton, witnessed this
incident.

Now as to the information on Big Nose George. I had some
litigation in Rawlins, Wyoming and had the good fortune of
meeting Dr. Lillian Heath. The doctor told me on tape that her
mother ran a boarding house in Rawlins. One of the boarders was
Dr. Osborne. She worked for Dr. Osborne as his nurse. When
they lynched Big Nose George, she knew the whole story. When
George was cut down the next morning, Dr. Heath was there.
The body was taken to the doctor's office and skinned and the
hide was tanned. She related that Dr. Osborne kept George's
brain in a jar of formaldehyde so that he could study the convolu-
tions. He gave to Dr. Heath the top of the skull and she used it as
a doorstop at times and as a flower pot at other times.

*   *   *

The refinements of civilization apparently had not been fully assimilated by Western society.

12. Ambergris is a resinous substance originating in the intestines of sperm whales and thrown out as debris on the shores of Africa, China, India, Ireland, and the Bahamas. Its musky aroma was added to perfume oils, soap, and other toiletries. Taken internally—usually through inhalation—it supposedly acted as an aphrodisiac and exhilarant. The fin-de-siècle era had a fascination for Oriental themes, exotic plants, ritual, and eroticism.

Dear Reader,

Writing romances is great fun for me. Like one of those daydreams that actually happened. And not because I was pragmatic enough to set a goal and work toward it. More like Alice in Wonderland, I fell into it.

I research first, one of life's great pleasures, and find enough material to write dozens of books. And from an initial, amorphous image, that research clarifies my characters and my new fictional reality. My characters seem alive to me as I write; they talk and I simply scribble down their words as fast as I can. I hope Trey, Empress, Hazard, and Blaze drew you back for a few hours into their nineteenth-century Montana world. My wish is to entertain and amuse, perhaps touch a kindred emotion, and in a small way bring to life a time long past. And to remind people of the beauty and power of love.

Best wishes,

Susan Johnson

P.S. I enjoy hearing from readers. If you have any questions or comments, I'd be delighted to answer them.

Route 2 Box 85
North Branch, MN 55056

BESTSELLING TALES OF ROMANCE